Lies You Wanted to Hear

Praise for *Lies You Wanted to Hear*

"Hard to believe Thomson is a first-time author, given the achievement of this novel. Compulsively readable and stunningly written, *Lies You Wanted to Hear* shows how the tiniest fissure in a relationship might become a canyon. Do we get what we deserve in a relationship? Can we ever receive what we truly need from the people we love? I'm still not entirely convinced that these characters are fictional; that's how much they lived and breathed on the page."

—Jodi Picoult, #1 *New York Times* bestselling
author of *Lone Wolf* and *The Storyteller*

"It is a rare novel that delves equally and fairly into the hearts and minds of both sexes, but that's just what James Whitfield Thomson has done in this riveting debut. *Lies You Wanted to Hear* is the searing tale of a wife and mother, a husband and father, both of whom are—like the rest of us—flawed, their animosity for one another only outweighed by their deep and abiding love for their children. No spouse or parent who picks up this book will be able to put it down. Nor will anyone else. This is a timely and important work."

—Andre Dubus III, *New York Times* bestselling
author of *Townie* and *House of Sand and Fog*

"In his gripping debut, Jim Thomson explores what happens when two characters, who bring out the worst in each other, fall in love. I loved reading about the extremes that Matt and Lucy are prepared to go to, and I loved how hard Thomson makes it to take sides. *Lies You Wanted to Hear* is a morally complex and thoroughly grown-up novel."

—Margot Livesey, *New York Times* bestselling
author of *The Flight of Gemma Hardy*

"A well-told narrative of complex characters and their troubled families."

—*Publishers Weekly*

"[An] effective debut... Thomson lays out the moral complexities underlying acrimonious divorces, taking care to make each side credible."

—*Booklist*

Lies You Wanted to Hear

A NOVEL

JAMES WHITFIELD THOMSON

Published by Sourcebooks Landmark, an imprint of Sourcebooks, Inc.
P.O. Box 4410, Naperville, Illinois 60567-4410
(630) 961-3900
Fax: (630) 961-2168
www.sourcebooks.com

Library of Congress Cataloging-in-Publication data is on file with the publisher.

Printed and bound in the United States of America
VP 10 9 8 7 6 5 4 3 2 1

for Elizabeth
another journey

The girl from next door, the borrowed child,
Said to me the other day, "You like children so much,
Don't you want to have some of your own?"
I couldn't believe she could say it.
I thought, "Surely you can look at me and see them."

—Randall Jarrell, "The Lost Children"

I barely got a smile, baby,
When I hung the moon for you.
Made the birds sing at your window.
You acted like you never knew.
You know you keep me guessin'
If I'm a good man or a fool.

—Johnny Joe Thibodeau, "Good Man Blue"

Prologue

New York City—January 1990

"I hate flying," the woman in the seat next to Lucy says.

"Me too," Lucy agrees, though it isn't true. She never worries about her plane crashing, not with all the human failings that tear lives apart.

As the plane starts down the runway, the woman whimpers and crosses herself, and Lucy reaches out and takes her hand. When they are safely aloft, the pilot making a slow, gentle turn northward, Lucy lets go.

"Thank you," the woman says. "I'm going to visit my daughter in New Hampshire and missed my connection. I didn't want to fly in this weather, but..." She shudders and gives herself a hug.

Lucy nods but doesn't respond. She is on her way home after three days at the midwinter conference of the American Library Association. She'd been hoping to catch the five o'clock shuttle to Boston but got stuck in traffic and ended up on the six; then the plane sat on the tarmac for nearly an hour waiting to take off and had to go back to the gate for deicing. If she's lucky, she'll be on the ground by eight.

The woman takes a sky blue ball of yarn from a canvas bag and goes to work, her knitting needles pecking like a pair of hungry birds. She's about fifty, wearing a purple sweat suit and matching reading glasses.

"I'm going as fast as I can," she says as she notices Lucy watching her. "But I don't think I'll finish it on time."

"What are you knitting?"

"A sweater for my new grandson. My *fourth*. No girls yet."

"Come on, you're not old enough to have grandkids."

"I got started early." The woman rolls her eyes. "*Way* too early. What about you? Do you have children?"

"Two," Lucy says. "A boy and a girl. Today's my son's birthday."

"Wonderful. How old?"

"Nine."

"Oh, that's a great age. Same as my grandson Conor." She wants to tell Lucy all about him and the other boys—long stories about their antics, one already a junior hockey star—and Lucy is grateful there are no more questions about herself.

When they land, the woman thanks Lucy for listening. Then she looks at her watch and says, "At least you'll be home in time to see your son blow out the candles."

Lucy smiles, trying to imagine what a joy that would be.

The taxi driver lets Lucy out at Le Lapin Vert, a little bistro on Centre Street a few blocks from her house in Jamaica Plain. She sits in the back with her suitcase under the table and orders escargots and a glass of chardonnay. There's a map of France printed on the paper place mats. In the summer she likes to rent a car and explore the French countryside. She keeps to the back roads, no plans or reservations. The taste of the escargots brings back memories of a restaurant in Venasque, a late dinner where she was the only patron, the chef joining her afterward for a cigarette and a glass of wine. Lucy studies the map on the place mat and conjures up images from her travels: the wild horses of the Carmargue, the cave paintings at Les Eyzies, the brightly colored anchovy boats at Collioure. She'd like to buy a cottage in St. Benoit someday and plant a small vegetable garden, go to the abbey every evening and listen to the monks chant vespers in the ancient crypt.

A handsome man in an Irish fisherman sweater smiles at her on his way to the men's room, as if they share a secret past. Lucy puts some money on the table and leaves without waiting for the check.

When she gets home, Frodo and Sam are asleep on the couch. Frodo yawns and tries to shake himself awake while Sam curls up against the light.

"Some watchdog you are," Lucy says as Frodo comes over and wags his tail. He looks like a cross between a boxer and a corgi: reddish-brown coat, short legs and a blunt snout, one bent ear, a tail that sticks straight up. When a man at the dog park asked what breed he was, Lucy laughed and said, *Albanian goatherd.*

Frodo goes to the back door, and Lucy lets him out into the yard. She takes off her heels and puts on a pair of slippers, checks the thermostat and turns up the heat. Sam comes into the kitchen and meows, and Lucy puts some fresh kibble in his bowl. The messages on the answering machine are from her mother and Jill and

Carla—one melancholy, one anxious, one offhand—each in her own way acknowledging what day it is, but none of them willing to come out and say it. The mail is nothing but solicitations and bills. Lucy pours a glass of wine, then goes to the study and sits at her desk, its walnut surface scarred with nicks and glass rings and one long burn from a cigarette ash that could have set the whole house on fire. In the lower left-hand drawer, there's a stack of leather-bound journals.

She takes out the one on top and opens it to the place marked by the thin red ribbon attached to the binding. For several years she wrote almost every day; now weeks go by without a word, her anger and sorrow shriveled to a hard kernel stuck permanently in the back of her throat. She smooths the journal open with the heel of her hand and does the math quickly on a slip of scrap paper, feeling guilty that she cannot recall the numbers instantly and recite them down to the minute. She writes with a fountain pen; there is something comforting in the permanence of the blue-black ink soaking into the page.

1-25-90 (6 years, 7 months & 15 days gone) Happy birthday, Nathan. Nine years old today! That is so hard to believe. I can almost see you laughing, a shock of dark brown hair falling across your forehead, your grown-up teeth still too big for your face. Did you have a party after school today or will you have to wait till the weekend? An afternoon of sledding on a snowy hillside (no girls allowed), hot chocolate and cake afterward, wet socks and gloves drying by the fire? Or will it be a picnic on a sunny beach, you and your pals playing Wiffle ball and riding your boogie boards in the surf? Is there a special present you're hoping to get? A Game Boy? Baseball mitt? One of those flashy dirt bikes with a banana seat? I remember the day I turned nine. My grandmother took me to the Plaza for tea. I wanted to live there like Eloise and play tricks on the staff. Do you remember Eloise? That was Sarah's favorite book. Yours was Goodnight Moon. You were only two, but you knew every word by heart. You liked to snuggle up close to me at bedtime and pretend you were reading. That was always my favorite part of the day.

Sam jumps up on the desk and nuzzles Lucy's hand. She looks at her watch. 9:53. She goes to the kitchen and refills her wineglass, doesn't bother to turn off the light in the study before she heads upstairs. On the bookshelf in the hall, she finds *Eloise* and *Goodnight Moon*. The copper washtub on the hearth in her bedroom is empty, no kindling or wood for a fire.

Lucy crawls under the covers in her clothes while Sam nestles beside her, purring and kneading. She opens a book and reads aloud. "In the great green room there was a telephone…" As the bunny is saying good night to the socks, Lucy hears Frodo barking in the yard. She groans and pulls the cocoon of blankets up around her neck.

"Sam?"

The cat cocks his ears and blinks at Lucy.

"Can you go down and let him in?" She scratches Sam under the chin. "*Please*, baby, go down and get him. I'm all tapped out tonight."

Part One

Chapter 1
Lucy

Cambridge, Massachusetts—July 1977

H is name is Matt," Jill said. "He drives this great little yellow fifty-six Thunderbird. You know, the one with the spare tire sticking up in back."

I was trying to ignore her, rearranging the uneaten cucumber slices on my plate while Jill scraped up the last few crumbs of cheesecake and licked them off her fork.

"You should see the looks on people's faces when he pulls up in that car." She let her jaw drop and made her eyes bug out. "Might as well be a gold carriage with four white horses."

"Sounds like a prince."

"Come on, Luce, don't be like that. He's a terrific guy. Just have a drink with him. What harm can it do?"

I shrugged one shoulder. Griffin took off four months ago, and Jill had been trying to fix me up ever since; any encouragement on my part and she'd have dates lined up for me like customers at a bakery on Saturday morning with numbered stubs in their hands. I lit a cigarette while Jill caught the waitress's eye and gestured for another piece of cheesecake.

"Cody called," I said. "He got us tickets for the David Bowie concert." Cody was my best pal from college. We dated for a few months until he admitted he was gay.

"Just this one time," Jill said, ignoring my attempt to distract her. "Please. For me?" She folded her hands like a beggar and tucked them under her chin.

"You little witch. You've set something up with him already, haven't you?"

She laughed. "Wednesday after work. The piano bar at the Copley Plaza. Just one drink. You'll thank me."

The guy Jill wanted me to meet was a Boston cop who played softball with her husband Terry. He came with the usual bona fides: nice-looking, great personality, loves his job, not on the rebound, which was more than I could say for myself. So why wasn't he already taken?

"Come on, Jill. A *cop*?"

"Yin and yang. You need a change. You can't spend the rest of your life waiting for that asshole to come crawling back."

"Funny, he's crazy about you."

"You have to forget him, Luce. The man skips town three hours after you have an abortion and you act like—"

"No!" I slapped the table and the dishes jumped and people nearby turned and stared. I lowered my voice. "Don't start with that shit."

"I'm sorry. I hate the way he treats you, that's all."

"I know I know I know. Believe me, Jilly, I don't want him back. I really don't. I just…I have to do this at my own pace, okay?"

She rolled her eyes, then plucked the cigarette from my fingers and took a guilty puff.

Jill was my oldest friend. We grew up two houses apart in a small town in Connecticut, dancing a *pas de deux* in the ballet recital, getting suspended in eighth grade for putting a dead mouse in Betsy Farrell's locker, coediting the high school yearbook. We both went to college in the Boston area—she to Lesley, I to BU—and shared an apartment for a year after graduation until she got married.

The waitress brought another slice of cheesecake. Barely five-two, Jill was five and a half months pregnant and had gained at least forty pounds already. Her appetite seemed to defy some basic law of physics.

"Look," I said, "it's not like I sit around every night, bawling my eyes out, waiting for Griffin Chandler to call."

"That's good to hear," Jill said. "You're down to what, five nights a week?"

I laughed and squeezed her chubby hand. A couple weeks ago, she had to go to a jeweler and have her wedding ring snipped off because it was cutting off the circulation and she couldn't slide it over her knuckle. Still, sometimes I'd look at her and feel sick with envy; if I hadn't had the abortion, our babies might have been born on the same day.

∞

My college roommate Rhonda got pregnant junior year. She had been dating two guys at the time and wasn't sure which was the father. It seemed odd to talk about the "father" when Rhonda had no intention of telling either boy about the pregnancy or including them in her decision. Rhonda's parents (like my own) had money, so even though this was before *Roe vs. Wade*, she didn't have to worry about going to some back-alley quack. For a few weeks it was all we could talk about. We considered ourselves feminists and railed about laws written by men to control our bodies and limit our options. Rhonda went to the Bahamas over spring break and came back with a tan. She said it was easier than getting your tonsils out; she had been expecting to feel some sense of guilt and loss, but mostly what she felt was relief. I can't remember if the topic ever came up between us again.

I had always assumed if I ever had an unwanted pregnancy I would handle it with the same aplomb as Rhonda, but the key word in that phrase is *unwanted*. When I realized I was going to have a baby, I was more ambivalent about having an abortion than she had been. The father in this case was Griffin, the man I loved, and if I carried the child to term, my life would be tied inexorably to his.

"Accident, my ass," Griffin said when I told him I was pregnant.

I had been on the pill but got mixed up and missed a day or two. He had no doubts about what I should do about the baby. Our quarrels got nasty. I cried and broke things and wouldn't let him touch me.

Jill found out she was pregnant about a week before I did. The happiest day in her life, she said, but when it came to my predicament, she was torn. She had been raised Catholic, and while she wasn't strictly opposed to abortion, she thought it should be an option of last resort. In spite of my feminist bent—which, for me, was more about how I wanted the world to be than how I actually lived my life—I found it hard to disagree. I was never comfortable with the die-hard stance of women who seemed to regard abortion as a high-priced form of birth control. Jill wanted me to have a baby, but not Griffin's; she hadn't wanted me to get involved with him in the first place.

Once I made up my mind to go ahead with the abortion, I didn't flinch. I found the clinic through a friend. Griffin drove me there on a Friday morning and paid the bill in cash. There were various forms and waivers, which the staff offered to explain, but I signed them all without a second glance. The doctor was a bald, middle-aged man who took my hand and asked if I was certain I wanted to go ahead with the *procedure*. It was the same word I'd been using when I thought about what I was about to do, trying to make something so elemental and irrevocable into something banal. I told the doctor yes.

I was home by noon, feeling groggy but not much pain. Griffin made me tea and sat on the edge of the bed; he said he'd been thinking about taking a road trip, a little alone time to get his head together. Jill had predicted he would bolt. I was afraid she was right, but I thought he'd have the decency to wait until I'd had a chance to shower and brush my hair, maybe hang around for a week or two and take me out to dinner, pretend our happiest days were yet to come. I told him to go, I could use some alone time myself. He didn't wait for me to change my mind. When I thought about it now, some part of me knew he had proven how heartless and selfish he could be; another (bigger) part kept hoping he'd realize how much he needed me and come running back.

I called Jill and she came to my apartment, and we talked and laughed and cried and slept in the same bed like we were back in junior high. I had some cramping and bleeding over the weekend but went back to work on Monday. Ten days later I crashed: night terrors, crying jags, the tapeworm of guilt. Griffin didn't call for over a month.

I forgot the name of the cop Jill wanted me to meet five seconds after she said it. Tom? Bob? Something short and common. Some people I knew still called the police *pigs*, but I wasn't as put off by the idea of going out with a cop as I'd acted with Jill. When I was in college, Rhonda and I got picked up by some off-duty cops who took us bowling and didn't act like jerks when we refused to let them take us back to their apartment. I had gone skeet shooting a few times with my dad, so I wasn't freaked out about the idea of dating a guy with a gun. As for the handcuffs…well, I tried that with Griffin once and liked it—a bonding experience, one of those little kinks in my sexual history I never divulged to Jill.

Close as Jill and I were, she didn't like to talk about sex. She had gone steady with Robby Durant all through high school but refused to say how far they went. Not far enough for Robby, I guessed, seeing him droop along beside her like a lost puppy. (As for me, I surrendered my virginity in the tenth grade to a boy so sweet and desperate he cried afterward, and it almost felt like love.) Jill dumped Robby for Scott Fowler freshman year of college; Bernie Katz stole Jill from Scott. Bernie was the captain of the Harvard squash team, a great guy who was crazy about her but not crazy enough to risk alienating his rich father by marrying a shiksa. Next up, Terry O'Shea. Jill never went six weeks without a boyfriend, convinced each time that this was *the one*. This time she was right. Terry was in his final year of law school at BC when they met; now he worked as an assistant district attorney. He was good-looking, thoughtful, incorrigibly cheerful, and one of the most boring men on earth. Terry could spend ten minutes telling you about the great deal he'd gotten on a new rider mower from Sears with a sixteen-horsepower engine, detachable grass catcher, and a three-year service guarantee. Being a friend of Terry's didn't automatically disqualify the cop from consideration, but I had a feeling he wouldn't be my type.

Of course, when I was being honest with myself, I knew there wasn't any type; there was only Griffin.

I hadn't mentioned it to Jill, but I had started going out again, not on dates, just drinking and dancing at some of the upscale bars and hotel lounges in Cambridge and Back Bay, lots of gigolo wannabes with their gold chains and bad cologne, out-of-town businessmen with silver money clips and pale outlines of wedding bands on their fingers. Occasionally I'd meet someone interesting and give him my number then kick myself if he didn't call back or turn him down if he did. One night I met a pilot who flew corporate executives around the country in a private jet. He was easy to talk to and told me a great story about learning to fly a crop duster from his father when he was still a kid. At the end of the evening, he drove me home and wrote down my phone number, ready to leave, it seemed, without so much as a good-night kiss. I asked him in for a glass of wine and put Van Morrison on the stereo. The pilot studied the prints on my living room wall—six framed woodcuts in bold colors depicting various Tarot cards—discreetly ignoring the photographs of Griffin and me on the bookshelf below.

"These are great," the pilot said. "Who's the artist?"

"My friend Cody. He's very talented. My favorite is the magician." I pointed.

"*Le bateleur.* My mother likes to give Tarot readings for fun."

"She's French?"

He nodded. "A war bride. She and my dad only knew each other for nine days when they got married."

The pilot's mother had been part of the French resistance and sounded like a fascinating woman. She was from Rennes, not far from Saint-Malo, where I'd spent two weeks as a teenager visiting a friend who had been an exchange student in our high school. The pilot and I were sitting on the couch. He kissed me tentatively; I responded in French. My sweater and bra were on the floor, my nipple in the pilot's mouth when he sat up abruptly.

"We don't have to rush into this," he said. "I really *like* you. I don't want to mess things up."

Great line, I thought. He may even have meant it. It was a caution worth noting; the self-help books don't advocate having sex with a guy you've known for less than three hours if you're interested in building a long-term relationship. But I wasn't thinking long-term. After months of wallowing in anger and self-doubt, I needed to be desired. I needed to find a way to put Griffin behind me. I got up from the couch and led the pilot into the bedroom.

Our lovemaking was quick and pleasant, nothing I'd celebrate or regret in the morning. Afterward, we were sitting on the bed, smoking, my head on his shoulder, his hand idly caressing my thigh when the telephone rang. I tried to ignore it, but my body grew taut, each ring more insistent than the last.

"You better get that," the pilot said, dejection in his voice, as if he knew as well as I did who was calling.

I picked up the phone and cradled it to my ear. "Nothing much," I said. "Just sitting here, thinking of you." Which was true.

I was still on the phone with Griffin when the pilot let himself out the door.

"Wear something sexy," Jill said. "That white Charlie's Angels one-piece or the salmon mini-dress."

"I thought you said this was just for a drink."

"Yeah but, you know…first impressions."

"What exactly have you told him about me?"

She laughed. "Very little. I didn't want to scare him off with the truth."

"So what if I really like him?"

"What do you mean?"

"Can I take him home with me?"

"You do and I'll wring your skinny little neck."

Chapter 2

Matt

It was the hottest day of the year, temperatures up over a hundred. A crushed Pepsi can kept the front door of the Sweet Spot propped open for ventilation. The place used to have live strippers when I began patrolling the Combat Zone, but now it was just private video booths, couple of minutes of porn for a quarter. I went in the open doorway and said hi to Lenny.

"Officer Drobyshev." He saluted from his perch behind the counter with an electric fan blowing on the back of his neck. He was reading a battered hardback copy of *The Mayor of Casterbridge*, elbows resting on a display case filled with sex toys.

"Scorcher today," I said.

"You're telling me. I got four, five more weeks of this shit, and the boss won't spring for a fucking air conditioner."

"How's business?"

"Couldn't be better. Summer, winter, guys never stop jacking off."

"You been checking IDs?"

"Please." Lenny frowned. "There are *real* crimes happening out there, my friend. Don't tell me Boston's finest give a flying fuck about a couple of guys giving each other blowjobs in a private video booth."

"The brass wants us to crack down. Undercover picked up a young hustler at the Pussy Cat last night. Third or fourth juvie this month."

"Enterprising youth. I'm sure he makes a helluva lot more money than I do."

I smiled. "How's the book?"

There were underlinings on the page, the margins filled with notes in minuscule handwriting in different color inks.

"Michael Henchard." He shook his head. "The trouble with the past is, it's never really *over*. Just keeps coming back and biting you in the ass."

Lenny had been working on his dissertation for years. He told me *Jude the Obscure* was one of the three greatest novels in the English language. I had a copy of the book on my nightstand but couldn't get into it. I preferred history—Sacco and Vanzetti, the Nuremberg trials, General Sherman burning his way across Georgia. Stuff that really happened.

I stepped through the black curtain to the peep-show booths in back. The room was divided into two narrow corridors with video booths on either side. The piney smell of disinfectant couldn't hide the human stench underneath. Several men lurked in the corridors. I turned my head and caught one of them staring at me. In the half-second our eyes met, the man's face seemed to change from desire to fear to shame before he turned away. What a life! Poor schmuck probably had a wife and three kids at home. I heard a guy whisper in the booth behind me and another man let out a moan. I pounded on the door with the heel of my hand.

"One person to a booth," I said and went back out front.

"Thomas Hardy, my friend." Lenny held up the book like a gospel preacher. "He understood how weak the human race is. Every fucking one of us."

Back on the street I checked my watch. Twenty minutes till knock off. That left me an hour after work to go home and shower and get ready for my blind date. I was supposed to meet her for a drink at the piano bar at the Copley Plaza. Not the sort of thing I did often, but Terry O'Shea's wife, Jill, cornered me at our last softball game and asked me to do it as a favor. The girl she set me up with was her best friend.

"Lucy's gorgeous," Jill had said. "Smart, funny. Body to die for."

"And...?"

"Terrible taste in men."

"Ah, no wonder you asked me."

Jill laughed. "No, no, that came out wrong. The last one was a total shit, that's all. She's been sitting at home, moping for months now. I figured if she went out with a really terrific guy..." She batted her eyes like Betty Boop. Jill knew how cute she was, even with all the weight she'd put on with her pregnancy.

I said okay to the blind date. She wasn't going to stop bugging me till I did.

"Anything else you want to tell me?" I said.

"Well, she's not..." She crinkled her eyebrows. "Let's just say she has an edge."

An edge was fine with me. The last girl I dated was as edgeless as fog. I met her as I was passing through Filene's cosmetics department. I was on my way to the basement to look for some shirts and she caught me ogling her cleavage.

"Would you care to sample the new fragrance from Chanel, officer?" She blocked my path. "For that special lady in your life."

"Sorry, I don't have one at the moment."

"Maybe I could offer some assistance?"

Some women have a thing about men in uniform. It's one of those unwritten perks that comes with the job, like never having to worry about getting a traffic ticket. Something to help make up for the scornful looks cops get sometimes from strangers on the street.

The Chanel girl and I met for coffee after work and ended up in bed that same evening. At first I was taken by her sunny disposition. She had been a cheerleader in high school and still had that chirpy, never-say-die spirit that keeps those girls leaping and chanting when it's cold and rainy and the home team is down forty-two zip. But after a while it got irritating. She didn't want to hear about the unsavory things I had to deal with on the job. I started calling her less and making excuses not to get together. One night over dinner, I told her I thought we should take a break.

"But why?" she said. "I thought we were doing so well."

I sank low in my chair and tried the it's-not-you-it's-me maneuver, but she kept probing.

"I don't know," I said. "I guess it's just…you're too damned *happy*."

"Not anymore," she said.

Out on the sidewalk, heat rose from the cement through my crepe rubber soles.

"Mr. Pleeze-man. Mr. Pleeze-man." A woman was yelling and waving her arms on the opposite side of the street. "You come quick."

I couldn't place her accent. She was short and round with dyed black hair. She didn't appear to be hurt, but the front of her yellow waitress's uniform was splattered with blood. I ran across the street, and she led me down an alley to a brick building with an apartment on the second floor. We hurried through her living room, and she pointed toward an open doorway.

"In there," she said. "My husband."

A hairy man was lying face down on the bed, naked except for the boxer shorts pulled down around his knees. Blood oozed from a lump the size of a tennis ball on the back of his bald head. For a moment I thought the man was dead, then he let out a loud snore. I felt so relieved I almost laughed. In five-plus years on the job, I'd found the dead body of a homeless man in an alley and another of a junkie who OD'd in the backseat of a car. But never a homicide victim. I wasn't anxious for my first.

"You did this?" I said.

"Yes."

"What happened?"

There was a shrill cry behind me. "No! Don't you dare!"

A girl ran into the room and tried to put her hand over the woman's mouth. The woman started yelling in another language, her arms flailing to fend the girl off. I got between them and told the girl to calm down. She was about fourteen, short and chubby, in tight cut-offs and a Sex Pistols T-shirt. Streaks of mascara ran down her cheeks.

I looked at the woman. "Tell me what happened."

The girl said, "I'll kill you if you say anything."

"I come home from work and find him and this little whore—"

The girl lunged, but I grabbed her around the waist and held her back.

"Shut up, Mummy. I mean it. Don't say another word or I'll come in your room some night and slit your fucking throat."

I said to the woman, "Is this your daughter?"

She nodded. I was still holding my arm around the girl's soft belly, which almost made me feel like a pervert myself. The man on the bed groaned and tried to roll over.

"We need to call an ambulance," I said.

By the time I talked to the detectives and got back to the station and filled out all the paperwork, I had less than fifteen minutes to get to the Copley Plaza for my date. No time to go home and shower and change. I had a pair of jeans and golf shirt in my locker. I asked Sergeant Barker what he thought I should wear.

"Go with the fuckin' uniform," he said.

"You think?"

"Listen to Sergeant Barker, boyo. This is who you are. She don't like it, fuck her and the appaloosa she rode in on." In Barker's thick Boston accent, there was an "r" at the end of appaloosa, none in his own last name.

"The uniform it is."

"What time you supposed to be there?"

I glanced at my watch. "Eight minutes. No way I'm going to make it on time."

Barker laughed. "Hop in the cruiser. We'll hit the fuckin' siren."

We pulled up to the Copley Plaza with our blue lights flashing.

"Check this out," Barker said, lifting his chin. A girl was crossing the intersection. "Maybe that's her."

"Maybe. Fits the general description."

She was wearing mules and a sleeveless mini-dress—small breasts with no bra, nipples and panties outlined against the pink cotton. Summer tan and Jackie O sunglasses, light brown hair hanging halfway down her back. Two guys stopped to watch her pass. Her walk was slow and casual, like a lioness sauntering down to the waterhole.

"No way you're that fuckin' lucky, boyo. That girl could melt the pennies on a dead man's eyes."

I grinned and started to get out of the car. "Well, here goes."

"You really think that's her?"

"I can only hope."

The doorman made a little bow as he held the door open for the girl. I followed her into the hotel. The piano bar was on the right. She stopped in the entranceway and looked around.

"Lucy?" I said behind her.

She turned, took off her sunglasses, and smiled. "Hello. You must be…?"

"Matt."

"I'm sorry. I'm terrible with names."

"Not my strong suit either," I said. A lie. I had a knack for remembering names and faces, which served me well on the street.

"I didn't expect you to be in uniform."

"Sorry." I looked down at myself. "I got tied up with a case and didn't have time to change." She had bright, mischievous eyes, gray-green with a dark ring around the iris.

"No, it's fine. A little *arresting*, but that's okay."

I cackled like a madman. Stay cool, I told myself. It felt like a pinball was ricocheting around in my chest. The Copley was one of the best hotels in the city. Plush chairs and low polished tables in the piano bar, half the patrons dressed to the nines. I wanted to walk into the bar with her and see all those heads turn our way, guys wondering how I got so lucky. But it probably wasn't a good idea.

I said, "I don't think the manager's going to appreciate me sitting there in my uniform. Might make some customers nervous."

"What do you suggest?"

Let's skip the small talk and go back to my place. Make love till we set ourselves on fire.

"I have a friend who's the owner of the Café Budapest. It's just a short walk from here. Have you ever been?"

"No, I've heard it's wonderful." We went back outside. "Look, mimes," Lucy said.

In the middle of Copley Square, a boy and a girl in white face and black leotards were sitting at an imaginary table eating an imaginary meal.

"Amazing," I said. It was hard to believe they could sit in those nonexistent chairs without falling down. The boy crossed his leg, balancing on one foot. The girl mime was trying to uncork a bottle of wine. She kept twisting and yanking the corkscrew and did a back somersault. Her partner hurried over to help, but he was more worried about the wine than the girl. They struggled over the bottle till it crashed on the sidewalk. The two of them tiptoed sad-faced through the broken glass. Then the girl cut herself and started hopping around, holding her foot against her chest.

I glanced at Lucy, wanting to share the moment, but she seemed far away.

Chapter 3
Lucy

T he first time I saw Griffin he was smoking a joint and talking on a pay phone in Harvard Square. He appeared to be about thirty—thin face with a patrician nose, strawberry-blond hair parted in the middle, charcoal gray slacks, beige turtleneck, and a navy blue blazer—one of those men who would look perfect in a rainstorm. I slid a dime in the phone beside him but couldn't get a dial tone.

"Sorry, Russell, but I can't do that," he said. "Have you taken economics yet? Supply and demand, my friend. Supply and demand."

He turned and smiled at me, eyes as blue as arctic snow, and handed me the joint. The first toke made my scalp tingle; the second one made me feel like I'd just stepped off a Tilt-A-Whirl.

"I don't have time for this, Russell." His eyes never left mine. "Six-fifty for the whole stash. Take it or leave it. There's a young lady standing here with a Mona Lisa smile who requires my attention."

He introduced himself simply as Griffin. It was Saturday, a cool afternoon in early May, my second year out of college. My mother, Amanda, had driven to Boston from Connecticut for the weekend and was staying at the Ritz. We were planning to go see the Renoir exhibit at the Museum of Fine Arts and have dinner after. I'd gone out to do some errands and lost track of time, so I stopped to call her and say I was running late.

"Plans change," Griffin said, flicking the roach into the street. He asked if I wanted to go get something to eat.

It didn't take much convincing. I called my mother and told her I'd come down with a bug, was feverish, and could barely get out of bed. Amanda went on about how sorry she was, how she'd been looking forward to spending the day together, even mused about coming to Cambridge to make me tea and soup, but we both knew she didn't mean it, no more than she believed my story about being ill. I had no qualms about standing her up; given the chance, she would have done the same.

I was eleven or twelve when I realized my mother was a drunk. My younger brother Mark and I learned to watch her and adapt to her shifting moods. My father basically ignored her tirades and dark silences until she went completely off the rails, at which point he blamed it on "exhaustion" and carted her off to a sanatorium to dry out. In my junior year of high school, Amanda decamped on a three-day bender with the twenty-six-year-old assistant tennis pro from the country club—one of her more public transgressions, right up there with the time she drove *into* the beauty parlor. The scandal probably would have ended most marriages, but my dad had his own counterweight of peccadilloes: speeding tickets, bimbo secretaries, a pied-à-terre in Manhattan. The tennis pro, whom I had a crush on and would gladly have run off with myself, lost his job; Amanda spent a few weeks at a spa. Like all family disasters, we never discussed the incident at home, not openly anyway.

Mark and I, who relied on each other for regular reality checks, learned early on that our parents' foibles were an invaluable legacy, a bottomless trust fund of bad behavior. Amanda and Roger Thornhill—everyone, including my mother, called him "Thorny"— had no illusions about their children being perfect; they assumed Mark and I would screw up from time to time, just as they did. No matter what the misadventure—wrecking the car (a Thornhill family tradition), stealing pills from Amanda's cache, getting caught in the TV room *in flagrante delicto*—the best defense was to pretend it hadn't happened. Or lie about it.

Griffin got a red Lord & Taylor shopping bag from the trunk of his BMW, which was parked on Mt. Auburn Street, and we walked up to the Hong Kong across from Lamont Library. The restaurant was empty except for an elderly couple near the window. We sat in a booth next to the tropical fish tank. The waiter brought us menus and we ordered drinks—Glenlivet for Griffin, a mai tai for me. When the drinks came, Griffin took the pink paper umbrella from my glass and spun it back and forth between his fingers; then he reached up and slipped the stem under my hair comb as if it were a flower, drew his head back, and gave me the once-over. He smiled his approval. I was half thrilled, half mortified, as if he'd put his hand up under my skirt.

He asked what I did when I wasn't picking up strangers in the Square. I told him I worked for the Harvard Class Report Office, editing the entries alumni sent in for their reunion books.

"About half the stuff we get is nothing but bragging," I said.

"Guys crowing about themselves, their kids, grandkids. The Cliffies are almost as bad as the men. Not that some of these people don't have reason to brag. We get responses from congressmen, Nobel Prize winners, businessmen with more money than God. Leonard Bernstein, Norman Mailer. That big tall actor…what's his name? The one who plays Herman on *The Munsters*. Can you believe he went to Harvard?" Griffin had one elbow on the table, his chin in his hand and his eyes fixed on mine. "Some guys write in and they can be really thoughtful or funny or sad. I mean, sometimes we'll get a submission from some guy who graduated thirty years ago, probably thinking he had it made; now he's been divorced three times and is working in a shoe store in Schenectady. We get stuff from Hare Krishnas, Black Panthers, you name it. Harvard has this thing about trying to keep up with all their alumni no matter what."

I couldn't stop babbling. The waiter brought mountains of food I didn't remember us ordering. Griffin wielded his chopsticks like a grasshopper; I wished I had a fork but was embarrassed to ask. A boy in a ratty Army jacket approached the table.

"Hey, Russell," Griffin said, "have a seat. This is Lucy. Will you join us?"

"Can't, man. I got to run."

Griffin sighed and looked at me. "The death of manners. He used to beg me to play catch with him when he was a kid." He slid the shopping bag out from under the table with his foot. The boy took the bag and handed him a wad of bills, which Griffin slipped into his pocket without bothering to count. It didn't occur to me that I was witnessing a felony, that a narc might walk in the door and arrest us. I suppose I could attribute my lack of concern to the times—dealing drugs in Harvard Square was as common as selling used textbooks—or to the fact that I was stoned, but it was more than that. Nothing mattered but Griffin. Maybe it was those blue eyes, the way he seemed to hang on every word when I talked. I couldn't explain the feeling; I just wanted it to last.

The waiter brought the check and a brown bag with the leftovers. Outside it was clear and chilly. I put on the sweater I'd brought in a canvas shoulder bag. Griffin and I both lit cigarettes, and we walked down to the river and sat on the grassy bank. A man in a filthy hooded sweatshirt was throwing a Frisbee to a brindled mutt with a blue bandana tied around its neck. The dog was swift and agile with an uncanny sense of timing, his body arching and twisting as he leaped to make the catch. Sometimes the Frisbee would sail into the river and the dog would swim out and get it. Griffin went over and spoke to the guy, then came back for the leftovers. He took the bag to the water's edge where the dog and the man shared the food. I stretched out on the grass and rested on one elbow. Griffin slipped off his blazer, and he and the man started taking turns throwing the Frisbee to the dog, the disc hovering at the top of its arc like a prop in a low-budget sci-fi movie, interplanetary orange with a purple outer ring. I lay back with my shoulder bag under my head. There was a drowsy hum of car wheels on Memorial Drive as I closed my eyes and thanked my lucky stars I wasn't slogging through the museum with Amanda.

When I awoke, the sun was sinking behind the stadium on the other side of the river. The man and his dog were gone, and so was Griffin. I stood up and brushed myself off, scouring the ground and my shoulder bag, hoping to find a note. A gust of wind made me shiver. As I reached up to refasten my hair comb, I felt the paper umbrella and removed it gingerly, careful not to tear the paper or break the fragile spokes. The umbrella was pink with a pattern of pale green bamboo shoots. I held the stem between my fingers, spinning it clockwise and counterclockwise as Griffin had done, trying to convince myself he'd gone off for a few minutes to make a phone call or buy a pack of cigarettes, but I knew he wasn't coming back.

Chapter 4
Matt

Sandor spotted me talking to the maître d' in the foyer of the restaurant.

"Matyas!" He rushed over and wrapped me in a bear hug. "Where have you been, my friend? Every day I am thinking, Where is Matyas? Maybe I should call police." He roared with laughter at his own joke. "Now, tell me, who is beautiful lady?"

"Sandor, this is Lucy Thornhill. Lucy, Sandor Toth."

"*Enchanté.*" He took her hands and kissed her on both cheeks. "Welcome to Café Budapest."

"Thank you," she said. "It's a pleasure to be here."

"You have known Matyas long time?" He put his arm around me.

She smiled. "About fifteen minutes."

"Ah, let me tell you, this man, he save my life. Without him, I am *lapcsánka.*" Sandor laughed and slapped his palms together. "Potato pancake."

He led us to a table in back and pulled out a chair for Lucy. A busboy filled our water glasses and lit the candles. There was a single red rose in a slender vase on the table. I had never been to Europe, but the restaurant had an Old World feel to it. Not lavish, more about class than money. The kind of place you see in the movies where Ingrid Bergman walks in and spies an old lover across the room. Two waiters in tuxedos came to the table. One brought a plate of bread crusts and feta cheese spread. The other had a bottle of Dom Pérignon and three glasses. The waiter popped the cork and poured the champagne.

Sandor held up his glass for a toast. "To good friends—and love."

When he left to attend to other customers, Lucy gave me a sly smile. "Jill didn't tell me you were the lost dauphin of Hungary."

I made a face. "It's embarrassing. He goes a little overboard sometimes."

"Is your real name Matyas?"

"No, just Sandor's way of pretending I'm Hungarian. He calls me 'nephew' sometimes, like I'm part of his family."

"How did you meet him? He said you saved his life."

"That's debatable."

"Tell me. I love stories."

"Sandor was down in the theater district, picking up tickets for some show. The guy has a million connections. He's always offering me seats to the Red Sox, Celtics, concerts, you name it. He parked his new Mercedes in an alley near the Wilbur and ran in to see the manager."

The waiter came with the menus.

Lucy finished her champagne. "If this stuff were eight bucks a bottle," she said, grinning, "the whole world would be drunk all the time."

I refilled her glass.

"Anyway, the place where Sandor parked was illegal, but he figured no big deal, he'd be back in five minutes. When he came out of the theater, he heard the Mercedes starting and knew immediately what was happening." I told her the car was a 450SL red sports coupe. The salesman at the dealership had warned Sandor the car was on top of the wish list for thieves.

Lucy spread some feta on a bread crust, tasted it, and nodded her approval. The waiter asked if we were ready to order our appetizers.

"You pick," she said. "I'm sure everything's marvelous."

I asked for foie gras and cabbage rolls.

"Sandor didn't stop to think. Just heard the car engine and charged down the alley. He's incredibly strong, like a little bull. He grabbed the thief who was getting in the car on the passenger's side and smashed his face down on the top of the door. The guy in the driver's seat threw the car in reverse and knocked Sandor down and jumped out of the car to help his friend. Sandor tried to get up, but the driver kicked him and broke his jaw. The other thief was dazed, blood spurting from his eye socket. His friend was trying to get him in the car when I walked by the alley."

Lucy's face was rapt. It was hard to look at her and keep my train of thought. She wasn't beautiful exactly, but incredibly sexy. Bewitching. Like she could twitch her nose and turn you into an armadillo.

"I saw Sandor writhing on the ground. It wasn't clear what the situation was, but something bad was obviously going down. I drew my gun and yelled at the thieves to put their hands on top of the car, which they did. Believe it or not, that's the first and only time since I joined the police force I've ever pointed my gun at someone."

"God, I can't imagine. Were you scared? Your adrenaline level must have been off the charts."

"It was definitely a rush. I don't think I had time to be scared.

More like I was super aware, trying to put all the pieces together. In the back of my mind, I kept wondering if the thieves had an accomplice, somebody about to come around the corner and shoot me in the back. Meanwhile, the guy lying on the ground *looked* like the victim, but I couldn't be sure. Luckily, everything turned out fine."

"Fascinating." She leaned forward. "I can see why Sandor's so grateful to you."

"I don't know. I tried to tell him I was just doing my job, but he's convinced the driver was about to back up the car and run over him."

"Excuse me, sir," the waiter said. He put our appetizers on the table. "Mr. Toth is recommending an excellent Chateauneuf-du-pape with your dinner this evening."

"Sure, why not." I looked at Lucy and shrugged again. "So I get treated like the lost dauphin."

The waiter brought our entrées and we savored our food. I'd been to the restaurant with a date three or four times and always brought my mother when she came for a visit. I didn't know how much it cost and didn't want to know. The menus at my table never had prices on them.

Lucy was wearing a thin silver chain with a turquoise pendant and matching turquoise earrings. She had a small brown birthmark shaped like an acorn just below her right collarbone that I couldn't stop staring at. It made me think of the term "beauty mark," which I had never really considered before. It was uncanny the way that tiny imperfection made her seem even more attractive. I tried to squelch my fantasies about seeing her naked and actually touching her smooth, tanned skin. Who was the idiot who let this woman go? Two old-fashioned silver combs held her long hair back from her face.

I said, "Are your hair combs antique?"

"Yes." She touched one then the other as if she had forgotten they were there.

"They're extraordinary."

"Thank you." She smiled, knowing I meant her. "They were my grandmother's."

I asked where she worked, where she'd gone to college. Her answers were short. She didn't want to talk about herself, though she mentioned that she had recently taken two courses at the Cambridge Adult Education Center—pottery and conversational French.

"I'm trying to find my *grande passion*." She pushed her food around with her fork, then muttered under her breath, "Something besides falling in love with assholes."

I let that one go, a conversation for another time.

"So what happened today?" she said.

"What?"

"At work? The thing that almost made you late."

I told her the story.

"The man was the girl's stepfather," I said. "Turns out he'd been molesting her for years. The girl was like a firecracker with the fuse lit. She seemed angrier at her mother than she was at him. And the mother...it was almost like she thought it was the girl's fault."

"I can see that. The girl blames her mother for letting it happen. A mother is supposed to protect her daughter, not let some pervert rape her. Meanwhile, the mother knows she failed—she's the one who brought that monster into the house—but she can't face it, so she turns on the kid."

"Huh? You seem to know a lot about this stuff. Are you a therapist or something?"

"No, no, I would make a *really* bad therapist." She laughed. "Just ask mine."

The waiter came by and refilled Lucy's glass. She was drinking much more than I was but didn't seem to notice me holding back. The last thing I wanted was to get drunk and do something stupid.

"Enough," she said. "This food is too good." She pushed her plate away. "Do you mind if I smoke?"

"No, not at all." I didn't smoke myself. I picked up the candle from the table and held it out for her. She touched my hand as a gesture of thanks and a little jolt of electricity went through me.

She said, "I read a book about sex abuse a few years ago. Turns out it happens everywhere. Rich people, poor people, black, white. One of those clubs without any restrictions. Like beating the shit out of your wife. Any two-fisted son-of-a-bitch can join."

Her face was flushed. She'd only taken a few drags on her cigarette, but she ground it into a crooked stub in the ashtray. Here was that edge Jill had mentioned, her anger so intense I got the feeling she might have been smacked around by some shithead herself.

She asked me how I'd decided to become a cop. I told her it was something I'd always been interested in. I went to community college near my home in Butler, Pennsylvania, and majored in criminology.

"I thought about going on for a four-year degree," I said, "but I felt a little burned out on school. Luckily, I had a high lottery number and didn't have to worry about the draft. I told my mom I wanted to do a little traveling and she was great about it. I'm an only child. My father died in a mining accident when I was a baby, and my mom raised me herself. We're real close, but she never tried to smother me. She told me to go see the country. She said she wished she could have done it herself." Lucy took out another cigarette. "The farthest I'd ever been away from home was a field trip to Washington, D.C. I had an old Rambler with a stick on the floor and headed west. I got a job in Minneapolis loading freight cars. When the weather got chilly, I headed south. The car gave out in Missouri, so I got on a bus and kept on going."

"Sounds neat."

"Yeah, it was. I worked odd jobs, bummed around for a year and a half. Got to see some interesting places, met some terrific people."

Lucy said, "So, in all your travels, what was your favorite place?"

I didn't have to think. "Puerto Rico."

"Really?" She narrowed her eyes. "Aww, that's where you fell in love."

"Fell in love with surfing," I said, not wanting to talk about my Puerto Rican girlfriend. "You can't believe how blue the water is."

She grinned and let me off the hook.

I told her about the retired Boston police lieutenant I met on the plane back to the States from Puerto Rico. When I mentioned my interest in law enforcement to the lieutenant, he offered to make a few phone calls on my behalf. Eight months later I had my shield.

Lucy said, "Did you meet Terry on the job?"

"No, through softball. He's good friends with a couple other guys on the team. I actually know Jill better. She talked me into coming to school and speaking to her fourth-grade class."

"And talked you into going out with me."

"Well, there're only three bachelors on the team." I smiled and took a chance. "The other two turned her down." It's always tricky, making a joke like that with a woman.

Lucy laughed. "The smart ones always do."

The waiter came by and asked if we wanted coffee or dessert. Lucy said just coffee. I ordered one of the house specials, chestnut purée with rum and whipped cream. She smoked her third cigarette. Sometimes when she took a drag, she'd hold the cloud of smoke in her mouth for a second with her lips parted, then curl her tongue and pull the smoke in. She seemed to do it unconsciously. I wondered if she had any idea how seductive it was.

"Impressive," she said, watching me dig into my dessert. She spooned a dollop of whipped cream from my plate and put it in her coffee. "I like a man with an *appetite*." As soon as she said it, she made a funny face. "Oh my god—" She covered her mouth with her hand, but a giggle squirted through her fingers. "I can't believe I just said that." She tried to suppress her laugh for a moment, then threw her head back and let out a husky, wine-soaked howl that made other people in the restaurant turn and stare. I reached across the table and interlocked my fingers with hers.

Sandor came to the table with a bottle of apricot brandy and insisted we share a glass. Lucy thanked him for his hospitality.

Sandor said to me. "You must bring your lady back."

"I will, definitely," I said.

He put his hand on my shoulder. "You want me to call taxi for you?"

"Yes, please," I said. "Thank you for everything."

Sandor took the rose from the vase on the table and handed it to Lucy. "Here is souvenir of your first visit to Café Budapest. You must come back soon." He looked as smitten as I was.

On the sidewalk, Lucy twirled the rose between her fingers. She snapped the stem in half and gnawed on the tough fibers until she'd broken it in two. Then she stuck the rose in her hair and struck a pose, one hand on her hip.

"What do you think?"

"*Me gusta.*"

She smiled. "Did that Puerto Rican *señorita* teach you Spanish?"

"Look at that sky," I said. It was dusk, the city bathed in a glow of red and purple.

Two businessmen walked by with their briefcases. One leaned toward the other and said something, and they both laughed. If the joke was on me, I didn't care. The cab pulled up to the curb. Lucy and I got in the backseat, and she gave the driver her address.

Lucy sat close and rubbed her hand softly on my thigh. "What else did the *señorita* teach you?"

I rolled down the window and let the warm air blow on my face. We drove along the river with the colors of the sky reflecting on the water. Couples were strolling along the Esplanade. I'd never seen the city look more beautiful. The driver crossed the bridge to Cambridge and made a few turns. Halfway down the block on Lucy's street, she pointed at a ramshackle house with a lopsided front porch, most of the balusters broken or missing.

As we got out of the cab, I asked the driver to wait.

"You're not coming in?" Lucy said, pouting.

"I better take a rain check." Since we'd left the restaurant, I had been debating with myself about what to do if she offered.

She leaned against me. "It's not raining, Matt." It was the first time she had said my name.

"You busy Saturday?"

"Come on, you don't want to wait that long."

She pulled my head down and kissed me. Her tongue tasted like brandy and cigarettes.

I said, "I should go." She tried to kiss me again. I held her shoulders, keeping her at bay. "I'm sorry, but I really need to go."

"Are you always so fucking *controlled*?"

"Please, Lucy, can't you see you got me dangling by a thread?"

She measured me for a second, then her eyes softened. "What time on Saturday?"

The cabbie drove me home to Mission Hill. When I tried to pay him, he said it was already taken care of. Sandor again. My roommate Kreider was asleep in his ancient recliner with the TV on, three empty beer bottles and an empty pizza box beside him on the floor. I turned off the television and carried the box and bottles out to the kitchen and put them in the garbage. Kreider was a cop in the harbor patrol division. A great guy and an unapologetic slob. He wandered around the apartment leaving trash and dirty clothes and wet towels behind like a molting lizard. I cleaned up after him and tried not to complain. Two years ago he asked me if I wanted to room with him. He had a terrific deal from the landlady who loved having cops as her tenants. The apartment was much larger than my old place and the rent considerably less. I had always been frugal. I put half the money I saved on rent in the credit union and the other half in a mutual fund. In another year or two, I'd have enough to make a down payment on a house or condo of my own.

I went to my room and tried to read, but all I could do was think about Lucy. I didn't like her asking if I was always so controlled, but I knew I'd done the right thing. She was drunk and I wasn't. I wanted to make love to her, not simply get laid. I was twenty-eight years old and I'd been around the block enough to know that sooner or later every romance turns into a negotiation. It's a matter of give and take. Give too little and you breed resentments, take too little and you start feeling used. How does a candlelight dinner stack up against changing the oil in her car? Is getting a blowjob worth the same as giving her a back rub? Before long you're both keeping a ledger. Tallying things up. I didn't want Lucy to wake up tomorrow with a hangover, wondering if she'd given too much. I wanted her to look forward to our next date as much as I was.

Chapter 5

Lucy

I was tempted to call in sick the morning after my blind date with Matt, but it was the slowest time of the year in our office, so I figured I could fake it through the day. Wearing sunglasses to hide my bloodshot eyes, I poured a cup of coffee and carried it to my desk, my coworkers giving me friendly, knowing looks but no one saying a word, not like that sadistic little dwarf pounding on the inside of my skull with a hammer—*Did-it-again. Did-it-again.* I lit a cigarette, straightened a pile of papers, and moved it from one side of the desk to the other. I picked at the callus next to the fingernail on my left thumb and tore it off with my teeth. Anita answered the phone at her desk across the room, then buzzed my line.

"So, how'd it go?" Jill said, all bright and cheery.

"It was all right."

"That bad, huh?"

"No, it was fine. He seems like a decent guy."

"Wow, you should get a job writing cards for Hallmark."

"What the hell do you *want* me to say? He's nice. We had a good time. He's just not…"

"Griffin."

Exactly, but I wasn't going to admit it. "It was one date, for Christ's sake. Why do you care so much?"

"About *you*? Sometimes I wonder."

"I'm sorry, Jilly. I haven't even had my coffee yet. He took me to the Café Budapest. It was lovely. They roll out the red carpet when he goes there."

"The red carpet?"

"I'll call you later and tell you all about it."

"Promise?"

"Promise."

I hung up the phone. Shit shit shit. Why was I so nasty to Jill? Matt was precisely what I needed in my life. I woke up this morning thinking about our date, how he jabbered away at dinner and didn't ask me a million questions, how he seemed, in the best sense of the word, like a *regular* guy: forthright, congenial, eager to please, but certainly no pushover. I liked the way he held his ground when I tried to seduce him into coming up to my apartment. He said I had him dangling by a thread, but I didn't believe that in the light of day any more than I did last night. He wanted to show me that he was in control, that he was going to take me to bed on his terms, not mine. That seemed to bode well for good times to come, but the possibility of good times with Matt made me feel like I was losing Griffin, losing not only what I wanted but what I knew: that ache, the habitual sting, like tearing the skin around my thumbnail till it bled.

All Jill wanted was for me to be happy. The key, according to my therapist, was for me to want it myself. My mother told me happiness was overrated. *Any fool can be happy*, she liked to say. *The hard part is feeling like you matter.*

Three years ago, the morning after that first impromptu date with Griffin, I was the one calling Jill, trying to make the whole episode sound amusing, though I left out the part about the Lord & Taylor bag of marijuana.

Jill said, "The guy is obviously a jerk, Luce. Be thankful you found out *before* you started going out with him."

But I was already second-guessing myself, wondering what I'd said or done to drive him away, what I could have said or done to make him stay. I'd had my fair share of boyfriends up to that point, but no one who left me yearning. I didn't envy Jill for having Terry, but I envied her certainty that he was her one and only. It seemed so arbitrary, a trick she played on herself. Why him when the possibilities were limitless?

As the week dragged on, I began to think I might never see Griffin again. Then, late Friday afternoon, I was standing by the copy machine at work when a man's voice behind me said, "Buy you a drink?"

I turned around and glanced at the clock on the wall. "If I don't get a better offer in the next eleven minutes."

Griffin grinned. He was wearing a starched white shirt with the top two buttons unbuttoned, jeans with a pressed-in crease, and an alligator-skin belt. I could feel my coworkers watching me. I wanted to kiss him; I wanted to kick him in the shins. He was smaller than I remembered, about my height and whippet-thin.

"I'll wait for you outside," he said.

I gave him a skeptical look.

"Honest." He put his hand on his heart. "Till Hell freezes over."

My own heart was pounding as I stood in the bathroom and brushed my hair. I smiled at myself in the mirror, feeling like I was fourteen again.

Spring had finally arrived; people were out in shirtsleeves and tank tops, pastel leaves unfolding on the trees. We tried one bar, then another, but they were so crowded we couldn't get in the door. Griffin and I walked across the Square to Harvard Yard and sat on the steps of Widener Library. He asked me how I'd been, and I said fine, keeping busy.

"What about you?" I smiled. "Got any more dope deals lined up?"

He grinned. "Nah, that was just a favor I was doing for friend. I like to consider it as an act of civil disobedience, my way of under-mining the establishment."

I bumped his tassel loafer (no socks) with my foot. "Come on, you look just like the establishment."

"It's all a big disguise. Makes it easier to operate behind enemy lines."

"Seriously, what do you do?"

"I have my own one-man PR firm—Griffin Chandler Strategies. Companies hire me to help them get publicity and improve their image, come up with clever ways for them to market their products."

"Do you enjoy it?"

"It can be interesting. Depends on the client. Sometimes I can't believe how much people pay me to tell them things they could have easily figured out for themselves. I've got plenty of work, but I've been getting antsy lately. I'm thinking about trying something new."

"Like what?"

"I don't know. See if I can get into promoting. Write the great

American screenplay. Go out to Hollywood and try to swim with the sharks."

"What will your screenplay be about?"

"Serendipity. A tragically bored young man meets a beautiful girl while he's talking on a pay phone, and they connect for one magical afternoon before fate intervenes."

"I can't wait to find out the rest of the story."

"A happy ending, for sure. That's what sells."

"Let's go back to the part about fate. Why did you leave me by the river like that?"

"Sorry, the dog with the Frisbee got into a fight with a schnauzer, and I had to help the guy take him to the vet."

I grinned. "Please. You can do better than that.

"No, really. I knew where to find you."

"You're not going to tell me, are you?"

"You want to know the truth?" He fixed those pale blue eyes on me. "When I came over and saw you sleeping on the grass, I felt like I'd stepped into a dream. You had one hand folded under your chin, your hair spread out around you like a silk cape. You looked so *amazing*. Like a pre-Raphaelite painting or a vision out of a Fellini film. I stood there for about five minutes just watching you sleep, thinking, 'Be careful, Griff. This is the real deal. You've never known a woman like this before. One kiss and all your hard-earned insouciance could be gone in a heartbeat.' I don't have any excuses, Lucy. I wasn't sure I could handle it, so I just…" He made a motion with his hand like an airplane taking off.

I narrowed my eyes for a second, then burst out laughing. "I can see why you went into PR."

"A little heavy-handed, was it?"

"Better than a sharp stick in the eye." I leaned over, kissed him softly on the lips, and waved bye-bye. "There goes all your hard-earned insouciance."

He flicked his hand. "Good riddance."

We kissed again on the stairs leading up to my apartment, then tumbled in the door and made love on the couch. His body was lean and wiry, almost no hair on his freckled skin. He had a tattoo on the back of his left shoulder, the first I'd seen on someone of his ilk—a lion with an eagle's head and wings, the gryphon from *Alice in Wonderland*. I traced the black lines with my fingernail. He took out a joint, and we smoked and drank wine and made love again.

It was after nine when we went out to dinner at a little Greek restaurant. Alan Griffin Chandler III told me he had grown up in Cincinnati and, like his father and grandfather before him, had gone to St. Mark's then Princeton. He said he'd majored in partying with a minor in English literature, his only regret being that he was never quite good enough to make the varsity tennis team. His father wanted him to go to law school and join the family firm, but Griffin said he had no interest in the law and even less in living in Cincinnati. Two weeks after graduation, he married his longtime girlfriend.

"I think we did it out of inertia," he said. "We came home from our honeymoon, moved into an apartment, looked at each other, and said, *Now what?* She worked as a buyer for a department store; I got a job with an ad agency. I don't think we had one whole week when we were really happy. We had so little in common. I wanted to travel; she didn't. She wanted kids; I didn't. Thank God, she never got pregnant. We lasted almost two years before calling it quits."

"Do you ever see her now?"

"About once a year. She lives in Belmont with her perfectly boring husband, cute little twin daughters, and a fat chocolate Lab. Everything she ever wanted."

When we got back to my apartment, my cat Rory was waiting at the top of the stairs. She had a long white coat with a regal black tail and an intricate black patch on her back. I picked her up and stroked her under the chin, and Rory purred like an old refrigerator. Griffin said he loved cats; his family always had at least three or four of them. He told me a long, funny story about a blue point Siamese named Minx, which Griffin's black sheep uncle Baxter claimed he had won in a poker game in Chicago. Minx supposedly had a cry that could hit high C and a knack for warning Baxter when bill collectors or angry women came to the door.

We smoked another joint and made love again. The first two times he had been rough, oblivious to my cues and muffled yelps of pain, but I reveled in the thrill of it, the proximate danger; no man, it seemed, had ever wanted me more. Then he slowed down and began to explore my body, bringing me to the edge and pulling back, teasing me, making me beg.

When I woke up Saturday morning, he was gone again. The note on the kitchen table said: *Had to run. I'll give you a call.* No tender closing, no name, not even a G.

I sat at my desk, drinking my third or fourth cup of coffee, wishing I hadn't promised Jill I'd call her back. I didn't want to talk about

Matt, not with Jill and certainly not with Carla, my therapist, with whom I had my regular appointment later that afternoon.

I started seeing Carla after I'd been dating Griffin for about four months. Being with him could be wonderful. He was well-read, loved opera and foreign films and avant-garde theater; he was a terrific skier and a patient instructor on the tennis court. We spent glorious afternoons sailing on the twenty-seven-foot sloop he kept at a dock down in Quincy. He liked to go shopping and buy me clothes and jewelry; he took me to Morocco, the Copper Canyon in Mexico, to Italy for my twenty-fifth birthday. We were from similar backgrounds, a world of money and privilege we sometimes scoffed at but never rejected. The first time we slow danced it felt like we'd been partners at the country club since we were eight years old.

But for all the good times, I never felt secure. He slept over at my place three or four nights a week, but rarely wanted me to stay at his—his way, I guessed, of maintaining a retreat that held nothing of mine. He had no office, only an answering service, and when he traveled on business, he often went for days without calling me. I assumed that he was being unfaithful, but I didn't ask, not in the beginning; I wanted to prove that I wasn't some possessive, demanding bitch. We experimented with various drugs, though plain old cannabis worked best for me. In time our lovemaking grew bolder, grittier. We coaxed and dared each other into trying new things, including a ménage à trois (which was basically a bore, the girl dull and mechanical and completely uninterested in me). But no matter how good the sex was, I couldn't shake the apprehension that something was missing. *Oneness.* The feeling after we made love that lying in bed next to me was the only place on earth he wanted to be. Maybe that was why I kept going back to him—or letting him back in—the hope that someday everything would be so perfect he'd never want to leave.

I tried to explain this to Carla.

She said, "What you're missing is *love*."

I looked at the floor and nodded, grudgingly.

Carla waited till my eyes met hers. "On both sides of the bed," she said.

∞

Anita buzzed my line for another incoming call. I picked up the phone.

"Lucy? This is Matt. I just wanted to tell you what a great time I had last night."

"Thank you. I had a good time too."

It was just like me to make that gratuitous qualification, *great* demoted to *good*. He stammered for a second, just enough for me to know he hadn't missed it. If the man had any sense, he'd forget about our date for Saturday and get out while he could.

Chapter 6

Matt

I woke up the morning after my blind date feeling like I'd drunk a bottle of Love Potion Number Nine. Lucy was bright, sexy, funny, everything a guy could want. All my caution was gone. I sang in the shower, dressed in my uniform, and danced my way out the door. People on the street smiled at me as if they knew. It seemed almost cruel that I would have to wait for two and a half days to see her again.

It didn't take long for doubts to set in. I regretted having talked so much. Women like guys who are reserved. Mysterious. The ones who keep them guessing. The evening must have been boring for Lucy. Maybe that's why she drank so much. Still, I was certain I'd done the right thing by not letting her entice me up to her apartment. There probably weren't many men who could have resisted the temptation. Then I started wondering if that was something she did often, get wasted and try to screw some guy on the first date. The thought made me sick to my stomach. I'd had several long-term relationships in my past, even lived with a nurse for a year, but there was only one other time in my life that I'd felt like I was in love.

In my travels after junior college, I went on vacation to Puerto

Rico with Carlos Tacoronte, a guy I knew from my job on a golf course in West Palm Beach. Carlos introduced me to his cousin Enid, who was a freshman at the university in Mayaguez. Enid was gorgeous. She could surf as well as any of the boys on the beach, and she delighted in my clumsy attempts to learn. The last night I was there we walked in the moonlight and she let me kiss her. A month later I was back on the island working on a construction crew for Carlos's brother. We dated for seven months before she dumped me for an Argentinean graduate student, and I went back to the States with a broken heart. It seemed like puppy love in retrospect, but I had kept my feelings closely guarded ever since. Now, after one evening with Lucy, I was ready to do cartwheels on the edge of a cliff.

The workday was long and slow, but I was looking forward to playing softball that night. We usually started at seven, but the weather was so hot they'd moved the game back to nine, hoping it would cool off after dark. After work I went home and washed my car. It was a classic yellow '56 Thunderbird with a V8-312 engine— removable white hardtop with porthole windows on the side, black and white upholstery, a pair of fuzzy dice hanging from the rearview mirror. The car had originally belonged to my uncle Joe. I was a toddler when my dad died, and my mom's younger brother Joe stepped in as a surrogate father. He took me bowling and fishing and duck hunting, to Pirates and Steelers games. I loved to go riding in the T-bird, squeezed in between him and one of his girlfriends on the bench seat. I told him I was going to get a car exactly like it when I grew up, and Joe said maybe he'd give me his. One day my mother heard me pestering him, asking how old I'd have to be to get the car.

"Now listen here, young man," Mom said, looking at me but

scolding us both. "Your uncle Joe had to work hard in the mine to *buy* that automobile, and I'm telling you right now there are two things that are never going to happen as long as I'm on this earth. Number one, you're never going to spend a single day working in a coal mine. Number two"—she held up two fingers—"I am not going to let Joe or anyone else *give* you something you should have earned for yourself."

Uncle Joe never married. He kept the T-bird in his garage in pristine condition and drove a junker to the mine. Four years ago, he called and asked me if I wanted to buy it. He said he was having a hard time getting in and out of the low seats with his creaky knees. I told him how much I loved the car, but there was no way I could afford it. He asked me how much I had in my savings account, and I said about twelve hundred dollars.

"What do you say we make it ten percent?"

"What?"

"Ten percent of your savings. A hundred twenty bucks." He laughed. "I won't take a nickel less."

The car was worth at least four grand. I tried to say no, but not very hard. When I went home to pick up the T-bird, I told my mother I had to hock my soul to the credit union to buy it from Joe. I know she didn't believe me. Her bullshit detector could have been certified for use in a court of law. But she didn't ask me about the car again. Maybe it was enough for her that I'd followed her first rule about not working in the coal mines. I know she wished I lived closer to Butler, but she loved telling people I was a *police officer*. She never said "cop." (I think she was one of those women who get starry-eyed over a man in uniform.) Occasionally she worried about the dangers of my job, but she knew they were negligible compared to being a miner. My father was a Marine who fought at Guadalcanal only to come home and get crushed by a coal car.

Strangers often stopped me to admire the T-bird. I refused to listen to offers when someone asked if it was for sale. The car was a legacy I felt honored and duty-bound to preserve. I changed the oil and tuned the engine myself, rented a garage to keep it off the street. Unfortunately, it wasn't a chick magnet for me like it had been for Uncle Joe. I wasn't a cool guy like him. I could never pull it off. I was too sincere with girls, too eager to please.

Actually, I was that way with everyone. When I got in trouble or mouthed off and acted like a smart aleck, my mother would get angry and dole out some punishment, but the worst punishment of all was for her to say she was *disappointed* in me. Mom was the bookkeeper for an insurance agency. I knew how hard she worked to raise me on her own, and I wanted her to be proud of me. That meant being good, not cool. A cool guy didn't raise his hand in class or mow his neighbor's lawn. Didn't hurry or get agitated or put himself out. A cool guy would never call a girl the day after a blind date to tell her what a great time he had. A cool guy would never go on a blind date in the first place.

Our softball team was called the Lobsters. We took an early five-run lead on the Uzis then let it slip away. The ball carried well in the thick night air, but guys looked like they were running underwater. After the game I gathered up my things and walked to the parking lot with Terry. He said Jill hadn't come because it was too hot and she wanted to stay home in the AC. I told him I had been hoping to talk to her about Lucy.

"Oh yeah, you went on that blind date with her. How'd that go?"

"Good. She's amazing. We're going out again on Saturday."

Terry nodded noncommittally.

"What?" I said. "You think I should stay away from her?"

"Look, don't get me wrong. Lucy's great. She's Jill's best friend. The two of them would kill for one another. She thinks I'm a total stiff, but I don't mind. All I'm saying is, *caveat emptor*, my friend. Women like her come with a price."

We stopped next to my car. I said, "She muttered something over dinner about falling in love with assholes. Can you expand on that a little? Jill said her last boyfriend was a total shit."

"Griffin? Yeah, Jill hated him from day one."

"What was he like?"

He shrugged. "Guess it depends on your perspective. He's a smart guy. Cocky, seems to be well connected. He's a good storyteller. To me he's like a character out of a Tennessee Williams play, one of those handsome rakes. Women know he's trouble, but that's part of the appeal."

"That's the kind of guy Lucy wants?"

"Like I said, it's part of the appeal." I grimaced as Terry leaned up against the Thunderbird, and he stepped away without my having to ask.

"Maybe I'll have to adopt a new M.O. Treat her like dirt and show her who's boss."

Terry smirked. "That might work."

As I drove home, I gunned the engine and cranked the T-bird up to eighty. Hand-me-down cool from my uncle Joe. I had a feeling I was going to need it.

$$\infty$$

Friday morning after roll call, I was told to report to Captain Antonucci's office. I had never been called in by the captain before, which made me a little nervous, but I couldn't think of any reason to be concerned. I saluted as I entered the captain's office. He waved it off and told me to close the door and take a seat.

"I'm going to get right down to business here, Drobyshev." He had my personnel file open on his desk. "I see from your record you got a community college degree?"

"Yes, sir."

"That's good, good. It says here you speak Spanish?"

I smiled. "*Sí, capitán.*"

He smiled too. "Schoolbook or street talk?"

"Street, sir. I studied it in high school, but I got pretty fluent living in Puerto Rico."

"Good, good. Let me tell you what I have in mind." He started talking about the school busing problems, how the department felt like it was under siege. Damned if we do and damned if we don't. The captain leaned forward and dropped his voice. "The commissioner wants me to put together a small task force. Officers who can go out into the neighborhoods and get the people back on *our* side. You know, talk to the priests and ministers, really get to know the merchants, spend some time at the boys' and girls' clubs. Cops used to do that kind of thing every day. We need to get a dialogue going, come up with some fresh ideas. Speaking Spanish will come in real handy."

"Sounds like a great opportunity, sir."

"It is, it is. I got some good feedback on you, Drobyshev. I think you'll be a great addition to the team. But I want to caution you— we're still in the planning stages for the next month or two. We don't even have a name for the task force yet. Everything I just told you is confidential. Not a word about it leaves this room. You understand?"

"Yes, sir. Thank you, sir."

I left his office and practically jumped up and clicked my heels. The job was a plum. I wished there was a way I could tell Lucy. Things were definitely turning my way.

Chapter 7
Lucy

I went to bed Friday night thinking about Matt, telling myself I'd be a good girl on our date the next evening and not drink so much. The phone rang about two in the morning—Griffin calling from a hotel in Denver. It was almost like he had a sixth sense that another guy was circling, or perhaps I had summoned him with my extrasensory need. He sounded stoned, maudlin. He told me he had just lost out on a big contract he'd been working on. Also, his father was having some serious heart problems back in Cincinnati. I tried to be sympathetic but couldn't think of much to say. He asked me how things were going and I said same-old same-old.

"You miss me?" he said.

"Every day." I didn't mean to be quite as sarcastic as I sounded.

"You've met somebody, haven't you?"

"Of course. You told me not to wait."

"Is he there now?"

"He just left."

"Was he good?"

"Incredible. One of the best."

"But you want more?" Griffin said.

"Always."

"Tell me what you're wearing."

"Just panties." The truth. "Nothing else."

"Touch your nipples."

A deep intake of breath, my pulse quickening. "Okay."

"Squeeze them," he said. "Dig your fingernail in a little."

I let out a soft cry.

"Now slowly move your fingers down across your belly."

And so on. I can't explain why this made me feel like I had a hold on him. Wasn't he simply proving the opposite?

The next afternoon Jill and I went shopping. When we stopped for a bite to eat, Jill put my hand on her stomach so I could feel the baby move. I asked if she knew if it was a boy or girl, and she said she had no idea. It seemed strange that the child could be inside your body and still be such a mystery.

Jill watched with disapproval as I tore a nub of skin from my thumb with my teeth. "You heard from Griffin, I guess."

"No. Why? I can still be neurotic without him." I smiled. "He hasn't called in weeks."

"Good. I hope he's gone for-evah."

"Me too." I tasted a drop of blood. "I'm going to fall in love with Officer Krupke."

"Maybe you *will*, Miss Smart-Ass."

"Jesus, wouldn't that be a trip?"

Which is precisely what I was thinking a few hours later as I took another hit on a joint and snipped the price tags off the new outfit I'd bought for my date. Matt was coming to pick me up at six-thirty. I showered and got dressed and went downstairs and sat on the porch to wait for him. We were going to see the new Woody Allen movie, *Annie Hall*, then out to dinner.

The heat had finally broken, a soft breeze stirring the air as Matt came walking up the sidewalk with a bunch of flowers in a green paper cone. He had broad shoulders and a long, determined stride. He waved when he saw me, then stopped at the bottom of the steps and spread his arms wide.

"This better than the uniform?" he said.

"Yeah, you look great." Still, it was a uniform in all but name: blue oxford shirt with button-down collar, khaki pants, polished weejuns, and a matching belt. "But, officer?" I said in my best Blanche DuBois. "How will you protect me? There are wicked men roaming the streets."

He growled and raised the paper cone like a club. "Flower power."

I fluttered my hand next to my cheek. "Oh my, how disarming."

His laugh was a sharp cackle—*ack-ack, ack-ack*—like a volley from a machine gun. "You're great at puns," he said.

"A legacy from my father. We'd try to one-up each other at the dinner table while my mother and brother sat there and groaned."

He handed me the flowers: calla lilies, white and rusty orange. I asked him to come up to my apartment while I put them in water. Halfway up the stairs I remembered the joint I'd smoked. I had a stupid grin on my face as I unlocked the door, the apartment still reeking, and imagined myself getting arrested *by* my date. Matt must have smelled the marijuana but acted like he didn't. I looked around for something to hold the flowers. I'd had a French crystal vase, an heirloom from my grandmother, which would have been perfect, but that *objet* met its end a split second after it sailed past Griffin's head. I think that was the time I found out he was screwing my friend Vanessa from work. The fight ended as usual with fevered sex, injury added to insult when I stepped barefoot on a shard of glass.

I found a ceramic pitcher I used for sangria, filled it with water, and put the calla lilies on top of a stereo speaker.

Matt was looking at Cody's Tarot woodcuts, the photos of Griffin and me craftily hidden away earlier in the day. I felt shallow but couldn't help thinking that Matt was rather plain, his face too round, nose too broad, deep-set brown eyes a little too close together. His best feature was his curly brown hair—and a big, easy smile.

When we went back downstairs, my first-floor neighbor, Mrs. Stansbury, was standing on a chair in the hall, straining to change a light bulb in the fixture overhead.

"Here," Matt said, "let me do that for you."

He took her hand to help her down, then hopped up and changed the bulb. Mrs. Stansbury thanked him with a look in her eyes like he'd just carried her out of a burning building. She was an attractive woman in her forties (no husband in evidence), who blew hot and cold with me.

My cat Rory was sitting on the porch washing her face with her paw.

"There you are, little girl," I said. "I've been wondering where you were." Mrs. Stansbury or the Lindells, who lived on the second floor, let the cat in and out of the front door as they came and went.

"She's beautiful," Matt said. "What's her name?"

"Rory. Short for Rorschach."

He squatted down and held out the back of his hand. "Hello, gorgeous."

The cat sniffed his hand, then ducked her head and began to nuzzle it.

"She likes men," I said.

He started to tease Rory, and she took a swipe at him with her paw.

"Now, now, Rorschach, don't get testy." Matt glanced at me for approval.

"You, sir, have potential," I said.

We walked down the street to his car, the yellow Thunderbird Jill had told me about. When we got into the theater, the only empty seats we could find together were in the second row. Matt hurried off to the lobby and came back with two sodas and a bucket of popcorn. The movie was wonderful, but I kept squirming in my seat with my neck craned up at the screen. Matt began to massage the back of my neck; his fingers were salty and greasy, but the gesture, like Alvy Singer's bumbling attempts at romance with Annie Hall, was so artless and sincere it was impossible to resist. I gave a sigh of approval and leaned in for more. When he laughed his peculiar laugh, people nearby took a peek at him, amused or annoyed, but he didn't seem to notice.

It was twilight when we exited the theater. We strolled through the Common to the Public Garden and talked about the movie. Matt said he liked it, but he thought *Bananas* and *Sleeper* were funnier. I said I thought it was Woody Allen's best film yet. I liked the way he kept reminding you it was a movie, turning to the camera and talking directly to the audience, then stepping back into the story. Matt and I began quoting our favorite lines from the movie.

I said, "I loved the part where Annie and Alvy are walking down the street and he stops and suggests they kiss for the first time so they can get it over with."

"Yeah, great line," Matt said. "I wish I'd've thought of that with you."

"When would you have said it?"

"When would I have had the courage? On the sidewalk after dinner, maybe, when you put that rose in your hair. When did I want to say it? About two seconds after I saw you crossing the street."

"I probably would've slugged you."

"Yeah?" He put his arm around me. "Then I would've cuffed you and taken you in."

I laughed. "Promises, promises."

We crossed the footbridge over the pond where the swan boats were tied up for the evening. A fat man was sitting on a bench playing "The Tennessee Waltz" on an accordion. I started singing along with the music, and Matt put a dollar in his instrument case.

"Milady," he said with a deep bow.

I curtsied and took his hand, and we began to waltz. It could have been a scene from a movie, more Frank Capra than Woody Allen, Matt a little ungainly, but his spirit trumping his awkwardness. I knew at that moment he was not going to sleep with me tonight to get it over with; he wanted a storybook romance, an old-fashioned courtship full of restraint and longing. A week ago I would have scoffed at such a notion as artificial and demeaning to women. Now I found myself thinking, *Why not give it a chance?* It would be something different, anyway. Like going to live in a commune, or being born again and putting your faith in Jesus. I had no illusions (or delusions) that this was True Love, not for me anyway, but it felt like happiness—pure, simple-minded joy. The trick was not to question it, or belittle it like Amanda; just put on my fool's cap and follow Matt's lead.

It was summer, the sun shone brightly, and I rarely felt blue. Matt called me every day. He took me to a Red Sox game and a Bee Gees concert. I went to a few of his softball games and met some of his friends; Jill and Terry had us over for a cookout with a bunch of other couples. Matt was at ease socially, and everyone seemed charmed by him.

I loved riding in the Thunderbird with the top down and the radio blasting, Matt shifting gears like a race car driver. One Sunday morning we were on the way to the beach at Plum Island—I was wearing shorts over a low-cut bathing suit—when a police car pulled us over in Ipswich. The cop was bald with a big potbelly. Matt showed him his BPD badge and the cop grinned. The cop's eyes were crawling all over me as he and Matt made small talk, but if Matt noticed, he didn't let on. Griffin would have reached over in mid-sentence and put his hand on my bare thigh. *Eat your heart out, pal. She's mine.* The thought made me wonder where he was right now, what he was doing. Probably tiptoeing out of some woman's apartment the morning after, on his way to someone else. He hadn't called in a few weeks. There were nights I wished he would.

The Ipswich cop patted the fender of the Thunderbird and tipped his hat goodbye. Matt said something to me as we drove away, but I was thinking about Griffin, remembering all the crazy places we'd made love: in a canoe on the Charles River, in the shadows at the far end of a subway platform, behind an armoire in a dusty antiques store while the shopkeeper and a woman haggled over the price of a Biedermeier chest. Sometimes I think we were hoping we'd get caught, as if we were trying to prove that our need for each other carried us beyond the usual boundaries of decorum and common sense.

Matt and I had been dating for a month and were still making out like high school kids. I made no initiatives and asked for no explanations, waiting to see how far he'd go. Close, but (alas, Dr. Freud) no cigar. Sometimes it felt like a game, silly and frustrating, but the anticipation kept my hormones percolating. The chemistry between us seemed fine, but I began to worry. What if it wasn't worth the wait? What if, after this great buildup, our lovemaking was a dud? Not a full-blown fiasco—one of those spectacular misfires we could both acknowledge and maybe even laugh about somewhere down the road—but something numbingly pedestrian, the sexual equivalent of Muzak or instant coffee, a vapid facsimile that only proves just how great the real thing can be.

When we got to the beach, I spread a blanket out on the sand and took off my shorts, my white bathing suit cut high on my hips. When I'd tried it on in front of the mirror that morning, I noticed that if I raised my arms or twisted my torso, you could see a tiny portion of my tattoo, which was on my lower tummy near the bend in my hip. Griffin had talked me into getting the tattoo one night in Portsmouth. At first I thought he was joking, but he said he'd get one too. Neither of us was drunk or high.

"You mean we each get a heart with an arrow through it? Mine says Griffin, yours says Lucy?"

"Whatever you want. They don't have to be the same."

We looked at the samples on the wall and leafed through a sketch-book of the artist, who said he could draw anything. I saw some birds

70

and butterflies I liked, but nothing that caught my fancy. I wanted it to be unique to Griffin and me; I also wanted it to go someplace on my body that only he would see. Griffin went first, agreeing to get his in the same place as mine. He chose his birth sign, Scorpio, which seemed a bit trite. I decided on a pink and green Chinese umbrella. The needle burned a little but didn't really hurt. The artist covered the tattoo with a bandage and warned me not to itch it or pick at the scab. A week later it looked beautiful. Even after Griffin left, I couldn't say I regretted it—in fact, quite the opposite—but I still felt self-conscious about Matt's seeing it and asking the inevitable questions.

Matt tried to talk me into going into the ocean at Plum Island, but it was too cold for me. He had long, well-defined muscles and a thatch of dark hair on his chest. I watched him dive into the waves and swim far out. When he came out of the water, he toweled off and sat down beside me.

"Would you like me to put some suntan lotion on you?" he said.

I was lying on my stomach. "That would be wonderful."

He dabbed some lotion between my shoulder blades, massaging my neck and shoulder muscles as he rubbed it in. His hands were strong and patient as he worked his way down my back and started on my thighs. I turned my head, one eye scrunched against the sun.

"You can do that all day," I said.

"Maybe I will."

I rose up on one elbow. "And night."

He kissed me softly and said, "Okay."

Walking along a secluded stretch of beach twenty minutes later, we detoured into the dune grass where we groped and fumbled and gasped. When we were done, we looked at each other and laughed with relief. It was far from perfect—sand where sand was never meant to be—but good enough to make me want to try again, *soon*. If he noticed my tattoo, he didn't say.

Chapter 8

Matt

I knew I was acting silly, but there were moments every day when I'd think about Lucy and get a big smile on my face. She and I saw each other three or four times a week, and I often stayed over at her apartment. Our sex life was better than anything I had ever dreamed of, though it annoyed me that she usually smoked a joint before we made love. She said she was like Annie Hall, marijuana made her relax. She tried to get me to try some, but that was a line I didn't want to cross. I was too straight, too much a cop. I never asked where she bought the stuff and didn't want to know. I figured if that was my only complaint, I had none at all.

Every Sunday without fail, I called my mother, but it wasn't until after Labor Day that I felt confident enough to mention Lucy.

"So," Mom said, "when will I get to meet her?"

"Sometime soon I hope. We could come to Butler for a long weekend. Better yet, why don't you come up here? It's been awhile. Let me buy you a plane ticket for your birthday." She was turning fifty-four in October.

She said that sounded wonderful. I liked hearing the excitement in her voice, as I knew she liked hearing it in mine. She wouldn't come right out and say it, but most of her friends had become grand-parents and she was feeling left out.

One afternoon on the job, I saw a skinny black kid snatch an old woman's purse and knock her down. Several people on the sidewalk rushed to the woman's side, and I took off after the kid. I had nearly lost sight of him as he ran through Chinatown when he tripped on a dolly stacked with orange crates and dropped the purse. I yelled for the truck driver pushing the dolly to grab him, but the trucker only managed to tear off the kid's T-shirt. The kid was limping as he took off again. I thought I was in pretty good shape, but my lungs were heaving and my leg muscles burned. I made one last burst and caught the boy, but he was sweaty and kept slipping out of my grip. I finally got my left arm wrapped around his neck.

"Hold still," I said.

"Get off me, motherfucker!"

I tightened my grip on his neck. "Just calm down. I'm gonna cuff you."

"Stop choking me, you fucking pig."

He kept kicking and flailing, and his elbow struck my cheek. I saw stars but didn't let go. Hooking the fingers of my right hand under the kid's belt, I lifted him off his feet and slammed him down on the sidewalk. There was a loud crack, and the boy screamed. I stood over him for a second then staggered away a few steps, put my hands on my knees, and vomited. I couldn't say if I was sick from all the running or the sight of the jagged bone protruding from the boy's arm.

The next day, several black community leaders went down to City Hall decrying police brutality, hoping to get their pictures in the newspapers. The department withheld my name from the press. The boy, who was fourteen years old, had been arrested several times before. Two officers from internal investigations interviewed me and told me not to worry. They said there were several witnesses to back up my story, and the old woman had broken her hip when the kid knocked her down. Despite these assurances, the incident shook me up. I remembered throwing the boy to the ground and *wanting* to hurt him. I knew there was a split second when I could have stopped myself and didn't. Lucy suggested I visit him in the hospital, but that was taboo, almost an admission of guilt.

A week went by. No one had filed a formal complaint with the department, but I was still worried about the repercussions. I didn't think I would lose my job, but the incident could cost me a spot on Captain Antonucci's task force. This wasn't something I could discuss with Lucy or anyone else. I didn't sleep well at night.

One afternoon I was standing on the corner of Tremont and Boylston, listening to a homeless man tell me about the fortune he'd lost in the rare coin business, when Sergeant Barker pulled up in a squad car.

"Hey, boyo," he said. He got out of the car, and the homeless man shuffled off. "Can you believe that?" Barker pointed at a billboard advertising *The Spy Who Loved Me*. "How could they pick a fag like Roger Moore to replace Sean Connery? You telling me that's the best actor they could come up with? Sean Connery is a legend. Did you see *The Man Who Would Be King*? Greatest fuckin' movie ever made."

"I'll second that," I said. Sean Connery and Michael Caine, a Rudyard Kipling story with John Huston directing. How could it not be great? I'd seen it three times and had been telling Lucy about it recently. I was hoping it would come on TV so we could watch it together.

We both loved to go to the movies but rarely agreed on what to see. I liked movies, she liked films. Movies were entertainment, stories that made you laugh or cry and kept you on the edge of your seat. Films had meanings and subtitles, slow, tortuous stories with bleak endings or no ending at all. Films were supposed to make you think, but they usually put me to sleep. We settled on a compromise, alternating between her choice and mine. A few weeks ago she dragged me to a double feature of *Persona* and *Cries and Whispers*. On the drive back to her place, I asked her if she'd noticed the bowl of free razor blades in the lobby for people who wanted to go home and slit their wrists. It took her a second to realize I was joking. We ended up having an argument, then laughed about it later.

I wanted nothing more than to make Lucy happy. For her part, she rarely showed that edge Jill had told me about. If she was hiding it, I didn't care. We treated each other with uncommon tenderness. Never bickered or took a stubborn stand over some petty principle or demand, as if we were afraid one ugly fight would tear us apart. It wasn't something we talked about. I didn't spend much time thinking about it either. We'd been together for two and a half months. The more trust and goodwill we built up in happy times, the better off we'd be when we hit the inevitable rough patch.

Barker jerked a thumb at the squad car. "Hop in, boyo. We have to run."

"What's up, Sarge?"

"Captain wants to see you."

"Now?" My mouth suddenly felt dry. "Is this about that kid whose arm I broke?"

He shrugged. "No idea. But you don't have to worry about that. 'Nucci won't hang you out to dry over that bullshit."

Not unless someone from City Hall was leaning on him. Captain Antonucci must have seen the concern in my face as I took a chair across from his desk.

"Listen, Drobyshev, that thing with the kid? The scumbag purse-snatcher?" His face was grim. "You don't have to worry about it affecting that other thing we talked about. I got your back all the way."

"Thank you, sir."

"But look, that's not why I called you in here." He started playing with a hockey puck on his desk, rolling it back and forth between his thumb and forefinger. "I got a call from your Aunt Sally a little while ago. Your mother...I'm sorry, I'm afraid she passed away."

I stared at the captain blankly. No words came into my head.

"She was at work. They said she just put her head down on the desk like she was taking a nap, and the next thing anyone knew, she was gone. She didn't suffer."

Blood pooled in my arms and legs, anchoring me to the chair. The captain kept talking, but I didn't hear what he said. He came around the desk and patted my shoulder. Then he walked me to an empty office with a couch and a desk and a telephone. Someone brought me a cold soda. I asked if I could be alone.

I sat on the couch and closed my eyes and thought about the last time I'd seen my mother. It was early April, a beautiful spring weekend. I helped her work in the yard and repaired the trellis for her roses. My last morning home I woke to the smell of bacon. When I came downstairs, I heard her singing a Fleetwood Mac song. She had a lovely voice. She was the only parent I knew who listened to pop music. My friends used to call her Mrs. D and liked to come to the house and hang out. I walked into the kitchen and said good morning, and she poured me a cup of coffee. She was making my favorite omelet with cheddar cheese, chopped onions, and red peppers. When the food was ready, Mom sat down, and we ate and talked and laughed as we always did. An ordinary morning together. I couldn't believe there would never be another. Surely if I conjured up enough details, piling them up like talismans, I'd go home and find that nothing had changed.

I went to the desk and called Aunt Sally, who wasn't actually my aunt but my mother's best friend. She sobbed the moment she heard my voice. I wanted to sob too, but I sat there holding the phone, saying nothing. Sally said they'd reached my uncle Joe in the mine, and he was going to help arrange things. She asked if there was anything special I wanted done, and I said I couldn't think of anything. I told her I'd be home as soon as possible.

"You call the minute you get here, honey," she said. "I don't care what time it is. And if you don't…if you feel strange being in that house all alone, you come stay with us."

I phoned Lucy next.

"Oh my god, Matt!" she said. "That's horrific. I'm so sorry. Where are you now?"

"Still at the station. I need to go back to my apartment and pack some clothes. I'm not sure whether I should fly or drive."

"How long does it take to drive?"

"Eleven, twelve hours. I guess there isn't any rush."

"You don't want to be on the road alone at a time like this. I'll go with you. I'll leave work right now."

As soon as she said it, I knew I didn't want her to come. I had no idea how I was going to act, whether I was going to break down or fly into a rage or plod through the whole thing like a zombie. Probably a little of each and none of it pretty. Besides, I didn't want Lucy's only memory of my mother to be a corpse lying in a coffin. It would be better if Lucy didn't come at all. But how could I tell her that? Wasn't this a time when I was supposed to need her most?

"Matt?"

"Sure, okay."

"Unless you'd rather be by yourself."

"No, no, I *want* you to come. I'm sorry. This is all…"

"I can't even imagine what you're going through. Listen, why don't we take my car so we'll have more room? I'll come to your place and pick you up. I'll drive. We'll talk—or not. Maybe you can get some sleep. Whatever you want."

"Okay. Thanks."

"See you soon."

"Lucy?"

"Yes?"

"I love you."

She took a deep breath. "Oh, Matt."

I pushed the button down on the phone. I still had the receiver in my hand, and I wanted to smash it down on the desk. I'd just taken the cheapest of cheap shots, the dead mother pity plea. Poor little orphan boy begging for love. I had no idea I could stoop so low.

Chapter 9
Lucy

Matt and I barely spoke on the long drive from Boston to Butler, no radio, just the dull whir of the highway, me trying not to chain smoke, trying not to feel like he wished I hadn't come. Now and again he'd reach over and touch me and give me an almost-smile. We got to his house around two in the morning and went to sleep in the double bed in the guest bedroom. In the middle of the night, I felt him spoon against me, and I pretended not to wake up as I scissored my legs and he slipped inside me, so gentle and dreamlike I wondered if he was even awake himself.

We were up early, and Matt started making phone calls, talking to relatives and the undertaker; then we went to the funeral home with his uncle Joe to pick out a casket. The "viewing," as it was called, began Friday evening and continued all weekend, three hours in the afternoon and three more in the evening, a steady stream of mourners. Matt never cried or wavered in his kindness, giving comfort to those whose grief seemed even greater than his own. Aunt Sally had placed several framed photographs of Matt's mother around the funeral home. She had a shy smile with a little V between her front teeth, the same round face as Matt, the same deep-set eyes—a face that seemed to have no connection with the body that lay in the coffin.

Matt's best friend, Dan Roble, told me Mrs. D's house was always the most popular place for their crew to hang out. He said he'd stop by just to talk sometimes, even when Matt wasn't home. Dan didn't have many stories about their high school escapades. He said he and Matt were both too shy to do much dating, too busy working part-time jobs to get into trouble.

When we weren't at the funeral home, people congregated at Aunt Sally's house where women brought endless supplies of food— pirogi, sausages, macaroni, dumplings, potato salad. Matt called these women The Ladies. They treated me like I belonged, their affection seemingly free of cattiness and suspicion, no snide remarks or probing questions, their goodwill so unconstrained I felt like I had wandered onto the set of an old television show.

The funeral service Monday morning lasted for an hour and a half, followed by the slow ride to the cemetery, the procession of cars stretching for several blocks, then another service at the graveside where they lowered the coffin. I hung back while Matt threw the first shovel of dirt, then others did the same. Matt wanted to stay and finish the job, but his uncle Joe talked him out of it.

We gathered at a restaurant where they'd set up a big buffet. I was sitting with Mr. Karski, who was Aunt Sally's father and had worked in the mines with Matt's grandfather. He started telling me stories about "the old country," which people talked about like a distant matriarch, the formidable babushka you missed terribly and were just as happy never to see again.

"Half my friends said they were Polish, the other half Russian,"

Mr. Karski said. "The border was always moving. We used to joke about it. Go to bed in one country and wake up the next morning in the other."

Aunt Sally, who was short and wide as a beanbag chair, came over and gave me a hug. "Don't believe a word he says, Lucy. The man could talk Satan into buying a crucifix."

"What would be wrong with *that*?" Mr. Karski said.

Sally saw the restaurant manager and hurried over to tell him something. This was clearly her show.

I said to Mr. Karski, "So you spoke both languages, Russian and Polish?"

"Oh sure, Russian, Polish, Lithuanian. A little Serb, a little English." He grinned, proud that he had only a slight accent. Some of the elderly people at the funeral seemingly spoke no English at all. "The Tsar, Nikolay Aleksandrovich Romanov, decided I was Russian and drafted me into the Imperial Army. I lasted four months before I deserted. I spent the winter hiding in a farmer's barn. Never spoke to the man or looked him in the eye, but he left me a crust of bread or bowl of something every day, enough to get by. I always wished I knew his name, so I could write him a letter and say thank you."

He finished his whiskey, his plate of food untouched. He was tiny with a full head of white hair and a tic in his eye, which I first mistook for a wink. I asked if I could get him another whiskey.

"No, no, one is enough for me," he said. "When an old man drinks, either he starts thinking he's young again and makes a fool of himself, or remembers how old he is and ends up getting sad."

I excused myself and went to get another glass of wine. One of

The Ladies intercepted me and asked me to come meet her daughter, who had just arrived from out of town last night. The people of Butler, Pennsylvania, were probably as corrupt as people everywhere else, bigoted, backbiting, quietly committing the seven deadly sins—gluttony seemed to be the local favorite—but the way they accepted me with open arms put to shame the vain, judgmental world I'd grown up in. *Who are his people?* my Virginia-bred grandfather used to say. I tried to imagine Matt coming home with me under similar circumstances, members of the country club making snotty inquiries about his peculiar last name, most of them dismissing him out of hand as soon as they learned he was a cop. Not that the people in New Canaan, Connecticut, had anything against the police, per se. My parents' crowd was staunchly Republican and firm believers in law and order, but cops, to them, were simply part of the large contingent of worker bees who trundled in from the vast elsewhere, people who were paid to keep our town safe and clean and educated.

Drinking had begun in earnest. A man got out his violin, and a group of spongy middle-aged men gathered around him and began to sing a doleful Russian song. Then the fiddler picked up the tempo, and the men started to dance, squatting like Cossacks, falling and laughing and trying again. The children quickly joined in, spinning and sliding across the polished wooden floor in their good clothes, the women looking on with mock disapproval and oceans of love in their eyes, a celebration of what was lost and what remained.

Matt smiled at me from across the room. The Ladies liked to tell me he was a *catch* (the kind of man your mother would want you to marry if you had a normal mother), and I'd nod and say, *Yes, he is*, as if it were all but settled, nothing but this tragic circumstance preventing us from making the announcement of our impending nuptials. For the past four days, I had been trying to imagine a future with him. Matt had told me he loved me, and I was touched that he'd taken the chance, but there were quiet moments when I found myself sitting alone, wondering only how fast and far I could flee. Maybe this was exactly what Griffin felt with me, a sense that, whatever we had, it was not quite right, not quite enough.

The closer I grew with Matt, the more I seemed to talk about Griffin with my therapist. A few weeks ago, Carla said she wanted me to make a list comparing the two men and bring it to our next session. I thought it was a ridiculous exercise, but once I got started, it became intriguing. I took a yellow legal pad and made two columns: *Matt/Griffin, tall/short, plain/handsome, dark/fair, sweet/acerbic, working class/privileged, Butler County Community College/Princeton, frugal/generous, loyal/philandering, loves me/probably doesn't.* The list went on and on.

I didn't write it down, but nowhere was the difference between them more pronounced than the way they made love. Griffin was demanding and inventive and uninhibited. He laid claim to me, took me, and did whatever he wanted. He took other women too and never tried to deny it. He would tell me who it was if I asked, which I did sometimes, wanting not just a name but details—every lick and hole, the pornographic montage—until I felt utterly debased and aroused and we fucked like it was the last days of Pompeii. I had kept most of this from Carla, out of shame, I guess, or maybe I was afraid she'd find a way to make me stop. It was reprehensible behavior, especially for a woman who liked to think of herself as a feminist. The only excuse I can offer is that I found him captivating, like Patty

Hearst and other victims who become attached to their kidnappers. On an intellectual level, I knew I shouldn't let him treat me the way he did, just as I knew I shouldn't love him (if, as Carla would say, it was even love at all), but Griffin, for all his considerable faults, took me places I had never been. Places I wanted to go back to again.

Matt was a gentle, diffident lover: patient, intent on pleasing me, his stamina heroic. He touched me as if I were something precious, something he was afraid he might break. At times he seemed to regard his own satisfaction as an afterthought. He never knew when I was faking, or perhaps he chose not to call me on it. I tried to nudge him into more aggressive, adventurous sex, a bit of fantasy and role-playing, which he did sometimes, but it made him uncomfortable. Yet, for all his solicitude and self-control, when Matt finally let go, he did so with complete abandon—grunting, snorting, roaring—no faking on his part. Matt *gave* himself to me, got lost in me and let himself be vulnerable, and when he was spent, he always said thank you. Then he would hold me or, more remarkably, let me hold him, content as any man could ever be. One night he said, *Forget the story about the snake and the apple. This is what got Adam and Eve kicked out of the Garden of Eden. God knew He couldn't compete.* How, in the name of reason, could I not love a man like that? As if reason had anything to do with love.

"Matt is Steady Eddy," I told Carla. "What you see is what you get. Griffin is always surprising me. He keeps me guessing. There's something about his unpredictability that pulls me in."

Carla shrugged.

"Is that wrong?" I said.

"This isn't about right and wrong, Lucy. It's about the kind of life you want." She handed me the list. "You missed one important difference."

"What?"

I guessed at one thing and another before she took the list back and wrote at the bottom: *here/gone*.

Matt and I were alone in his house the evening after the funeral. He started to go through his mother's papers, trying to sort out what he should take back to Boston when we left the next morning. The files were neat and well organized (like mother, like son), notes on the documents written in a small, precise script. She had left everything to him in her will, no outstanding debts, the mortgage and car paid off. Matt picked up a black leather folder with a brass clasp, his mother's insurance policies.

"Check this out and tell me what you think." He handed me a policy.

It was a thick document with lots of fine print and legalese, but all you needed to know was on the first page.

"It's for fifty thousand dollars," I said.

"You're sure?"

"That's what it says."

He shook his head in disbelief. "There's two more here, one for fifteen thousand, another for forty."

"That's incredible."

"I know. It's way too much money. It doesn't make any sense."

"But that was her business, right? She knew what she was doing."

"I guess. She worked for the agency for twenty-six years. I talked to her boss, Barry Ledyard, at the funeral home. He wrote the policies, but he never said anything about this."

"That's not the place to talk about money, Matt. It's only seven-thirty. Why don't you call him and ask?"

Matt seemed hesitant.

"I'm going to get a glass of white wine," I said. "You want anything?"

"Wine sounds good."

When I came back from the kitchen, he was on the phone. I heard him saying goodbye to Mr. Ledyard, thanking him for his help.

"It's what we thought," he said. "The policies have a total value of one hundred five thousand dollars. The money's all tax-free. He said I should have a check in a few weeks."

I handed him the glass of wine. "That's wonderful. What an amazing gift."

"Yeah, pretty fucking ironic, huh?" He spread his arms wide, wine sloshing onto the rug, and let out a self-mocking laugh. "Here I am, an orphan in Fat City."

He ground the wine spot into the rug with his shoe. I led him to the couch, and he leaned his head on my shoulder, the wineglass still in his hand. I stroked his hair, hoping he would let go and cry.

"This is crazy," he said. "First I meet you and fall in love. Then the captain calls me in and says he wants me to serve on some new task force." I hadn't heard about that before but didn't interrupt. "Just to make sure things don't get too routine, I chase down some kid and break his arm so bad he needs a plate and umpteen screws. Ten days later my mother drops dead. Now I find out I've inherited more money than I ever thought I'd have in my life." I kept stroking his hair. "It all seems so fucking *random*." He lifted his wineglass as if he were making a toast, his hand wrapped around the bowl. "Just life, I guess."

The glass exploded in his hand.

"Matt!"

He rolled off the couch and stood up, looking at his hand as if it were a curiosity, some bloody urchin dredged up from the deep. A shard of glass protruded from his palm.

"I'm going to need stitches," he said.

On the way to the hospital, he made me promise I would corroborate his story, saying that he stumbled and fell. In the emergency room, he joked with the doctor and nurses about being a klutz. The doctor said he was fortunate he hadn't cut an artery; it took eleven stitches to close the wound.

I tried to talk to him about it when we got back to the house.

"I don't know," he said. "I can't explain what came over me."

"It's normal. You just needed to feel something."

He gave me a contemptuous look. "Believe me, I've had way too many *feelings* already."

"Matt, I'm sorry. I—"

"Forget it."

"No, that was an idiotic thing for me to say."

"*Forget* it, okay?"

I let it go. But part of me wanted to provoke him and have one of those fights we'd both been so careful to avoid, the kind where ugly thoughts get spoken aloud and you are knocked back by what you've heard and what you've said, unsure how much was true, both of you knowing that the fight was not simply inevitable, but necessary. I wanted to quarrel and get it over with and find out what we were really made of. But not now, not after all that Matt had been through. The next day we drove back to Boston and acted like the incident with the wineglass had never happened.

∞

Three days after we got home from the funeral, Jill had her baby, a little boy named Terrence Kyle O'Shea Jr. They planned on calling him TK. When Matt and I went to visit them in the hospital, Matt looked at the baby and beamed. He asked Jill if he could hold him, then picked him up with gentle nonchalance like it was something he did every day.

"Hey, TK," he said. "What do you think about your first day out here in the big wide world? Everything fine so far? This is easy living, kid. Enjoy it while you can. Pretty soon your old man's going to turn you into a Red Sox fan and make you miserable for the rest of your life."

Jill's mother and sister were in the room with us. They smiled at me the way The Ladies did, reminding me that this guy was a catch.

Matt and I went back to my place and made love. The next day I realized I'd forgotten to take a pill. I wasn't sure when, sometime in all the commotion of the past week. I felt a twinge of guilt but didn't say anything to Matt. It wasn't like I *wanted* to get pregnant. Not like the last time.

Chapter 10
Matt

The new task force was called Together with Trust—TWT. Good name, bad acronym. Rank-and-file cops, who viewed us with a tinge of jealousy and suspicion, quickly dubbed us the "twits." My partner was a nineteen-year veteran named Javi Veliz. The two of us hit it off immediately. We were assigned to the Roslindale and West Roxbury neighborhoods, which Javi knew well. He had a great knack for drawing people out and getting them to vent. We spent a lot of time talking to small-business owners, listening to their problems and trying to get them to hire some of the neighborhood kids part time. Javi was an entrepreneur himself. Over the years he had built up two businesses of his own, a flower shop and a three-car limousine service.

One evening Lucy and I went out for a drink with him and his wife, Colleen. Colleen was first generation Boston Irish. She was tall and skinny, with green eyes, red hair, and a face that turned pretty when she smiled. Javi and his family had come to Boston from Guatemala when he was six. With his long nose and copper skin, ink-black hair and trim goatee, he could have passed for a Saudi prince or a South American drug lord. He and Colleen told us they were high school sweethearts.

"The only girl I've ever kissed," Javi said.

Colleen rolled her eyes. "My father wasn't exactly happy with the situation. He called Javi the blankety-blank little spic the first two years I went out with him."

"Now it's just the spic," Javi said, laughing.

"The only thing that saved him was being Catholic," Colleen said.

They had three daughters and a son. Colleen said they'd been having trouble with their boy recently. He got caught skipping school, and she and Javi were trying to decide how to punish him.

"He's a good kid," Javi said. "A little dreamy, that's all. I was a *criminal* when I was his age."

Lucy and I chuckled.

"He isn't kidding," Colleen said.

Lucy said, "Do tell."

"Master cat burglar," Javi said. "I'd find a cellar door unlocked, crawl up a fire escape to an open window. In and out quick, though things got dicey once in a while." The waitress came by, and we ordered another round. I'd already heard a lot of Javi's stories, but he seemed to be ratcheting things up for Lucy.

Javi said, "One day this cop, a big burly guy named Jimmy Bohan, catches me with a pocketful of stolen watches. Bohan knew my papi. Poor guy drove a cab twelve hours a day, six days a week. All he wanted was for us kids to live the American dream. Finish school and get a decent job, get married and have a bunch of kids. Bohan's got his hand on my arm like a vise. Wants to know what my father's gonna say when he hauls me in. I'm thinking, Forget about getting sent up to Thompson's Island, man. First thing my papi's gonna do is beat the living shit outta me. Then he's gonna stick my ass on the next plane back to Guatemala so I can work twelve hours a day on my uncle's chicken farm."

Javi lit a cigarillo with his gold lighter, then Lucy's cigarette. She leaned forward, the top two buttons of her Western shirt undone, and I saw him take a peek.

"Bohan took the bag and let me go. Said he'd jump on my head with both feet next time I stepped out of line. Lesson learned. I ended up becoming a cop."

"That's a wonderful story," Lucy said, touching his arm. "A lot of police officers wouldn't have been so compassionate."

I said, "What happened to the watches?"

"That's the best part. The day I graduated from high school, Bohan gave me this." He pushed up the cuff of his sleeve to reveal a rectangular-faced Cartier with a tiny sapphire in the stem-winder. "Creative rehabilitation, partner. That's how you reach tough kids in the neighborhoods."

"Winning hearts and minds," I said.

Javi chuckled. "Nah, man, *con amenazas y sobornos*." He translated for the women. "With threats and bribes."

Lucy said, "Do you guys speak Spanish to each other on the job?"

"Depends on the topic," Javi said. "We switch back and forth. Spanish is a *romance* language. We use it to talk about women and food. English is for sports, money, and police work. Politics and religion are off limits in any language."

"What do you say about us women?" Lucy said.

He gave her a killer smile. "Only how much we love you."

"Good answer." She was getting drunk.

Colleen said, "Where did you learn Spanish, Matt?"

Before I could respond, Lucy said, "In Puerto Rico. From a pretty *señorita*."

"Enid," Javi said. "I've heard about her."

"A *need*, indeed," Lucy said. "He can't mention her without blushing. If she shows up here, I'll scratch her eyes out." She meowed and clawed the air and grinned at me.

"I think it's wonderful you learned Spanish," Colleen said. "I wanted Javi to teach our kids, but he couldn't be bothered."

"I love Latin women," Lucy said. "They have so much *flair*. They're so up front about everything." She pulled her shoulders back and stuck out her tits.

"*Si lo tienes, muéstralo*," Javi said. "If you got it, flaunt it."

"Yeah," Colleen said, shaking her head. "You should see his sisters."

The conversation drifted to other things. At the end of the evening, Javi insisted on paying the bill.

In the car on the way to Lucy's, I said, "Well, you put on quite a show."

"A *show?*"

"With Javi."

"I was being friendly with your partner. Isn't that what you want?"

"Not like you're gonna take him into the back room and fuck his brains out."

"Oh please."

"That's how you were acting. Getting him to light your cigarette, letting him look down your shirt. Colleen and I were sitting there with our jaws hanging open."

"Listen, if I wanted to…" She looked away for a moment, then turned back to me. "I'm sorry. I was just having fun." I didn't say anything. "Don't be mad, Matt. *You're* my guy."

"Am I?"

She sighed and put her head on my shoulder. Why did I try to make her say it twice?

Later, in bed, Lucy said, "Tell me about the *señorita*." She never said the name even when she knew it. It was always the *señorita*, the nurse, the Chanel girl.

"She was short and muscular. Pretty face, frizzy brown hair."

"With that smooth, whiskey-colored skin."

"Yes," I said.

"And dark nipples." I nodded as she unbuttoned the top of her nightgown and let it fall open. "Were they like big chewy gumdrops or hard little jujubes?" She pinched her own.

I reached for her, but she moved away.

"Tell me," she said.

"Little and hard." My body felt light, caught in the spin of her game.

"Did she like you to bite them?"

"Yes." A lie.

"Show me."

I nipped her and she let out a sharp yelp. I had never been with a woman so bold. She wanted words, fantasies. *Tell me how the nurse sucked your cock*, she'd say. *Did she like it from behind?* I responded meekly. A disappointment, I know. Sometimes she begged me to hurt her. She didn't say how. One night I bit her on the shoulder until she cried out in pain. She had a purple bruise for a week, which neither of us mentioned.

She pushed my head lower. I kissed her belly. She had a tattoo of a Chinese umbrella in the bend of her hip. The first time I saw it I asked her what it meant. *Something for a rainy day,* she said.

She was one of a kind. Fantastic. Beyond explanation. I felt like a man on a high wire. Like that crazy Frenchman who walked between the towers of the World Trade Center. I hate heights. I have to turn away when they show footage of him bouncing on the wire, taunting the police, defying the wind. One little slip and he was a dead man. But if you asked him, I'll bet he'd say it was the one time in his life when he never felt more alive.

∞

One day after work I got a call at my apartment from Sandor.

"Matyas, why you don't come see me and bring your beautiful Lucy? Don't tell me you break up with her."

"No, no, Sandor, she's fine. Everything's fine. I've been real busy." I hadn't been to the Café Budapest since a week or two before my mother died.

Sandor told me he'd gotten stopped the night before for speeding. It was on the Jamaicaway. He was doing sixty in a thirty-five-mile-an-hour zone. "When officer ask me for license and registration, I tell him I know I am speeding, sir, but, please, do you know my nephew, Matt Drobyshev." He chortled. "The policeman, he give me funny look and say, 'You're Drobo's uncle?' 'Oh yes,' I tell him. 'My sister's boy. My *favorite.*' The policeman, he say, 'You need to slow down, Pops. Tell Matt Richie Harrington says hello.' You see, Matyas, you save me again."

"Richie and I were at the academy together. He's a good guy. We play basketball at the Y sometimes. I'll tell him thanks."

"Yes, please. Now I want to repay you. Yesterday someone give me tickets for—"

"Come on, Sandor. You do too much for me already."

"No, no, listen. I have two tickets for *Annie* in New York for next week. Saturday night. Everybody in restaurant is talking about it. They say is best show in years. You take your beautiful Lucy."

"Sandor, I…"

"Please, you take."

"Sure, okay. Lucy will be thrilled. You're too good to me, Sandor."

"No, no, I am not lying what I say to policeman, Matyas. You are part of my family."

"Thank you, uncle," I said, choking up.

I wanted to tell him about my mother's death, but I didn't know how to begin. The funeral had been over a month ago. Every time I thought about her, I felt a tightness in my chest. I missed her voice. I missed simply knowing she was there. At times something would happen, nothing dramatic, just some funny incident on the job or a story I heard, and I'd wish I could call her up and tell her about it. More than anything, I wanted to talk to her about Lucy.

I hung up the phone and saw a cockroach scurry across the floor. Living with Kreider was becoming untenable, and I had been thinking about getting my own apartment. Actually, my real goal was to get a place with Lucy, but I was wary of rushing her. I considered telling her I was going to buy a condo with my mother's insurance money and see how she reacted. If she wanted to take the next step and move in together, she'd find a way to let me know. For all my hesitation, I felt like we were getting closer every day. She was more open and affectionate. Sometimes she spoke of "we" and "us." She had stopped peeling the skin off her thumbs, even gained a few pounds. She still hadn't said "I love you," but when she did, I'd know it was true.

I waited a few days before I told her about going to New York. I wanted to make sure I had everything lined up. I said it was a surprise, just be sure to bring something special to wear for the evening. She laughed and said she couldn't wait.

We went out to Wellesley to see Jill and Terry and the baby. We were in the living room drinking wine and eating cheese and crackers. Lucy sat sideways on the couch with TK resting on her propped-up knees.

"I can't believe how *alert* he is," she said to no one in particular. The baby was staring at her with his big blue eyes. "Yes, little man, I mean you. You. You. You." Each time she said it, she kissed him on the tip of his nose.

I was sitting on the floor beside her; Elton John was on the stereo, singing "Bennie and the Jets." Lucy held TK's tiny hands, moving them back and forth to the beat of the music. I took a sip of wine. Lucy smiled at me, then reached out with her thumb and brushed away the red wine whiskers from the corners of my mouth.

It was an offhand gesture, but it seemed as intimate as anything she had ever done in bed.

Chapter 11
Lucy

It was December first, the sky dark at quarter to five as I crossed the intersection at Harvard Square with my fellow jaywalkers, drivers honking their impatience. Every Thursday after work, I'd walk ten minutes up Mass. Ave. for my appointment with Carla. Some days the idea of sitting down with her while she cajoled me into talking about the can of worms I called my life was more than I could bear; other days our sessions were my refuge, as if she were the only person on the planet who would let me be completely honest and give me an honest response. Today I was of both minds. At lunchtime, I had gone to a clinic and peed in a cup, my period long overdue; tomorrow I'd call them and find out what I already knew. I still hadn't told anyone and figured I might as well start with Carla.

Carla was vintage Cambridge, one of those stringy earth mothers who dressed in neo-peasant cotton, no makeup, long salt-and-pepper hair, two broken teeth on one side, which gave her a goofy smile. She had worked for an international aid organization in Africa and was married to a Nigerian man with skin the color of carbon paper. I had no idea what Carla's credentials were; there were no framed diplomas or certificates on her walls, just a great collection of African masks.

I arrived at her office a few minutes early and sat in the anteroom and thumbed through a copy of *Newsweek* with President Carter's beer-swizzling brother Billy on the cover. Behind the closed door, the woman who had her regular appointment just before mine let out a manic laugh. Ten seconds later, Carla's office door swung open, and the woman came out with her arm in one sleeve of her coat, a look of horror and relief on her face as if she'd nearly been run over by a bus. She and I had been nodding at each other every week for several years but had never exchanged more than a hello. I hated to admit it, but it always made me feel better imagining her problems were worse than mine.

When I went into the office, Carla paid me a rare compliment, saying I looked "becoming" today, and I wondered if I had acquired a bloom in the early stages of my pregnancy, never mind that I'd been throwing up every morning for the past two weeks. We made small talk for a few minutes, and I told her Matt was taking me to New York for a big weekend.

"Lucky you," she said. "To do what?"

"I'm not sure. It's a state secret. He was really cute about it. Told me to be sure to bring an evening dress and a couple of casual outfits. That's all he would say."

"You think it's something big?"

"You mean some life-altering question? He's been dropping hints. I think he's going to ask me to move in together."

"What will you say if he does?"

"I don't know. *Maybe?* It's a big decision." As if having his baby weren't.

"What's holding you back?"

"He's a good man, Carla. I don't want to hurt him."

100

"Give him a little credit. He knows what he's getting into."

"Not really." She didn't catch the hint, or chose to ignore it.

"You and Griffin never actually moved in together, did you?"

"Not officially." He spent most nights at my place but never gave up his own apartment.

"So moving in with Matt would be a big deal for you?"

"Very." My eyes shifted to the wall behind her desk. "I see you've got a new mask."

She turned to admire it. "Yes, it's from the Igbo people." The face was white with stark black lips and two black pipes protruding from either side of its mouth, black rings around the eyeholes, a black dog perched on top of its head.

"I love it," I said. "It's really scary. The masks are such a neat part of coming here."

"Some of my clients tell me they're put off by them."

"Yeah, I can understand that. Too many eyes watching you."

She smiled and said, "Let's get back to Matt. Tell me again why you're hesitant to move in with him."

"Like you said, it would be a big deal. Plus, I'm not sure I'm in love with him."

"Have you told him that?"

"I haven't said I was. I guess that's the same thing."

"But he's told you?"

"Once."

"And you liked hearing it?"

"I was touched, yes. Granted, it was two minutes after he told me his mother died, but I give him an A-plus for courage. He knows how skittish I am."

"Skittish maybe. But you're the one who's in control."

"You think I'm afraid of letting myself be vulnerable?"

"Are you?"

"Not with Griffin I wasn't."

"But now…" she said.

Now I'm fucking pregnant! It doesn't get any more vulnerable than that. I found myself shutting down, not wanting to tell her my secret; I managed to mumble and dodge my way through the rest of the session without letting her draw it out of me.

I walked home from Carla's and got in my car and drove straight to Jill's. She was on the couch in the great room off the kitchen, nursing TK. She touched her finger to her lips for me to be quiet. I took off my coat and sat in the big armchair.

"Is he sleeping?" I said softly.

Jill nodded. "Little bugger's been cranky since he woke up this morning. This is the first time he's been down all day." She unhooked the baby from her breast and tucked him into the corner of the couch beside her.

"I was in the neighborhood," I said. I picked at my thumb.

"This isn't about your trip to New York with Matt tomorrow, is it?" Count on Jill to cut to the chase. "Please tell me you haven't backed out."

I shook my head.

"So, how bad is it?"

I took a deep breath. "I'm pregnant."

"Okay." Her expression was unreadable.

"It's not official. I get the test results tomorrow, but all the signs are there. Backache, tender boobs, morning sickness. My boss brought a cup of hazelnut coffee back from lunch yesterday, and I had to race out of the office to keep from puking at my desk."

"You're going to tell Matt this weekend?" It sounded like a question, but it wasn't.

"Yes."

She leaned forward. "And keep the baby?"

"Of *course*, Jilly." It devastated me that she might think I wouldn't.

She let out a whoop and rushed over and hugged me. Seconds later we were all crying—her and me and the baby—then Terry walked in the door, and Jill and I started laughing, fat, happy tears streaming down our faces, and he looked at us like he'd wandered into a loony bin.

"It's a girl thing," Jill said. She scooped up TK, who had decided to take his discontent to the next decibel, and handed him to Terry. "He's been asking for you all day."

I grabbed my coat. "I have to go," I said to Jill. "I'll call you later."

I drove home feeling an enormous sense of relief. Now that I had said it—*I'm pregnant*—I couldn't conceive of my life in any other way. This baby was a blessing. Matt would be euphoric when I told him, not like the last time when Griffin and I had such horrible fights. After the abortion, I had a recurring nightmare in which I kept finding the dead fetus in various places around my apartment. It was tiny as a pearl and perfectly whole. I would come across it in an ashtray, beneath my panties in the bureau drawer, caught in the strainer in the kitchen sink. Now, as I drove home, I had an unshakable feeling that I was carrying a girl, a daughter who would live and grow, giggle and sing and call me Mommy. Life didn't have to be complicated; happiness was there for the taking. I had known that since my second date with Matt. How could I look into the eyes of our child and not love her father?

$$\infty$$

I called the clinic Friday morning, and a nurse confirmed that my pregnancy test was positive. She calculated the due date as July 19. I sat at my desk, grinning like the Cheshire cat, doodling 7-19-78 on a notepad, trying to imagine the look on Matt's face when I told him. Should I do it over dinner or matter-of-factly as we were strolling down the street? In bed after we'd finished making love? I wondered if the other women in the office could guess what I had been talking about when I was on the phone with the clinic, and almost wished that they could.

When I got to my house after work, Mrs. Stansbury was in the front hall sorting through the mail. I said a cheerful hello, but she scowled and handed me a catalog and a few envelopes. Her snub took me a little aback; she'd become much more amiable since Matt the Light Bulb Changer started coming around. I glanced through the mail as I walked up the stairs to my apartment on the third floor, happy to see that one of the envelopes was a blue aerogram, a rare letter from my brother Mark, who was working in New Zealand.

"Hey, babe," a voice above me said.

I looked up, so startled I dropped Mark's letter and nearly lost my balance.

"Oh my god, Griffin, what're you...?"

"Sorry." He stood on the landing, grinning, the apartment door open behind him. "I didn't mean to make you jump out of your skin."

I picked up the letter and charged up the stairs, pushing him aside as he tried to put his arms around me. He followed me into the apartment and closed the door. His parka was lying on the coffee table. Through the doorway of my bedroom, I could see my half-packed suitcase sitting on the foot of my bed. Matt was coming to pick me up in less than an hour.

I spun around. "Griffin, this is insane. You can't come barging into—"

"Lucy, I'm sorry." He lifted his empty hands. "You're right, I should have called first. I tried ringing the bell, but you weren't home, and I still had my key so I…" He gave me a coy shrug. He'd grown a short beard, more red than blond.

"This is unbelievable. What do you *want*? What are you doing here? You've been gone for eight months. Then all of a sudden you show up and *what*? We pick up where we left off? Or are you just passing through, looking for a quick fuck?"

He seemed genuinely hurt, a look I was unfamiliar with. "I came back to see you. I just want to talk."

"Talk? Really? What was that clever little maxim you used to say? The more time we spend talking about us, the less us-ness there is to talk about."

"Come on, baby, just listen. I've had a lot of time to think since I've been gone, and there's one thing I know for certain—no matter how fast I run or how far I go, every road keeps leading me back to you."

I rolled my eyes.

"I know you're skeptical," he said. "Hell, you *should* be. But here's the simple truth. I love you, Lucy. I love you and I need you in my life. I tried a hundred different times to say that over the telephone, but I was afraid you wouldn't believe me. Afraid I wouldn't believe it myself. I had to come here and say it face to face. If it's too late, I…" His head drooped in desolation.

I would have given a queen's ransom to hear him say this six months ago. But what did it matter now if his words were true?

"I'm sorry, Griffin. You need to go."

"I don't want to lose you, Luce."

"Please, go."

He stared at me for a moment, then nodded and held out his hands. "A kiss for the road?"

"Go." I took a step backward; I didn't want him to touch me. "Get the fuck out of here!"

He nodded, then angled his head toward the doorway of the bedroom. "Looks like you're going somewhere for the weekend?"

I shrugged.

"What's his name?"

"What difference does it make?"

"Just tell me his name."

"Matt. His name is Matt."

"Are you in love with him?"

"He's everything you're not, Griffin. Gentle, reliable, honest, *faithful.*"

"That's not what I asked."

"Yes, I'm in love with him."

He took out a cigarette and offered me one. I shook my head, and he shrugged and lit his own. "What time is he picking you up?"

"In about forty-five minutes." There was a ripple of panic in my throat. "I want you to go."

106

"No, I think I'll hang around and meet this fellow. Congratulate him on winning my girl."

"Please, Griffin, don't do this."

"Lucy, I came back for *you*. I'm not going to turn around meekly and walk out of your life."

I was on the verge of tears, my voice a whisper. "Please, you have to go."

"All you have to do when he gets here is look me in the eye and say, Griffin, this is Matt. This is the man I love." He took a drag on his cigarette. "That's it. You do that and I promise you'll never see me again."

"Get out of here, you asshole!" I put my hand on my head and clutched a fistful of hair. I felt like I was in a high school play, gesticulating, overacting, saying my lines all wrong. I wanted to walk offstage but I didn't know which way to turn. I had a feeling I was about to do something incredibly stupid—maybe screw up my entire life—and nothing could make me stop.

Chapter 12
Matt

All the stars were aligned for my weekend with Lucy in New York. I had the tickets Sandor had given me for *Annie*, a late dinner reservation at Sardi's, a room booked for two nights at the Plaza, which cost me nearly a week's salary. Lucy had a thing about the Plaza where her grandmother used to take her for tea, so I tried not to be concerned about the money. My mother's insurance policies had left me sitting pretty. Time for me to quit worrying about every nickel and spend a little on the woman I loved.

On the way home from work, I stopped in the lingerie department at Jordan Marsh and bought Lucy a short silk negligee, off-white with embroidered blue flowers. I pictured Lucy coming out of the hotel bathroom in the negligee with her hair falling across her shoulders. Tomorrow we'd take a ride through Central Park in one of those horse-drawn carriages. Go to the Museum of Modern Art, which Lucy was always raving about.

When I got to my apartment, Kreider was sitting on the couch drinking a beer and holding the telephone to his ear. He made a conciliatory grunt into the phone, then looked at me and mouthed, *Women.* I went to my room and put my gun in the safe. I took a shower and dressed and packed my suitcase. Double-checked my wallet to make sure I had the theater tickets. Kreider was still on the phone as I headed out the door.

Traffic was heavy on the way to Cambridge. I never liked being late, but Lucy wouldn't mind. She considered punctuality a minor character flaw. I climbed the rickety porch steps and rang the bell, waiting for her to buzz me in. She'd been saying she was going to give me my own key but still hadn't gotten around to it. I assumed that was a line she wasn't ready to cross, but I didn't want to make an issue out of it. I rang the doorbell again. Mrs. Stansbury from the first floor appeared in the hallway and opened the front door.

"Hello, Mrs. Stansbury."

"She isn't up there."

"Excuse me?"

"I saw her go out." Her words were terse. "She left about a half-hour ago."

I looked at my watch. Twelve minutes late. Maybe Lucy's doorbell was on the fritz. I said, "You mind if I go up and check?"

Mrs. Stansbury stepped aside. "Suit yourself."

I went up the stairs two at a time. There was an envelope thumbtacked to the door with MATT written on it. I tore open the envelope.

Dear Matt,

I'm SO SORRY, but my mom's gone off the deep end AGAIN. She's really outdone herself this time, and I had to rush home and help my dad. I called your house, but the line was busy. I'll try to catch up with you tonight or tomorrow morning and give you all the gory details. Sorry to spoil the weekend. I was REALLY looking forward to it.

xoxo,
Lucy

I leaned against the wall and read the note again. Lucy had left bowls of cat food and water for Rory in one corner of the landing. I folded the note and put it in my pocket. She had told me stories about her mother—the affairs and car accidents, drunken scenes at the country club. This was obviously something serious, but I was hurt and confused. Why not wait another half-hour for me? We were driving through Connecticut anyway. I could understand why Lucy might think the circumstances were too touchy and embarrassing to bring me into the mix since I hadn't met her parents yet. For all I knew, she hadn't even told them about me. But we could have talked along the way. I could have stayed in a motel in case she needed me.

Still, if she and her father got things under control, maybe I could still drive down tomorrow and take her to *Annie*. Not the weekend I'd planned, but it might give her a break from the drama. The only thing for me to do now was to go home and wait for her call.

When I got to the bottom of the stairs, Mrs. Stansbury was standing in her doorway.

"Thank you," I said, smiling. "She left me a note. Have a nice weekend."

As I started down the porch steps, she opened the front door and said, "Did the note mention who she left with?"

I was on the sidewalk before the words registered. I stopped and turned around.

"Ma'am?"

"Lucy. Did she tell you she went off with her old beau?"

"What're you talking about?"

"She took off with her ex. I forget his name. Skinny blond guy."

"Griffin?"

"That's him. Something about him always rubbed me the wrong way."

"Did she…?" My words trailed off, my worst fears confirmed. It wasn't that I had guessed that Lucy had run off with Griffin. But from the moment I first read that note, I had a feeling it was her way of leaving me. I had been deluding myself for months, trying to make myself believe she could love me. Maybe not as much as I loved her, but enough—something more than *xoxo*. I stood there trying to come to grips with the situation. I knew I had lost her. But how can you lose something you never really had?

Mrs. Stansbury said, "You seem like such a nice young man. Fine-looking police officer. I'll bet there are a million girls dying to go out with you. Don't waste your time on that tramp." She put her knuckles to her lips. "I'm *sorry*. That was a horrible thing to say. What you do is your own business."

I ran my fingers through my hair.

She said, "Would you like to come in for a cup of coffee?"

I sat in Mrs. Stansbury's living room while she made coffee in the kitchen. The room looked like something out of a magazine, stylish and modern and virtually unlived in. There was a black leather sofa and a white shag rug. Copies of *Gourmet* were fanned out neatly on the chrome-and-glass coffee table. A red enamel gas heater sat on the hearth in front of the bricked-over fireplace.

Mrs. Stansbury brought a tray with bright blue mugs and a matching sugar bowl and creamer. She handed me a mug. I put cream in my coffee and three spoons of sugar.

"Have you lived here long?" I said.

"Nineteen years. My husband Johnny and I moved in when he came home from the army." She stirred her coffee and held up the mug. "Cheers."

"Guess you've seen a lot of other tenants come and go."

"Not as many as you might think." She sat down in an armless rocking chair that appeared to be made from a single piece of red lacquered plywood. "We had the same three couples here for years. The Sizemores and their daughter on the second floor, Professor Wertz and his wife on the third. We were all so friendly back then. Now everyone keeps to themselves."

"Are those your sons?" I pointed at the photograph of two dark-haired boys on the mantel.

"My nephews. My brother's boys. Unfortunately, my husband and I couldn't have children. That's me and Johnny on our honeymoon in the other picture. Salisbury Beach."

In the photograph she looked lovely in a sleeveless summer dress. The man was wearing white pants and a flowered shirt. He had one arm around her waist, a cigarette in his hand, and a white Borsalino cocked over his eye.

"Weren't we dashing? Well, *he* was anyway. Could have had any girl he wanted." She bit one corner of her lip. "Which is exactly how it turned out. Now Johnny lives elsewhere. He has *friends* as he calls them. Pretty, young friends. I'll say this for the man though, he still pays the rent. I run into him on the street sometimes and he gives me a big hug. He used to beg me for a divorce, but I'm Catholic, so I never would. Now I'm the best excuse he's got. It wouldn't surprise me if he showed up on the doorstep tomorrow, asking to move back in."

"Would you let him?"

"Of course, he's my *husband*. I might make him sleep in the other bedroom for a few nights though." She grinned. "I hope I haven't shocked you, being so frank. Young people think they *invented* love, which I suppose they did. Trouble is, it's like smoking. Once you get started, it's hard to stop."

I sipped my coffee. "Has he been coming around much lately?"

"Johnny? No, he never…Oh, you mean Griffin? Here I am blabbering on and on, and you, poor thing, you're dying by the minute. No, to answer your question. As far as I know, he showed up this afternoon for the first time in ages. I can't remember the last time I saw him. Tell the truth, I don't think Lucy knew he was coming. I could hear her yelling at him all the way down here."

"Do you think…? Maybe she didn't want to go with him."

She shrugged, willing to let me believe whatever I wanted. "You and Lucy seemed so happy together. I think that's what made me angry, the thought of her going back with that creep again. I probably shouldn't've said anything and let the two of you work out things for yourself. I never paid one bit of attention when people warned me about Johnny. Resented it, actually."

"No, that's okay. I'm glad you told me. It's always better to know the truth, right?"

"Oh, I don't know about that. Sometimes I think I'd be a lot happier today if I'd've just kept the blinders on. A lot of women do." She stopped to consider the possibility. "More coffee?"

"No, thank you."

"Maybe you need something a little stronger?"

"No, I think I better be on my way." I stood up. "Thanks for everything, Mrs. Stansbury."

"Please, call me Ida. You know, I don't even know your name."

"Matt. Matt Drobyshev."

"Well, Officer Matt Drobyshev, it's a pleasure to finally have a chance to talk with you. I wish we could've had our little chat under different circumstances, but…Say, would you like to stay for dinner? I've got some nice lamb chops in the fridge. I'm a great cook, but I rarely get a chance to entertain."

It didn't occur to me until that moment that she was making a pass at me. Her eyes left no doubt. Maybe this was what she had in mind all along. I met her gaze frankly. I didn't want to diminish her by playing dumb. She had a voluptuous figure and a bold, inquisitive mouth. For a moment I let myself indulge in the fantasy, her full, creamy breasts spilling out of the negligee I'd bought for Lucy. Why not stay? Perhaps it was the perfect twist in this soap opera, each of us finding a way to debase ourselves.

"Thank you, Ida, but I need to go."

She walked me to the door. In the hallway she kissed me on the cheek.

"For luck," she said.

Chapter 13
Lucy

Griffin and I drove north in my car with the radio playing; he was driving, neither of us talking. He insisted he wouldn't leave the apartment till Matt came. I grew frantic, not wanting a confrontation, and said I'd spend the night with him if we could go somewhere else. We were on 95 just south of Portsmouth where we'd gotten our tattoos when I suddenly felt hungry. Griffin pulled off the highway and stopped at a diner. We sat in a narrow booth with green vinyl seats and a jukebox mounted on the wall. Griffin put a quarter in and punched some buttons, but there wasn't any sound.

The waitress said, "Sorry, it's broken."

Griffin shrugged and gave her a grin. "Maybe you could sing something for me instead."

"Not till I get off work, hon." She was about fifty and plain as a spoon.

I ordered comfort food: meatloaf with mashed potatoes and string beans, applesauce and warm dinner rolls on the side. Griffin began telling me about his travels, including a hilarious story about a commune in New Mexico where a bunch of hippie holdouts who thought nothing of dropping acid or smoking peyote referred to refined sugar as "white death." When I asked him if he had ever made it to Hollywood, he said he'd managed to get a few interviews with agents but quickly realized the place was mostly smoke and mirrors. I ate heartily as he talked. When the waitress asked if we wanted dessert, I ordered peach pie with vanilla ice cream, and she gave me a smile as if she knew my secret. Jill had gained sixty-eight pounds during her pregnancy; maybe I could match her and end up just as happy. I took a cigarette when Griffin offered, my first in over a week. I was determined to stop smoking, to quit drinking too, but this wasn't the time to try to hold the line. The nicotine gave me a buzz.

Back on the highway, we lost the radio station we'd been listening to. I scanned the dial, but all I could find were talk shows and country music. I finally got a station out of New Brunswick that played big band music, Count Basie and Duke Ellington, Sarah Vaughn singing "How High the Moon." Griffin and I hadn't talked about where we were going. I just got in the car and told him to drive, a million thoughts spinning around in my head.

What are you supposed to do when you come home, having just learned that you are officially pregnant, and find your ex-boyfriend in your apartment? Then the ex, whom you haven't seen in eight months, tells you he wants to make a life with you, which is probably complete bullshit but exactly what you've been hoping to hear him say since the day he left. And, of course, he gets jealous when he realizes you have a new boyfriend, who (minor detail) happens to be the father of the child you are carrying—something neither he nor the ex knows anything about. So you say you're in love with the new guy, though you're not at all certain, but you want to hurt your ex for abandoning you, only he turns the tables and tells you all you have to do is say the word and he'll be gone. Which may or may not be a bluff, but you don't want to risk losing him again, so you leave a note for the new boyfriend, who may be the sweetest man on earth, hoping he'll be stupid enough to believe your lies. But all you've bought is a day's reprieve at best, because tomorrow you're going to have to make some hard decisions, which, let's face it, has never been your strong suit.

We passed the York exit in Maine. I hadn't asked, but I figured maybe Griffin planned to stop at a motel outside of Biddeford near a flea market where we'd gone a few times. That's where I'd found the silver hair combs with the intricate latticework I wore the night I met Matt, the same ones I was wearing now. When Matt admired them, I said they'd belonged to my grandmother, the lie coming as easily as my next sip of wine. In my family, lying was as basic as condiments—mustard on your hot dog, tartar sauce on your fish sticks. Actually, I hadn't lied much to Matt, not unless you counted the lies of omission, like not telling him about the abortion or the story behind my tattoo. Anything that brought Griffin into the picture was basically verboten. I didn't want to reveal how much Griffin had meant to me, which, I suppose, was another way of lying, not just to Matt but to myself.

I tried to remember exactly what I'd said in the note I'd left on the door, wondering what Matt's reaction might have been when he read it. He wasn't a fool. Chances are he'd seen through my ruse and had already begun to hate me. But I hadn't given up hope that I could get away with it. If I called him tomorrow and gave him some wild story about Amanda, maybe he'd fall for it, his gullibility

and concern only proving how much he loved me. Or maybe he'd
be a little suspicious, wondering why I hadn't waited for him, why I
wouldn't let him help me in my time of trouble the way I'd helped
him through his mother's funeral. If he began to question me, I'd
have to admit, Yes, I was conflicted. Yes, I was running. But only
for one night, only for enough time to try to come to grips with my
beautiful, scary secret. *Our secret.* His baby and mine.

It started to rain. The radio station faded and Griffin found
another, drumming his hand on the steering wheel to an Allman
Brothers song. I began to feel sick to my stomach. I was still thinking
about that note. Was it worse to keep the lie going or to tell Matt the
truth? Sometimes the truth can be much crueler than a lie.

The song on the radio ended. Griffin said, "Penny for your thoughts."

"Nothing special."

"Must be Matt, then."

"Don't be a dickhead." I hated that he was right.

He laughed and squeezed my thigh. "Oooh, I *love* it when you
talk dirty."

"Pull over!"

"Jesus Christ, Luce, can't you—"

"Please, Griffin. Pull over quick! I'm gonna throw up."

We were in the passing lane. Griffin cut in front of a tractor-
trailer and skidded onto the shoulder of the road, wheels fishtailing
on the wet macadam, gravel pelting the underside of the car. The
first eruption came as I flung myself out the door. Then I fell to my
hands and knees, Griffin squatting beside me, holding my hair back
from my face as I heaved, and heaved again.

At the motel I took a long, hot shower and came out of the bathroom in jeans and a baggy sweatshirt, my hair in a ponytail. Griffin was sitting on the bed watching TV with his shirt off, smoking a joint. He had a new tattoo on his left bicep, four black Chinese characters still blistered with scabs.

He said, "Feeling any better?"

"Much. Must have been something I ate."

"I got you a can of ginger ale from the machine."

"Thank you. What're you watching?"

"Nothing. You can turn it off."

I switched off the television and sat next to him on the bed. He handed me the ginger ale, then put his arm around me and kissed my cheek.

"You want a hit?" He offered me the joint.

I took one toke, then another, happy to get high without Matt's silent chiding. Just this once wouldn't hurt the baby. I made a silent vow to throw away my stash of weed when I got back to the apartment.

I touched Griffin's arm. "What does your new tattoo say?"

"It's just some Chinese characters I like."

"Come on, tell me."

"Promise you won't laugh," he said. I nodded and crossed my heart. "It says *I love Lucy*."

I burst out laughing. "Oh, Griffin, you never quit, do you?"

"Not when it comes to you."

I leaned against him. Then we were kissing, his hand under my sweatshirt, my nipples tender and swollen.

He said, "This is why I came back, baby." He lifted the sweatshirt and took one of my breasts in his mouth. He unsnapped my jeans and slipped his hand inside my panties. "This is all that matters." His fingers were familiar. Accurate. "This is what we do best."

I shuddered with pleasure then pushed him away. "No, Griffin. I'm sorry. I can't do this."

"I'm not giving you up, baby. Not without a fight."

"It's complicated."

"No complications, Lucy. Just give me one more chance."

"Griffin, I'm pregnant."

"Well." He thought about it for a second, then shrugged. "We know that can be fixed."

I nodded, a rueful twist to my mouth, then dug my fingernails into the new tattoo and raked them down his arm.

"*Motherfucker!*" He raised a fist to hit me but let it fall. "You crazy bitch!"

I sobbed and covered my face with my hands. "Take me home. I want to go home."

He tried to hold me, but I got up from the bed.

"Lucy, I'm sorry. I—"

"No, it's okay."

"Christ! What a stupid fucking thing to say." Blood ran down his arm. "I'm sorry. I know how bad you felt the last time."

"No you don't. You have no fucking clue what I went through. You've never asked me one single thing about it. Not then, not today." I could feel my voice getting stronger. "You don't want me, Griffin; you want to *win*. You just want to prove to yourself that I still want to fuck you." I pulled the sweatshirt over my head.

"Okay, fine, prove it. Make this the *coup de grace*. The fuck to end all fucks."

"Please, baby, stop. I'm sorry."

"No, I mean it." I stepped out of my jeans, naked except for my panties. "Come on, let's make this the fuck we'll never forget. You want to do it here or go somewhere else? You want to get kinky? Find a roadhouse and screw me on the pool table in front of thirty other people? Great, let's go. I'll do anything you want."

"Lucy, I—" The look in his eyes went beyond contrition, almost as if he were afraid of me.

"Then what? What'll we do for an encore, Griffin? We have great sex, but so what. What's the point? Carla's right. This isn't love, it's an addiction."

"Not for me." He stood up and put his hands on my shoulders. "I know *exactly* where I belong."

"For God's sake, Griffin, try being honest for once. We're not in love. What you and I have is like gambling. Like we're in a casino running from one slot machine to the next, pulling those handles, hoping we'll hit the jackpot. And the thing is we *do*. We win big! Lights flashing, bells clanging, silver dollars spilling onto the floor. But it's never enough. We're never satisfied."

"Isn't that what we want, baby? That hunger? The way we keep pushing each other, always looking for ways to make it new. That's what keeps us fresh, Luce. I can't find that with anyone else, and neither can you."

It became a battle of wills. I couldn't wear him down or hold on to my anger. I sat next to him on the bed and dabbed his bloody arm with the sheet. He began to kiss me and run his fingers through my damp hair. I told myself he wasn't a bad man, only weak, and so was I. It was useless to resist. I needed to do this and get it over with so I could walk away and never look back.

I guess it was all those months apart that made our lovemaking seem so good. Maybe we were some inseparable cosmic pairing like earth and moon, or Eros and Psyche. Except I was pregnant with another man's child. When it was over, I hid my nakedness with the sheet and hugged my knees to my chest.

Griffin lit a cigarette. "Come on, don't get all moody on me."

"Moody? This is real life, Griffin. I'm going to have a *baby*." His face went slack, the conquest over and reality settling in. "You have to let me go," I said. "I don't know if things will work out with Matt. It could be a complete disaster, or maybe we'll live happily ever after. I don't know, but I have to *try*." I touched his cheek. "Think about it, Griffin. You're not going to settle down with me and someone else's kid. You couldn't even do it when it was your own. Please. Let me go. Stop reeling me back in."

He took a drag on his cigarette. I couldn't tell what he was thinking.

"You want to go back now?" he said.

I nodded, afraid I might change my mind.

We got dressed and headed back down 95. One of my silver hair combs was missing. I couldn't find it after I took my shower at the motel; it wasn't in the car either. It probably had fallen from my hair when I was puking on the side of the road. I took the other comb from the pocket of my jeans and ran my fingertip over the lacy whorls.

Chapter 14

Matt

I drove home from Cambridge with my heart in my throat. On the way I kept thinking about two things Mrs. Stansbury said. The first was that before today she hadn't seen Griffin in ages. The other was that she'd heard Lucy yelling at him. At least Lucy hadn't been deceiving me for weeks or months, though a cynic (or a realist) might say she dumped me and bolted with Griffin the minute he came back. But what was she yelling about? I pulled over to the side of the road and took out Lucy's note. I kept trying to read between the lines, hoping to find some clue that she had acted against her will. As if Griffin had come back and kidnapped her and forced her to write it. I kept wanting to believe she was something other than a cold-hearted bitch.

When I got back to my apartment from Cambridge, Kreider was coming out the front door carrying his gym bag.

"Hey," he said, "I thought you were headed for the Big Apple?"

"Change of plans. Lucy had to go home to her parents' for the weekend." I congratulated myself on the innocuous response.

Kreider asked if I wanted to go to the Y and play some hoops. I said sure and went to grab my stuff. We rode in his car. I hadn't played in any of the Friday night basketball games since I'd started seeing Lucy. Most of the guys were in their twenties and thirties, but there were a couple of older guys who were still pretty good. We played full court. No refs, no harm/no foul, a rough, punishing game that helped me get my mind off Lucy. As I was going up for a rebound near the end of the evening, a sergeant from the crime lab gave me a hip check and I landed hard on my left shoulder. Some guys on my team started pointing fingers, saying it was a cheap shot. When the sergeant told them to go fuck themselves, Paki Epstein walked over and doubled him over with a quick punch to the stomach. Paki was a wiry little guy who could dribble like Earl the Pearl. No one knew what he did for a living, but there were rumors he used to work as a bag man for the Winter Hill Gang. The sergeant didn't try to retaliate, and we decided the game was over. As I was getting dressed, my shoulder hurt so much I could barely raise my arm. I didn't mind. It was another distraction and fit my mood.

A bunch of us went to a bar in Back Bay. Free drinks for Paki and me. Someone at the table ordered a Perfect Manhattan. Nice bit of irony given where I was supposed to be going. I had no idea what was in the drink but said I'd take one too. We laughed about Paki's punch and bragged to one another about our exploits on the court. I drank the Manhattan quickly and ordered another. My shoulder burned deep in the joint. The second drink made everything fuzzy. Kreider picked up a girl with stupendous tits and a face like a ferret.

I got up and went to the bathroom. While I was washing my hands, I looked at myself, bleary-eyed, in the mirror and let out a groan. I left the bar without returning to the table. I walked a few blocks and began to shiver. The temperature must have dropped twenty degrees in the past hour. I was wearing only a light jacket, my head turtled in the upturned collar. A few taxis passed, but I didn't try to flag them down. I wondered what Lucy and Griffin were doing right now, then tried to chase away the images. I felt less anger and jealousy than a vast, unfathomable emptiness. I windmilled my left arm to get the kink out of my shoulder, or to punish myself with the pain. Lucy had tried to warn me not to fall in love with her, but I kept ignoring the cues, pretending I didn't know how it would end.

This wasn't a matter of taking the road less traveled. Anyone with an ounce of curiosity could do that. This was about knowing exactly where the road will lead and taking it anyway, believing you could change your fate. She was everything I ever desired. There were times when we were making love or talking over dinner or simply sitting in a movie theater holding hands that I felt so *connected* my entire body seemed to be filled with light. And I would often find myself thinking, *I'll bet some people have never felt like this in their whole lives, not even once.* Now it occurred to me that Lucy probably had never felt that way about me. Not even once.

A working girl stepped out of the shadows and said, "Hey, handsome."

"Hey," I said and kept walking.

"I could show you a good time," she called after me.

Halfway down the block I considered turning around and going back to her. Or driving to Cambridge and knocking on Mrs. Stansbury's door. Either/or—at least I'd be doing something. But I kept walking, not half as drunk as I wanted to be.

∞

I was dozing in front of the TV when the telephone rang. I had a hunch it was Lucy and thought about not picking up. She'd wonder where I was, wonder if I knew the truth. I wished we had an answering machine so I could hear her tone of voice. Would she try to keep the lie going? How would I react if she did—or didn't? I still felt empty, no energy for anger, not yet anyway. It's the way all dupes feel I suppose. You want to blame the swindler, but somewhere in the back of your mind you've known all along the deal was too good be true.

I answered the phone on the fifth ring.

"Matt? It's me," Lucy said. "Sorry if I woke you up."

"No, no, it's okay. I've been hoping you'd call."

"Thanks, I…Boy, what a wild day." She was trying to sound frazzled and relieved at the same time.

"How's your mother?"

"Better. She's…"

"What?"

"It wasn't her, Matt. It was me."

"What do you mean?"

"I'm sorry I left that note. It was a terrible thing to do. There wasn't any crisis with my mother."

A dash of honesty. I didn't say anything.

"Matt, this weekend… I've had some big things on mind. Maybe you have too. It's no excuse, but I haven't been feeling well the past few weeks. It was horrible to leave you a note like that, but I wanted…I needed some space. I got scared and ran. I'm so sorry." She changed to the voice of a naughty little girl. "Can you forgive me? I don't want to lie anymore."

"Where'd you run to?"

"Nowhere. Just drove around. I'm home now. Can I come over? We need to talk."

"Talk about what?"

"Us. The future."

She really thought she could get away with it. "Will that include Griffin?"

She let out a soft cry. "Oh, Matt." Which was the same thing she said the first time I told her I loved her. I let her dangle in the silence. "How did…? I swear I was going to tell you."

"Right."

"Please don't hate me. I *tried* to get him to leave, but he wouldn't. I was afraid of what might happen if he was still here when you came to pick me up." I said nothing. "I know how cruel and stupid I've been. All I can do now is be honest and hope you'll forgive me. Griffin showed up out of nowhere. I hadn't seen him or talked to him in months. We had a long, rocky relationship. The last time I saw him I…Listen, Matt, *you're* the one I want to be with. Please, let me come over and I'll tell you everything."

"I'll come to Cambridge," I said and hung up.

I drove like a madman. Lucy left the front door open so I could let myself in. She was waiting at the top of the stairs in black flannel pajamas, shoulders hunched, her hands tucked under her armpits. Her skin was pasty and her eyes full of remorse. She wanted a hug, but I brushed past her. The apartment smelled of fresh coffee. I went into the kitchen and sat down, and she poured me a cup.

"Are you hungry?" she said. "I could make you cinnamon toast."

"Okay."

She put bread in the toaster. Neither of us spoke. Her hair was pinned up carelessly. A long strand fell across her cheek. The yellow-and-white-striped canisters on the counter had come from my mother's house. Lucy had admired them, and I said she should bring them home. She sprinkled sugar and cinnamon on the toast, then sat down across the table.

"You're not eating?" I said.

"I'm feeling a little queasy."

A nasty retort came to mind, but I didn't say it. She reached for my hand, then withdrew hers when I failed to meet her halfway.

"Look, Matt, what I did today was the worst thing I've ever done in my life. You have every right to be furious, but *nothing* happened with Griffin. Nothing I'm ashamed of." She looked me directly in the eyes. "I didn't have sex with him. We argued and talked and argued some more. There's a lot of history there. Some stuff that never got resolved. But that's all over now. You have to believe me. I belong here with *you*, Matt. This is where I want to be."

I gave a skeptical shrug, as if to say, *So what if I believe you? The damage is already done.* She bit her lip, on the verge of tears. Truth was, I wanted to believe her. A few hours ago, I would have given my soul to have her back, but I wasn't ready to let go of my anger. Rory came into the room, and Lucy bent down and scratched her ears.

"There are two things I have to tell you," she said. "One bad, one good, at least from my point of view. God, I wish I had a cigarette." She had picked her thumbs raw again. "First, I had an abortion last March. It was Griffin's baby. He took off that same day, and I didn't see him again until this afternoon. The second thing is…" She took a deep breath and let it out slowly. "I'm pregnant again. No matter what you decide, I'm not going to have another abortion."

"Holy shit! Are you positive?"

She gave a brave smile. "I got the test results today. We're going to have a baby, Matt. Me and you."

I went around the table and kissed her and said her name. Then I sank to the floor, my face pressed against her belly, and began to cry.

"I love you, Matt." She was crying too. "I do. I really, really do."

Part Two

Chapter 15

Lucy

Jamaica Plain, Massachusetts—January 1981

W hen the bacon fat began to sizzle, I scraped the onions and mushrooms from the cutting board into the frying pan and stirred them with a wooden spoon. Amanda, who had arrived a half hour before, was sitting at the kitchen table, sipping a glass of sauvignon blanc. It was a few days past New Year's, and she and my father had just come back from a vacation in Peru. As soon as they got home, Amanda called and asked if she could come for a visit, which I assumed meant she needed to get away from Thorny for a while. A shopping bag full of presents she'd brought was sitting in a corner of the kitchen.

"Amazing," Amanda said, watching me slice a cucumber into thin, translucent slices.

"What?"

"You're so *domesticated*."

I mooed. Eight months pregnant with my second child, I'd spent the morning cleaning the house—definitely not my forte as Matt was quick to point out—now I was making dinner from a special recipe I'd gotten from Sandor. It was the same housewifely thing Amanda might have been doing herself thirty years ago, the parallel not lost on either of us.

"You disapprove?" I said.

"Not at all, dear. You're obviously quite good at it."

"Tell me about Peru," I said.

"Oh, there were some wonderful moments. Machu Picchu is divine. You're on top of a mountain surrounded by ruins, and it's so *spiritual* you're half expecting some ancient god to appear." She lit a cigarette, and my nerve endings tingled at the smell. I'd quit smoking when I got pregnant again, but still had the urge. She continued telling me about their trip.

I diced a yellow pepper for the salad. To Matt's delight, I'd become a pretty good cook since we'd gotten married though I rarely derived much enjoyment from it. The dinners were only for him and me. At two and a half, Sarah was a finicky eater, her diet consisting mostly of Cheerios and peanut butter and jelly. Matt and I were at odds over the issue. She was a healthy, happy kid, and I assumed she'd start eating other foods as she got older. I felt it was a waste of time and energy to try to get her to eat things she didn't like; Matt thought she should take a bite of everything on her plate. He and Sarah often got into a battle of wills, which he (silent cheer) rarely won.

I said to Amanda, "How's Daddy?"

"Fine. The same. Still kicking up his heels."

"Are you worried?"

"Not a bit." She took off her camel's-hair jacket.

"And you're still trying to keep up with him."

"Oh honey, I'm too tired for that nonsense anymore," she said, which probably meant she was on the prowl. I pictured her sitting in the club car on the train to Boston, talking to some salesman, laughing her silvery laugh. She was fifty-six, her beauty fading, but she had an air that gave off a hint of danger.

I looked out the window at the windblown snow banking half-way up the ladder of the wooden swing set in the backyard. The check that my parents had given Matt and me as a wedding present was so generous we'd bought a fixer-upper in Jamaica Plain. Built in 1904, the house was shabby and in need of updated wiring and plumbing, but otherwise sound. There was oak flooring in every room, a working fireplace in the master bedroom. I loved the panels of stained glass on either side of the front door and the plaster medallion shaped like a fruit basket around the base of the light fixture in the dining room. Matt and his pals from the police department who moonlighted as tradesmen had worked tirelessly to get the house in shape. The first thing they did was to renovate the apartment on the third floor, which tenants reached by a stairway at the back of the house. We rented the apartment to a couple named Derek and Robin Nevins, who were also expecting their first child. Robin's baby, Emily, was born six days after Sarah.

Sarah and Emily burst through the back door with Robin, their faces rosy from the cold.

"Nanda!" Sarah ran to Amanda, who scooped her up onto her lap. "How's my little angel?"

"Good. Me and Em had ice cream."

"Brrrrr. Ice cream in the middle of winter?"

"Mm-hmm. I like double fudge. Em likes plain old banilla."

Amanda looked at Emily. "Good choice. Vanilla is my favorite too."

Painfully shy around strangers, Emily was peeking out from

behind Robin's pant leg. Robin and I were practically raising the girls like twins, a double stroller to take them for walks, toys and books and clothes migrating from one place to the other till it was hard to remember whose was whose. Sarah was the first to talk, then translated Emily's gibberish. They begged to sleep in the same room every night, a treat Robin and I reserved for special occasions. Now that was all about to change. Derek, a medical researcher, had gotten a job in Texas, and they were moving at the end of the month. A touch of panic flickered through me when I thought about their leaving. Robin and I traded time taking care of the girls, but she assumed more than her fair share, cheerfully dismissing my concerns.

Much as I loved my daughter, I felt like an inept and impatient mother. I managed okay for Sarah's first year; she nursed gently and regularly, took long naps during the day, and slept soundly through the night. Back then I had time to relax. I read and worked in the garden and started a few small projects around the house. The struggle began when Sarah became a toddler. For me the problem was simply that I didn't know how to play. I would sit on the floor with Sarah among the dolls and stuffed animals and brightly colored plastic toys that whirred and squeaked and plinked "Eine kleine nachtmusik" over and over, and time stood still. Thank goodness for *Sesame Street* and *The Electric Company*—Sarah mesmerized by the television for an hour and a half, an occasional pun thrown in to amuse the grown-ups—which gave me a chance to fix supper and get a few things done around the house. What baffled me was how much pleasure Robin and Jill (who recently announced she was pregnant with her third) seemed to get from hanging out with toddlers. Did they really enjoy it, or were they just faking? I could never find a way to ask, afraid the question might seem disparaging or show my unfitness as a mother. I'd read articles in women's magazines telling me I was not alone, with advice to mitigate the boredom and irritability, but nothing to assuage the guilt. I loved watching Sarah grow and discover new things, loved listening to her unfiltered, often hilarious comments on the world. But I needed more. I never should have let Matt talk me into quitting my job; now here I was, pregnant again, playing the role of the happy homemaker for Amanda, who knew all too well how poorly the apron fit. If I weren't worried about harming the baby, I'd get drunk with her at supper tonight, or sneak off and smoke a little dope (if I still had some).

When Matt came home from work, Amanda gave us the presents she'd brought from Peru: hand-knitted wool sweaters for Matt and me, a stuffed llama for Sarah, a beautiful cotton blanket for the unborn baby. The llama was white, with a dark brown tuft of hair between his ears. Sarah said he looked like a bowl of ice cream with chocolate on top, and we dubbed him Sundae.

After dinner, Amanda insisted on cleaning up. I was sitting at the kitchen table with my tired legs propped up on an adjacent chair. Sarah's squeals of laughter filtered down from the second floor where Matt was giving her a bath.

"He's so good with her," Amanda said.

"Yes, he is." He was good at almost everything, which wasn't always easy to live with.

"You got lucky."

"I know."

Amanda emptied the wine bottle into her glass. "Is this one going to be your last?"

I shrugged.

"How many does he want?"

"At *least* three."

"Oh dear."

I couldn't claim that Matt had talked me into this pregnancy. He wanted to have another baby and I did too, mostly because I didn't want Sarah to be an only child. My brother Mark and I had been very close growing up, especially as teenagers, though as adults, we had drifted apart. Mark spent most of his time abroad. I hadn't seen him in four years, our communications limited to an occasional phone call or letter, but I couldn't imagine having grown up without him. He had been my ally and confidant, my biggest fan and the first one to call me on my faults, a bulwark of sanity in the family asylum. I wanted a sibling like him for Sarah, someone to turn to when her hormones started raging and her parents became the enemy. To me, this second child seemed like the most precious gift I could give to my daughter—compensation, perhaps, for the inadequacies I felt as a mother. Depending on my mood, the gesture seemed touchingly noble or incredibly stupid.

Amanda finished loading the dishwasher. "Honey, if you want to, you could just go ahead and get your tubes tied. Matt doesn't have to know."

"I can't do that, Mom. We're just gonna have to fight it out."

"Fight what out?" Matt said. He had Sarah in his arms, Sarah holding the llama.

"Nothing," I said.

Matt shrugged, content not to know. No doubt he assumed it was some problem between Amanda and me. Having grown up with a mother whose capacity for love and understanding and a firm guiding hand had become the stuff of legend, Matt seemed perplexed by the strife in my family and a little self-righteous about the harmony in his own. He felt his upbringing gave him a distinct advantage over me when it came to raising children, and I, given my own maternal ambivalence, was inclined to agree. As for getting my tubes tied, Matt was so happy with the prospect of our second child, it seemed unkind of me to toss that issue into the mix when the baby hadn't even been born yet. I figured we'd work it out in time, which was indicative of how we both operated, as if avoiding the hard stuff was almost as good as not having the hard stuff at all.

Sarah took the binky from her mouth. "It's not nice to fight."

"No it isn't," Matt said.

Amanda held out her arms and took Sarah from Matt. "Can Nanda read you a story and put you to bed?"

Sarah nodded enthusiastically. It amazed me how the two of them had bonded. Had my mother been this relaxed when Mark and I were kids? Why couldn't I remember her as anything other than a crabby, impatient witch with a drink in her hand? When Amanda took Sarah up to her room, Matt squatted next to my chair and began to rub my weary legs.

"Good day today?" he said.

"Yeah, fine."

"That was a terrific dinner."

"Thank you."

"Guess you're pretty worn out?" It was his way of saying, *Any chance of our making love tonight?* Throughout my pregnancy, I'd been deliciously horny, which Matt never failed to appreciate, but lately I'd been feeling too tired to do much about it.

"Don't worry. I'll take care of you." I leaned forward to kiss him, but my belly stopped me short.

Matt made up the difference between us. "Do you have any idea how much I love you?"

I smiled. Sometimes I wished I didn't; I never quite felt like I repaid him in kind.

Around noon on Friday, the seventeenth of January, my water broke, and I went into labor two weeks early. I called the police department, and they said they'd try to get in touch with Matt as quickly as possible. Meanwhile, Robin got a neighbor to take care of Sarah and Emily while she drove me to the hospital. Things happened so quickly—twenty-three minutes from arriving at the hospital to giving birth—that Robin ended up staying with me the whole time. The baby was a boy. I was in my own room with him when Matt finally arrived. The baby was much smaller than Sarah had been, with a weak, mewling cry. After they did a few tests, the doctors determined he was so jaundiced that they took him away and put him in a special crib, naked, under an ultraviolet light. He looked like a tiny surfer with his down of blond hair and brownish-yellow skin. We named him Nathan Alexander Drobyshev.

When the baby and I came home from the hospital, the house was decorated with colored ribbons and helium balloons. Sarah and Emily huddled close to me, watching him nurse, touching his tiny fingers and toes. Rory the cat didn't like the commotion of the homecoming but was curious about Nathan in a way she had never been about Sarah. The first night I put the baby to sleep, Rory cuddled up underneath the bassinet as if she were standing guard.

Matt took a week off work, cooking and doing the laundry and looking after Sarah and Emily while Robin and Derek got ready for their move. The thought of Robin's leaving upset me so much I had refused to advertise the apartment for rent. I told Matt I didn't want a bunch of strangers traipsing around upstairs while our friends were still living there. This was true, but I knew I was engaged in a bit of magical thinking: if the place wasn't rented to someone else, there was still a possibility Robin and Derek would stay. The day the moving truck arrived, Sarah and Emily were inconsolable, and so was I.

Nathan nursed voraciously, as if he knew how small he was and was anxious to catch up. My nipples were cracked and sore, and I began expressing my milk, which I gave to him in a bottle while I healed. When he wasn't feeding, he was colicky, never sleeping for more than an hour or two at a time. I started smoking again, much to Matt's dismay. Friends phoned and I had nothing to say. I stopped getting dressed in the morning and spent entire days in my bathrobe, fending off Sarah's pleas to go here or there. I would ask her if she missed Emily, knowing it was wrong to bring up the subject, but it was almost as if I wanted her to be as sad as I was. She'd nod and her lip would quiver, but she had an innate resilience and curiosity, and three minutes later she'd be cheerful again while I retreated deeper into my despair.

Matt did all the grocery shopping, but I couldn't bring myself to cook. I'd make tuna fish sandwiches for dinner or call Matt and ask him to bring home some takeout food, rarely eating anything myself. One Saturday afternoon when Nathan was seven weeks old, Matt went off somewhere with Sarah and the baby to give me a break. I took a Benadryl in hopes of getting some sleep, but it didn't seem to be kicking in. I decided to soak in the tub. Naked, I caught a glimpse of myself in the bathroom mirror, my skin loose and sallow, lips chapped, dark circles under my eyes—thirty years old and going on fifty. I got a pair of scissors and began to chop off my hair, thick sheaves dropping into the sink. Matt came home and found me curled up and shivering on the tile floor.

$$\infty$$

"Postpartum depression," the doctor said. "In a few months you'll be fine."

"Months?" I didn't how I was going to get through the rest of today.

He gave me a patronizing smile. "How's your husband handling this?"

"Matt? He's been great. He does as much as he can." Which, along with his relentless good cheer, sometimes made me resent him all the more.

"Can you get some outside help on a regular basis? Maybe a few hours in the afternoon?"

I shrugged. I wanted Robin back. I wanted to hear my daughter's laughter and feel like she wasn't mocking me. I wanted not to shrink with revulsion when Matt tried to pull me close. I wanted to wake up one morning and get dressed like a normal person and look out the window and see the sun shine.

"You need to get out of the house. Treat yourself to a movie, go to the beauty parlor. Things like that."

I shrugged again and touched the scarf on my head, thinking the beauty parlor remark was gratuitous.

"Meanwhile," the doctor said, "I'll start you on antidepressants. You'll have to stop breast-feeding, but I think it's for the best. The medication won't take effect immediately. A week, maybe a little longer. Check back with me in a month. If you're still feeling blue, we'll up the dosage."

I felt a sudden loathing for him. Blue? No, doctor, blue would be a vast improvement. This is the total absence of color, unless you're counting black.

Chapter 16

Matt

For the first time I could remember, my life was a bore. The TWT task force had been disbanded about six months before Nathan was born, and Javi retired to his flower shop and limousine service. I passed the sergeant's test and was transferred to media relations. My new job was to talk to reporters about the department's criminal investigations. The trick was to give the press enough details to write their stories without jeopardizing the case. High-profile crimes were handled by people far above my pay grade, but Captain Antonucci assured me the position was good for my career. I worked from eight to four-thirty and could slip away from the office any time I wanted.

That proved to be a godsend in the darkest days of Lucy's postpartum depression—six or seven months when she walked around like a zombie. She tried a number of different doctors and prescriptions, but nothing seemed to work. Everything I heard and read said the condition was chemical, hormonal, but it felt personal to me. As if she'd spun a web around herself to keep me and the children out. For months our sex life was nonexistent. I didn't stray, but I had my share of fantasies. I had two porno tapes that I'd hid in the basement, but I'd only watched snippets a few times late at night. I didn't want Lucy or, God forbid, Sarah to wander downstairs and catch me.

Nathan was almost a year old now, and Lucy professed to be back to normal. We'd started making love now and again, but it was perfunctory on her part. She could have doubled as one of those blow-up dolls Lenny sold at the Sweet Spot down in the Combat Zone. She may have come out of her depression, but she had not come back to me.

Marcy Feldman came through the open door of my office and asked me if I'd consider looking over a speech that the commissioner was planning to give to a group of real estate agents.

"Sure, I'll look it over," I said. "What kind of feedback do you want?"

"Just make sure none of the facts about the crime rate reduction are too ridiculous." She grinned back over her shoulder as she walked out the door. "Thanks, Drobo."

Marcy had long been one of my fantasies. About a month ago I'd run into her at a bar after my old roommate Kreider talked me into coming to the Y for a game of basketball. It was the first night I could remember being out alone in more than a year. Marcy ended up in a booth beside me. She knew I was married. Her thigh brushed against mine, and I started getting hard. She handed me a pack of matches to light her cigarette. I excused myself to go to the men's room. There were condoms in a vending machine on the wall. I put in two quarters and slipped the foil package in my pocket.

My heart pounded as I walked toward the table. Marcy gave me a knowing smile, but I couldn't go through with it. Maybe she was making it too easy. I'd always been good at resisting temptation. I put a ten on the table to pay for the drinks and said I was sorry, it was late, I had to go. Marcy pouted and pushed her glasses up on her nose with her middle finger. On the way to the car, I dropped the condom in a trashcan. It was the closest I had ever come to being unfaithful to Lucy. Driving home, I felt righteous and horny and glad I hadn't gone through with it. The sad part is, I'm not certain Lucy would have cared if I strayed. Sometimes I felt as if she expected me to cheat on her—that she believed a *real* man would go off and get what he needed from someone else. I was still deeply in love with her, but how long could I wait for her to come around?

I was reading the commissioner's speech when a familiar voice in the doorway said, *"Necesito una cita, sargento?"* Do I need an appointment, sergeant?

I looked up. *"Solamente una genuflexión, mi hijo."* Just genuflect, my son.

I stood up and came around the desk to meet Javi. We grinned and shook hands and patted each other on the shoulders. I considered Javi one of my closest friends but couldn't remember the last time I'd seen him.

"How's that little boy of yours?" Javi said.

"Nathan? He's terrific. Getting bigger every day."

"That's great, man. And Sarah? Lucy?"

"Good. Real good."

I could hear the hollowness in my voice. I had tried to hide Lucy's troubles as much as possible from everyone.

We walked over to Jake Wirth's to have lunch, best Reuben sandwich in town. Javi said his family was great. Same with his business ventures.

"What about you?" he said. "You like that desk job?"

"It's a paycheck, Javi."

"You could put in for a transfer. Get your ass back out on the streets."

I shrugged. I knew I'd gotten lazy.

Javi said, "How many years you got in?"

"Almost ten."

"Long way to a pension, man. You ever think about turning in your shield and doing something else?"

"Sometimes. I don't know." It wasn't just the job; my whole life seemed governed by inertia. Except for the joy I got from the kids, I couldn't remember the last time I'd felt really alive. Maybe in that bar with Marcy.

We finished our sandwiches. Javi lit a cigarillo.

"Listen, I didn't drop by today just to chitchat. I got this new business going. A real winner, but I need somebody to run it. Somebody I can really *trust*."

"You can't run it yourself?"

"I'm flat out already, man. We're opening another flower shop, adding a fourth car to the limo service."

"So what's the new business?"

"Escort service."

"That *definitely* would be interesting."

"I'm serious."

Javi strung me along for a minute before he told me the story. "Couple months ago I get a call from a guy who tells me he's bought a painting. Early impressionist, which didn't mean a thing to me. The sale was private. The guy says the painting's in Mainz, West Germany, and he needs someone to fly over there and bring it back to Boston. Right away, my wheels start turning. Sounds like money isn't an object, but why doesn't he just use a commercial shipper? I figured it might be something shady. One of those paintings the Nazis stole from the Jews or something."

"How'd he get your name?"

"One of my limo drivers. Anyway, I figured it's worth checking out."

Javi said he arranged to meet with the man at his house in Cohasset overlooking the bay. Javi was completely up front with the guy and asked him where the painting had come from. The man had all the documentation. His lawyer had already contacted customs and everything was set for the painting to come back to the U.S. The guy told Javi there were shipping companies that routinely handled this sort of thing, but he wanted his own man on the job.

"I had a good feeling about him," Javi said. "No airs. Completely up front. Only took about ten minutes for us to work out the details."

"How did you decide what to charge?"

Javi chuckled. "He shouldn't have let me see his house before he asked. I told him five hundred a day plus expenses. He said he thought that sounded fair."

I let out a low whistle.

A week later, Javi flew first-class to Germany and checked into a hotel in Mainz. The next day, an art expert picked him up and took him to see the painting. The French countryside at twilight with a horse-drawn carriage. Javi said it was so beautiful it gave him chills. He had no idea how much his client had paid for it, which he said was probably just as well or it would have made him too nervous. He and the art expert watched workmen pack the painting in a crate, then a driver took him and the painting to the airport in Frankfurt for a nonstop flight back to Boston. Everything had been worked out with the airlines in advance. Javi stood on the tarmac while they loaded the crate into the cargo hold and waited for the ground crew to close the hatch. He was the last passenger on the plane and the first one off.

I said, "Were you carrying?"

"You bet. Little Smith and Wesson thirty-eight in a shoulder holster."

"You think there's a real business in this? How often does someone need an escort for a painting?"

"More than you realize. But it's not just paintings. There's jewelry, antiques, dogs, *children*. Rich people talk, amigo. They have this tight little club. A couple weeks after I got back from Germany, I got a call from a woman who asked me if I'm the guy who transports *valuables* around the world? Sure, I tell her, I'm your man. This time it's a jade parrot going from Singapore to New York. I wrapped it up in an old bathroom towel all taped up with duct tape and kept it in a gym bag the entire way home." He grinned. "I felt like I was Sam Spade in *The Maltese Falcon*. Except it was first-class air tickets, five-star hotel. I'm telling you, Matt, this business is *very* real."

I started asking questions, not trying to hide my enthusiasm. Javi laid out his plan. He wanted me to manage the business and work as the primary courier. Once I learned the ropes, I could cut back my trips and concentrate on building our clientele. There wouldn't be much overhead, just a small office with a desk and a telephone in the back of his flower shop in Brookline. We would use ex-cops as couriers and pay them on a per diem basis. Javi said he needed an answer from me ASAP. He was starting to get inquiries about more trips every week.

I said, "I'd be giving up a lot of job security if I quit the force."

"Yes, you would."

"In exchange for?"

"Equity. Seven percent a year till you own forty-nine percent. As far as salary goes, let's say ten grand. You'd be paid as a regular courier for the trips you make yourself—half to you, half to the business—plus you'll get a small commission out of every other courier run."

"Give me a guesstimate, Javi. How much could I make?"

"Conservatively? I'd say about forty-K." Nearly double my salary as a cop. He let me think about it for a second. "Tell you what. I'll guarantee that figure your first two years on the job. If you can grow the business, who knows? Sky's the limit."

I finished my coffee. I wasn't sure how to ask the next question, but Javi read my mind.

"We'll have a lawyer put it all in writing," he said. "That's the best way to avoid any misunderstandings down the road."

"What's the business called?"

"Discreet Courier Service. DCS, Limited. Makes it sounds intriguing."

I took a deep breath and let it out slowly. "Definitely intriguing. I'll need to talk things over with Lucy."

"Of course," Javi said, smiling. He knew I was already hooked.

When I went back to the office, I called home and got Brenda the babysitter. After Derek and Robin moved away and Lucy fell into her depression, I convinced her we should find someone to live in the apartment who could help out with the kids. Brenda seemed ideal. She had an easygoing disposition and had worked for another family for a year as a full-time nanny. Brenda was taking evening courses at a community college and only wanted a part-time job. We offered her free rent in exchange for caring for the kids five afternoons a week.

"I expect Lucy home about four," Brenda said on the phone. There was some banging in the background. "Wait, hold on a sec." She came back on the line, laughing. "Crisis averted."

"You have school tonight?"

"Nope. You need me to watch the kids?"

"Just for a couple of hours. Say, seven to nine. I want to take Lucy out to dinner."

"Sure, no sweat."

I asked Brenda not to say anything to Lucy. I wanted the evening to be a surprise.

On the way home, I bought flowers. I had tried this often when she was sick. Most times she barely acknowledged them. Other times she'd look at the flowers like they were just one more thing she had to deal with, as if they came with an expectation too heavy to bear. They'd sit in a vase, wilted and rotting, until I threw them away myself. I was bewildered, wondering where she'd gone. One day in the car, the kids asleep in the backseat, I caught her eye and said, *I miss you.* She lit a cigarette and stared absently out the window. *I miss me too.*

When I got home from work, Lucy said she was tired and didn't feel like going out.

"Come on, honey," I said. "Take a nice bath and lie down for a while. I'll put the kids to bed. We'll go see Sandor." I kissed her forehead. "Like the old days."

"Okay, what's going on here?"

"What, can't I take my beautiful wife out to dinner?"

She laughed. "Sorry, Matt, but you're the worst liar in the universe."

I told her about lunch with Javi and his business proposal. Lucy got excited. She told me it sounded great, that Javi was a man I could trust.

"Take the job and don't look back," she said. She was more animated than she had been in months. There was color in her cheeks. Her hands fluttered with excitement as she talked.

And I was thinking, *There* she is. There's my Lucy. Her short hair accented the strong line of her jaw and made her gray-green eyes look even bigger. She was wearing a striped cotton jersey with no bra. My gaze lingered on her body, which had begun to fill out again. Until a few months ago, she had been alarmingly thin, her breasts shriveled, hipbones protruding. She would walk across the bedroom naked, indifferent to my concern or desire.

I called Brenda and told her we'd be staying in. After the kids had eaten, Lucy gave them a bath and put them to bed while I went to a local Thai restaurant for takeout. When I got back, I smelled a trace of marijuana. I didn't know she'd started up again. I felt a pinch of anger and put it aside. We talked easily over dinner. Lucy had found a bottle of champagne in the basement, a leftover present from Nathan's birth. She smiled gaily as she popped the cork. We toasted new ventures and happier times. The champagne made us giddy. Soon we were kissing and tugging at each other's clothes. We stumbled into the living room, and I pulled her down onto the Persian rug. She straddled me, rocking gently, a half-smile on her lips. I touched the acorn-shaped birthmark below her collarbone with my fingertip.

"Please, Matt," she said, riding me harder, her fingernails digging into my shoulder. "*Please.*"

I slapped her firmly on the ass a few times, and she acted like she got what she needed.

Afterward, we sat on the couch watching *Brideshead Revisited* on television, neither of us paying much attention.

I said, "You know, if I take this job with Javi, I'm going to be traveling a lot. At least for the first year or two."

"Meaning?"

"Nothing. It'll be different, that's all. I'll miss you and the kids. We've never really been apart before. Not more than a couple days a year."

She lit a cigarette. "And you're wondering if I can handle it?"

"No, honey," I said automatically, though the idea had crossed my mind. At least twice during her depression, she had confused her medications and fallen asleep, leaving the children untended. The first time, which I didn't learn about until several weeks after the fact, the woman next door noticed Sarah playing alone in the yard after dark. When she brought her inside, she found Lucy passed out on the couch. Nathan was in his crib, naked and crying. The second time, Jill told me she came for a visit and saw Sarah standing on a chair by the stove, trying to figure out how to turn on the burner so she could fix Nathan a bottle. "I was just thinking it will be hard on both of us."

"No, that's okay, I know what you mean. You have every right to be concerned. I've been a shitty mother, shitty housekeeper.

Shitty wife. If it weren't for you, this family would have fallen apart a long time ago."

"Whoa! Where did *that* come from?"

"From reality. Careful observation of the parties in question. Don't tell me you haven't noticed."

"Honey, you went through a rough patch, is all. We're in this together. When you're down, I help you. If I'm down, you help me. Isn't that what marriage is all about?"

She gave me a skeptical look.

"Isn't it?"

"When are you ever down, Matt? When are you ever anything less than perfect? You don't smoke, don't do drugs. Never drink too much, hardly ever swear. Christ, you never even look at other women."

"Is that what you want? You want me out there running around with another chick?"

"I want you to be *human*. I want you to fuck up sometimes, like me and everybody else."

"I'll do my best."

"Thank you."

She took a drag on her cigarette, then looked at it in disgust and stabbed it out in the ashtray.

"I'm sorry, Matt. You don't deserve this."

"No. I don't."

Later, for the first time in more than a year, she curled herself around me in bed. As she fell asleep, I tried to forget the nasty things she had said. I knew her anger was mostly aimed at herself. We had some things to work through, but we'd made a start. Maybe the new business venture with Javi would help us get back on track.

Chapter 17
Lucy

Lincoln Halstead stepped to the front of the line at the hostess station, ignoring the others who were waiting to give me their names. "Table for four, Lucy."

"I'll do my best," I said.

"Thanks, doll." He palmed me a bill.

The hoi polloi were stacked three deep at the bar, but A. Lincoln Halstead, defender of the rich and famous, had no intention of waiting. Tillie, the owner of Garbo's, didn't want to keep him waiting either.

It was mid-August, and I had been working at Garbo's for four months. In the spring, I told Matt I wanted to get a job, something to get me out of the house and make me feel useful. The timing wasn't great. Matt was up to his eyeballs getting the courier business established, but we had Brenda to take care of the kids, and he agreed that going back to work would be good for me. He said he wanted to see me smile again. I tried to convince myself that we had come through my long depression with no lingering issues or resentments—we didn't bicker or snipe at one another, there were no major disagreements about the house or children—but things still felt unresolved. I wanted him to hate me a little the way I hated myself for all I'd put us through.

This wasn't something we could talk about. The Grand Inquisitor couldn't have made Matt admit to any resentments of his own; he just plowed ahead with his amiability and relentless optimism, consumed by the challenges of the new business, making it up as he went along, coming home and telling me about his successes and blunders, flying off to Florence and Tokyo and Buenos Aires. I had never thought of him as a risk-taker, but he'd left a cushy job with the police force to step into the unknown, and he deserved whatever success he found. My pride in him was exceeded only by my envy.

The first place I went to look for a job was the Class Report Office at Harvard. My old friends were glad to see me, but there were no openings. Several publishing companies told me they might have some freelance work, but nothing came through. I finally got the job at Garbo's through Sandor, who was a friend of Tillie's. Tillie was a blunt woman about sixty who chain-smoked Parliaments, and the two of us hit it off immediately. She offered me a job as the lunchtime hostess, eleven to three-thirty, Monday through Friday, the perfect schedule for me. The restaurant catered to athletes and politicians and other celebrities. Not much intellectual stimulation, but rumors and gossip wafted through the place like the smell of fried clams.

I glanced at the tip Lincoln Halstead had given me—a twenty— and led him and his minions to a table. (He had slipped me a hundred once, back when he still thought he could get in my pants.) We were so busy the wait for ordinary customers stretched out to over an hour. The highlight of the afternoon was three guys with English accents dressed like lost rockers from the Ziggy Stardust tour who were ordering Mouton Rothschild at two hundred dollars a bottle.

When I got home from my shift, there was a note from Brenda on the kitchen table saying she'd taken Sarah and Nathan to the playground. Brenda did a good job with the kids, who adored her, but I felt like she judged me constantly and found me wanting as a mother. It was never anything direct—Brenda was too smart for that—just a look or a veiled question. Matt, in her eyes, could do no wrong. I lit a cigarette and checked the answering machine. The first message was from Jill, checking in. The second message was a hang-up—a distinct pause before the caller broke the connection—which had happened several times earlier in the week. I erased the messages and opened a bottle of pinot grigio. Knowing the look I'd get if Brenda saw me with a wineglass in the middle of the afternoon, I poured the wine into an orange plastic tumbler.

On the way upstairs, I caught a glimpse of myself in the full-length mirror in the foyer. I stopped and sucked in my tummy and brushed the front of my skirt. Tillie expected me to dress up for the job, and I enjoyed wearing stylish clothes, putting on makeup and jewelry. For the first time in ages, I felt attractive again, the feeling affirmed by the men who flirted with me at the restaurant. I leaned closer to the mirror and examined the crease between my eyes. When I frowned, the crease deepened, and I tried to smooth it away with my thumb. Amanda had the same crease, which was permanent now, time and alcohol and cigarettes taking their toll.

I went upstairs to change clothes. Matt was away in Madrid and due home tomorrow afternoon. The courier service was growing steadily, but Matt still did most of the traveling himself. For the past several months, he had been gone two or three nights a week. Meticulous as ever, he marked his trips on the calendar in the kitchen and always left a phone number of the hotel where I could reach him. I never begrudged his time away; it gave me a chance to be alone with the children, bathing them and reading to them before I put them to bed. After doubting myself as a mother for so long, I'd begun to feel competent. Needed.

When Matt first started going on the road, I hoped, as I'm sure he did too, that his travels would rekindle some romance between us. I imagined horny homecomings when we couldn't wait to be alone. Or, perhaps, accompanying him on a trip somewhere—Venice, Barcelona—just the two of us in a luxury hotel, the theater, museums, breakfast in bed. No hint of that yet. Matt grumbled about the time away, saying he was looking forward to the day when other couriers would take all the trips and he could be home every night with me and the kids. Perhaps it was my vanity or complacency, but with all his absences, I rarely gave much thought to the idea that he might stray.

Then, a few weeks ago, as I was gathering his shirts to take to the dry cleaner's—he always wore a coat and tie when he traveled—I pricked my finger on something sharp and found an earring post poking through the fabric of the breast pocket of one of the shirts. The earring was unique, a red stone set in a gold leaf-shaped setting. I was actually more surprised than hurt at finding it. In some ways, I didn't blame Matt; our sex life, which had dwindled to nothing during my depression, had not exactly come roaring back. There were no lipstick stains on the shirt, just the faint whiff of another woman's perfume. I stuffed the shirt in the laundry basket and put the earring in my jewelry box along with the other lost sisters of my own that I couldn't bring myself to throw away.

A few nights later after I found the earring, I said, "I just want you to know that I know what you've been doing."

I was sitting sideways on the couch in the living room, Matt in an overstuffed chair.

"What're you talking about?" he said.

"That you've been unfaithful." I tried to sound matter-of-fact, but that word, *unfaithful*, was larded with rebuke and self-pity. "I found her earring in your shirt pocket."

Matt stared at me for a moment, then looked away, his face stricken with guilt. When he looked back, he said, "Lucy, I…" He tried again but couldn't speak.

"Is this serious or just a one-time thing?"

"Just once, but it's not what you think."

Of *course* it was only once, that "forgotten" earring probably a cry for attention. Even so, I gave my lip a skeptical curl, savoring my victimhood; it had been so long since I felt righteous about anything.

"Honey, I didn't actually…I was in a restaurant and—"

"Please, spare me the details."

His eyes welled with tears. I let him dangle for a moment, then smiled sadly and opened my arms. "Come."

He knelt beside me, and I stroked his hair. I thought about that night in the kitchen of my apartment in Cambridge when I told him I was pregnant with Sarah. I had lied then and said nothing had happened with Griffin. I wasn't about to confess to that now, but didn't his betrayal make us even? I came from a family of serial adulterers; this was nothing we couldn't work through.

I kissed him. "I haven't been much of a wife, have I? I need to take better care of you."

We went upstairs and made love and fell asleep. When the baby woke up crying in the middle of the night, Matt got up with him and didn't come back to bed.

The next morning he was quiet, unable to look me in the eye. I assumed he felt guilty and ashamed, and I let him be. At dinner he acted like everything was fine, but after the kids were in bed, it all came boiling out.

"Is that it?" he said. "Is this whole thing over for you?"

"What do you mean?"

"You think I slept with some other woman, and you just sit there and act like nothing happened. How can you be so fucking nonchalant?" His tone turned to mockery. "Matt cheated on me. Tsk tsk, naughty boy. I hope he doesn't do *that* again."

"Sorry," I said, caught off guard. Wasn't I the injured party? "You said it was only once. I didn't want to make a scene and have some horrible fight."

"Why not? Aren't you jealous? Don't you want to start throwing dishes? Don't you want to strangle me? If this isn't worth fighting about, what is?"

"Guess I'm not the dish-throwing type." The moment I said it, an image of the crystal vase I'd flung at Griffin sailed through my brain. "I was trying to give you the benefit of the doubt. You made a mistake and said you were sorry. What was I supposed to do? Kick you out of the house? File for divorce? Is that what you want?"

"I want you to *care*, Lucy. I want you to act like this is something more than me forgetting to take the garbage out. I want—"

"You never forget to take the garbage out." I was teasing him, trying for a little humor to take the edge off the situation.

"Yeah, that's right. I forgot. I'm perfect. I don't smoke, don't do drugs, never look at other women. Well, not this time. I looked and she looked back. We went up to my hotel room and fucked our brains out. I ate her—"

"Stop! You don't have to be cruel."

"*Cruel?* I'll tell you what's cruel. We're dying here, and you act like there's nothing wrong."

"I know things were rocky during my depression, but we got through it, Matt. We've been doing okay."

"I don't want *okay*, Lucy. I want us to be great. I've been crazy in love with you since the day we met. I don't want to lose you. To lose us! I don't want some half-assed marriage where I cheat and you cheat and we smile and have friends over and act like everything is peachy keen. Is that what you want? Lies, secrets, denial? Your parents all over again?"

I let him rant without trying to defend myself. What he said rang true. He was a good man, a terrific father. I liked being married to him and loved him as best I could, but it would never be enough for him. His love for me was almost more than I could bear. As I stood there listening to his complaints, I knew with absolute certainty that one day our marriage would end. It was only a matter of time before Matt looked at me with disdain or utter indifference and said that he was tired of trying, that he didn't care anymore. But not now, not this time. He was still striving, his anger and frustration still laced with the yearning. It was a feeling I knew all too well, the belief that if you did everything perfectly—listen, fuck, laugh, pretend—you could win over your lover and make him realize this was the only place on earth he wanted to be.

Matt railed on until he wore himself out. Since then, neither of us wanted to bring up the subject again.

∞

I was pulling on a pair of jeans when I heard the front door open.

"Mommy?" Sarah called from the front hall.

"I'm upstairs, sugar pop. I'll be right down."

"We picked some *flowers*."

"Really? I can't wait to see."

I slipped on a T-shirt and went downstairs with my wine in the orange plastic tumbler.

Sarah presented me with a bunch of daylilies. "A nice lady had them in her yard and said we could take some home."

"Oh, thank you. They're so pretty."

Nathan said, "Up, Mama." I handed the flowers to Brenda and unbuckled the stroller and lifted him up.

"How's my big boy? Did you have a good day?"

"We *always* have a good day," Brenda said.

I wiped an imaginary smudge of dirt from Nathan's cheek, took the flowers back, and told Brenda she could go. Out in the kitchen, I gave the kids a snack. Sarah got out her coloring book and crayons and went to work on a picture of Snow White and Dopey. She had changeable gray-green eyes like mine; otherwise, her face was all Matt. Rory jumped up on the table, and I shooed him off. Sarah watched me pour some more wine into my tumbler. Maybe it was my imagination, but she seemed to have Brenda's look of disapproval in her eyes.

The telephone rang. I picked it up and said hello.

"Hello, Lucy," Griffin said.

Chapter 18

Matt

The stewardess woke me to say we'd be landing in twenty minutes. It was a Saturday morning in mid-October, and I was escorting ten-year-old twin girls from New York to see their father in Madrid. Damita and Dalila Flores-Crane. I couldn't tell them apart. They were tall and lanky and as beautiful as their mother, Ariel Crane, an internationally famous model. The twins already knew they had the world by the tail. Their father, Hector Flores, had been a mid-level player on the pro tennis circuit when he married Ariel. Several years ago, the couple's divorce provided rich gossip for the press. Now, Hector ran one of his industrialist father's companies. I'd made two previous trips with the girls. This time, Hector had invited me to stay for the weekend so we could play golf and go fly-fishing.

On my last trip, we'd had dinner together at his villa. The twins had gone to bed, and Hector and I sat on the veranda in the cool blue light of the swimming pool.

"I see you are a married man," Hector said in English. He had been educated in England and had no trace of a Spanish accent.

"Yes."

"And your wife, is she beautiful?"

"Very."

"I'm sorry." He put his hand up. "No offense. I only mean that beautiful women, so many of them have a way of…"

"Cutting your balls off?"

He laughed. "And putting them on a string. But when she walks in the room and all the men turn their heads, you feel your chest swelling up with pride. Those are my *cojones* she's wearing around her neck."

"We're willing victims, I guess."

"Yes. And now my daughters?" Hector put his palms together and lifted his eyes to heaven and asked God to protect *los inocentes*. He didn't mean the twins.

We stayed up late, talking. Hector started telling me about his divorce. He said it wasn't as sordid as the stories in the tabloids, but there was no way to fight it. Suing to refute the rumors only gave them some validity. Hector was mortified, but Ariel didn't seem to mind. Her career had taken a dip, and she relished being in the limelight again. The most absurd part of it all, he said, was that he still missed her. I was grateful for his openness. I couldn't conceive of the anguish I would feel if Lucy and I split up. A few months ago, she had found that stray earring in my shirt pocket. I wanted to talk with Hector about it, but I couldn't bring myself to say a word.

I had met the woman in a restaurant in San Francisco. Like me, she was dining alone. We traded glances, and she asked if I'd care to join her. She was Japanese, with a lovely face and a heart-shaped mouth. I liked the way she kept tucking her silky black hair behind her ears. The red stone in her gold earrings matched her lipstick. She said her name was Shirley. I said mine was Fred. She was a site manager for a company that installed trade show booths.

I said, "Does the job keep you on the road a lot?"

"Constantly."

"Me too." I said I was a salesman. Medical supplies.

"I loved traveling for the first few years, seeing new cities, trying different restaurants. Now?" She playfully puffed out her lower lip. "Too many nights sleeping alone."

It was strange the way women had been coming on to me in the past year or so. That rarely happened when I was single.

Shirley lived in Portland, Oregon. She said she had two sons, both in college. She wore a wedding ring but didn't mention her husband. I was wearing my ring too. I didn't say anything about Lucy and the kids, and she didn't ask. Conversation with her came easily. She told me her family had been sent to an internment camp during the war.

"They sent your whole family?"

She nodded. "My parents, my three younger brothers and sisters. Aunts, uncles, cousins. We kids had a ball."

"Were your parents bitter?"

"More *confused*, I'd say. They were very patriotic. My grandparents came to America before the turn of century. I'm named after Shirley Temple, for goodness' sake. As I got older I tried asking questions, but the camp was a taboo subject."

I ended up telling her about the death of my mother and how much I missed her. "It's odd," I said. "I think that's the first time I've really been able to talk about it with anyone."

"Sometimes it's easier to talk to a stranger."

"Then I guess that person's not a stranger anymore." Terrible line, but she was kind enough not to laugh.

We left the restaurant and walked along the waterfront. Even in late July, the air was chilly and dank. Shirley was tiny, barely up to my chin. She shivered, and I took off my sports coat and put it over her shoulders. (I was glad I'd left my gun with the concierge in a safe back at the hotel.) We stopped to look at the seals swimming in the harbor and lounging on pylons, barking for food. Shirley snuggled close to me with her cheek against my chest. I kissed the part in her hair. I loved the smell of her, the newness. Passersby would have seen us as two people in love. I wished I hadn't lied about my name.

She was staying at the Fairmont. I was at the Mark Hopkins across the street. I hailed a cab. My heart thumped as I held her in the backseat—one beat for desire, the next one for guilt.

We crossed the lobby of the Fairmont. When we got to the elevators, she turned and said, "Thank you for a lovely evening, Fred. I've had a wonderful time, but we need to end it here."

"Why?" There was disappointment in my voice and relief in my chest.

"I don't know. Instinct. You're new at this." I didn't reply. It probably wouldn't have taken much to change her mind. "Blame it on the wifely code of honor. A bit of moral gymnastics, I suppose, but I don't want to be the first."

She stood on her tiptoes and kissed me with her pretty mouth. As the elevator doors began to close, she tucked her hair behind her ears, and I noticed one of her earrings was missing.

When Lucy confronted me a few days later, she had already assumed the worst. I tried to explain but only halfheartedly. How could I prove that nothing had happened? It was like Hector said about the stories in the tabloids: the harder you tried to refute them, the more they seemed true. Besides, I had *wanted* to sleep with Shirley. Only her good sense had kept me faithful. As Lucy glared at me, I felt vile and ashamed. I was afraid she would ask me to move out and say she wanted a divorce. But after a few sarcastic remarks, she was ready to drop the whole thing. She said she hadn't been a good wife; it was her fault as much as mine. We went upstairs and made love, and I was in the absurd position of feeling like I'd gotten off easy for a crime I didn't actually commit. Then I got suspicious. Lucy almost seemed relieved by what I had done. I lay awake feeling agitated, wondering what she was trying to hide. Perhaps she was having an affair herself. But then why bring up the earring at all? Why not simply stash it away and use it to assuage her own guilt?

I got up with Nathan in the middle of the night, then slept in the spare bedroom. The next day Lucy acted like nothing had happened. Everything back to normal, if not more so—bacon and eggs on the table for breakfast, a kiss before I left for work. I obsessed about it all day. I kept thinking about the rage and jealousy and unbearable physical revulsion I would feel if I knew she had cheated on me.

Then I finally realized she already had. It was the night she'd gone off with Griffin and left that note tacked to her door. She'd fucked him, knowing she was pregnant with our child. Fucked him and lied about it. I'd had the same thought back then but quickly put it out of my mind. I was too much in love and believed what I wanted to believe. Now I felt as much revulsion with myself as I did with her. How could I have been such a fool?

It took me a long time to calm down. Maybe she hadn't lied about that night with Griffin, but I still couldn't understand her reaction to my supposed infidelity. I wanted more than a pout and a shrug.

I wanted all those crazy, conflicting emotions that love brings. The anger that comes from being betrayed.

In the end, I wasn't sure who had been hurt more, her or me.

$$\infty$$

When the plane landed I got our bags and took the twins through customs. Hector was not at the gate. A woman called out their names and hurried toward us, high heels clicking on the terrazzo floor. The girls ran to her shouting, *Tia, tia.* She introduced herself to me as Hector's sister Alma. She said there had been a crisis at one of their factories. Hector had gone to Zaragoza yesterday and wasn't sure when he'd return. Alma told me she was taking the girls to see their grandparents in Castellón for the weekend, but I was welcome to stay at Hector's villa. The cook was there. Arrangements had been made for me to play golf at Hector's club.

The idea of being there alone did not appeal to me, and I politely declined. Pan Am had a flight leaving for Boston in an hour. I was disappointed that Hector had to cancel, but maybe it was all for the best. Lucy had taken Sarah and Nathan to her parents' house for the weekend. I could fly home and catch up on my paperwork. It wasn't easy trying to balance work and family. When I wasn't traveling, I liked to get home by five-thirty so I could take the kids off Lucy's hands. Even with Brenda's help, it often seemed like she was about to unravel.

It was four in the afternoon when the plane arrived in Boston, a balmy Indian summer day. My car was in the airport parking lot. (I still owned the T-bird but rarely drove it. Now I had a Volvo.) Traffic was light. I breezed through the tunnel and got on Storrow Drive.

My office was in the back room of Javi's flower shop in Brookline. I collected a bunch of paperwork from my desk and headed home.

I did a double take when I saw Lucy's car parked in the front of the house. She had said she and the kids were leaving for her parents' yesterday. I felt my pulse quicken, my thoughts whipsawing between suspicion and dread. There weren't any messages from her with the answering service. Maybe Lucy had gotten into one of her classic battles with Amanda and cut the visit short. I parked across the street and got out of the car. The sound of Lucy's laughter stole through an open window in our bedroom on the second floor. For a minute or two I stood on the sidewalk, trying to decide what to do next. I wanted to believe my wife was at home with our children, but I couldn't hang on to that illusion.

Our front door opened into the foyer. There was a staircase on the right and a long hall to the kitchen straight ahead. Lucy was coming down the hall in a silver-blue kimono I had never seen before. She had a green beer bottle in one hand and a glass of red wine in the other. For an instant, I found myself thinking what great legs she had.

"Matt, you're home," she said, trying to sound casual.

"Yeah, Hector had to cancel our weekend." I put my bags down. "Are the kids here?"

"No, they're still with my folks."

"Is that beer for me?"

She looked at the bottle, then handed it to me. "Yes, perfect timing." Her voice was giddy, her eyes glassy and filled with fear.

"Let's go upstairs."

"Matt, we have to talk."

"We can talk upstairs."

"Please, Matt, let's just—"

I lifted my chin. "Go!"

She didn't move. I grabbed her upper arm, and wine spilled out of the glass and made a dark stain on the front of her kimono.

"Please," she said. "Please don't do this."

I squeezed her arm tighter and led her up the stairs. The staircase rose half a flight and turned left. Griffin was standing on the landing at the top in bare feet and blue jeans with the tails of a white shirt hanging out.

"You must be Griffin," I said.

"I am." He had the same stoned eyes as Lucy.

I gave him the beer. "I think this is for you."

Lucy said, "Please, Matt, let's all go downstairs and talk."

"Sure, okay." I eased past Griffin. "I just want to check out the crime scene first."

They followed me into the bedroom. The sheets on the bed were rumpled; Lucy's black panties lay on the floor. On the nightstand was a bong, a bottle of baby oil, and a hairbrush with a thick, smooth handle. I looked at Lucy and back at the nightstand. I clutched my stomach and bent over double and let out an anguished cry.

"*Matt!*" Lucy rushed over to me. She put her hands on my shoulders and started rubbing the back of my neck.

Her touch felt repulsive, but I didn't have the strength to move away. I was gasping, unable to catch my breath. Lucy said something, her face near mine, but I couldn't make out the words. I knocked her down and grabbed a fistful of hair and slapped her twice.

"Matt, stop!" she screamed, her arms flailing as I tightened my grip on her hair.

"What's the matter, honey?" My face was close to hers, spit flying as I spoke. "I thought you liked it rough."

I saw a flash of green out of the corner of my eye and felt a burst of pain in my left ear. I let go of Lucy and staggered and fell to one knee. Griffin was standing over me, still holding the broken beer bottle. He tried to kick me, but I caught his foot, and he lost his balance and went down hard on his back. I lunged for him, but he crabbed away from me. Bits of glass dug into my palms. I stood up but was having trouble keeping my balance. Strobe lights flashed behind my eyes. Warm blood ran down the side of my face and under the collar of my shirt. I thought for a second I'd gone deaf, no sounds whatsoever in my head. Then there was a loud crash as Griffin knocked over the fireplace tools and scattered them across the hearth. Lucy was slumped against the bed like a discarded doll. Her eyes were filled with terror, her face and chest freckled with blood. Her kimono had come undone. I could see the umbrella tattoo and the dark triangle of hair between her legs. When I turned back to Griffin, he was holding the poker from the fireplace in his right hand. My eyes locked on his.

"Bad idea," I said. Then I reached under my sports coat and pulled out my gun.

Chapter 19
Lucy

"N anda! Mommy!" Sarah said. "Watch me. Watch!"

She was riding her Big Wheel like a scooter, one foot planted on the seat, the other pumping the pavement of the driveway to pick up speed.

Amanda puffed on her cigarette. "Be careful, sweetheart."

Sarah turned her head to make sure we were watching and stretched her leg out behind her like a bareback rider; then she steered the Big Wheel past the rhododendron onto the lawn, dove and rolled over a few times, and came up laughing.

It was Saturday morning. I had driven down to New Canaan with the kids yesterday afternoon to spend the weekend. That was the ploy, anyway. I told Amanda I'd called the answering machine at home early this morning and gotten a frantic message from Tillie saying she needed me at the restaurant. Amanda knew I was lying but didn't question me. Sarah did another trick with the Big Wheel.

"I have to get going," I said. I was holding Nathan on my hip, an overnight bag at my feet.

"Go. I'll be fine." She hesitated for a moment. "Are you sure you want to do this?"

"I trust you, Mom. You're great with them."

"Thank you. But that's not what I meant."

"Don't worry. You taught me well."

She pursed her lips. "You're right, I'm no one to talk. But you're swimming in dangerous waters, honey. People get hurt."

"Sounds like you have some regrets."

"Oh yes, bushels full." She handed me her cigarette and took Nathan in her arms. "Guess you have the right to collect your own."

"Are you disappointed or envious?"

"Little of both, I suppose." She smiled. "You look like you're glowing at the moment. Depends on how it all works out."

I picked up my overnight bag and put it in the back of my station wagon.

"I'll call this evening to check in. Oh wait, I almost forgot." I unhooked Nathan's car seat. "Do you want me to put it in your car for you?"

"No, I can do it." She took the car seat from me and set it on the ground.

I kissed Nathan, then called out to Sarah to come say goodbye. "You be good for Nanda. Help her take care of your little brother, okay?"

"I will," Sarah said.

I gave her a hug and a kiss. When I got in the car, I rolled down the window and said to Amanda, "If Matt calls..."

"I'll give him your love," she said, being snide and protective in the same breath.

It was quarter to eleven, leaving me plenty of time to drive back to Boston and meet Griffin at two. I stopped at a service station for gas and cigarettes and got on the Merritt Parkway. Tommy Tutone was on the radio, singing Sarah's favorite song—"867-5309"—impossible not to sing along. I wondered how many thousands of prank calls it had spawned, kids dialing the number in every area code across the country. Prank calls were a rite of passage for Jill and me back in junior high. We'd call the homes of girls in rival factions, boys we had crushes on. *8-6-7-5-3-0-ny-ay-yine.*

A horn blared as I started to change lanes. I hadn't seen the car in the blind spot on my left and had to swerve to avoid a collision. The driver gave me the finger as he went by.

I missed Jill. The *old* Jill—mischievous, irreverent, blunt—not the one with the perfect house, perfect husband, three perfect kids (and hoping for more). We still spoke on the phone a few times a week but didn't see each other much. Jill had a way of talking about the world that put me in a silent rage. She couldn't understand why everyone wasn't living a perfectly happy life like her own, as if mistakes and misfortune were acts of will, something that only happened to people who were stupid or careless or selfish. She tried to be supportive when I fell into my black hole of depression, but I couldn't shake the notion that she believed I was being self-indulgent. God knows what she'd be saying now if she knew about the affair with Griffin.

It was hard to keep my composure the first time he called. I hadn't heard from him since the night we fled my apartment in Cambridge nearly five years before. He had been on my mind from time to time, but mostly it was a matter of curiosity, wondering where he was and what he was doing, wondering if he'd settled down and gotten married, wondering if he ever thought about me. Our first conversation was short. I agreed to meet him in Quincy Market for breakfast the following Monday morning.

He was standing outside Faneuil Hall in a gray suit, checking his watch.

"Lucy," he said softly, almost shyly, when he saw me. He took both my hands and kissed me on the cheek.

I smiled. "Hello again."

He stepped back, still holding my hands, looking at me with those ice-blue eyes, and I had that same dizzy, Tilt-a-Whirl feeling I got the first time we met, no joint to blame it on this time around. We went into a restaurant and sat down; the waitress brought a pot of coffee to the table and filled our cups.

"You cut your hair," Griffin said. "It looks terrific. Everything about you…" He shook his head, one of the few times I'd ever seen him stuck for words.

We ordered our food and ate and talked. I told him about my job at Garbo's, about my depression and Matt's career change, showed him pictures of Sarah and Nathan. I asked if he was married, and he said no, never even came close. He told me his father had died a few months after I last saw him. At the funeral, he ran into an old friend of the family who was putting together a deal to build a luxury retirement community in Key Biscayne and talked Griffin into coming on board. Things had gone exceedingly well, and they were able to replicate their business model in Annapolis; now Griffin had moved to Boston to lay the groundwork for their third facility.

He said, "Tell you honestly, I wasn't too keen on the idea of coming back to Boston. I couldn't stand the thought of living around here and not being with you."

"Some things never change," I said, scoffing at his bullshit but loving the kick it gave to my ego.

"No, they don't." He gave me a grin. "And aren't we glad?"

I laughed, reaching for his hand across the table, and I felt like myself again—the person I *liked*, the one I used to be—which defied all logic given my tortured history with Griffin. Half an hour later, we were going at it in the darkened stairwell of a parking garage, my skirt hiked up around my waist. Some so-called experts say that having an affair has nothing to do with sex; the physical stuff is simply an expression of some deeper longing. But it sure *feels* like something you need. You love the rush, and when it wears off, all you can think about is how and when you can get it again.

Griffin and I met once or twice a week. It was easy to arrange, especially with Matt's business trips. The guilt I felt had more to do with the kids than Matt, but I needed to talk about my affair with someone. I called Carla and said I wanted to come in for a tune-up. My last session with her had been shortly after Matt and I were married.

Carla had gotten her teeth fixed; otherwise, everything was the same. I spent the first fifteen minutes in her office chattering nervously before I told her about Griffin

Carla nodded as if she already knew. "How long have you been seeing him?"

"About a month." It was closer to three.

"And you don't want to stop?"

"Not exactly."

Carla picked a few pills of lint from the sleeve of her sweater and weighed them in her hand. "Lucy, what do you want to come of this? How do you want things to work out?"

"I don't know. That's why I'm here, so you can help me figure it out."

"Let me ask you a simple question: Do you see yourself staying married to Matt for the rest of your life?"

"I love him, Carla. He's a good man, a terrific fath—"

"That's not what I asked."

I shrugged. "No, I guess not."

"Then the only issue is how and when to end it."

"I don't want to hurt him. I really don't."

"Please, let's not get on that merry-go-round again. Do you really think you're going to find a *nice* way to break his heart?"

"He cheated on me too. It was a couple months ago, with some woman he met in San Francisco." I told Carla about the earring I'd found but not about the fight afterward, Matt raging at my indifference, scrabbling for some proof of my love.

Carla suggested he and I go see a marriage counselor and get everything out on the table. I asked if she could take us on, but she said that wouldn't be appropriate—she preferred being my advocate.

"You mean you're on *my* side?" I said, kidding her.

She smiled. "You don't make it easy, Lucy. Some of the choices you make." She made a funny sucking sound with her new teeth. "You have a way of…"

"Fucking things up."

"You're very good at it."

"It's a gift."

I stopped at the service area on the Mass Pike. When I came out of the stall in the ladies' room, there was a girl about twenty-five standing barefoot by a sink in a bra and panties, a pair of jeans and a brown T-shirt folded neatly on the floor by her feet. The girl splashed water on her worn, once-pretty face and ran her fingers through her greasy blond hair. She had the firm, slender body of a runner, but her back and thighs were scarred with cigarette burns, several of them still pink and raw. The other women in the bathroom pretended to ignore her as they traded sidelong glances of pity and aversion. The girl stoppered the drain with a wad of tissues, filled the sink with water, and began to lather her underarms with liquid pink soap from the plastic dispenser. I stood at the sink beside her and washed my hands.

"Long journey?" I said.

Her eyes met mine in the mirror. "All the way from hell."

"Anything I can do to help?"

She gave me a crooked smile, as if to say, *You must be joking.*

I said, "Is he waiting for you outside?"

"Please, leave me alone."

"I could give you a ride somewhere."

She seemed to consider it for a second, then shook her head. She lifted one dusty foot and put it in the sink, turning the water brown as she scrubbed between her toes. I dried my hands with paper towels, unable to get her to meet my eyes again. I started for the door then went back.

"I mean it," I said. "I'm going to Boston. I know a women's shelter where I can take you."

"*What?*" the girl said, raising her voice. "You think me and you can just waltz out of here and drive away? No way he's gonna let that happen. Even if we got lucky and gave him the slip, I guarantee you he'd chase us down. Run your car off the road and kill all three of us."

A plump, tanned woman in a yellow tennis dress was standing by one of the stalls, listening, a concerned look on her face.

The girl turned, her foot still in the sink, and glared at the woman. "Any man ever love *you* that much, fat-ass?"

I left the bathroom. There was a nervous Leon Trotsky look-alike with a scruffy goatee and wire-rimmed glasses standing by the vending machines who I assumed was the abuser, but it could just as easily have been the paunchy fifty-year-old in the John Deere baseball cap playing a video game. I bought a cup of coffee at the take-out counter, my hands still shaking when I got back in my car. Eventually the man would murder that poor girl and stuff her body in a Dumpster. Or maybe they'd grow old together, locked in their grotesque dance.

I got in my car and turned up the radio, John Cougar Mellencamp singing "Hurt So Good." I lit a joint and felt the fever of anticipation; this was the first time since the affair began that Griffin and I would have some extended time together rather than a few stolen hours. We were going to meet at my house, then head off to an old inn in the Berkshires. Whenever I heard Mellencamp asking his baby to make it hurt so good, it sounded like a perfect theme song for Griffin and me. Maybe the girl in the bathroom felt the same way about her guy, some warped concept of love.

Last week, Matt and I had the kids in the car when the song came on the radio.

"What's that mean, Mommy?" Sarah asked.

"What, sugar pop?"

"'Hurt so good.' Things that hurt you are *bad*."

"Yes, they are, but sometimes…well…"

I pictured myself bent over a red vinyl chair next to the mirror in a motel room, watching Griffin spank my ass with a hairbrush.

"Sometimes good things hurt a little, honey," Matt said. "Like when I go away on my business trips and I miss you and Nathan and Mommy. When I call home and hear your voice, it makes me happy because you're excited and you tell me what you've been doing all day, and I feel really good. But I'm kind of sad too because I wish I was there so I could read you a story and tuck you in bed and kiss you good night. So, that phone call is kind of sad and happy at the same time. It hurts me not to be with you, but it's still good. You understand?"

Sarah nodded. Matt was always coming up with stuff like that. He didn't give me a smug look, but to me it felt like he was showing off.

Two days before, I'd had another session with Carla, talking in circles, ready to leave ten minutes after I got there. I said Matt was too perfect. I was tired of trying to love him, tired of the burden of being loved. How could anyone live with all that devotion and understanding? The scale was tilted so far in my favor it felt like an unbearable weight, a fortune I was compelled to squander.

"Matt *embraces* me," I said. "I know it's supposed to make me feel safe, but it's suffocating. He wants us to melt into a giant blob of togetherness. With Griffin, it's the complete opposite. It's like he frees me to be myself."

Carla asked if I'd said anything to Matt about seeing a marriage counselor. I said I hadn't, and she made me promise I would.

Up to the moment when Matt came through the front door, I hadn't worried about getting caught—*caught* was just a word, an abstraction like *right* or *wrong*, conveniently disconnected from my actions—and yet it's clear in hindsight that I had gotten careless, almost as if I had wanted it to happen. When Griffin arrived, I invited him in, eager to show him the house, so stupid and cocky that I tried on the kimono he'd brought in a gift box; then we fired up the bong and one thing led to another. I was very stoned, coming down the hall with a wineglass in one hand and a beer bottle in the other; for a moment, I thought Matt was a hallucination, his head haloed in the light from the stained glass behind him. I handed him the beer. He didn't look surprised or angry, and I thought then that he'd set me up, his entrance arranged for maximum effect. I begged him not to go upstairs, but he marched me ahead, his fingers so tight on my arm, they left five purple bruises. Griffin was standing at the top of the steps. It felt like I was in a movie, everything in slow motion, and I kept thinking I could fix it, just make the camera stop rolling and change the script entirely.

Matt went in the bedroom and looked around and let out a cry like a wounded animal. He was bent over, clutching his stomach. I rushed to help him, but he threw me down and slapped my face. A searing pain shot through my skull as he coiled my hair in his fist. He raised his hand to hit me again; then I saw Griffin out of the corner of my eye, and there was a grisly, crashing sound, and my body seemed to fly across the room. I must have blacked out for a moment. When I came to, I was propped up against the bed with my legs splayed, the neck of the broken beer bottle near my foot. Griffin was standing by the fireplace with the poker in his hand; Matt was in the middle of the room with blood streaming down the side of his face. He gave Griffin a weary, disdainful look, then he reached in his jacket and took out his gun.

"Take it easy, pal," Griffin said. "I'm putting this down, okay?" He squatted and laid the poker on the hearth very gently, then stood up again and raised both hands.

"Kick it under the bed," Matt said, his voice cold and lethal.

"What?"

"Use your foot and slide the poker under the bed."

Griffin complied, never taking his eyes off Matt. I scrunched up my legs and tried to cover myself with the kimono.

Matt turned to me, his eyes so sad I wanted to hold him. "I never had a chance, did I?"

I couldn't speak. I wanted to tell him that wasn't true, one more lie before he finally stopped loving me. He put the gun back in his holster. Griffin was eyeing him warily, his back to the fireplace. I cowered as Matt took a step toward me and picked up the neck of the bottle. A drop of blood fell from his chin onto my bare knee.

"Watch out for the broken glass," he said.

He glanced around the room as if he might have forgotten something, then slowly walked out the door. I called for him to wait, but he didn't look back.

Chapter 20
Matt

No one knows how they're going to act in a situation like the one with Lucy and Griffin until it happens. Thankfully, most people never have to find out. Sometimes I think it was pure luck that kept me from turning it into a front-page story—*Ex-cop shoots...* I pressed a handkerchief to the wound above my ear and got in my car and drove to the hospital. The nurse in the emergency room asked me what happened, and I said I'd slipped on some wet tiles in the bathroom and hit my head on the edge of the sink. She had me lie down and shaved my scalp and put some ice on the cut to stanch the bleeding. The doctor was a young black woman with a clipped British accent. She picked two slivers of green glass from the wound but didn't question my story. When she applied the antiseptic, my whole body shuddered from the pain. The doctor closed the wound with nine stitches and wrapped a bandage around my head. She wanted to keep me in the hospital for a few hours for observation, but I refused and signed the waivers to check myself out. The nurse cautioned me to take it easy and stay off my feet.

It was dark outside. I got some clean clothes from the suitcase in my trunk and changed in the hospital bathroom. I felt like Humpty

Dumpty, all stitched up and broken beyond repair. Images kept popping into my head—Lucy in the kimono, the bong and the baby oil and the hairbrush on the nightstand, the flash of green as Griffin swung the beer bottle, a drop of blood falling onto Lucy's bare knee. I drove west on the Pike, intent on going to Connecticut to pick up Sarah and Nathan. I had no idea what I would say to Amanda and Thorny or where I would take the kids.

I stopped at a HoJo's near Worcester for a cup of coffee. Luck was with me, getting that far without wrecking the car. The next thing I remember is waking up in the backseat of the Volvo, shivering. The HoJo's was closed. I found a packet of aspirins in my dopp kit and took three to ease the pounding in my head. I got off the turnpike at the next exit and went to an all-night diner. The waitress brought me coffee. She said there was a motel a half-mile down the road. I took a room and slept fitfully, my dreams dark and troubled, but each time I awoke to reality, I wanted the dreams back.

In the morning, I drove back to my office in Brookline. Andrea, the flower shop manager, was working out front, making up a wedding bouquet. She winced when she saw me. My ear and the whole left side of my face were purple and swollen. I gave her the story about slipping in the bathroom, and she said "ouch" and touched my arm. I wondered if she believed me or was just being kind. I couldn't imagine ever telling anyone the truth about what had happened. It made me understand why so many rapes go unreported. There's too much humiliation, the details too sordid and degrading, people wondering if this was something you brought on yourself. The phone in the office rang, but I didn't pick up. When I called the answering service, the operator told me my wife was trying to reach me.

I went to the Holiday Inn on Beacon Street a few blocks from my office and booked a room for a week. I tried to do some paperwork, but my ears were ringing, and there was a stabbing pain behind my eyes. The packet of aspirins was empty. I went down to the gift shop and bought some more and came back to the room and fell asleep. When I woke up, it was seven in the evening. I took a shower and let the water run over my head. The bandage came off, and I dabbed the wound dry with a towel. The stitches pinched my skin together in a puffy, crooked line, and I didn't bother to cover them again. The left side of my face was purple as an eggplant.

I got dressed and went outside. The sky was hazy, the air turning cold. I walked and walked and ended up on the Esplanade. A tour boat was sailing slowly up the river, spreading its soft wake. I wished I could turn my mind off and make all those sickening images go away. I wondered when Lucy's affair with Griffin had begun. Was it before or after she had found that earring in my shirt? Maybe that was why she had reacted so mildly, a two-minute show of indignation and a giant sigh of relief. I suppose it didn't matter when it started. Either way, the earring gave her the perfect excuse to act out her fantasies and something to relieve her sense of guilt. I felt hollow as a gourd. Everything inside me had shrunk into dry, lifeless seeds. I rattled when I walked.

Tomorrow or the next day I'd get in the car, go to the house, and do *what*? How would I act? What would I say? Would I fly into a rage or whimper and whine? Lucy would be remorseful, eager to make amends. She'd probably cry and tell me how sorry she was, and all the while she'd be thinking, *Come on, Matt. Be honest with yourself. When was the last time I said I love you, let alone showed it? Think about it. We should never have gotten together in the first place. It's like we jumped in a wagon and started rolling downhill, both of us knowing it would end badly but not knowing how to stop. You're a good man, Matt, but you're no fun. I want something else. I'm not saying what we had was all bad. We still have our two beautiful children. You have to believe me when I say I never wanted to hurt you. I'm sorry for what I've put you through. Right now you probably think you can never forgive me. What happened in our bedroom was the scariest, ugliest five minutes of my life, but maybe it was a ghastly blessing in disguise. Now that it's over, there's no chance for illusions. We don't have to pretend anymore.*

She left three or four more messages with the answering service. It gave me a sense of satisfaction, being in control, making her wait. I went to the house Monday afternoon and knocked on the front door. Lucy gasped when she saw me. She was still in her work clothes, red blouse and billowy black pants. Tears came to her eyes as she surveyed my face.

I said, "Are the kids still at Katydids?" The day-care center.

She nodded.

"I'll go pick them up and hang out with them for a while. Take them for something to eat."

She nodded again. "Matt, I—"

"We're not going to talk about it. Not now, not ever." Until I said it, I had no idea that this was my plan. No idea if I would be able to hold myself to it.

"Okay," she said. I turned to go. "Matt, don't you think—"

"No!" I wheeled around and pointed my finger. "Don't say one fucking word." I liked seeing that she was afraid.

"It's about the kids."

"What about them?"

"It's just…I mean…your face." She grimaced. "I'm afraid you might scare them."

"This is reality, Lucy. *Our* reality. The world we made for them." But I knew she was right. It pissed me off that I hadn't considered it. Did I think I could just show up at day care looking like Frankenstein? I glared at Lucy. "So what am I supposed to do? Wait for my face to heal before I see the kids?"

"It's up to you. I don't feel like I have a say in the matter right now."

"That's right, you don't."

I made a vow never to spend another night in that house. I stayed in the Holiday Inn for two weeks, then found an apartment in Roslindale. It was on a busy street, the interior shabby, but I took it because it was furnished and available immediately and only a mile and a half from Lucy's. The apartment was on the second floor above a bakery. The best thing about it was waking up to the smell of fresh bread and cinnamon buns. There were two bedrooms, a living room, and a big eat-in kitchen. The landlord let me put in a set of bunk beds, which the children loved. Lucy and I managed to hide most of our rancor from the kids. We told them we were having trouble getting along and had decided to live apart for a while. I'm not sure why we felt the qualification was necessary. We both knew the breach was permanent. Just to ease them into the change, I suppose.

I wanted to have the children with me as much as possible. With all the traveling I did for my job, it was hard for me to stick to a regular schedule, so Lucy and I made one up on a weekly basis. Sarah and Nathan usually spent every other weekend with me and several weekday nights as well. Lucy had them for the long Thanksgiving weekend; Santa came to my place Christmas morning. I felt a sense of pride that Lucy and I had been able to make these arrangements without seeing a lawyer or a counselor. Nothing to brag about, but a far cry from standing in your bedroom with a gun in your hand.

In early February I picked up the kids and drove them to my place. They had adjusted quickly to the new arrangements. Nathan was too young to understand what was happening, and Sarah had stopped asking when Mommy and I were going to get back together.

"Cool bus," Nathan said, pointing. He was two and a half and loved trucks and buses.

"Yes, that's right," I said, looking at him in the rearview mirror. "A ssschool bus."

He was sitting in his car seat in back, Sarah up front beside me, holding Sundae the llama in her lap.

"What color is the school bus, Natey?" Sarah said.

"Well-wo."

She giggled and looked at me. "Well-wo. I love how he says that."

"Me too."

"Natey?" She peeked around the seat. "Do E.T."

He shook his head.

"Come on, Natey. Pwease. Pwetty pwease."

"Ell-wee-ot," he said in a scratchy voice. "Ell-wee-ot. E.T. phone home."

I cracked up.

"I taught him that," Sarah said.

"That's wonderful, sweetheart. Maybe we can get him a job in the movies."

Sarah and I laughed as Nathan said it again.

We all went candlepin bowling that evening. I loved these times together. Just the three of us. Things seemed so much easier without Lucy, as if she didn't belong.

The next morning I took them back to her place. There were often details to discuss about schedules and finances, but I refused to talk about the breakup. We had settled into a stiff cordiality salted with my occasional sniping and sarcasm. Lucy rarely retorted. She seemed content to let things work out slowly, but she had begun to grow frustrated.

One day she said, "Matt, I know how angry you are. Okay, fine, get it out! Call me a slut. Say whatever you want. But sooner or later we have to *talk*."

"Not really."

"Arrrgh. Sometimes you can be so smug and self-righteous I want to scratch your eyes out."

"That actually might help," I said, looking her up and down as if she were something I'd scraped off my shoe.

She took the blow and didn't strike back. I'd won that round, but I knew it wouldn't be long before she started to forgive herself. Pretty soon she'd be rewriting history, telling me we were both to blame. I realized I needed to hash out an agreement while I was still ahead.

As I was leaving Lucy's house one morning, I said, "I just want to let you know. I've been thinking about getting in touch with a divorce lawyer."

"Okay." I'd caught her off guard. "What brought that on?"

"Nothing. I don't know. I figured we might as well get on with our lives."

"Have you considered mediation?"

"You mean working with an arbiter?"

"Yes, my friend Prissy from work told me she and her ex went to some guy in Cambridge. She said it was great. No lawyers bickering back and forth, wasting a ton of money."

She went on talking about the advantages of mediation while I stood there nodding, agreeing that it sounded like a good idea. But I had lost my train of thought. I felt like I'd been blindsided when she said *Prissy*, the way her mouth puckered, the little wrinkle between her eyes. She was all I'd ever wanted. I couldn't imagine loving another woman the way I had loved her.

Still loved her. Everything I had been doing since the breakup was a sham. My anger at her was real enough, but all I'd wanted was a sign, a little hint that she'd take me back, and I would have come running. It was such a revelation, so absurd and inarguably true, I actually thought about telling her. Then I saw something shift in her eyes and I realized she already knew. She'd known all along. Everything she had been doing since the breakup was calculated to make sure I kept my distance. She was humiliated by the way things had ended, but she wasn't going to offer false hopes. I suppose you could say it was her gift to me. She was finally being honest, but that left me with nothing.

She said, "Would you like me to get his name?"

"Who?"

"The mediator. The one my friend used."

"Sure, I guess it's worth a try." I smiled. "We can start throwing stones at one another later if we have to."

She smiled too, as if we'd finally made a little progress, but her eyes told me she knew it was a warning. I had a much bigger pile of stones than she did.

Chapter 21
Lucy

I got the names of some mediators," I said, handing Matt a sheet of paper with a list of five professionals, three men and two women. He glanced at the list but didn't say anything. "The first one is the one Prissy and her ex used. She said he was excellent, really fair and easy to talk to, but I don't have a preference. Anyone you're comfortable with is fine with me."

It had been four months since he'd come home and caught me with Griffin. I still didn't know (and probably never would) if it was happenstance or something he had planned. He refused to talk about it, not just the incident in the bedroom but what had gone wrong in our marriage. I let him take the lead in our interactions. For the most part he was cold and reserved, though there were times when he would make a cutting remark or simply look at me with such scorn I wouldn't have been shocked if he'd spit in my face. But he had begun to mellow lately, smiling and laughing as we got the kids ready to go to his place, telling me about a trip to Istanbul, asking me about work. I could sense he kept hoping for a sign that I wanted him back. I pretended not to notice. I had tried to tell him I was sorry, but sorry for what? For the scene in the bedroom? For breaking his heart? For not being the woman he wanted me to be? All that and more, but not sorry our marriage was over. It was such a relief not to have to *try* anymore. When Matt came by last week, saying he was thinking about contacting a lawyer, I brought up the possibility of working things out through a mediator, and he seemed to agree that it was the sensible way to go.

He folded the list I'd given him and put it in his back pocket. It was Friday afternoon, the start of a long weekend. Matt was taking the kids, and I wouldn't see them again until I picked them up from day care Tuesday after work. I didn't know anything about his living arrangements (though I'd gotten some tidbits from Sarah), and I made it a point not to ask. It made me feel guilty sometimes, the way I looked forward to these weekends off, but I told myself they refreshed me and helped me focus on the children when I was with them.

"You kids ready?" Matt said.

"I am, Daddy," Sarah said, putting on her coat, always eager to please.

"What about you, Nate-ster?"

Nathan laughed with delight as Matt picked him up and tossed him in the air.

"Their bags are by the door," I said.

"Did you remember to pack their boots?"

"Shoot. No, I'll get them." He had mentioned the boots on the phone an hour before because he wanted to take them sledding.

Matt shook his head and gave me a condescending smile. I felt like kicking myself. I made lists, put reminders on the refrigerator, even wrote notes on the back of my hand, but I still forgot things sometimes. Nothing critical—not like the T-shirt of a cartoon-strip woman with her hand on her forehead, *Oh my god! I left the baby on the bus!* Just an occasional missed appointment, a lost permission slip, enough to make Matt secure in his unspoken assessment that he was the better parent. Which he was. Hadn't I admitted as much before everything fell apart?

He was always so sure of himself as a father. It wasn't hubris, just a kind of knowing. He never seemed to forget anything, never lost his temper, always seemed to know the right thing to say or do. I loved my children beyond measure, but I had a hard time finding my rhythm with them, as if mothering were a dance and I had to keep looking down at my feet, my good intentions no substitute for self-assurance and grace. I could be short and irritable one minute, over-indulgent the next. The books on child-rearing said you had to be consistent and evenhanded, but a mother isn't a robot. One day the kid might get in your purse and cover his face with lipstick and you'd think it was the funniest thing you'd ever seen; catch him at it the next day when you're feeling tired and irritable and you're liable to scream at him like he'd just drowned the cat. Some nights I would lie in bed, thinking about things and wishing I had a "do-over," as Sarah and her friends would say. At Carla's suggestion I had begun keeping a journal, not only about the kids and being a mother but everything, all my worries and doubts, just letting my thoughts flow freely, puzzling things out. I wrote nearly every day, which seemed to help.

Matt picked up Nathan's bag; Sarah insisted on carrying her own. I followed them out the front door onto the porch. The air was frigid, icicles hanging from the gutters. I pulled my sweater tight around my shoulders. Sarah jumped down from the third step, fell on her butt, and got up laughing. As Matt started down the steps with Nathan, I saw Griffin getting out of his car a short way down the street. He wasn't due at the house for over an hour.

"Hey, Griff," Sarah called and ran to him.

Griffin looked stricken; I'm sure I did too. Matt turned and glared at me. Sarah took Griffin's hand and tugged him toward the house. "Come on, Griffin. Come meet my friend, Daddy."

In another context, it would have been cute as kittens, but Matt wasn't smiling. A week later, I got a summons from his lawyer.

Matt's attorney's name was Norman Claxton. Griffin made some inquiries and discovered he worked in a two-man firm, but no one seemed to know much about him. The one name that kept coming up when people talked about the best divorce lawyers in Boston was Arthur Hoyt, who represented Joan Kennedy last year in her divorce from Teddy. People said Hoyt was a bulldog, the kind of lawyer you love to have on your side. I talked to my father, and he said this wasn't something to leave to chance, hire Hoyt and he would cover the bill. I called Hoyt's office, explaining that I had needed to talk to him as soon as possible, and the secretary told me to come in the next morning. The office was on the forty-third floor of Sixty State Street, a few blocks from Garbo's. Hoyt's secretary came out to the reception area to greet me and ushered me into a conference room overlooking the harbor, one of their staff following close behind with a tray of pastries and a pot of coffee. There was a polished mahogany table with six plush leather chairs, signed lithographs on the walls, a beautiful oriental carpet on the floor. The secretary apologized, saying that Mr. Hoyt had just taken an emergency phone call and would be about twenty minutes late, then left me alone. I poured myself a cup of coffee and gazed across the harbor at the planes flying in and out of the airport.

"Sorry for the delay, Mrs. Drobyshev," Hoyt said, bounding into the conference room. He shook my hand and took a seat across the table, a yellow legal pad in front of him.

"That's okay. Please, call me Lucy. Thank you for seeing me on such short notice."

"Certainly." He *looked* like a bulldog: barrel chest, a square head with heavy jowls, thick folds of skin around his small brown eyes. He glanced at the legal pad, nothing but my name written on the top line, and put a double line under Lucy. "My secretary tells me you'd like me to represent you in your divorce."

"Yes. People say you're the best lawyer in town."

He frowned. So much for flattery. "How long have you and your husband been separated, Lucy?"

"Four months."

"Children?"

"Two. A girl four and a half and a boy who's just turned two."

"I understand it was your husband who initiated the divorce?"

"Yes, well, legally. On an emotional level, I guess you could say the breakup was mutual."

"And he has retained Norman Claxton as his counsel?"

"Yes, I believe that's his name."

"I'm not familiar with Mr. Claxton, but I never underestimate an adversary. My people will find out everything I need to know about him. Do you expect this to be a difficult divorce?"

"I'm not sure. I hope not."

He stared at me for a moment, as if he were trying to assess my character—was I a gold-digger? would I be bitchy or weepy?—and I wondered what he thought he saw.

"I don't deal in hope, Lucy. I deal in the *law*, which, despite its many arcane twists and turns, is about as real as life gets. So let's dispense with hope and concentrate on the task at hand. You wouldn't have come to me unless there was a great deal of money at stake or you thought this was going to be highly acrimonious. How would you characterize your situation?"

His bluntness was intimidating. "My husband is very angry. I don't want...Our breakup was pretty ugly. I was—"

"No, not now." He waved his hand impatiently. "I have another client waiting. You and I will have plenty of time to talk. I'm going to pass you along to one of my paralegals. I need you to sit down and talk with her. It will probably take several hours. If you can't do it today, make an appointment to meet with her as soon as possible. She's going to ask you a lot of questions about yourself, your husband, your marriage, what you believe caused your breakup. Try not to be offended if the questions seem too personal. This is a very personal business. I want you to tell her everything. Anything you can think of that might be relevant. Above all, I need you to be completely honest. Pretend you're under oath. If you've been having sex with the next-door neighbor, male or female, I need to know about it. If you've been hopped up on diet pills for the past three years, I need to know that too. This isn't about good or bad, it's about the facts. I don't like surprises. The more I know, the better I can represent you. The paralegal will record everything you say. Don't worry about privacy; this is all subject to attorney-client privilege. No one but myself, the paralegal, and my secretary will ever see it." He tapped his pen on the legal pad. He hadn't taken a single note. "Do you have any questions?"

"Well, I…"

"You'll think of plenty, I'm sure." He stood up. "The paralegal will go over our billing rates with you. We ask for a ten-thousand-dollar retainer to get started. I hope that won't present a problem."

"I thought you didn't deal in hope."

Hoyt smiled for the first time. "I don't. That's why I ask for the money up front." The retainer was even higher than I had guessed it would be. "If you're concerned about the total cost of the divorce, let me say that it will depend almost entirely on how much disagreement there is between you and your husband. Sometimes these things start out reasonably well, and all of a sudden the couple is fighting over custody of the pet iguana and who gets to take the kids trick-or-treating on Halloween. Are you and your husband still on speaking terms?"

"Minimal at the moment."

"Good, keep it that way. One of my biggest problems is having some client make an agreement without consulting me first. A couple gets talking, maybe shares a glass of wine—heaven forbid they sleep together. Next thing you know my client gets snookered."

He opened the door of the conference room for me and walked me out into the hall. "Do you work, Lucy?"

"I'm the lunchtime hostess at Garbo's."

"And your husband?"

"He runs a courier service. Mostly international deliveries. He used to be a cop."

"Hmmm."

"Is that a good hmmm or a bad one?"

"Let's say it's neutral. Be glad he's not a doctor or we'd really be in trouble."

"Or a lawyer?"

"You got that right," he said, laughing. "Have a nice day."

Two weeks later, I gave a deposition in the same conference room overlooking the harbor—Matt's attorney, Norman Claxton, Hoyt, a court reporter, and myself. Hoyt's paralegal had spent an hour with me the day before going over the facts a second time, particularly the more damning issues: the affair with Griffin, smoking marijuana, my depression and the medications, the incident in our bedroom. She said it would be rough. The lawyer would be aggressive, and the questions would feel quite invasive; the important thing for me was not to be nervous and simply tell the truth.

The court reporter swore me in. Claxton spent a few minutes establishing some basic facts and dates about my life. About forty-five, he looked like a holdover from the Eisenhower administration: brown three-piece suit and rimless eye glasses, Adam's apple bobbing above his red plaid bow tie, Brylcreemed hair combed straight back.

"So, Mrs. Drobyshev, it is my understanding that you have had a relationship for a number of years with a man named Griffin. Could you please state his full name?"

"Alan Griffin Chandler the third."

"And when did you first meet Mr. Chandler?" His words were formal, but his accent was pure Queens.

"In the spring of 1974."

"How would you describe your relationship with him, Mrs. Drobyshev?"

"Our relationship was okay, the usual ups and downs. We had a lot of fun."

"Did the two of you live together?"

"No."

"But he often stayed at your apartment?"

"Several nights a week."

"In fact, Mrs. Drobyshev, he had a key to come and go as he pleased?"

"He had a key, yes." Hoyt was sitting next to me. I half-expected him to interrupt Claxton and say there was no need to go this far back, the information was irrelevant to the divorce, but Hoyt kept silent.

"During this time, did you and Mr. Chandler use any illegal drugs?"

"We smoked marijuana occasionally."

"Where did you obtain the marijuana?"

"Griffin got it. From a friend."

"Did Mr. Chandler ever sell any marijuana himself?"

"No." Only on the day we met. Claxton was obviously fishing, but his questions came much too close to my secrets.

"While you and Mr. Chandler were having *a lot of fun*"—his voice dripped with sarcasm—"did the two of you indulge in any other illegal drugs such as cocaine, Quaaludes, LSD?"

"No."

"Would Mr. Chandler confirm this if he were questioned under oath?"

"Yes."

Claxton gave me a half-smile. "And would you say that you and Mr. Chandler had a sexually open relationship, Mrs. Drobyshev?"

"Not at all. We were committed partners."

"But there were mutual infidelities?"

I glared at him. "No."

"Neither of you had sexual relationships with other people?"

"He did. I did not." I needed a cigarette. I chewed on my right thumb, which pulsed and burned.

"What about a ménage à trois?"

"*No!* Jesus, where are you coming up with all this ridiculous stuff?" I had never told anyone about that night. The paralegal said the questions would be invasive, but I wasn't expecting anything like this. I kept hoping Hoyt would jump out of his chair like Perry Mason and tell Claxton to stop bullying me, but he just sat there playing with a paper clip with a bored look on his face.

Claxton asked me how I met Matt, then turned to my friendship with Jill and Terry. Jill was devastated over what had happened between Matt and me. Feeling as if she herself had been betrayed by my secrecy, Jill called me an idiot and berated me for weeks, but we'd been talking more lately and getting closer again. I wondered if she had said anything to Matt that would put me in jeopardy, but Claxton's questions along this line were innocuous, and he went back to asking me about Griffin.

"When you got pregnant for the *first time* in 1977, were you certain it was Mr. Chandler's baby?"

"Yes."

"And when did you abort that child, Mrs. Drobyshev?"

I answered the question and glanced at Hoyt. His expression didn't change, but I knew what he was thinking. I hadn't mentioned the abortion in my interview with the paralegal. It was before I ever met Matt and didn't seem important.

"Did you and Mr. Chandler break up after the abortion?"

"Yes, it was a difficult time for both of us."

"In fact, he abandoned you the same day as the procedure?"

I shook my head.

"Please answer the question aloud."

"No." I took a sip of water and found it hard to swallow. "He didn't *abandon* me. It was very emotional. We both needed to be alone to think about things and get a little distance."

Claxton said, "Did you know you were pregnant with Mr. Drobyshev's child when you rekindled your romance with Mr. Chandler in December of that same year?"

"I did not *rekindle* anything. I hadn't spoken to Griffin in months. He barged into my apartment and wouldn't leave. I was frightened. We drove off and spent a few hours together, and I came home immediately."

"Why were you frightened?"

"Matt was coming over to take me on a date for the weekend. He can be jealous. I was afraid the situation might get volatile."

"Did you have sexual relations with Mr. Chandler that evening?"

"Absolutely not."

"And he will corroborate that under oath?"

"If he tells the truth."

Claxton smirked. "This was the same evening you told Mr. Drobyshev that you were pregnant again. With *his* child this time?"

"Yes."

"And you were absolutely certain the child was Mr. Drobyshev's."

"I've already answered that."

"Did you continue to see Mr. Chandler after your tryst in December?"

"It wasn't a tryst. I *told* you, he showed up at my apartment unannounced. After that night I had no contact with him whatsoever."

"Not until you began your affair with him last summer?"

"Yes."

Claxton took a moment to shuffle through his papers. "During your marriage to Mr. Drobyshev, did you continue to smoke marijuana?"

"Occasionally. Not during my pregnancies. I didn't even smoke cigarettes then."

"How did your husband feel about your habit?"

"The cigarettes?"

"Marijuana."

"Matt didn't care for it. He was a police officer the first few years we were married. He was concerned I might get caught."

"And you were *not* concerned? You knew it was against the law."

"It seemed like a minor vice. It helped me relax."

"In fact, you were rarely able to make love with your husband unless you got high first."

"That's not true." I couldn't believe Hoyt just sat there playing with a paper clip. He hadn't said a word or taken a single note since the deposition started.

"Let me ask you about your current relationship with Mr. Chandler," Claxton said. "Does he ever spend the night at your house?"

"Sometimes. Once or twice a week."

"Does he ever stay over when your children are there?"

"No."

"Never?"

I hesitated. Griffin didn't stay with me unless the kids were at Matt's, but he had stopped by the house one evening after they were asleep. We got stoned, then went upstairs and made love. We were still in bed when Sarah awoke from a bad dream and crawled in beside me. When Griffin rolled over, Sarah said, *Daddy?* She didn't say anything about it to me in the morning. I wasn't sure she even remembered, but she might have told Matt. Could Claxton depose a four-year-old? He may have been trying to trick me into admitting something he had no way of knowing, but I couldn't risk lying. I felt like I had a neon sign imbedded in my forehead, blinking off and on—*Fuck up! Fuck up! Fuck up!*

"He stayed over once," I said.

When Claxton began to ask about my postpartum depression, his tone turned solicitous. I said the illness came out of nowhere, a dense fog that made the whole world seem muted and muddled. "It was horrible," I said. "The only emotion I felt was sadness. I could hear my daughter talk and laugh, but nothing seemed to *translate*, like she was speaking in some language I couldn't understand."

"Did you seek medical attention for your condition?"

"Yes, I saw several doctors who prescribed antidepressants."

"And there were times—at least two, I believe—when those medications caused you to fall asleep and neglect your children?"

"I don't remember." I felt like I was going to throw up.

"You don't remember waking up to find your friend Jill in the house and your three-year-old trying to turn on the stove to make a bottle for her little brother?" This was another thing I hadn't told the paralegal.

"I was *sick*, you sadistic son-of-a-bitch! I didn't know what month it was." Hoyt put his hand on my arm to quiet me down. I took a breath and tried to be calm. "The only thing I know about those incidents is what Matt and Jill told me. The one with the stove scared me so badly I threw all my pills away."

"How did your husband react to your troubles?"

"He was concerned, of course. He helped me get through them."

"So concerned, in fact, that Mr. Drobyshev tried to make sure the children were never left alone with you?"

Was that true? I said it wasn't.

Claxton said, "While you were depressed, did you continue to use marijuana?"

Back to the drugs again. This was obviously a big part of his strategy. "No."

"But you began to smoke it again when you got well?"

"Occasionally."

"Do you and Mr. Chandler still indulge in marijuana?"

"No." I wondered if they could force me to take a drug test.

He paused and looked over his notes. "Have you ever smoked dope in front of your children?"

"No, never. For Christ's sake, what kind of witch hunt is this?" I turned to Hoyt. "Is he *allowed* to make all these horrible accusations?"

"We'd like to take a fifteen-minute break," Hoyt said.

Claxton nodded. "Certainly."

Hoyt led me to his office. I lit a cigarette. He frowned but didn't tell me to put it out, then he turned his back to me and watched a plane take off.

"I'm sorry," I said. "I know there were some things I forgot to tell your paralegal. But it's not as bad as that man is trying to…I understand what he's doing. He wants to take my kids away." He turned around, his face unreadable. "I'm a good mother, Mr. Hoyt. I love my children. I take good care of them. You have to believe me."

"It doesn't matter what *I* believe. Our job is to convince a judge you're a competent parent."

I was heartsick, too scared to cry. "Please tell me he can't take my kids from me." I couldn't see an ashtray anywhere and tapped the ash from my cigarette into my palm.

"Come on, Lucy, I need you to be tougher than this. You're no saint. Neither is anyone else, including your husband. Just answer Claxton's questions as directly and unemotionally as possible." There was a hint of a smile on his face as he handed me a plastic cup for the ashes. "This game has barely begun."

Chapter 22
Matt

A copy of Lucy's deposition was in my mailbox when I got home from a trip to Mexico City. Norman Claxton had gone after her hard and got her rattled. I was beyond the point of being repulsed by the sordid details, but one line of questions from Hoyt, her attorney, was troubling. He asked Lucy how she felt about my having a gun in the house, and she said she didn't mind because I kept it in a safe down in the basement.

Atty. Hoyt: *Did Mr. Drobyshev ever forget to put the gun away when he came home?*

Mrs. Drobyshev: *Just once.*

Atty. Hoyt: *Would you please elaborate?*

Mrs. Drobyshev: *This was about six months after he started working for the courier service. I was out with the children, and when I came home he was sleeping on the couch. I guess he was so tired he took his sports coat off and lay down with the gun in his shoulder holster.*

Atty. Hoyt: *So the gun was still in the holster when he was sleeping on the couch?*

Mrs. Drobyshev: *Actually, the gun had fallen out of the holster and was lying on the rug.*

Atty. Hoyt: *And you picked it up?*

Mrs. Drobyshev: *No, our daughter Sarah did. She picked it up with both hands and pointed it at me and said, "Look, Mommy, Daddy dropped his gun."*

Atty. Hoyt: *How old was your little girl at the time?*

Mrs. Drobyshev: *About three and a half.*

Atty. Hoyt: *What did you do when she pointed the gun at you?*

Mrs. Drobyshev: *I was holding my son, Nathan, in my arms. I tried to be very calm and casual and said something like, "Oh, thank you, honey. Please give Mommy the gun." Meanwhile, I thought I was going to wet my pants.*

Atty. Hoyt: *What type of gun was it?*

Mrs. Drobyshev: *I'm not sure. I don't know much about guns.*

Atty. Hoyt: *So you don't know if the safety was on?*

Mrs. Drobyshev: *No.*

Atty. Hoyt: *What did you do with the gun after you took it from the child?*

Mrs. Drobyshev: *I put it on a high shelf behind some dishes in the kitchen.*

Atty. Hoyt: *Did you mention this to your husband when he woke up?*

Mrs. Drobyshev: *Yes, of course. I had to give him back the gun. But I didn't say anything about Sarah picking it up off the floor.*

Atty. Hoyt: *Why not?*

Mrs. Drobyshev: *I felt bad for him. He was mortified about not putting it away the minute he got home. He was under so much stress from his job I didn't want to make him feel worse than he already did.*

Claxton had penciled exclamation points in the margin next to some of Lucy's answers. I'd completely forgotten about the incident. I was ninety-nine percent certain Lucy was lying about Sarah picking up the gun, but that wouldn't be easy to prove.

∞

My deposition took place in Norman Claxton's library. It was a dingy, cluttered room with books and file folders piled everywhere. A single dirty window looked out on a brick wall about three feet away. Hoyt started off with questions about my work as a cop, then moved on to the courier service. When he asked me where I stored my gun, I said I always kept it in a safe. Then he questioned me about the time the gun had fallen out of the holster while I was asleep on the couch. When I said I didn't believe Lucy's claim that Sarah had picked up the gun, he paused but didn't press the issue.

Hoyt asked me to describe my apartment.

After I did, he said, "So Sarah and Nathan sleep in bunk beds?"

"Yes."

"And you feel that this is a proper sleeping arrangement for a little boy and girl?"

"Of course. They love being in the same room together."

"I take it Sarah sleeps in the top bunk?"

"Yes."

"Aren't you concerned about her falling out?"

"Not at all," I said. "The bed has a safety bar."

"But she still has to climb in and out in the middle of the night if she needs to go to the bathroom?"

"She's an agile little girl, Mr. Hoyt. Millions of kids her age sleep in bunk beds. You're trying to insinuate there's a danger when it's perfectly safe."

Hoyt smiled and Claxton frowned, a warning for me not to get confrontational.

"I'm just trying to establish the facts, Mr. Drobyshev. Isn't it true that there are many nights when Sarah doesn't sleep in her bed at all?"

"She goes to sleep in her own bed every single night."

"But she often wakes up and comes into your bed, doesn't she?"

"Sarah's been having bad dreams lately. Sometimes she gets frightened and crawls in next to me."

"Do you still sleep in the nude, Mr. Drobyshev?"

I glared at him. Lucy and I often slept naked, especially in the summer. "No, in my underwear. Boxers and a T-shirt."

Hoyt nodded. "What about bathing? Do you ever take a shower with your children?"

"Yes, I do."

"And you see nothing inappropriate about showering with a little girl who is almost five years old?"

"Sarah is not aware of sex yet. I have no intention of making her feel self-conscious about something that seems perfectly normal to her."

Hoyt said, "She may not be aware of the details of sexual reproduction, but certainly you would agree that she knows the difference between the two sexes?"

"Of course."

"What does she call your penis?"

I scowled at him.

"Mr. Drobyshev?" Hoyt said.

"Willie. She calls it my willie."

The morning after my deposition, Claxton called and said that Hoyt had reached out to him with a tentative settlement. Claxton asked me if I could come to his office. He didn't want to discuss the details on the phone.

"I'm not backing down," I said, sitting across the desk from him. "I want full custody of the children."

"I know what you *want*, Mr. Drobyshev. What I'm trying to tell you is the family courts in Massachusetts are reluctant to take away a mother's custodial rights."

"They must do it *sometimes*. The woman is a whore and a pathological liar. She can't get through the day without smoking a joint. She's been a totally unfit mother. Isn't that what you proved in the deposition? I've read it three times. You completely eviscerated her."

"I agree, the deposition doesn't cast her in the most favorable light. But Mr. Hoyt has raised some questions about your parenting as well. You may believe these issues are without merit, but—"

"Without merit! They're trying to suggest I'm molesting my own daughter, for Christ's sake. I can't believe I was married to that woman for five years. It's like she just crawled out of a sewer."

"This certainly could get uglier, Mr. Drobyshev. Please, just calm down and listen. Let me tell you the terms of the proposed settlement before you reject it."

I clenched my jaw in anger.

Claxton looked at his notes on a legal pad. "You and Mrs. Drobyshev would have joint legal custody. The children would stay with you half the nights on a flexible schedule just as they do now, depending on your work demands. You cede your half-ownership in the house in lieu of child support, which, in my opinion, is an excellent deal for you. Major expenses for the kids like camp and medical bills would be split equally between you. Mrs. Drobyshev is willing to forgo any claims on the money from your mother's insurance policies or your equity in the courier business. This would be a no-fault divorce. You sign the papers, and one year later, the divorce automatically becomes final."

"I want custody of my children."

"That could only happen if this case were to go to trial."

"Fine. Let's go to trial."

"Look, Mr. Drobyshev, your wife has been indiscreet and self-indulgent. We can put Mr. Chandler on the stand, and he may occasionally tell the truth. We might even be able to find a few neighbors or acquaintances to testify against her. But going to trial is a roll of the dice. Judges can be very arbitrary. I've had cases where the rulings were so capricious and fundamentally at odds with the facts, I thought I'd stepped into the wrong courtroom. If we turn this into a custody fight, the first thing the judge is going to do is appoint a guardian ad litem for the children. Do you know what that is?"

"I've heard the term, but no, not exactly."

"A guardian ad litem—a GAL—is usually a social worker or a psychologist, someone who acts as your children's advocate before the court. He, or sometimes she, will interview you and your wife. He'll inspect your homes, watch how you interact with the children, talk to the teachers at the day-care center. With all the issues that have come up in the depositions, he's probably going to want an independent psychologist to interview the children as well. It's a very thorough process. When he's done, the GAL will submit a report to the judge."

"He can talk to anyone he wants. You say these people are *professionals*? Good. A chimpanzee could see what a terrible parent Lucy is."

"You're missing the point. Once the GAL gets brought in, we have no idea how he might interpret the situation. It's highly arbitrary. One of the kids could say something to the psychologist that turns this whole thing on its head. The GAL might be someone who hates guns or feels like you travel too much in your job or just can't stand the fact that you happen to be wearing a striped tie with a plaid sports coat. It doesn't matter if you walk on water; we can't control what the GAL thinks, and we can't control what he says to the judge."

"I'm in the right here, Mr. Claxton. I want you to fight for me."

"I *am* fighting for you, and if you insist on having a custody battle, I will give it my all. I just want to make sure you understand what we're facing. These custody fights can be brutal. He said, she said; he did this, she did that. Experts weighing in on both sides, your children being interrogated by total strangers. The more contentious it gets, the more inclined the court is to find that neither parent is doing a good job. A judge might even decide it's better for the kids to put them in foster homes until he makes his ruling. I'm not saying you can't win, Mr. Drobyshev; I'm simply saying we could spend the next year or more wading through mud, which will probably cost you upwards of thirty or forty thousand dollars, and when it's all said and done, there's a good chance you won't get custody, and we'll wind up with an agreement that isn't much different from the one we have today."

"I don't care about the money. Not when it comes to my kids."

"You need to consider what you're trying to accomplish here. Are you trying to do what is best for your children, or are you trying to punish your wife? Granted, the woman has not been a model citizen or a model parent. She's made some poor choices, but she's not a criminal. Besides, even if you were to win full custody, she will still be the mother of your children. You're going to want her to see them and have as good a relationship with them as possible. You may not like her or respect her, but she's not going to *disappear*. You need to focus on making the best of this situation going forward."

I slapped my palms on my thighs and stood up and paced around the room.

"I try to give my clients the best advice I can, Mr. Drobyshev. If you don't agree with what I've been telling you, please feel free to consult someone else. Perhaps you should take a copy of your wife's deposition and shop it around. I guarantee you, you won't have any trouble finding another attorney who would salivate at the opportunity to take this case to trial."

He looked at me coldly. The man didn't seem to have an emotional bone in his body.

"Like I said, this agreement is more than fair. Frankly, I think you'd be a fool not to take it, but that is your decision, not mine. Why don't you go home and mull it over, talk to some friends or acquaintances who have gone through troubled divorces of their own. Give me a call when you know how you want to proceed. Whatever decision you make is fine with me."

I was so agitated when I left his office I kicked a watercooler in the hall. It already had a few dents in it, probably from other men like me.

I had two friends who had gone through contentious divorces. Randy Fallon was an old friend on the police force, and I remembered how he had complained about his divorce settlement. When I told him what Claxton had advised me to do, Randy said, "Your lawyer must be one in a million, not wanting to soak you for every penny. I paid mine over twelve thousand bucks and still wound up getting screwed." Randy's pension from the BPD was being garnisheed by the court for child support. He said the deal I was being offered from Lucy's attorney sounded like manna from heaven.

Craig Hildebrandt served on the TWT task force with Javi and me. He had been divorced twice. He and his first wife split amicably, no kids. Craig and his second wife had a little girl he adored, but the marriage was a disaster. His wife was an alcoholic who cheated on him with another cop. She got arrested twice for shoplifting. Craig fought for custody, but the judge let her keep the child as long as she provided the court with proof she was attending AA. "Your attorney's right, Matt," Craig said. "It's not worth all the money and heartache. I was so angry for a while I swear I thought about trying to find someone to knock her off. But she found Jesus and things worked out okay in the long run. I'm not a big fan of all the religious stuff, but it helped her get her shit together. She's actually turned out to be a pretty good mother."

I called Claxton and told him to draw up the papers. I can't exaggerate the bitterness I felt when I signed them.

∞

In late March, a month after the divorce had been filed, I got a call in my office from Katy Bowen at Katydids, where the children went to day care.

"Maybe it's my mistake, Matt, but isn't Lucy supposed to pick up the kids this afternoon?"

"Yeah, hasn't she come yet?"

"Nope. No sign of her."

It was quarter to six. When it was Lucy's night to have the kids, she usually picked them up no later than five. I asked Katy if she had called Garbo's.

"Yes, they told me she left around four. I called the house too, but got the machine."

"Okay, I'll come right away and take the little monkeys off your hands."

It was Tuesday. I was supposed to have them tomorrow night and Thursday. My two weekday nights with Sarah and Nathan varied according to my work schedule. I made sure I spoke with Lucy in advance and kept Katy up to date. Either Lucy had forgotten it was her night or written it down wrong in her daybook. I hopped in my car and drove to Kaytdids, my tires slipping on the trolley tracks in the rain.

"I have no idea what happened with Lucy," I said to Katy. "It concerns me that she hasn't called."

"Eh, she probably just got confused about the schedule. Happens with parents more than you think." She laughed. "I've had to take my share of orflings home for supper."

I bundled up the kids and put them in the car.

Sarah said, "How come Mommy forgot to pick us up?"

Because your mother is a total fuck-up. You'll figure that out for yourself pretty soon.

"She just got confused, honey. We all make mistakes sometimes, even mommies and daddies." Wasn't that the way the experts said you should play it? Never belittle the ex to your children. I wondered how long I could keep up the charade.

I took the kids to dinner at an Italian restaurant. Afterward, I drove slowly down Lucy's street. I thought I'd see if she was home yet and knock on the door. The house was dark except for the lights in the third-floor apartment. I circled the block and decided to take the kids into the house and wait for her to come home. It would piss her off to have me invade her space like that, but I didn't care. She had messed up again, and I wanted to embarrass her.

I parked out front. I knew it wouldn't be hard to get in. Chances are Lucy hadn't changed the locks, and I still had a key for the house on my key ring. It was just like her not to ask for it back. The key fit, and I took the kids inside. I played with Sarah and Nathan till eight-thirty. Then I gave them a snack and read them a story before putting them to bed.

Alone downstairs, I went into the study. Lucy's desk was a mess. I poked around a little, trying not to disturb anything. In one of the drawers, I found a leather-bound journal, a diary of sorts. I glanced at one entry, which happened to be about Amanda, then put it back.

I'm not sure if I resisted the temptation to stop reading out of some qualm of conscience or because I didn't want to see what Lucy said about me. I wandered into the living room and sat on the couch. I started to read a *Newsweek* article about South Africa but couldn't concentrate. I went to the kitchen and drank a glass of water. Back in the living room, I saw my car keys partially lodged between the couch cushions. I retrieved the keys and lifted the cushion to see if any coins had also slipped out of my pocket. As I was putting the cushion back in place, I noticed a small dark hole on the under-side—an unmistakable cigarette burn that had smoldered deep into the stuffing. I wondered when this had happened. Lucy had bought the couch last summer when we were still together. There were smoke alarms in the house, but even so. I imagined myself barging into my lawyer's office, holding up the cushion. *What about this, Claxton? See this hole! Is this proof enough to get some judge to acknowledge that my children are in danger? Am I supposed to sit around and hope they're lucky enough to be staying with me when she burns the fucking house down?*

"Daddy?" Sarah stood in the doorway with Sundae in the crook of her arm.

I put the cushion back, burnt side down. "What's the matter? Can't sleep, sweetie?"

She nodded.

"You want to play a game of Parcheesi?"

She smiled and nodded again and ran to get the board.

"We gonna have a bet?" she said. She was not yet five but already fiercely competitive.

"Okay, let's see. If *you* win, you get another cookie before you go back to bed. If *I* win…you have to buy me a new car?"

She giggled. "It's a deal." And put out her hand to shake.

Sarah won fair and square. She ate the cookie, then I carried her back upstairs and tucked her in bed.

"Will you stay here till I fall asleep?" she said.

"Sure, I won't move an inch."

She curled up with Sundae, and I smoothed her hair as she drifted off. I tiptoed out of the room. Outside Nathan's open door, I stopped and listened for his soft, wet breath. The lights were off in Lucy's bedroom, but the door was open. I hadn't set foot in that room since I'd come to collect my clothes and personal belongings. I turned on the light and went in. The bloodstained rug was gone, but little else seemed to have changed. I sat on the bed. The faint smell of Lucy filled me with an unwanted sense of longing. I went over to her dresser and opened the top drawer where she kept her bras and panties. In the back, in its usual place, was her stash of marijuana. The fat buds were still a little green, a sweet odor oozing from the clear plastic baggie. I closed the drawer and gazed across the room. Lucy had put some new photographs on the mantel. Sarah in a princess dress, Nathan on a swing. The photo in the center, in an inlaid wooden frame, had been taken outdoors in the snow—Lucy holding Nathan in her arms and Griffin with Sarah on his hip. They were all smiling brightly, their cheeks rosy from the cold. A handsome, happy family. Lucy could've just as easily kept the old photo of the four of us and pasted a cut-out of Griffin's face over mine. I turned the photograph facedown on the mantel.

I heard the front door open.

"Matt?" Lucy called from downstairs. "Matt, is that you?"

"Be right down."

She was at the bottom of the stairs with her coat on. Griffin was behind her in a brown leather bomber jacket taking off his driving gloves. They'd brought in several fancy shopping bags and placed them on the floor by the coat tree.

"Would you please tell me what the fuck you're doing here?" Lucy said.

"You forgot to pick up the kids at day care." I gave her a sarcastic grin. "I thought I'd do you a favor and bring them home."

"I didn't forget anything. I don't know what kind of shit you're trying to pull here, Matt, but it's your night to have them. I could have you arrested for trespassing."

I was about to say how strange it was that Katy had made the same mistake I did, but I held my tongue. Lucy was about to flip out. I didn't want to get in a shouting match and wake the kids. I had signed the divorce papers, but I still wasn't ready to give up the fight. Of course, there were smarter ways to go about it than breaking into her house. What I'd done was needlessly provocative, and it would give her an excuse to shrug off her guilt and embarrassment when she finally figured out she was in the wrong.

"I'm sorry," I said. "I guess I screwed up."

She thought I was being snide. "I mean it, Matt. Next time I'll call the police."

"No. No, you're right. I'm sorry. It was stupid. My mistake."

She hesitated, suspicious of my quick capitulation. "Well…okay. But you can't come in here like this. We're divorced now. This is *my* house. The lines have to be clear."

"I know, you're right. Here." I took the house key from my key ring and handed it to her. "It won't happen again."

"Everything's cool," Griffin said, a stupid smile on his face. He put his arm around her shoulder. His woman now. I wanted to grab him by the front of his bomber jacket, pick him up, and hang him on the coat tree. I tried not to let my animosity show on my face.

I turned to Lucy. "You want me to get the kids and take them home with me?"

"Don't be silly. It's perfectly fine if they stay here. I'll take them over to Katydids in the morning." It was ludicrous to see her playing the dutiful mother.

"Okay, thanks. Excuse me. I think I left my jacket up in Sarah's room." I turned and took the steps two at a time. I went into Lucy's bedroom and righted the photograph on the mantel.

When I came back downstairs, Lucy held out the jacket. "It was in the kitchen," she said, her eyes narrowed with suspicion, trying to figure out what I was up to.

She followed me onto the front porch and stood there watching until I got in my car and drove off. She'd be a little spooked by what I'd done, but she'd look around the house, see that everything was the same, and forget about the whole thing in a day or two. That was my hope, anyway. What an idiot I was for not taking the kids home with me in the first place and calmly pointing out her mistake to her tomorrow.

I stayed up late playing solitaire, thinking how much better everything would be if Lucy simply vanished. I didn't wish she was dead, just *gone*. Out of our lives completely. Or the other way around. Maybe I should take the kids and run. Disappear. Start over. New names, new place, no more screwups from her to deal with.

I wasn't ready to cross that line, but it was time for me to get smart. No more grandstanding. It was foolish to put her on guard like I did tonight. From now on I'd play the part of the model ex-husband. The perfect co-parent. Easygoing, nonjudgmental, eager to compromise. I needed to win back her trust before I could violate it again.

Chapter 23
Lucy

After Matt drove off, I came back in the house still holding his key. "Talk about *weird*," I said to Griffin. "What the hell do you think that was all about?"

"Aah, don't sweat it. He's just having trouble letting go."

We went into the kitchen. "He must have been looking for something. Or checking up on me. I need to get the locks changed. He might have another copy of the key."

Griffin uncorked a bottle of wine.

I got my daybook from my purse. "Look," I said, "Tuesday, 'M' for Matt. It was *his* night to have the kids."

"You don't have to prove anything to me, Luce."

"I know. I just hate him accusing me like that. He keeps trying to make me out to be a bad mother."

"Come on, forget about it." He handed me a glass of wine. "Time to celebrate. Happy birthday."

"Thank you."

My birthday actually wasn't until Thursday, but Griffin was going to be out of town on a business trip, so we were celebrating early. His gift was to take me shopping. He picked me up after work and we went to a half dozen high-end stores where he watched me try on various outfits and lingerie, his eyes filled with delight when I came out of the dressing room looking like a model or a classy hooker. I could feel myself blushing as I showed off a lacy black teddy with a thong bottom. *Bingo*, he said, clapping his hands. I said, *You just want to buy this so you can tear it off me.* And he said, *True, so true.* The teddy cost ninety-eight dollars. Griffin delighted in spending money on me. Much as Matt loved me and occasionally bought me a thoughtful gift—a colorful wool shawl or a wide leather belt with hammered tin buckle—his first priority was to find a bargain. He couldn't buy anything without considering the price first, not even an ice cream cone or a pair of socks. His frugality wore thin. It almost seemed like a birth defect—congenital cheapness—as if he'd been born with a cut-rate soul.

Griffin and I took our wineglasses upstairs. As we walked into the bedroom, I said, "Matt's been in here, spying on me."

"How do you know?"

"I just do. I can *feel* it. It gives me the creeps. Like there's mold oozing over everything."

"Don't worry about it. You were great with him. Clear, straightforward. The poor bastard's still madly in love with you. He'll get over it in ten or twenty years."

We undressed and got in bed, the lamp still lit on the nightstand. I kept scanning the room, trying to see if anything was amiss, resisting the urge to check the closet and dresser drawers. I imagined a scene out of a creepy black-and-white movie, Matt taking a pair of scissors to my underwear. But that wasn't like him. Tonight was an anomaly he wouldn't repeat; I could see it in his face. For all his lingering resentment, he was, at heart, a rational, economical man, which is precisely what my lawyer understood when he proposed the divorce settlement. It was a deal Matt couldn't resist.

I turned out the light and snuggled up next to Griffin. He had been spending nearly every night with me since the divorce was finalized. His emotional support over the past six months was no illusion, and I was beginning to believe that he could love me—and stay. We were a couple now, no different from millions of others who had tried and failed before they got things right.

The next morning Katy asked me if I'd gotten the schedule worked out with Matt.

"Yeah." I smiled. "His mistake for once."

"Really? I had it on my calendar that it was your night."

"You did?"

"Yes," Katy said. "I called him at the office and he came right over."

"Well, he wound up admitting it was him."

Katy shrugged. "I guess he gave me the wrong dates to put in my book."

I thought about rubbing it in the next time I saw Matt, but it was enough to watch him slink away last night like a petty criminal.

Nothing said more about Griffin's commitment to me than his relationship with the children. He thought they were a hoot, especially Sarah. She was a tomboy and a daredevil, always rolling and tumbling, begging to go faster and swing higher. Nathan was more of a watcher, a little timid and often cranky. I don't think I fostered it, but he had a tendency to cling to me. Griffin and I bought a pair of bicycles with child seats on the back and took the kids for rides through the Arboretum. One Saturday morning he showed up with a trampoline in two big boxes. He carried the boxes out to the backyard and put it together with Sarah acting as his helper. Rory the cat sat on the fence watching them like she was Queen of the May.

"You guys ready?" Griffin was jumping lightly up and down on the trampoline. "I had one of these when I was a kid." He sprang up effortlessly, did a back flip and landed on his feet, tried a front flip but couldn't hold the landing. "Out of practice," he said, laughing.

"I want to do it," Sarah said.

I lifted her up. As soon as she got on, she started bouncing as high as she could, utterly fearless, while I stood there holding my breath, afraid she'd go flying off into the bushes. When it was Nathan's turn, he walked around, unsteady on his feet like a little drunk, lost his balance and got up giggling. Falling down was the best part for him. Sarah and Griffin begged me to take a turn, but I wanted no part of it. Griffin bounded down and put his arm around me as we watched Sarah and Nathan knock each other down over again and again.

My neighbor Nancy Prince, whose backyard was separated by a low wooden fence from mine, stood on her porch and waved. Nancy had an eight-year-old daughter and a teenage son who sometimes did odd jobs for me, raking leaves and shoveling the sidewalk. She and I didn't talk much, and I had never discussed the breakup with Matt with her, but she must have heard some gossip. I wondered what she was thinking as she looked across the yard and saw Griffin with his arm around my shoulder. I leaned into him, as if to prove to her (or to myself) that there was no mistake in what she was seeing.

∞

Over the past year, Amanda had developed a condition that caused the septum in her nose to collapse. She could only breathe through her mouth, and her voice was so raspy it was hard to understand her on the telephone. Worse, perhaps, was her wounded vanity, her nose smooshed in like an old prizefighter's. She went to several doctors before she found a surgeon at Mass. Eye and Ear who came up with a solution, a procedure that left her with a little dent in her nose but nothing off-putting. In early May she called me and said she was coming to Boston for a checkup. The two of us had been getting closer since my marriage had fallen apart, and I enjoyed having her stay with me. Some nights we'd sit in the kitchen, talking and getting buzzed on white wine; sometimes Griffin joined us. Amanda had confessed to me recently that, much as she cared for Matt, Griffin was obviously more my type—hers too—a man "with the devil in his eye," just like Thorny. For once I admitted she was right.

The plan was for her to pick up Sarah and Nathan at Katydids after her doctor's appointment and take them to the Aquarium. She was so good with them that it almost made me jealous. About two-thirty in the afternoon, I got a call at work from a lieutenant in the Braintree Police Department saying they had Amanda in custody.

"One of our officers stopped Mrs. Thornhill for driving erratically on Route Three," the lieutenant said. "She refused to take a breathalyzer, but her eyes are glassy and her speech is slurred."

"Oh my god. How are the children?"

"They're fine. One of the female members of our administrative staff is looking after them. We're hoping you can pick them up soon, or we'll have to get social services involved."

"Yes, of course. Thank you. What about my mother?"

"She wasn't happy when we brought her to the station, but I'd say she was more confused than belligerent. We'll release her to your custody, but she'll have to come back to court at a later date."

"Thank you so much. I'll take a cab immediately and drive her car home." He gave me the address.

I wondered how Amanda ended up in Braintree, which was about fifteen miles south of the Aquarium. She must have gotten on the Southeast Expressway and kept going. I sat in the cab with my mind racing, furious at her and even more furious at myself. She was just doing what she had always done. How many times had she driven drunk with my brother Mark and me in the car when we were kids? She seemed to have gotten her drinking under control lately. Still, I should have said something to her about never drinking when she had Sarah and Nathan in the car. What if this had happened a few months ago? I imagined Claxton looking at me with disdain over his rimless glasses: *Had you been aware of your mother's drinking problem, Mrs. Drobyshev? Isn't it true that she had been hospitalized for alcoholism on numerous occasions? Didn't Mrs. Thornhill once crash her automobile through the plate glass window of a beauty parlor, causing considerable property damage and injuring a female patron?* Yes. Yes. Yes. *And you still let her drive your children around?*

I could recite my mother's excuse before hearing it: Amanda saying her sinuses were still blocked, the pressure so bad when she woke up this morning it felt like her teeth were falling out, so the doctor at Mass. Eye and Ear gave her some capsules—a little something to go along with her prescriptions for high blood pressure, high cholesterol, and depression. At lunch she'd treated herself to a gin and tonic, *just one*, which was understandable after everything she'd been through—a mistake in hindsight, of course, but the doctor should have warned her not to drink with those pills or she never would have gotten behind the wheel with the kids in the car and driven on these dreadful highways with rude drivers and signs pointing everywhere except the place you wanted to go.

Or maybe she'd say, *I'm sorry, I'm a drunk, what I did was horrible. Time for me to go somewhere and dry out for a while.*

Ultimately, what Amanda said to me didn't matter; the issue was what I would say to Matt when he found out. *If* he found out. The trick was how to get the kids to keep it a secret. Nathan could easily blurt something out, but he'd follow Sarah's lead. If she didn't say anything about the incident, chances are he wouldn't either. But what if Matt caught me trying to keep it from him? This was a man who *never* made mistakes or bent the rules. Last week I'd gotten a lecture for letting Sarah sit in the backseat without a seat belt. Maybe the best way to mitigate the damage would be to tell him myself.

I paid the cabbie and went into the police station. Amanda looked so old when the lieutenant brought her out to me. She was meek and downcast, muttering apologies as I gave her a hug. The officer handed me her keys, and I walked her out to the car. By the time I came back out with the children she was curled up in the front seat, asleep, a shiny trail of drool running down her chin. The kids started giggling as they imitated her snores.

Sarah said, "Are they going to make Nanda go back to jail?"

"Oh no, honey. Nanda's sick. She just took the wrong pills, that's all. The policemen will understand." I was almost ready to believe it myself. "But you know what? Nanda's going to be embarrassed by all this. She'll be worried people will say she did something really bad." I lowered my voice to a whisper. "Maybe we shouldn't tell anybody."

"You mean keep it a *secret*," Sarah said.

"Yes, kind of. Just keep it to ourselves." I was trying to split hairs with a preschooler.

"Not even tell Daddy?"

"Not Daddy. Not *anybody*. That's what makes it a secret."

"Okay," Sarah said.

I could only hope.

Matt was planning to take the children to Disney World the second week in June; he said he heard it was a good time to go, just before most schools let out. It was all the kids could talk about. They'd be gone from Friday to Friday, and I was hoping Griffin and I might be able to take a vacation of our own, but he had arranged some meetings in Dallas that couldn't be changed.

One afternoon I was talking to one of the mothers I had met at Katydids, and we set up a Friday sleepover for her daughter at my house.

It was interesting to watch the girls interact. Naomi wasn't bossy, but she had a rich imagination and definitely took the lead, which was a surprise to me given Sarah's personality. I could hear them chattering in Sarah's room long after I'd turned out the lights. In the morning Griffin played with them on the trampoline. I sat on the back steps smoking a cigarette with Nathan between my knees. Naomi was frustrated that she couldn't do a flip like Sarah, but she loved doing belly flops and back flops over and over.

The phone rang in the kitchen. Griffin and Sarah were on the trampoline together, Naomi waiting her turn. I put Nathan down at the bottom of the steps and said to Naomi, "Could you watch him a sec while I get the phone?"

"Yes, ma'am." She was polite to a fault.

I was about to open the back door when I heard Sarah shriek and Griffin shout her name. I turned around to see her arcing high in the air, her arms and legs pinwheeling as if she were trying to fly. She landed in the grass between the trampoline and the swing set and let out a heart-stopping scream.

Griffin leaped down and cradled her in his arms, his face stricken.

Sarah was crying, "My arm, my arm. Ouch, my arm."

I rushed to them and took Sarah from Griffin and hugged her to my chest. "Oh, honey, you're okay, you're okay. Let me see. Show me where it hurts. I'll kiss it and make it better."

She was wailing so hard she could barely catch her breath. "I want *Daddy*," she said.

Chapter 24

Matt

My job was a godsend. During the dark days of the divorce, it gave me something challenging to focus on and kept me from spending all my time being angry and feeling sorry for myself. I cut back on the number of trips I made but still spent a lot of nights and weekends in the office when I didn't have the kids. Javi gave me free rein. I was the primary contact with clients, managed the couriers, and coordinated all pickups and deliveries. I did the payroll, taxes, and billing.

"You gotta pace yourself, partner," Javi said the last time he dropped by the office. "Why don't you hire a bookkeeper?"

"Nah, I'm okay for now."

I handed him the latest financials. He gave them a once-over and let out a whistle. "Can't argue with the results. Lean and mean."

"Lean maybe, but definitely not mean." There were days when I felt like a toady dealing with some of our clients.

I had to keep reminding our couriers that we had *clients*, not *customers*. Our personnel consisted of four men and a woman who specialized in escorting children. They were all ex-cops Javi and I knew from the force—reliable, trustworthy people who occasionally needed a little polishing. I'd correct one of them and get an eye roll or a sarcastic salute. *Listen*, I'd tell them, *we're professionals. That's why we wear coats and ties and fly first class. You want customers, go deliver pizzas.* The parameters of the job were defined by our name— Discreet Courier *Service*. It was important for the clients to see us as savvy, no-nonsense operatives, but we also had to know when to bow and scrape.

The first time Javi told me about DCS, at lunch at Jake Wirth's, he mentioned the painting he brought back from Germany that was so beautiful it gave him chills. I didn't think about it much at the time. I was more interested in the business opportunity. But I soon learned what he meant. My third trip as a courier took me to London, where I picked up a painting by a Dutch artist named Salomon van Ruysdael. It was a river scene—two men in a rowboat with a cloudy sky and tall, overhanging trees. It was a small oil on an oak board only about eighteen by twenty-four inches, but you could get lost in that world. Not all the pieces I transported had the same effect on me. Some antiquities seemed to be valuable only because they were old, and as far I was concerned, most of the abstract paintings were the emperor's new clothes. But our clients paid huge sums of money for the artwork we transported and I wanted to learn more.

I was never much of a museumgoer. Before this job the only exhibit that ever really knocked my socks off was the treasures of King Tut. Then, as a courier, I started visiting museums in the cities where I traveled. In Frankfurt I came across *The Geographer* by Johannes Vermeer, a painting of a man standing by a window with a pair of dividers in his hand, that mapmaker's tool for measuring distances. It was a small canvas about the same size as the van Ruysdael. The light coming through the window looked so real the paint seemed to glow. I stopped in the museum shop to buy a print of it to hang on the wall at home, but the reproductions didn't come close to capturing the magic of the original. The difference was so startling I went back into the museum and stared at the painting. In the end I bought a postcard of the picture and put it in a drawer in my office. It was the first of many. Reminders of the real artworks I wanted to go back and see again.

We had gotten a call recently to pick up a collection of daguerre-otypes in Amsterdam, and I decided to take the trip myself. I had never been to the Netherlands and wanted to see the Vermeers and Rembrandts and go to the Van Gogh museum. I was also curious about the red-light district where the prostitutes displayed themselves in windows, waiting for johns. I couldn't quite see myself hiring a prostitute, but maybe it was time to start. My sex life had been nonexistent since Lucy and I split. Maybe I could make it a theme trip—fine art and whores.

A week before I left, I went to an opening for several new artists at a gallery on Newbury Street. I didn't care for that sort of thing, but Billy Tuttle insisted I come and meet a potential client. Billy was a dealmaker in the Boston art world and a good source of business for DCS. The prospect he wanted me to meet was Pamela McDermott, a furniture heiress from North Carolina. She was about fifty, a short, pudgy platinum blond upholstered in a red leather pantsuit. When Billy introduced me, she eyed me up and down like I was a slave on the auction block. We had only exchanged a few words when someone came along and spirited her away.

"So," Billy said, raising an eyebrow, "what did you think?"

"What? Of Pamela? Billy, you don't mean…?"

"How much do you want the business, pal?"

"Not that much."

"Ah, a man with *standards*." He said it like it was a four-letter word. "Actually, she can make that sort of thing quite interesting."

"Billy? I thought you…" Were gay.

He laughed. "Come on, Matt. You know I try to make *everyone* happy."

"Yes, you do, Billy," a woman said behind me. "I couldn't get this big ox to give me the time of day."

Billy grinned. "Hello, Marcy." He kissed the police commissioner's assistant on both cheeks.

She turned to me, a glass of wine in her hand. "Sergeant Drobyshev."

I bent down and gave her an awkward one-sider. I hadn't seen her since I left the force a year and a half ago. I'd thought about looking her up from time to time, remembering our flirtation in the bar, but never got around to it.

Billy said, "You two know each other?"

"Vaguely," Marcy said. She was wearing a tight blue dress. She'd put on a little weight, done something different with her hair.

The three of us made small talk for a few minutes before Billy moved on.

"Surprising to see you here, Matt," Marcy said. She sipped her wine. "I didn't know you were an art lover."

I shrugged. "Trying to drum up business. What about you?"

She said one of the artists was an old friend from her hometown in New Jersey. We walked across the gallery to look at his work. The canvases were mostly cityscapes, very dark. Each painting was divided into five or six distinct parts, but somehow they all fit together.

Marcy said, "What sort of business are you in, Matt?"

I began to tell her and got carried away, talking too fast, trying to impress her. She looked terrific in that blue dress. I paused to take a breath.

"Fascinating," she said.

"Sorry."

"No, I *mean* it. Sounds romantic, flying all over the world."

"Yeah, it's neat. I get to meet some interesting people. The ones who live behind the high hedges and gates with security cameras."

She finished her wine. I asked if she'd like me to get her another.

"Can we make it a real drink?"

"Sure."

She gave me the claim check for her coat. It was a short black trench coat with wide lapels and a belt she cinched tight around her waist. I imagined her walking across the room, naked beneath the coat. It was a chilly evening with a light rain falling as we walked down to the Ritz. I got Bailey's on the rocks; she ordered a Dewar's neat. She told me she'd left the commissioner's office at the end of last year.

I said, "So where're you working now?"

"I'm in-house counsel for a high-tech start-up on 128. The salary isn't much, but they gave me great stock options. Half the time I don't know what the hell I'm doing, but I'm hoping the company goes public before anyone finds out."

"Did you get recruited for the job?"

"No, nothing as glamorous as that. Things got complicated in the commissioner's office and it was time to get out. Now, if you want to know why..." She finished her Dewar's. "That requires another drink."

I signaled the waiter.

"Oldest story in the book," Marcy said. "Married guy, three kids. You see his name in the paper sometimes. We couldn't go out in public, I couldn't take him home to meet my parents. I threatened to leave him, he promised to leave his wife. All the while I'm wondering how a smart, reasonably attractive chick like me could be such an idiot. He's calling me, writing me, feeding me lines they couldn't get away with in a bad soap opera. Meanwhile, I'm hanging on every word like it's Shakespeare. Get me drunk enough and I'll recite some for you."

"You ended it?"

"Not exactly. His wife got suspicious, so we're taking a break. If I hold on for the next five or ten years, he might actually leave the bitch. No, that's unfair. I've met her. She seems perfectly lovely. Of course, if he dumps *her*..." She smiled forlornly. "...he'll probably start shacking up with some twenty-four-year-old intern."

"Sorry."

"Nah, don't be. I did it all by myself." She gave me a look that said, *But I'm here with you*, and ran the tip of her finger around the rim of my glass. "Okay, it's your turn now."

Which I took. My story was not a short, self-mocking version like Marcy's but the whole sordid saga. She was the first person other than Norman Claxton I told about the incident in the bedroom. I went step by step. Spared no details. It was a purging of the first order—vile, unseemly, humiliating. Another round of drinks came.

Marcy slouched in her chair, a look on her face that said it was okay for me to use her like that. Perhaps listening was what she did best.

"She's a lousy mother," I said. I had been talking nonstop for at least half an hour. "I was blind to it when we were married. I loved her. We were a family, so I gave her the benefit of the doubt. Now I look at her and realize she doesn't have a fucking clue. She packs overnight bags for the kids to come to my house, and she's always forgetting something. Underwear, sweater, extra pair of shoes in case it rains. It isn't just little things. One day I get a call at the office from the director of the kids' day-care center. Matt, where's Lucy? We're about to close. She hasn't picked up the kids. Shit! I have to drop everything and go over and get them. What if I had been out of town? What was the director supposed to do? Take them home with her and keep them overnight?"

I finished my drink—my fourth—and kept going. "The woman is a fucking menace. It's like she doesn't have a motherly bone in her body. She lets the kids ride in the car without their seat belts. Lets them eat those disgusting sugar-coated cereals with so much food dye the milk turns pink. A month or two ago, I caught Sarah with a candy cigarette holding it just like her mother. Like she can't wait to have a real one. Maybe she can drop ashes on the furniture like Lucy. Burn the fucking house down. I don't know what to do, Marcy. The whole thing's tearing me apart. I've *tried* talking to her. Sometimes she'll roll her eyes and tell me to chill out, or get pissed off and go into some convoluted explanation of why she's right. Half the time it's like she doesn't even understand what I'm talking about. I might as well be speaking Norwegian. It's like she's off on some other planet."

"What a nightmare, Matt. Even with all that, your lawyer says you still can't get custody?"

"That's what he says. I paid him a small fortune to tell me, Sorry, pal, doesn't matter if she's a ditz and smokes pot and fucked around on you. She's still their *mother*. No judge in the Commonwealth is going to take those kids away from her." I threw up my hands in frustration. "You want to know what the saddest part is? It's good advice. He's absolutely right. I've talked to other guys who've gone through it. They all say the same thing. That's the way the court works in Massachusetts. Divorced fathers get the shaft every time. There are men out there who are paying forty percent of their salary in child support, and they aren't even allowed to see their kids."

I came close to telling her I had been thinking about disappearing with Sarah and Nathan. Taking off and leaving all this shit behind. But saying it out loud would make it too real—a wish morphing into a plan. Maybe I didn't bring it up because I didn't want her to tell me the idea was insane and try to talk me out of it.

I went on a little longer until I wore myself out. Wore Marcy out too. I'm pretty sure she would have taken me home for a pity fuck, but I didn't try.

The next week I went to Amsterdam. I told Lucy I wanted to stay a few extra days, and she said that was fine. She knew I'd make it up to her. I'd been Mr. Nice Guy since the night I stole into her house. Lucy responded to my display of good humor like a gracious big sister. *So, how are you, Matt? Seems like the business is*

going well. Is that a new sports coat? Looks good on you. The kids are over the moon about going to Disney World. At least she had enough tact not to ask if I was seeing anyone, but I could tell she wanted to. The quicker I moved on with some other woman, the easier her life would be.

Amsterdam was a welcome break. I felt calm and unhurried. All the ranting to Marcy seemed to have drained some of the vitriol from my system. It was mid–May, bright sun every day. I missed the tulip season, but there were flowers blooming in every window box and public park. It seemed like everyone spoke English. I told the man who was my contact for the sale of the daguerreotypes about my interest in the museums and Dutch painters, and he offered to be my guide. Being with him was like getting a college course in art history in two days. He drove me to The Hague about an hour away to see the two Vermeer paintings. *Girl with a Pearl Earring* was nice, but the *View of Delft* looked like it was painted by God. I bought a postcard of the landscape to add to my collection. That night I wandered through the red–light district. Some of the women were gorgeous. I'm sure it would have been a rush to be with one of them, but I was holding out for something that wouldn't leave me feeling like a loser ten seconds after I'd gotten my rocks off.

I delivered the daguerreotypes to my client at his country estate in Vermont. On the way back to Boston, I called Lucy to remind her that I'd be picking up the kids at day care.

"How was Amsterdam?" she said.

"Great. Fabulous city. You and Griffin should go. You can buy pot in the stores just like cigarettes."

She didn't react to the dig. "Listen, Matt, I'm glad you called. I didn't want to bother you while you were away, but Sarah had a little accident."

"What kind of accident?"

"Nothing serious. She fell off the trampoline and broke her wrist."

"Jesus Christ! You think that isn't *serious*?"

"It's a simple fracture, Matt. Kids heal fast. She won't be in a cast long."

"How did she fall off the trampoline?"

"You know how fearless she is. A little daredevil. I think she's going to be a stuntwoman when she grows up. Griffin was showing her how to do tricks, and she bounced too high and flew off."

"Griffin was on the trampoline at the same time as Sarah?"

"I just said that. He was teaching her a new flip."

"Why wasn't he spotting her? She only weighs about thirty-five pounds. I don't think she can bounce very high on her own."

Lucy sighed in exasperation. "It was an *accident*, Matt. The kind of thing that happens to kids everywhere, every single day."

"Just bad luck, huh? A twist of fate."

"If you want to blame me, fine, go ahead. I knew you would anyway. You're the perfect parent. Nothing bad ever happens on your watch."

"No, it doesn't. I wonder why."

"Look, Sarah's fine. She cried for about three minutes. We took her to the hospital, and she charmed everyone. She thinks her cast is really cool. You can sign it and tell her what a terrible mother I am."

"I think she already knows."

"Asshole." She hung up.

I was at a pay phone in the back of a restaurant outside Manchester. I got in my car and drove down 93, muttering to myself like a lunatic. I pictured myself in Norman Claxton's dreary office, listening to him tell me exactly what Lucy had just said on the phone, that accidents like this happen to kids every day.

When I got to Katydids, Sarah ran up to me and jumped into my arms. "Daddy, Daddy! Look! I broke my wrist." She held up her cast like she'd won first prize.

"Ohhh, honey, I see. How did it happen?"

"Me and Griffin were playing on the trampoline and I flew off."

"Does it hurt?"

"Nope. I cried for a minute, but the doctor said I was real brave."

"Well, I'm glad you're okay." She didn't understand the danger Griffin and her mother had put her in. A different kind of fall and she could have broken her neck.

"Look at all the names on my cast. Me and Mommy saved a place for you." The cast was covered with names and smiley faces with a white rectangle prominently left blank on top.

"Thank you." I put her down. "Let's get a pen so I can sign it." I went over to a table where there were a bunch of markers. "What color do you think I should use? How about pink?"

"Noooo, you're a boy. You can't do pink." She handed me a green marker.

"Okay, green. My favorite color. Just like your hair. Do you want me to write Daddy or Matthew Drobyshev?"

"Daaaddy, all you ever do is *tease* me."

"Aw, I'm sorry, sweetheart. Do you want me to stop?"

"Yes." She nodded, a serious look on her face, then laughed and threw her arms around my neck. "No."

I went outside and got Nathan from the playground. On the way home we stopped at Star Market to get groceries for dinner. I was in the produce section with the kids in the cart when I ran into Richie Harrington, my old friend from the police academy. He was in uniform. We chatted for a few minutes, and he signed Sarah's cast.

After Richie left, Sarah said, "Why aren't you a policeman anymore, Daddy? Didn't you like it?"

"No, I liked it fine. But I got a chance to go into business with Javi and wanted to give that a try."

"When you were a policeman, did you arrest people and make them go to jail?"

"Sometimes. If a bad person was trying to hurt someone or breaking the law."

"Nanda got arrested."

"She *did*? That's too bad. Is that what Mommy told you?"

"No, we were *with* her, Daddy."

"You guys and Mommy?"

"Just me and Natey. She was taking us to the 'quarium and she got lost and the policeman stopped her car and made her go to jail."

"All the cars were beeping," Nathan said. "The policeman said Nanda was going too slow."

I said to Sarah, "When did this happen, hon?"

"I don't remember, Daddy. Before I broke my arm. Mommy had to come pick us up. She says Nanda's sick and can't drive any more till she gets better."

"Well, I hope she gets better real soon."

Sarah was quiet for a moment, then said, "Daddy?"

"What, sweetheart?"

"Don't tell anybody what happened to Nanda. Mommy says it's s'posed to be a secret."

The next day I called a friend in the police department and asked him to contact the RMV and see if he could find any traffic citations in the last few months for Amanda Thornhill. He got back to me after lunch. The arrest had been made by the Braintree Police. The charge was operating under the influence. Amanda had refused to take the breathalyzer. She'd been driving drunk with my kids in the car.

I stewed over the information about Amanda's arrest all afternoon. Then I had to go to a meeting with a wealthy blue blood on Beacon Hill. He was a stickler and inherently mistrustful, one of those clients who keep asking the same question in different ways, trying to trip you up. I left the meeting in a foul mood and walked across the Common and had dinner in Chinatown. When I got home, I was still agitated. I tried to relax in front of the television, but I couldn't stop thinking about Amanda's drunk driving. Lucy knew what her mother was like. How could she expose the children to such danger? One distracted glance, one errant turn of the wheel or a slow reaction on the brakes, and they could have all been killed. I lay awake long into the night, obsessing over Lucy's failings. Never mind the drugs and adultery; she seemed to lack the most basic parental instincts for keeping the children out of harm's way. The drip, drip, drip of her poor judgment and neglect was pushing me over the edge. Maybe I could go back to Claxton and have him file a petition with the court detailing all the reasons why I should have full custody. But

I couldn't keep Sarah and Nathan away from Lucy entirely, and no court in the land could make her wake up and suddenly become a good mother. She and the children had been fortunate so far, but it was only a matter of time before there was some tragedy.

The kids and I were leaving for Disney World in seventeen days. My only option was to take them and run. Get away and never look back. I kept trying to talk myself out of it, trying to find a reason why I should wait or take some other tack. But this wasn't a decision you come to by sitting down and making a list and weighing the pros and cons. It was something more visceral. Like believing in God. Or falling madly in love on a blind date. You can't deny what's in your heart and pretend it isn't there. This is your fate. You have no other choice.

Part Three

Chapter 25

Lucy

Matt seemed as excited as the kids about going to Disney World. I was grateful that he wanted to take Sarah and Nathan, but I couldn't understand why any semi-intelligent adult would want to stand in hour-long lines in the scorching Florida sun waiting to catch a ride with Mr. Toad or listen to little robots sing "It's a Small World" eighty-seven times. Better you than me, I thought as he told me about his plans. If this was another way for him to prove to himself that he was the better parent, I was happy to concede. *Sure you don't want to come along?* he said, teasing. At least he could joke with me sometimes now. He had said some nasty, accusatory things on the telephone, when I told him about Sarah's broken wrist, but he backed off the next time I saw him. I guess he figured we were stuck with one another, and it didn't make sense to keep the fight going.

He came to the house Friday after work to pick up the kids for the Disney trip. They were leaving bright and early Saturday morning, and I had their suitcases packed and ready to go. I could sense Matt's desire to go through the bags to see if I'd forgotten anything, but he resisted the urge. He was always checking on me, monitoring my behavior to see if I'd done things right. He used to do this behind my back when we were married, my faults furtively corrected to keep from embarrassing me; now he often did it openly to make a point.

Summer had finally arrived. I held Nathan's hand as I walked him to the car. Sarah had Sundae under her arm, the llama's white coat matted and gray with wear, the seams stitched to keep the stuffing from falling out. Since she'd gotten over her addiction to peanut butter and jelly, Sundae was her only fetish. She couldn't go to sleep at night without him, the llama traveling back and forth between Matt's place and mine.

I buckled Nathan into his car seat. "Call me," I said to Matt.

"Of course. How about Sunday evening?"

"Sure, that'll be fine." I gave both kids a hug and a kiss. "Have a great time, guys. You be good for your daddy, okay?"

They said goodbye, and I stood on the sidewalk, waving, as Matt drove away.

Griffin was somewhere in New Jersey and wouldn't be home until eight. I went in the house and gathered up a load of laundry and put it in the washer down in the basement. Then I poured a glass of wine and lit a cigarette and sat on the back steps reading *Middlemarch*. I'd been working on the book for weeks, not because it was difficult or boring but because it was so good I didn't want to finish. Rory sat on the step below me, her tail swishing back and forth as she watched a squirrel hop from branch to branch in the maple tree. She had gotten too old to catch anything but still had the desire. I picked her up and scratched her tummy.

"Nathan's going to be away for a whole week, Ror. What're you going to do?" Her devotion to the boy was uncanny. She'd slept by his bed every night since we brought him home from the hospital. Now, when he went to Matt's house, Rory came to me at bedtime, meowing, asking where he'd gone.

Griffin and I had a quiet weekend. He had to go to Dallas on Monday morning. Matt called from Orlando Sunday evening and put Sarah on the phone.

"We're having so much fun, Mommy. We went on lots and lots of rides. My favorite was Space Mountain. Daddy said Natey was too little to go on it, so he found a big girl to go with me. Then we saw Snow White and Cinderella, and Minnie Mouse came over and gave Natey a hug. My cast got real itchy, but Daddy put some baby powder under it and now it feels okay."

Nathan didn't understand about the phone yet, but, with a little coaxing from Matt, he said, *I love you, Mommy.* When Matt got back on the phone, he told me the lines for the rides were longer than expected, but the kids were having a fantastic time.

"What about you?" he said. "How's everything back home?"

"Fine. No complaints."

"Good. We're going to a water park tomorrow for a change of pace. I'll call you in a few days. Which is better, Tuesday or Wednesday?"

"Tuesday. I'm going to the movies with Anita on Wednesday."

"Well, okay." He cleared his throat. "So long, Luce."

"Bye. Have fun."

Monday was an easy day at Garbo's, but Tuesday turned into a bear. I came home exhausted, had a glass of wine, and took a nap on the couch. Amanda called. She hadn't lost her Connecticut license over the drunk driving ticket in Braintree, but the incident had scared her into going to AA. I was proud that she was finally being up front about dealing with her drinking problem. I had a light dinner, then paid some bills. I assumed Matt would call about seven-fifteen as he had on Sunday. When I hadn't heard from him by eight, I phoned his room at the hotel, but there was no answer and I left a message for him to call me as soon as he got in. Another half-hour went by, and I started to get concerned. It wasn't like Mr. Reliable to forget, and Nathan was usually sound asleep by eight-thirty. When Matt was planning the trip, he told me he might drive over to Palm Beach to see his old friend Carlos, the guy who had taken him to Puerto Rico years ago. I thought he might have done that and gotten stuck in traffic coming back to the hotel. By nine o'clock, my concern turned into full-scale worry. I called the hotel again and asked to speak with the front desk.

"Excuse me, I've been trying to reach my husband, Matthew Drobyshev. He and my children are staying in room fourteen twenty-nine. I've left several messages. Would you please make sure that's the correct room number?"

"Certainly, ma'am. Excuse me for a moment while I confirm that for you." The girl had a pathologically cheerful voice. "Yes, ma'am. That's right. Fourteen twenty-nine."

"Is it possible my messages aren't getting through to him?"

"Would you like me to try the room myself?"

"Please."

She put me on hold and came back a minute later. "I'm sorry, Mrs. Drobyshev. There's no answer."

"He was supposed to call me. I was sure he'd be there by now.

Could you possibly have someone go up to the room and check and see if he's there?"

"I'm not sure I…Would you like to speak with the shift manager, Mr. Bender?"

"Yes, that would be great."

I repeated my concerns to Bender. He was accommodating but cautious, no doubt familiar with the kind of guests who were having affairs or dodging creditors. He agreed to have someone check Matt's room and call me back. It took him fifteen minutes.

"I'm not sure what to tell you, Mrs. Drobyshev," he said. "Your husband's room is empty. No clothes or suitcases. It appears as if no one has been in the room since housekeeping made up the beds this morning."

"But he's still registered?"

"Yes, until Friday. Perhaps he decided to take the children on a side trip without checking out and is planning on coming back."

"Do people do that?"

"Well, yes, if our guests want to keep the special weekly rate. They'll often go over to Busch Gardens in Tampa or someplace like that for a night and not bother to tell us."

I didn't know what else to ask, so I thanked him and hung up. It wasn't like Matt to do something like this. On the edge of panic, I phoned Jill and told her the situation.

"Come on, Luce," she said. "Don't get yourself all worked up. I'm sure there's a perfectly reasonable explanation."

"Like what?"

"Like what the manager said about going to Busch Gardens. Or what you said about visiting his friend in Palm Beach."

"But he would've called, wouldn't he? You know Matt, he never forgets *anything*. Do you think I should call the police and find out if there were any accidents reported?"

"No. Well, maybe it wouldn't hurt to check if it would make you feel better."

I called the Orlando Police Department. They had no record of any serious accidents either with Matt's name or with unidentified persons. The officer took my number and called back ten minutes later to say that he had inquired with the state police and their search had come up empty as well.

"There's nothing you can do except try to relax," Jill said when I reported back to her. "Have a glass of wine and go to bed. I'm sure it'll all work itself out tomorrow."

Griffin called to check in. Like Jill, he thought I was overreacting.

I managed to get a decent night's sleep, but the minute I woke up I started worrying. This was the first time I could remember that Matt had let me down. That was a testament to his character, but his unwavering *rightness* had always felt like a reminder of what I could not be for him. Maybe now he'd decided to turn the tables and let me see how upsetting it could be when someone disappointed you and left you hanging.

I was pouring myself a cup of coffee when the phone rang.

"Mrs. Drobyshev. This is Ernie Glickman, the general manager at the Royal Palm Hotel in Orlando. I'm following up on the conversation you had with our night manager. Have you heard from your husband and children yet?"

"Not yet. I'm very worried. I contacted the Orlando police to see if there might have been an accident, but…I don't know. It's not like him not to call."

"Well, our records show he is still a registered guest in our hotel. I don't mean to alarm you, but I checked with housekeeping, and they informed me that no one has been in the room since the beds were made up Monday around ten-thirty in the morning."

"*Monday?*"

"Yes, our staff leaves complimentary chocolate mints on the bed pillows every day when they've finished making up the room. I've spoken personally with the housekeeper on that floor, and she distinctly remembers that the candy, along with the rest of the room, was untouched yesterday morning. It appears that your husband and children have not stayed here the past two nights."

"Oh my god. I don't...Have you...?"

"I'm not sure what to tell you, Mrs. Drobyshev. As I said, your husband is registered with us until Friday. There's no unpaid balance on the room. Perhaps he decided to go elsewhere without informing us."

"Or informing *me!*"

"I'm sorry," Glickman said. "We've left a note in the room asking him to call the front desk immediately if he returns."

I hung up. I was standing in the kitchen with a cup of coffee in my hand. For hours I'd been grasping at the possibilities, hoping one of them would make sense; then my heart stopped as I thought of something Matt had said Sunday night. He told me he was taking the kids to a water park the next day. But Sarah couldn't go swimming with her cast on. I leaned against the counter, my knees weak as if I were dizzy, but my mind was perfectly clear. I threw my coffee cup and watched it shatter against the wall.

"He's *gone*, Jill," I screamed into the phone. "Matt's taken the kids. Nobody's seen them."

"Wait! What? What do you mean?"

"He's kidnapped them. He left the hotel without checking out."

"Please, Luce, try to calm down. Tell me exactly what you found out."

I told her about the call from the hotel manager. "The hotel room's empty. Matt and the kids haven't been there since Monday morning. When I spoke to him Sunday night, he said they were going to a water park the next day. But don't you see? He must've been lying. Sarah can't go swimming with a cast on her arm."

"I don't know. I—"

"*He's fucking disappeared, Jill!* He's never going to let me see my kids again."

"Stop. Please. Let's try to think this through. There has to be a reasonable explanation."

"I need my kids, Jilly. I need to hold them."

"I'm coming right over, Luce. I'll be there fast as I can."

Three yellow-and-white striped canisters were on the counter beside me. I stared at them for a moment, then swept them onto the floor. Matt had said they'd been one of his mother's favorite possessions, but he would have left them in Butler if it wasn't for me. Since the funeral he had gone home only once to deal with her things and settle her estate. I was the one who sent Christmas cards to Uncle Joe and Aunt Sally. Matt *never* talked about his mother, never even hung her picture on the wall. I'd always assumed it was too painful for him. Now I saw his bloodlessness; he could simply turn the page and move on, just as he did with that boy whose arm he'd broken. He told me there was a moment when he really wanted to hurt the kid, an instant when he could have stopped himself but didn't. I remembered how he had felt guilty for a day or two then had seemed to forget about it. I hadn't thought about that incident for a long time, until now. I should have brought it up when he was blaming me for Sarah's broken wrist. Was that his justification for stealing the kids, her accident on the trampoline? He was quick to condemn me for my faults without ever seeing his own. In my mind I kept hearing him say, *So long, Luce.*

It was a warm summer day, but my teeth were chattering. I went upstairs and put on a pullover and a pair of sweatpants. From the bedroom, I called work and said I wouldn't be in. I told Tillie I had a problem but couldn't explain it now, and she obviously heard something in my voice that kept her from asking me anything more. Thank God Jill was coming. I couldn't be alone.

I suddenly thought of Thorny in New York. His secretary told me he was in a meeting, but I said it was an emergency and I needed to speak with him immediately.

"Daddy! Listen. I need your help." I tried to be clear and direct, explaining what I was sure was going on. Matt and the kids were getting farther away every minute. "Please don't think I'm crazy. This is *real*, Daddy. I know it in my heart."

There was no hesitation in his voice. "We have people here at the firm who can deal with this sort of thing. Keep your phone line open. I'll have someone call you within ten minutes."

It took less than five. A man from the Pinkerton Detective Agency asked me a few questions; then he said he would be sending someone from their Boston office within an hour to interview me and get photographs of Matt and the kids.

I went back downstairs. When Jill came, she didn't try to offer

any mitigating explanations for Matt's whereabouts. We were cleaning up the mess from the broken canisters in the kitchen when the
Pinkerton man arrived. He and Jill and I sat in the living room. I
gave him several photographs of Matt from last summer and a studio
portrait of Sarah and Nathan I'd had taken on a whim at Sears a few
months before. I told the detective about Matt's not calling and what
the hotel manager in Orlando had said about the room being empty.

"Can you find them?" I said.

"Let's not get ahead of ourselves, Mrs. Drobyshev. It's Wednesday;
your husband isn't due back in Boston until Friday. With a little
luck, he'll call today with some lame excuse and all this will be a
welcome waste of time."

"In other words, you think I'm overreacting."

"No, not at all. You were wise to get us involved so quickly. If
he *has* abducted the children, the sooner we start looking, the better
chance we have of finding him. Meanwhile, I'm going to have to ask
you some questions to see if we can come up with anything else that
could help our investigators."

The interview was exhaustive. I tried to be brutally honest. If the
detective or Jill—who knew most of it but was undoubtedly hearing
some of my starker admissions for the first time—thought I was a
lousy wife and mother, I didn't care. I was past the point of lying
about any of it; I just wanted to see my kids again. The detective
took copious notes. He said it was important to know that Sarah had
a cast on her arm because it made her stand out and people would
remember her. Before he left the house, he got paged on his beeper.
He asked if he could call his office in private, and I showed him to
the study.

When he came out, he said, "Well, I wouldn't call it good news exactly, Mrs. Drobyshev, but it's a start. Airline records show that your husband and children took a flight to Memphis, Tennessee, Monday morning."

"Memphis?"

"We'll get our people down there on this immediately." He stuffed his notes in his briefcase. "Memphis. Smart move. Middle of the country. Means we'll have to cover a lot more ground." He was thinking aloud; then he looked at my face and realized his mistake. "But don't worry, we'll find them."

"*Will* you?"

He forced a reassuring smile. "We're good at what we do."

I called Thorny and told him what I had learned. He said Amanda was on her way to the city to meet him and they'd catch the next shuttle out of LaGuardia for Boston. I didn't try to act tough and tell them not to bother. Jill stayed with me until they arrived and promised to come back the next day. I was supposed to go to the movies with my friend Anita that evening, but I called her to cancel, saying I'd come down with a summer cold. I couldn't bring myself to broadcast what I so desperately didn't want to be true.

Griffin called at some point. He wasn't due back until Saturday. He offered to fly home, but I said he should stay and finish his business, everything would probably be resolved in the next day or two. Maybe I was testing him, hoping he'd insist on coming home. He said okay, he'd wait to hear from me. As I hung up the phone, some part of me realized I didn't want him here right now. In my mind I was already blaming him, thinking how none of this would have happened if he hadn't come crashing back into my life. Which was both irrational and true. As the day wore on, when I wasn't blaming him—or hating Matt—I was blaming myself. Hating myself, certain that everyone would be whispering about what a horrible mother I had been, saying I *deserved* to have the children taken away. Chances are most people already believed that anyway.

Every minute felt like an hour. I was chain smoking and chewing my thumbs raw, my mood swinging between catatonic silence and screaming rage. I couldn't eat, didn't want to sleep. Each time the phone rang, I was filled with a sudden hope, believing it was Matt come back to his senses. I wouldn't let anyone stay on the line for more than a minute, afraid Matt would call and get a busy signal and change his mind. Thorny spoke with the phone company Thursday morning and arranged to have a second line for outgoing calls installed that afternoon. Amanda called Tillie for me and explained the situation but asked her to keep it quiet for now. Tillie said I could take all the time off from work that I needed.

Late Thursday afternoon a man from the Pinkertons called and talked to Thorny. One of their detectives had spoken with a clerk at the bus station in Memphis who said she had sold tickets on Tuesday to a man she was certain was Matt. She remembered the little girl with a cast on her arm. Matt paid in cash. She wasn't positive, but she was pretty sure he bought tickets to Little Rock. The Pinkerton man said it was a huge break; his detectives were only two days behind and were going to start posting fliers with photographs of Matt and the kids. Thorny authorized them to offer a twenty-five-thousand-dollar reward to anyone with information that led directly to "the recovery of the children." That was how the Pinkerton man wanted it worded; he wanted to make sure we didn't call it a kidnapping.

Matt and I had agreed he could take the children on vacation to Disney World. Flying off to Tennessee wasn't something we'd talked about, but as long as he brought the children home on Friday when he was supposed to, it would be hard to claim that he had broken any laws.

"Oh my god, Daddy," I said. "Twenty-five thousand dollars."

"Don't worry about the money, sweetheart." He put his arm around me. "We want to catch the son-of-a-bitch. That's all that matters."

I was awed by the way he had taken charge of the situation and touched by his concern. It was so much more than I had expected, and I think he may have even surprised himself. He was not a doting father or grandfather, but this violation had struck a nerve. This wasn't the usual Thornhill fiasco, someone screwing up with their foibles and bad habits; this was an assault on the whole family. As I watched Thorny's steely resolve, I understood for the first time why he'd fared so well on Wall Street.

On Saturday, after the deadline had passed, Thorny and I went to see the Boston police. We were careful not to mention that Matt had been a cop, fearing they would automatically close ranks around him and put us at a disadvantage. If the sergeant who listened to our story recognized Matt's name, he didn't let on. He laced his fingers over his broad chest and pretended to be interested.

When we were finished, he said, "Listen, folks, I sympathize with you. I really do. I can see how hard it must be for you with all this waiting. But you have to understand, he hasn't been gone that long.

Cases like this usually resolve themselves in a couple weeks. The parent gets tired and runs out of money; the kids are whining to go home. So he calls some friend or family member who talks him into doing the right thing. Bottom line is, your ex-husband was supposed to come back yesterday. I know it seems like a long time to you, but we have to let this thing run its course."

Thorny said, "Couldn't your department get in touch with your colleagues in Orlando, where the children were staying last? Or Memphis? We know their father took them there."

"I'm gonna be honest with you, sir. Police departments don't have the manpower to run around dealing with stuff like this. Do you have any idea how often some parent gets ticked off and takes off with the kids? We're talking about beaucoup cases. There are hundreds of them here in Boston every year. We file a missing persons report and hope for the best. If our officers ran around trying to chase those people down, we wouldn't have any time left to go catch the bad guys."

I wanted to spit on him. Since when were kidnappers not the bad guys?

Thorny said, "Do you think we should contact the FBI?"

The sergeant shrugged. "Good luck with that."

That afternoon the man from Pinkertons called. He said they'd gotten hundreds of leads, most of which proved to be dead ends. But one had come in from a motel clerk in Arkadelphia, Arkansas, who recognized Matt and the kids from the flier. She said Matt was growing a beard. He registered for the room under the name of Gerard Betz and stayed Tuesday night. He was driving a blue 1977 Chevy Malibu. The woman from the motel said there was no reason for her to take down the license number—the motel didn't require that from their guests—but she remembered the car because her brother had one just like it. Using this information, the investigators were able to trace the car to a dealership in Little Rock. The used-car salesman remembered Matt well and said he'd paid cash for the car. He was also able to give the detectives the license number.

Thorny thanked the Pinkerton man and reminded him that Matt spoke Spanish so he might be headed for Mexico. Not to worry, the detective said. They had people south of the border where Matt and the kids would stand out more than they did in the U.S. With all the information they'd gathered, the Pinkerton man didn't think it would take long to track him down.

I tried to feel confident. Looking at the Rand-McNally atlas, I traced the road from Little Rock to Arkadelphia with my fingertip and followed it down into Mexico. There were still moments when the entire situation didn't seem real, as if Matt were engaged in a grotesque practical joke.

Jill arrived with her kids, all three of them bright-eyed and rosy-cheeked. She had been coming to see me every day. Amanda paraded the kids out into the backyard while Jill and I talked in the kitchen. I poured some iced tea for her and told her what the Pinkertons said.

"They'll find them," Jill said. "I know they will."

"Do you really think so, Jilly?"

"Absolutely. I really do."

I began to cry for the seven hundredth time. Jill reached across the table and held my hand. "I know it's hard, but you have to stay positive, Luce. You *have* to."

"I know." But in my head I was screaming, Can't you see this is killing me? You have it all, you mindless sow—devoted husband, perfect kids, vice-president of the La-fucking-Leche League. My life is a total wreck. Half the time when you look at me I know you're thinking it's all my fault. And it *is*. It really is.

"Jill," I said softly, "did Matt ever...? I mean, you two have always been so close. He never said anything to you about...you know, doing anything like this?"

"Oh, Lucy." Her eyes filled with tears. "I love you. You're my best friend. How could you even think such a thing?"

"I don't know I don't know I don't know." I rocked in my chair and covered my face with my hands. "They're *gone*, Jilly. Really gone!"

Chapter 26
Matt

"Can we go to IHOP for breakfast?" Sarah said. "Mommy likes to take us there."

I looked at my watch. It was quarter to seven Monday morning, our bags packed and ready to go. "Sure. We have time before we go to the airport. I saw one just down the road."

"We're going on another airplane?"

"Yep, we're going to a zoo. A big zoo."

Nathan said, "I wanna see monkeys."

"Sure, we'll see lots of monkeys and lions and tigers and polar bears. You guys'll love it."

Sarah said, "Are we coming back to Disney World?"

"No, honey. We've been on all the rides and stuff. Let's go have some new adventures."

"Okay."

I was relieved. I was afraid she was going to balk or start asking questions about why we were leaving here and going on an airplane that wasn't taking us home. "Did your arm itch last night, hon?"

"Just a little."

"Well, let's sprinkle some more baby powder under your cast this morning just in case."

I looked around the room to make sure I had everything. Then we walked down the hall to the elevator. I was carrying my bag and Nathan's over my shoulder and pushing him in the umbrella stroller. I had gotten a small suitcase with wheels for Sarah that she could pull herself, Sundae strapped on top of the suitcase with a bungee cord.

There was a teenage bellhop at the concierge's stand by the door. "Need some help with the bags, sir?"

"No, we're fine, thank you." It was a stupid mistake. I should have gone out one of the back doors to the parking lot. Chances were the boy wouldn't remember us. He probably saw hundreds of guests a day. Still, I had to be more careful. I hadn't checked out of the room so it would seem like we were still staying at the hotel.

The kids asked for pancakes with strawberries and whipped cream at the IHOP. I said fine. Anything to keep them happy. This wasn't the time to take a hard line on what they ate. There was a jar of crayons on the table and paper place mats for them to color. As we waited for our order, I kept chiding myself for that brief exchange with the bellhop. That was actually my second stupid mistake. I had told Lucy we would be going to a water park today. I was trying to sound casual, in no rush to get off the phone. From the hotel window, I happened to be looking down on the blue neon sign for Cleo's Splashatarium, and the lie came slipping out. How could Sarah go to a water park with a cast on her arm? Fortunately—or, rather, true to form—Lucy didn't pick up on it.

I parked the rental car in the regular lot at the airport and locked it. The agency would discover it eventually. I had made the decision to go to Memphis before I left Boston. I heard they had a good zoo, which would be nice for the kids and make them feel like they were still on vacation. My next stop was still unplanned. From Memphis, I could go in any direction. I had no specific route or destination in mind. I figured I'd make it up as I went along, as if the randomness of our journey would make us harder to find. When I booked the airline reservations on the phone last night, I had been worried about using our real names for the tickets. I had a fake Massachusetts driver's license, but it didn't match the name on my credit card if the agent at the airport asked for my ID. A single man with two small children paying cash for one-way tickets could raise a red flag with the airline. It wouldn't matter if the authorities began their search in Orlando or Memphis. I'd just be spending a few more hours as Matthew Drobyshev.

It was strange watching myself turn into a criminal. All the stealth and paranoia. The last two and a half weeks in Boston had been incredibly stressful. I slept no more than two or three hours a night, wrote down almost nothing on paper. I had never been a good liar, and sometimes when I talked to Lucy, I was afraid she could see inside my head. The things that concerned me most were money and how I would go about changing our identities.

I actually had plenty of money. With some wise investment advice from Thorny, I'd managed to more than double my mother's life insurance payout in five and a half years. I had nearly a quarter of a million dollars, and the divorce settlement let me keep it all. My investments were mostly in stocks and mutual funds. Once I made up my mind to run, I sold everything and transferred the money to my bank account. The trick was making sure I had access to it in my new life. I couldn't convert the money into cashier's checks or stock certificates because they had to be made out to a specific individual, and I didn't know what name I'd be using. I considered asking Uncle Joe to hold the money, or my old friend Sandor, whom I didn't see much anymore but still felt close to. I knew I could trust them, but doing so would put them in a compromising position if the police came around and started asking questions. Javi had become my best friend, but I couldn't tell him I was abandoning DSC. I made sure the books were immaculate and left him with a schedule of upcoming trips and detailed client records.

In the end, I felt that it was best to have all my money in cash, but I didn't want to risk carrying it all with me and having it get lost or stolen. On the Sunday before I left for Disney World, I drove up to Monadnock State Park in New Hampshire and buried four plastic watertight containers, each holding fifty thousand dollars, in separate locations, and made a carefully drawn map. The rest I took with me, almost thirty thousand dollars in hundred dollar bills.

I wasn't quite sure how I'd go about creating new identities for the kids and me. I'd seen TV shows about people using some dead person's name and birth date, but I didn't have time to explore that angle. Besides, I needed to do it for all three of us. I tracked down a small-time criminal from my days as a cop. For a thousand dollars I bought a fake driver's license and three blank Massachusetts birth certificates, complete with the state seal, knowing I could fill them in with any names I wanted.

The kids loved the Memphis zoo. We had dinner and stayed in a motel room nearby. Lucy wouldn't know we'd gone missing yet, but I was already starting to look over my shoulder. Tuesday morning I bought bus tickets for Little Rock. I paid cash and didn't have to give the clerk my name. Nathan and Sarah fell asleep sitting side by side on the bus, while I was across the aisle from them with an empty seat next to me. I looked out the window at the green fields of Arkansas, a state I had never been to. The man in the row in front of me was snoring loudly. I glanced down at my feet and noticed a brown leather wallet. I assumed it belonged to the snoring man and had slipped under his seat. I picked up the wallet and found it was stuffed with cash. The man went on snoring. Tucked among the business cards and credit cards was a Tennessee driver's license. Unlike the licenses in most states, it had no photograph. The man's name was Gerard Betz. I slipped the license into my pocket. Betz awoke and stretched his arms over his head.

I stood up and looked over the seat. "Excuse me, but I think you dropped this." I handed him the wallet.

He gave it a quick glance to make sure the money was there. "Jesus, thanks, my friend. I woulda been up the shit's creek without a paddle." He pulled a fifty-dollar bill from the wallet. "Can I offer you a token for your honesty?"

"No, no. Please. You would've done the same for me."

He didn't ask twice. "'Course I would. That's what makes this country great, right? People bein' good neighbors. Doin' the little things." He offered his hand to shake. "Thanks again. What's the name, friend?"

"Dan. Dan Roble." My old pal from high school, the first name that popped into my head.

"I'm Gerry Betz." He was forty-three according to his license but looked much older. Sun-tortured skin and huge veiny nose. "Where you headed, Dan?"

279

"Little Rock."

"Business or pleasure?"

"Family." I shook my head. "Definitely not pleasure. I have my two little ones with me."

"Say no more, my friend. I got three ex-wives and doin' my best to make it four. My problem is I'm a *romantic*. I just can't do like these young people nowadays, takin' all the good stuff without makin' any promises."

"Those promises can get expensive."

"You're tellin' me." He laughed. "I guess that's why they sound like prayers. You feel so damn good when you're sayin' them. Then you just go back and do what you always done."

"Daddy?" Sarah said. "My cast is itchy."

I asked a man in the Little Rock bus station if he knew of any good used car dealers. He directed me to a Chevy dealer a short cab ride away. I had already decided to use Betz's license for identification instead of my fake Massachusetts ID. It would probably be days before Betz missed it, and he wouldn't think to ask if someone had used it to buy a car. It took me less than twenty minutes to pick out a blue 1977 Chevy Malibu, which cost six hundred fifty dollars. For an extra twenty the salesman said he could have all the paperwork back from the registry in two hours.

"How'd you break your arm, sweet pea?" the salesman asked Sarah.

"I flew off the trampoline," she said proudly.

"Awright! Does it hurt?"

"No, just itches."

I took the kids to a small amusement park, and we spent the night at a motel in Arkadelphia. I doubted if Lucy would do anything more than shrug when I didn't call that evening as I promised I would. She'd assume I forgot or was being spiteful. It wasn't like she really wanted to talk to the kids. Asking me to call was just a way for her to act like she was being a good mother. She was too busy fucking Griffin to think about anything but herself.

The air conditioner in the motel didn't work very well. It must have been over ninety even after the sun went down. I kept scratching my neck. I hadn't shaved since Friday. My whiskers were flecked with gray. Legally, I still wasn't a fugitive, but I looked like a bandito on the run. In the morning I shaved a distinct line under my chin to make it clear I was growing a beard.

Sarah picked up a brochure for the Arkadelphia Aquatic Park from the rack in the motel lobby. "This looks like fun, Daddy. Can we go there today?"

"We'll see."

The woman behind the desk said, "Whatcha do to your arm, punkin?"

I didn't like the way the cast kept calling attention to Sarah.

We had a great time at the water park. Nathan was timid about most things, but he loved the water. I let Sarah get her cast wet so it would be easier for me to remove later that evening. The doctor said she'd have it on for a month. It had been three and a half weeks, but taking it off a few days early wouldn't do her any harm.

When we got back on the road, I felt a strong pull south toward Mexico. But I figured that's what Lucy would expect, so I headed west instead. I stopped at a motel outside of Norman, Oklahoma. The sun and water had tired the kids out, and they both fell asleep shortly after dinner. I cut off Sarah's soggy cast with a pair of surgical scissors I'd bought at a pharmacy. I kissed her and rubbed some lotion on her dry, flaky skin. I could still hear Lucy dismissing the broken arm as the kind of thing that happens to kids every day. As if Griffin bouncing on the trampoline at the same time as Sarah wasn't the cause. I watched television with the sound down low and reminded myself of all the reasons why she couldn't be trusted with the children.

We spent one night in Wichita, another in Kansas City, where we went to see the Royals play the Twins. Sarah kept asking to talk to Lucy. I pretended to call and leave messages on the answering machine. I held the phone out and told the kids to say I love you, Mommy. Saturday morning I was keenly aware that I'd passed the deadline for returning. Lucy would have figured out there was a problem by now. I had no idea what she would do. Or *could* do. I doubted if she'd be able to convince the police to start looking for me immediately. They had bigger fish to fry, but my paranoia kicked in to high alert. I had purposely stayed off the interstates and stuck to the back roads, careful never to go over the speed limit. I didn't want to get stopped for some routine traffic violation and have some local cop get suspicious.

After three days the car had taken on a lived-in quality—road maps on the dashboard, toys and trash scattered about, one of Nathan's T-shirts, wet with drool from a recent nap, air-drying on the seat. My beard had begun to fill in. It definitely made me look older, maybe a bit more mysterious. In the late afternoon both kids were cranky and kept asking when we were going home. I stopped at a Dairy Queen in Bloomfield, Iowa. We got ice cream cones and went to the weedy picnic area around back. Three teenage girls were sitting at the next table feeding peanuts to a squirrel. The animal would scamper up close, hesitate, then quickly take the nut from their hands. When Nathan tried to say *squirrel*, it sounded like *curly*, and that became the animal's name. One of the girls let Nathan take a turn feeding him. As Curly was about to snatch the peanut, Nathan got so excited he lunged forward and the squirrel scratched him on the finger. Nathan howled. The scratch was tiny, barely enough to draw blood. One of the girls ran into the Dairy Queen and came out with a first-aid kit. She put some antiseptic on the scratch and covered it with a Band-Aid. Another girl picked him up and started swinging him around to get him laughing again.

When the girls left, I said, "We're lucky you only got a little scratch, Natey. Does it hurt?" He shook his head. "I'm sorry. I shouldn't've let you feed him."

Sarah said, "It was an accident. Curly didn't mean it."

"That's right," I said. "Do you know what an accident is, Natey?"

"Bad."

"Yes, accidents are bad. And they happen so fast, when you're having fun and least expect it."

"Like flying off the trampoline," Sarah said.

"Exactly." I'd been obsessing for the past three days, trying to come up with a context in which to frame my story for the kids. Now it began to unfold like it was telling itself. "That accident didn't turn out so bad. Just a cracked wrist. But if you had fallen a different way, it could have been much worse. You could have hit your head on the swing set or broken your neck like that boy from Katydids who crashed into a tree with his sled. Now he's paralyzed and can't walk."

"Christopher," Sarah said. "His mother brought him to visit us in his wheelchair."

"Yes, that's so sad." I didn't know how much of this Nathan was taking in, but Sarah understood the gravity of the conversation. "Listen, kids, this is really, really hard to tell you. I've been worried because I couldn't get in touch with your mother. Last night when you were sleeping, I made some phone calls and I found out there was a terrible accident. Your house in Jamaica Plain? The one where you live when you're with Mommy? It caught on fire and burned down."

Sarah's eyes widened. "From smoking?" Her question reaffirmed my fears about Lucy.

"Yes, from smoking. I guess Mommy fell asleep and left a ciga-rette burning." I pulled Sarah onto my knee. "Sometimes an ash drops, and it's just a little tiny spark. Then suddenly it catches fire, and everything burns really fast. The firemen came but there was nothing they could do. No one could get out of the house...and Mommy died."

"Nuh-uh," Sarah said. "You're telling a fib."

"I'm sorry, sweetheart. It's true. Mommy's dead."

"Don't *say* that!" She tried to claw my face. I clutched her arms and held her tight. She stopped struggling and began to sob. Nathan looked confused. Then all three of us were crying and hugging. An elderly couple who were about to sit down at the next picnic table gave us a concerned look and walked away.

I got the key for the bathroom and took the kids in and wiped their faces.

Sarah said, "Did Griffin die in the fire too?"

I hadn't thought about him until she asked. "Yes, he did." I'd have lit the match myself.

"And Rory?"

"Yes, I'm afraid old Rory is gone too. It's what they call a total loss, honey. Everything is gone. Pictures, toys, books, clothes. Good thing you brought Sundae on the trip with you."

Nathan said, "I want Mommy."

My heart was breaking. This was the cruelest thing I had ever done. Monstrous. Unforgivable. Necessary.

Sarah said to me, "Is Mommy up in heaven now?"

"Yes, Mommy's in heaven with the angels, smiling down on us."

We got in the car and drove on. Sarah whimpered. I touched her cheek, and she took my hand and squeezed my fingers.

From the backseat, Nathan said, "Play the radio, Daddy."

I looked at Sarah with questioning eyes to ask if it was okay. She nodded, her lips pinched as she fought off the tears. I turned on the radio. "You pick, Sar."

She scooched forward in her seat and pressed the buttons till she found a station she liked. Nathan seemed to love any kind of music, but she was a rock 'n' roll girl. A song by The Police came on, "Every Breath You Take." She knew all the words. Nathan tried to sing along too. I knew there would be more tears, but the two of them were already adjusting to life without their mother. I was living proof that a child could have a great upbringing with only one parent. Who knows what sort of father mine would have been? He might have been a bully or a bigot. One thing for certain, I didn't spend my youth slouching around, bemoaning how miserable my life was without him.

Sarah said, "Are we going to go back home, Daddy?"

"No, sweetheart. Everything's changed. Not like it was before. It would be too sad for us to go back to Boston." It was the only true thing I'd said.

∞

We spent another four days on the road. I took the kids to another amusement park, a carnival, and a county fair—busy places with lots of families where we wouldn't stand out. The days tired them out, but the nights were harder. Sometimes they woke up and cried for their mother. Both of them began to wet the bed. I needed to find a place where we could stay for a while and settle into a routine. Small towns were out of the question. Too many people asking questions, wanting to know where you were from. The anonymity of a big city offered a much better chance to slip quietly into a new life. Next stop Chicago.

On the bulletin board at Loyola University, I saw an ad for a furnished apartment for six months starting July first, which was only a week away. The professor who was subletting the apartment had a wife and two small children, so the place was ideal for the kids and me. It was in a large building with lots of people coming and going. I could tell the professor was desperate to find a tenant. Perhaps he sensed a little desperation in me. We'd left Boston for Disney twelve days ago, but I felt like we had been on the run for months. I got a motel room while we waited for the apartment to be available. Not an hour went by when I didn't worry about getting caught. It seemed remote, but I kept thinking the authorities might be able to trace me through the Chevy Malibu, so I put it in a covered parking lot and began using cabs and public transportation. The day before we moved into the new apartment, I drove to Milwaukee, removed the license plates, and left the car parked on the street with the keys in the ignition, no identifying papers in the glove compartment. The kids and I rode the train back to Chicago. Another adventure for us.

"You know what?" I said on the train. "We're living in a new city now. We're moving into a new apartment. I think we should pick new names."

"Pretend names," Sarah said.

"Yeah, but we can keep the new names if we like them."

Nathan did his ET impression, and we started calling him Elliot. Sarah wanted to be Alex Owens like the girl in *Flashdance*. The movie was rated "R," but that hadn't stopped Lucy from taking her to see it. Sarah loved to bop around to the video of the theme song when it came on MTV. I chose Adam for myself. I liked the name and the not-so-subtle idea of being a new man. Owens seemed like a good last name. Common enough but not too common. One day some girls at the playground teased Sarah and said Alex was a boy's name. She got upset and wanted us to call her Mary. Then Rachel. Then Eloise. Some names didn't last an entire day. Finally, I suggested she go back to Sarah and make it different by dropping the *h*. She liked that idea. Sara, Elliot, and Daddy (Adam) Owens. It became a game, using our new names. We corrected one another if we slipped up. In a few weeks we no longer had to.

I bought an old typewriter and filled in the birth certificates. I left the middle names for the kids blank. I kept Sara's birthday the same. She was turning five in mid-July, and I didn't want to try to convince her that she misremembered the date of her birthday. For Elliot, I changed it from late January to early February. For their mother's maiden name, I wrote Lucille Anne Padley. I typed in my mother's October birthday for my own, which made me a month younger.

With my new identity and established address, I applied for a Social Security card. For all my paranoia, I knew enough about government bureaucracies to know that a low-level clerk buried under mountains of forms in a neon-lit cubicle would not launch an investigation to inquire why a thirty-three-year-old man had never needed one before. A few weeks later, my card came in the mail. Using my new name and Social Security number, I got an Illinois driver's license and bought a three-year-old Jeep Cherokee.

Sara and Elliot adjusted well. They stopped wetting the bed, and I took them shopping for new clothes and toys. They rarely mentioned Lucy. When they did, it was mostly Mommy liked this or Mommy used to let us do that. One day Sara asked if we could go visit Nanda and Thorny. I told her Nanda had gotten sick again, like she did the day the police stopped her, and now she was in heaven with Mommy. I said Thorny was too busy at work to see us. She got sad for a minute and didn't ask again. For little children the world is a mysterious, magical place unencumbered by logic or doubt. They believe in the Easter Bunny and the Tooth Fairy. They believe that Santa Claus flies around in a sleigh with a sack full of Hot Wheels and Barbie dolls and Darth Vader sabers, delivering gifts to millions of children in a single night while pausing at virtually every house for a snack of cookies and milk. But a child's magical world isn't always kind and good. There are monsters and dragons, ghoulies and ghosties and things that go bump in the night. For every prince charming and fairy godmother, there's a witch or a troll or a hungry wolf lurking in the shadows. For every Peter Pan there's a Captain Hook. They believe what their parents and other adults tell them. No doubt the kids would ask me questions about Lucy when they got older, but by then they would have only hazy memories of the life we'd left behind. They were Sara and Elliot Owens now. Day by day the make-believe world we created over the summer became more real. I didn't say much about Lucy, but when I did I praised her to the hilt. She was already becoming a legend—attentive, patient, creative, amusing. The perfect mother they never had.

I registered Sara for kindergarten and found a day-care center for Elliot. He was shy, and I wanted him to meet other children.

I missed working. It was tough to leave the courier business when things were going so well, to say nothing of the equity I had built up in the company. But I didn't dwell on it. I was determined to push on without regrets and got a job as a laborer with a construction crew. Then I met a master carpenter named Paolo Agrillo, who agreed to take me on as his helper. I explained that I was a widower with two small children. I said it in a way that implied it was a painful subject, and Paolo wasn't the type to ask more. I liked working with my hands, and Paolo was happy to teach me. He said that every piece of wood was alive, and our job was to make it sing.

The professor's wife kindly left me a list of babysitters. One was a teenage girl who lived on the fifth floor of our building, and Sara and Elliot took a liking to her immediately. I began to treat myself to an occasional Saturday night out at the movies. One evening I stopped in a club and struck up a conversation with an attractive woman. She gave me her phone number, but I never called. I didn't want to get close to anyone who might start asking questions.

As the weather got chilly in October, I began to worry about the cash I'd buried in New Hampshire. I wanted to get it before the ground froze. Regardless of whether I flew or drove, I didn't want to take the kids to the park with me when I retrieved the money, and I couldn't leave them alone in a motel room. Hiring a stranger in New Hampshire to look after them for a few hours was out of the question. It would be better to have them stay in Chicago while I went east. But I was wary of leaving them with a teenage babysitter in Chicago, even if it was for only one night.

I mentioned my problem to Paolo in a casual way, not saying why I needed to go back east. Paolo had a big Italian family. He said one of his daughters or daughters-in-law would be glad to take care of Sara and Elliot, there were so many cousins floating from house to house they'd hardly notice if two more were added to the mix. I told him how grateful I was. Paolo, Javi, Sandor, Uncle Joe—I'd always been lucky to find friendship and guidance from other men. I felt bad thinking how, in the end, I'd abandoned them all. Not Paolo, not yet, but it was only a matter of time.

I told the kids I had to go away overnight on business. Elliot got a little clingy, afraid perhaps that I would disappear like his mother. But Sara reassured him, and Paolo's grandchildren distracted him as I slipped out the door. Going back through Boston was out of the question. I had no desire to return to the scene of the crime. Instead I flew to Albany and rented a car. Then I drove to New Hampshire and retrieved the money easily, no FBI agents sitting in the trees with binoculars and loaded weapons waiting to apprehend me. Halfway back to Albany, I got a motel room. I had been thinking about Uncle Joe before I left Chicago. Sitting in my room that night, I wrote him a long letter explaining what I had done and why. I told him I was sorry I couldn't contact him personally and hoped he'd understand. In the envelope I included the key for the T-bird along with the title, signing it over to him. I told him exactly where it was located in Boston and said the rent for the garage was paid up through the end of the year. The next morning, I mailed the envelope from a little town in Vermont.

Sara liked school and made friends easily. Elliot's day-care center was excellent. I loved working for Paolo. Things were going well, but I couldn't shake the feeling that my past would catch up with me. One day a man stopped me on the street, and the instant before he began asking for directions, I was sure he was going to say my real name. Every time I relaxed and let my guard down, some sixth sense seemed to slap me awake. In November I considered looking for a new apartment in Chicago in anticipation of the professor's return, but something told me it was time to move on. I couldn't put my finger on it, only that I had a vague sense that the net was closing in.

As we were loading our stuff into the car a few days after Christmas, the wind stinging our faces, I said to the kids, "Enough of this cold weather. I think we should go find some sunshine."

Sara gave me a funny look, then said, "Okay, Daddy." She seemed to want to get back on the road as much as I did.

Chapter 27
Lucy

Y ou have to eat something, babe," Griffin said. "Why don't you take a shower? Put on a nice outfit. I'll take you out to dinner."

I shook my head. It was a Wednesday, June 29, nineteen days since I last saw Sarah and Nathan. I was living on coffee and ginger snaps, smoking three packs of cigarettes a day; my fingers were chewed to open sores. I had probably lost ten or twelve pounds but didn't have the energy to step on the scale to find out. Sometimes I'd wander around the house saying the children's names aloud, as if they were playing hide-and-seek. I went into their rooms and sat on the floor and read their books, wound up a music box, buried my face in the sheets on their beds and inhaled the sweet smell of their bodies.

Griffin came by in the late afternoon and said, "Let's go out to dinner tonight. It'll do you good. I'll take you to Maison Robert."

"Please, Griffin, no. I can't." Can't get dressed, can't eat, can't imagine leaving the house knowing the telephone might ring.

Amanda was upstairs taking a nap; Thorny had gone back to work in New York but stayed in contact with the Pinkertons. The detectives had been so positive in those first few days after the abduction.

They'd posted thousands of fliers with pictures of the kids and Matt (including a mock-up of him with a beard), but aside from that motel in Texas, they didn't get a single credible lead. *It's a big country,* the Pinkerton man said. *We're dealing with an ex-police officer. He obviously knows how to cover his trail. I'm guessing he's already changed his name again, maybe ditched the car. Frankly, at this point, it's going to take some luck. A slipup on his part or some vigilant citizen who recognizes him and the kids from one of our fliers.* All of this must have been costing Thorny a fortune.

"Please, Luce," Griffin said, his voice tipping from compassion to frustration. "The kids aren't going to come back any sooner with you…"

"With me what? Sitting around feeling sorry for myself?"

"I didn't say that."

"But that's what you *think*. You think I should get over it. 'Oh shit, lost my kids. Bummer. Well, guess it's time to move on.'"

"You have to start taking care of yourself, Lucy. You need to be strong so you can see this thing through."

"You just want me to get strong so you can start getting laid again." He got a pained look in his eyes. We hadn't made love since the kids left. I said, "I'll suck you off if you want."

Griffin forced a smile. "I've got to run over to my apartment and get some paperwork." He put his hand on my shoulder like a pal. "I'll bring back some ice cream."

I hugged him around the waist and buried my face in his neck. "Thank you."

I poured myself a cup of coffee and sat at the kitchen table, and Amanda came downstairs and sat down across from me without saying a word. She looked as bad as I did, her body a shrunken walnut. She had started drinking again, not even trying to hide it. The weather outside was lovely, but we sat at the kitchen table, smoking and playing cribbage. Then Thorny showed up, and I hadn't even remembered he was coming. Like Griffin, he said it was time for Amanda and me to stop moping around. He told us to shower and get dressed, he was taking us out to dinner.

At the restaurant Thorny said there was nothing new from the Pinkertons. After the police had turned us away, he began trying to get the newspapers interested in the story. *The Globe* balked, but an editor at the *Herald American* was intrigued by the idea that Matt was an ex-cop. Last Thursday, six days after the kids were due home, the paper had run a short article on page five along with the studio portrait of Sarah and Nathan I'd given the Pinkertons, Sarah with one arm around her brother and the other holding Sundae. The caption beneath the photo read: *Where Are They? Sarah Drobyshev, 4, and her brother Nathan, 2, have been reported missing by their mother.*

Ex-cop disappears with children

A former Boston police officer has been reported missing by his wife, along with their two children. Matthew Drobyshev, 35, was last seen when he picked up Sarah, 4, and Nathan, 2, on Friday, June 10, to take them on vacation to Disney World.

The children's mother, Lucy Drobyshev, 32, of Jamaica Plain, told investigators her husband and children were due to return on June 17. They had a brief telephone conversation two days after he departed, and she has not heard from him since.

Authorities say they currently regard the matter as a domestic dispute between the parents, who are separated and share custody of the children. Sources say relations between the couple were extremely bitter during their initial breakup but had improved in recent months. Their divorce agreement will not become final until next year.

A police department spokesman said he did not believe the children were in danger or that there had been any foul play. No criminal investigation has been initiated at this time.

Matthew Drobyshev was a Boston police officer for ten years before going into business with a private courier service. His former district commander said he served with distinction. Lucy Drobyshev works part-time in a restaurant.

I was livid when I read the article. The newspaper had taken the same stance as the police, calling this a domestic dispute instead of a kidnapping, as if this were simply a disagreement between Matt and me. Thorny had been trying to get them to run a follow-up article along with a picture of Matt, but so far they had refused. He offered to buy a full-page ad, but the editor said it was against the paper's policy, the *Herald American* was a news organization and couldn't let private quarrels play themselves out in the press.

The waiter brought our food to the table, and I found myself eating a little of the chicken breast and rice pilaf I had ordered. Amanda picked at her food and drank.

"Listen, Lucy," Thorny said. "I'm getting worried about you. I want you to go back to work, honey. It will be good for you. Help take your mind off things."

"I'm sorry, Daddy. I can't."

"Sure you can. Take another week if you need to, but..." He paused to make sure he had my full attention. "This isn't negotiable."

Or what? I almost said. I didn't think he would stop funding the search or rescind the offer of a reward. I wiped the tears from my eyes. Deep down I knew he was right. "Okay. I'll try."

"Good girl." He turned to Mom. "Amanda? You can stay up here in Boston for a few days until Lucy goes back to the restaurant, then I want you home. With me." She nodded tamely. I wondered how different our lives would have been all along if Thorny had been as involved and caring as he'd been in the last few weeks.

Tillie asked me if I wanted to work my way back into my job at Garbo's slowly and just come in one or two days a week. I said I wanted to try to tough it out and work full time but she should have backup ready in case I faltered. Her niece, who was home from college for the summer, had filled in for me while I was gone. By the end of the first day, I was so tired I thought I was going to faint, but Thorny was right, the work helped to distract me and made the time go by faster. The staff at Garbo's and many of my regular customers must have known what happened, but none of them said anything directly to me about the kids. That night I slept better than I had in a month. Amanda left two days later.

Griffin and I began to make love again. He, like myself, was expecting little, I suppose, and we got little in return. None of his old moves seemed to work. My sorrow had changed everything. It was like an open, cankerous wound, so hideous and painful and utterly perverse that it would draw us up short at the most intimate moments, as if it were impossible to ever find joy again.

One day Griffin showed up and said he had a surprise for me. He made me sit on the back steps with my eyes closed and said he'd be back in a second.

"Okay," he said. "Open them."

He laughed and placed a russet-colored puppy in my arms.

"Oooooh my goodness." I drew the puppy close and nuzzled my cheek on his soft fur.

"He's a mutt from the pound. They're always the smartest dogs."

The gift was so touching and so spectacularly wrong, I didn't know whether to cuddle Griffin along with the dog or call him a fucking moron.

Griffin said, "Maybe we can teach him to catch a Frisbee."

That line was a clincher, remembrances of our first date and that brindled dog on the banks of the Charles. The puppy had an adorable face with a black, punched-in nose. My eyes welled with tears as I thought of how excited Sarah and Nathan would be if they could see him and hold him.

I named the puppy Frodo. He was curious and excitable, but it only took a week to housebreak him. The following week Griffin hired some men to put up a stockade fence to enclose the backyard so we could let him run free. Frodo yipped at the squirrels and birds and tried to play with Rory, who kept her distance.

∞

July dragged on into August, the air so heavy it held you down like an unseen hand. Early one evening Jill came by with her kids—TK, Maeve, and Ryan—all of them with energy to burn. Jill and I sat on the back steps watching the two older ones bounce on the trampoline while Ryan chased Frodo around the yard. I lit a cigarette. I could feel Jill's silent admonition—she didn't like me smoking around the kids even when we were outdoors—but she didn't call me on it. I took a few puffs on the cigarette and put it out. Jill let out a weary sigh and wiped the sweat from her neck. She was wearing a sleeveless dress and sandals, her fleshy arms and swollen ankles a clear sign that she was pregnant again.

I put my hand on her knee and smiled. "You can tell me about the baby, Jilly. I may be a basket case, but that doesn't mean I can't be happy for you."

"Thanks. I'm sorry. I kept wanting to say something, but the timing never seemed right."

"Sure, I understand." It was only in the past week or two that I'd been able to step outside myself and see how gingerly people were treating me. No one wanted to see me crumble before their eyes. The fact that I was able to accept Jill's apology and not react to it with withering venom or abject tears seemed like a small step forward.

Matt and the kids had been gone for a little more than two months. The Pinkertons still had several detectives on the case, but there wasn't much for them to do except to keep circulating the fliers in various cities and towns and hope they got lucky; a father raising two small children on his own didn't automatically raise people's suspicions. Thorny and I were talking about it, and he said he understood the detectives' dilemma. With new names, Matt and the kids could be anyone. I said it didn't matter if they changed from Drobyshev to Betz or Smith or whatever, the kids wouldn't say their last names much anyway, but they would still be Sarah and Nathan. *It isn't just the last name, Luce,* Thorny said, *he's probably changed their first names too.* I hadn't allowed myself to think of that before. It seemed unspeakably cruel; Matt was erasing the children's past lives entirely at the same time he was erasing me.

I had spoken to Carla briefly on the phone a few times since the abduction but hadn't been to see her. One day she called and said she wanted to get together, it didn't have to be a therapy session in her office, she'd be glad to come to JP simply as a friend. I was moved; she sounded a little undone, as if she felt partly responsible for what had happened. We went for a walk around Jamaica Pond. It was odd seeing her outside the confines of her office. I had flashes of anger as we talked, but mostly I was despairing, portraying myself as Matt's lawyer had in the deposition—bad wife, bad mother.

Carla stopped and held my gaze. "It's not your fault, Lucy." I didn't believe her, but it was nice to hear her say.

"There had to be something I did that pushed Matt over the edge." I picked up a rock and tossed it into the pond. "Sarah's broken wrist, I guess. I shouldn't have—"

"Stop blaming yourself, Lucy. What Matt did was *wrong*. It was an act of insufferable hubris and spite. When the law catches up with him, he's going to pay."

"*If* they ever catch up with him."

"Come on, don't give up hope."

"You have to help me, Carla. I try to be strong, but how can I go on?"

"Do you want to start coming to see me again?"

I nodded, and she said, sure, as often as I like; she'd call when she got back to the office so we could set up an appointment. As she was leaving she gave me a hug.

"Have you been writing in your journal?"

"No, not a word."

"It's terribly painful, I know, but it's one of the best therapies there is. Don't hold back. Write whatever comes into your head.'"

That evening I got out the journal I'd started when I was going through the breakup with Matt. Carla was right; it had been great therapy and had helped me to sort out my thoughts and feelings about my failed marriage. I'd found it much harder to lie to myself with a pen in my hand. Things became much clearer when I saw myself making the same excuses over and over, or tried to avoid writing some truth I knew in my heart but didn't want to put into words. I guess that's why I had avoided writing anything since Matt took the kids.

The last entry I'd made was a few days before the abduction. I had written about how well Amanda had been doing since her drunk driving arrest. As I leafed back and read over some previous entries, a sickening thought came over me. What if Matt had found the journal in my desk drawer that night he came into the house with the kids? There was so much there to condemn me, so many ugly thoughts about him, all my doubts and insecurities about being a parent. Maybe that was when he decided to steal them.

I picked up a pen and wrote:

8/16/83 (2 months & 6 days gone) Please, Matt. Please bring Sarah and Nathan home. I won't press charges. I won't ask where you've been. I promise I'll be a good mother. Just let me hold them again.

That was all I could manage before I broke down.

8/19/83 (2 months & 9 days gone) I went to see Carla today. I talked and cried and raged at Matt. Raged at myself. I should have known what he was up to. He was so anxious to get away. I never should have let him take the kids to Disney World. If I hadn't been so fucking blasé and had insisted he call me every night, maybe…

The phone in the hall just rang, "the kids' line" as I call it now. I ran to pick it up, and it was some woman looking for a Mr. Fletcher. She apologized when I told her she had the wrong number, and I said it was okay. I've been trying to learn not to take my anger and disappointment out on other people. Every time that phone rings my heart starts beating a hundred miles an hour. I no longer believe that Matt will come to his senses and bring the kids home, but I keep thinking Sarah will call. I taught her the phone number in case she got lost. She's very smart and could have easily remembered the digits, but I wanted to make it fun and see if I could turn our phone number into a word the way businesses do in their advertisements. Call 1-617-PLUMBER or 1-800-RENT-A-CAR. Our number is 244-6673, which spells BIG NOSE. Sarah giggled when I told her, and she made up a rhyme: Big nose, ice snows, jiggy wiggy piggy toes. But I didn't explain to her about dialing one first or an area code. I didn't teach her about calling collect. I had warned her about the dangers of talking to strangers, the usual stuff you say about not taking candy or getting in someone's car. But I never said, Be careful of Daddy too. He's angry at Mommy and might tell you lies and say mean things about me and take you far away.

Sarah Caroline Drobyshev. Nathan Alexander Drobyshev. Where are you now? Who are you now? Sometimes I want to stuff some clothes in a sack, close the door behind me, and wander the country, searching for you.

One of the truths I couldn't dodge in my journal was that Griffin and I no longer fit. For me, he was a constant reminder of everything I'd done wrong. It was foolish to blame him for ruining my life, but he was the catalyst, and I harbored a secret belief that I'd get the kids back if he were gone. He had started spending most nights at his own apartment now, and our lovemaking was scant and lifeless. We tried to talk about the future but couldn't sustain it. At least he had enough sense not to suggest we have a child together. Sometimes he'd come by after work and go out in the yard and do flips on the trampoline in a dress shirt and tie. Our only real connection seemed to be through the puppy.

Griffin tried to talk me into going to Nantucket for the long Labor Day weekend. I made excuses, saying I didn't want to deal with the crowds or sit in traffic, but I simply couldn't imagine leaving the house for three days with the telephone untended. He kept pushing and I pushed back, but he had no desire to keep the fight going. We had come to a crossroads and both of us knew it.

He said, "I'd like to make it easy for you, Luce, but this is your call. I don't want to be the one to say it first."

"Say *what*?" I gave him a sad smile.

He smiled too. He opened a bottle of wine and poured us both a glass as if we were celebrating. "You could shame me into sticking around if you want."

"I know. For a little while anyway." I lit a cigarette. "Are you relieved?"

"Actually, I was trying to fall in love with you."

"That may be the most honest thing you've ever said to me."

"Never a bad time to start good habits, as my Uncle Baxter used to say."

"Is that the uncle with the Siamese named Minx?"

"The very same. I'm amazed you remember. Can you believe that old cat is still going strong? Twenty-three years old and blind in one eye, but her fur's still as silky as a kitten."

I laughed. "You and your stories, Griffin. Do you have any idea which ones are true?"

"I try not to get hung up on minor details, baby. Life's better that way."

I think we both felt a sense of relief that it was over, our losses dwarfed by the realization that we no longer had to try.

The morning after Labor Day, I stood by the open window in the kitchen, smoking and drinking a cup of coffee. Stray leaves and twigs were scattered on top of the trampoline, the swings on the monkey bars rocking gently in the breeze. Sarah always wanted you to push her as high as she could go, squealing with delight as the ropes jerked at the top of their arc. Frodo was in the yard digging a hole under the maple tree. Beyond the fence Nancy Prince's tomatoes were bright red on the vines. When the kids were still here, Nancy's daughter Lindsay, who was eight or nine, would occasionally come over and play with Sarah and Nathan in the yard. The blinds on the windows on the second floor were raised, and I could see Nancy sitting on the edge of a bed braiding Lindsay's hair. I refilled my coffee cup and cinched the tie around the waist of my bathrobe and sat on the porch steps in front of the house, watching the children go by with their backpacks and lunch boxes. Two girls smiled and said hi to me then quickly looked away. I didn't try to hide the tears that were rolling down my cheeks. Today would have been Sarah's first day of kindergarten.

2/4/84 (7 months & 25 days gone) Thorny has been encouraging me to take a vacation, someplace warm and sunny, blue ocean, white sand beaches, and piña coladas. He just wants me to get out of the house to try to take my mind off the kids. The Pinkertons say the case is still open, but I know they've stopped looking. Photographs of missing children have begun to appear on milk cartons along with their names and the date they disappeared. It's part of a nationwide campaign started by the parents of a boy named Etan Patz, who left to catch a school bus in Manhattan one morning and was never seen again. Thorny tried to get Sarah and Nathan's picture on one of the milk cartons. He was told they were not publicizing "family abductions" at this time. Apparently, there are about 200,000 of these abductions every year, but the focus of the milk carton campaign is on the kids who have been taken by strangers. It makes me angry to think that my case is diminished because I know who stole my kids, as if it's not a crime but a misunderstanding.

My old pal Cody crawled out of the woodwork the other day. We went to a movie then to the IHOP after and talked for hours and he made me laugh, which sometimes still makes me feel guilty. Cody is in love with a nineteen-year-old boy, unrequited so far. He says if it doesn't work out, he wants us to move in together and live in celibate bliss, cook great meals in the evening with show tunes playing on the stereo. I told him it sounds like heaven.

On my way into the Star Market, I saw a notice on the bulletin board for a group called GrieveWell. It said that anyone dealing with grief was welcome, but the primary focus of the group was for parents who had lost a child. Their meetings were at the Unitarian Church in JP, which probably meant there wasn't a strong push toward Jesus and the healing power of prayer. I'd gotten way too much of that from well-meaning souls over the past eight months. I wanted to believe God would send my kids home to me, but when I tried to pray, I felt like a fraud, asking Him for something only when there was nowhere else to turn.

I waited several weeks before going to my first meeting of GrieveWell. There were two men and six women including me that evening. The group had been meeting for about seven months. People were friendly and asked me if I wanted to tell my story and I said no, maybe next time. Two of the women, one black and one white, had sons who were killed in gang violence; one man's twenty-year-old son had committed suicide. There was a woman named Winnie who had come to her first session the week before. Her husband and two young daughters were killed by a drunk driver, which I remembered reading about in the newspaper, a guy plowing into them head-on on the turnpike. The driver, whose blood alcohol level was twice the legal limit, was driving with a suspended license and walked away from the accident with only minor injuries. Winnie, who was about my age and very well spoken, was a dean at Wheelock College. She said it was a shame Massachusetts didn't have the death penalty, which was what the man deserved, but the most he'd probably end up with was two or three years in jail for vehicular homicide. I'm not sure why, but I felt a bond with her—maybe it was her incandescent anger and the fact that she flayed her fingers like me—and I thought we might become friends.

At the next meeting, Vernon, the man whose son committed suicide, wanted to talk. His wife had recently discovered that her father, who died when she was seven, had taken his own life, but the family had kept it a secret from her. She had been blaming Vernon for their son's death, telling him he coddled the boy too much and hadn't taught him how to face the world like a man. Now she admitted there was a long history of depression in her family. Vernon said it felt like a huge weight had been lifted from his shoulders. He told us he tried to get his wife to come to the GrieveWell meeting with him, but she wasn't ready yet.

"This is a real breakthrough, Vern," Maureen said. She was the one who had founded the group and acted as its leader. "When a loved one dies, we often look for someone to blame—doctors, God, another family member, the deceased, ourselves. But we have to learn to put that aside. The key to healing is forgiveness."

"I'm never going to forgive the man who killed my husband and kids," Winnie said. "He is to blame. Completely."

"Like whoever stabbed my son," a black woman said.

Things got heated; Maureen let people vent. Winnie was so filled with rage her whole body quivered. I listened and didn't say anything, but after the coffee break I decided to tell my story. I left out some of the ugly details like the scene with Matt and Griffin in the bedroom but didn't try to mitigate my own culpability in the failure of my marriage. I told them I had made mistakes, but ultimately I didn't know why Matt had taken the kids.

People were kind and supportive. Most seemed surprised that the police had no interest in pursuing the case. One black woman snorted, saying the cops always looked out for themselves. She said the police weren't interested in solving her son's murder; they just figured it was one less gang-banger on the street.

Winnie was listening quietly. She hadn't spoken since the break. Finally, she fixed her gaze on me and said, "Excuse me, Lucy, but would you please tell me what the fuck you are doing here?"

I was stunned, unable to respond.

"Please, Winnie," Maureen said. "There's no need to be rude."

"Rude? What could be ruder than her coming here and whining about her missing children?" She glowered at me. "My husband and daughters are *dead*. You understand dead, don't you? I watched the undertakers lower their coffins into three black holes in the ground. It doesn't matter if your kids are in Texas or Arizona or China, they're still alive. They're out there somewhere. You still have *hope*."

Several people tried to intercede on my behalf, but I said, "No, wait, it's okay. I understand what she means." At least Winnie hadn't said I deserved my fate. To her, there was a pecking order in the world of grief, and mine was a second-class sorrow.

I said, "Winnie, what happened to your family is horrific. Unthinkable. That drunk driver changed your life in a split second and shattered your world into a million little pieces. Nothing will ever bring your husband and daughters back again, so you think I'm lucky. I'm sure you wish you could trade places with me because I still have hope. And you're right, I do. In some ways it's all I have. I wake up every morning and try to make myself believe today's the day I'll get my kids back. Sometimes I can almost see their faces as they come running into my arms. But nights are different. At night I sit at the kitchen table with my cigarettes and a glass of wine and ask myself a simple question: Am I still a *mother*? How can I be a mother with no children to call me Mommy? No little ones to hold in my arms? Maybe their father will come to his senses and realize the kids need me as much as I need them. Maybe he'll bring them back to me tomorrow. Or next week. Next year. I *try* not to lose hope. But here's my question: How long am I supposed to keep hoping? Two years? Five years? Twenty? Give me a number, Winnie. How long do I have to wait till I can be as sad as you are?"

Chapter 28
Adam

Encinitas, California—June 1996

T he graduation party had been going for about an hour. I put a fresh bowl of guacamole and tortilla chips on the picnic table and threw some empty soda cans in the trash. It was a beautiful June evening, the smell of sage in the breeze. The sun lingered over the ocean as if it didn't want the day to end. The band on the back deck was playing "Maybe Baby," Sara and her friends jitterbugging on the lawn. Some of the kids were still wearing their mortarboards, tassels swinging to the beat. The band called themselves The Indolents. What they lacked in talent they made up for in style—double-breasted chartreuse suits, flamingo pink shirts, and skinny black ties. The lead singer, Ajit Banerjee, liked to say his one goal in life was to be known as the Bengali Buddy Holly. Ajit had been Sara's on-and-off boyfriend since the tenth grade. On, as of this afternoon, though that could have changed by now. I was smart enough not to ask.

We lived in the hills north of San Diego about a mile from the coast. A stand of cypresses hid our small stucco house from the street. Unlike most of our neighbors, we had no garage or swimming pool, but the lot was nearly five acres—a broad expanse of grass sloping down to a grove of lemon trees. Hummingbirds darted among the flowers on the firebush in the daytime. Skunks and raccoons prowled the grounds at night. Real estate developers had offered me ridiculous sums of money to subdivide, but I never gave it serious consideration. This, I often reminded myself, was as close to paradise as I would ever get.

I had no idea where the kids and I would end up when we left Chicago. We spent five months in Phoenix then moved on to Seattle. From there we went to Houston, Miami, Atlanta. The longest we stayed in one place was eleven months. I liked each city in its own way, but something always made me leave. Sometimes it was an omen, like the couple I caught a glimpse of at Pike Place Market in Seattle who I could have sworn were Amanda and Thorny. Other times it was just a hunch, a feeling that it was time to go, though I was always concerned that a sudden departure might make people suspicious. The kids whined a little when we moved but got over it quickly. When we came to Southern California, I promised myself I'd stop running. Elliot was seven, Sara just turning ten. I wanted to create a stable environment for them. Let them stay in school from one year to the next and hang on to the friends they made. I felt like I needed some stability for myself as well. I had become a good carpenter and had ideas about starting a contracting business of my own. I told myself I wanted to meet a woman I could connect with, someone I could trust, maybe even marry. But that was probably a lie.

Most of the women I met were single mothers, divorcées whose children went to school with Sara and Elliot. Virtually every woman had the same reaction when she found out I was a widower raising the kids on my own. She'd give me a look of pity and admiration, then fall all over herself making offers to help. *Feel free to drop the kids off at my place anytime. Do you do your own cooking? I have some wonderful dishes I could teach you to make. If you ever need someone to talk to Sara about, you know, girl stuff…* I never ceased to be astounded how a woman could be kind and predatory in the same breath. My first serious involvement was with a legal secretary in Atlanta. She had big blue eyes and a body that turned my brain to tapioca. Her husband had walked out on her when she was seven months pregnant, and she had to keep taking him back to court for child support. We started spending a lot of time together. Conversations came easily. She was a Braves fan and liked to go to their games. She and her daughter occasionally stayed over at my place for the night, which was a first for me. But she was in a hurry. She wanted to move in together and start making plans. I guess I was running from her as much as anything when we left Atlanta. I told her I had a great business opportunity in California that I couldn't pass up, but she knew I was lying. She cried and said, *I was hoping you'd be different.* I said, *I was hoping so too.*

In the eight years the kids and I had been in California, I'd had three long-term relationships, but they all fizzled out. Sooner or later my girlfriend would tell me I just wasn't *there* for her. She'd say she wanted to get closer but could feel me holding back. I didn't talk about Lucy, but it wasn't uncommon for a girlfriend to accuse me of being hung up on my dead wife. She'd say she needed something more from me. Like love. Commitment. I accepted the blame and didn't fight back. Sometimes she'd suggest we go see a counselor, but I said I believed a relationship either worked or it didn't, you couldn't fix it by talking. Sooner or later she'd get frustrated and leave. I never asked her to come back. When she was gone I missed her the way I missed an old car, remembering the things I liked and forgetting the problems. I'd mope around for a month or two then start going on test drives.

My current girlfriend, Gwen, had been Elliot's eighth grade math teacher. She flirted with me on parents' night, but I waited till the school year was over before I asked her out. She was only twenty-nine, petite and sassy, and still believed in love.

I went in the house to call the pizza shop and check on my order for the graduation party. The man on the phone said the last batch had just gone in the oven; the delivery van would be there in twenty minutes. I stood by the open window in the kitchen. Out on the deck The Indolents segued into their theme song—a catchy rockabilly tune called "Unchained Malady."

> *My girl's depressed and anorexic,*
> *I'm bulimic and dyslexic,*
> *And we caught a little STD.*

> *But we got shrinks and pills,*
> *To cure our ills,*
> *And we're filming it all for MTV.*

None of it was true, thank heaven. Ajit and Sara's romance was famous for its melodrama, but they were great kids. He was a terrific soccer player and class valedictorian who would be going to Yale. Sara was yearbook editor and captain of the golf team. Seeing what other parents went through with their teenagers, I felt blessed. Sara and I were as close as a father and daughter could be. We bantered constantly, but it was all in fun. We liked to surf and golf and watch old movies together. We played fierce games of Scrabble and cribbage for penny a point. Most important, we talked. Sara confided in me and valued my advice—no topics off limits except Ajit and sex, which was fine with me. There was an unspoken trust between us. From the window I could see her laughing and dancing, the world at her feet. She was headed off to Stanford in the fall. I tried not to dwell on it, but I knew I'd miss her terribly when she left.

The Indolents finished their song and a cheer went up from the crowd.

Ajit bent toward the microphone. "Hey, all you high school grad-u-ates." The cheer got louder. He savored the moment, then put up his hand. "All right, all right, the night is young. Let's not get crazy." There was a trace of Calcutta in his accent. He took out a handkerchief and wiped the sweat from his dark, handsome face. "Now we'd like to slow it down a little. We have something new we've been working on. Something smoo-o-th and mellow." He played a soft jazz riff. "But we need a real musician to come up here and help us out."

I felt my heart catch, hoping.

Ajit looked to his left. Elliot walked across the deck slowly, oboe in hand, his eyes fixed on his feet. Ajit fluttered his handkerchief and bowed like a courtier. Whistles came from the crowd. Some of the girls called Elliot's name, affectionate and teasing. The yard went quiet as Ajit checked the tuning on his guitar.

"This one's by Elliot," Ajit said. "It's called, 'Ask Me Later.'"

He played the same jazz riff, this time with more feeling. One by one the other members of the band joined in. The first notes from Elliot's oboe were sweet and haunting, like a summons from an enchanted world.

Elliot was fifteen. He was tall and thin and shy, just finishing the ninth grade. Teachers said he was bright but unfocused. His schoolwork was sloppy and mediocre. Pressuring him didn't do any good. He was never flip or defiant but had a quiet, stubborn streak. Sometimes it seemed as if he were completely self-contained. He had a few pals in school but preferred to be alone. Sara was his only real friend and confidante. Much as I loved him and knew he loved me, I felt like I was always reaching out for him and he was pulling away. He had no interest in sports. I stayed up half the night one time teaching myself one of his video games, but he didn't want to play it with me. He enjoyed reading novels like *Dune* and *The Lord of the Rings*, but the oboe was his true calling.

When Elliot was in the fourth grade, a woodwind quartet gave a performance at his school. He came home and couldn't stop talking about the oboe. He said it sounded spooky, like the desert at nighttime. I bought a used instrument and found a teacher to give him lessons. Within a year the teacher told me his potential was unlimited. The teacher said, *It isn't just the fact that he has perfect pitch and can memorize long, difficult pieces. His technique is so nuanced and mature. The oboe is like a fickle woman—you have to know how to read her moods. Otherwise, all you get is screeching and whining.* He tutored Elliot for three years, then recommended a woman who was a professional oboist to help him get to the next level. Elliot studied with her for only a few months, then stopped going. He refused to say why. I couldn't get him to try a different teacher or go back to the first. He wouldn't join any of the youth chamber societies in the area or play in the school band. But he kept practicing, often as much as four hours a day. He had a stack of milk crates filled with sheet music, hundreds of cassettes and CDs. I bought him a high-quality tape player to record his own work. He picked up a used flute at a music shop and started playing that too. Most of the time he practiced in his room with the door shut, but some nights he'd go out on the back deck, as if he were inspired by the moon. When I praised him, he'd just smile and shrug. He'd never write a piece and say, *Hey, Dad, listen to this.* It was almost as if the music was his way of keeping a diary, playing for himself alone. This song with The Indolents was the first time he had ever performed in public.

I eased out the side door of the house. I wanted to find some inconspicuous place in the yard where I could watch him play. As I started to walk around the side of the house, a car pulled into the driveway. It was Gwen with the cake, late as usual.

"Hey, darling," she said, slamming her car door. "I had to—"

I tapped my lips with my fingertip. Gwen's eyes lit up when she heard the sound of the oboe coming from the backyard. She stood on her tiptoes and gave me a kiss.

"This is *amazing*," she whispered. "Did you know he was going to play?"

I grinned and shook my head. I took her hand and started to lead her to the backyard. Another car pulled into the driveway behind Gwen's. I looked over my shoulder. It was a dark blue Crown Victoria—unmarked, unmistakable. Two plainclothes detectives were sitting in the front seat. The driver cut the engine while he and his partner remained in the car, talking. What I felt wasn't fear so much as sadness. I had been expecting this day for thirteen years. I believed it was never a question of if but when.

Gwen squeezed my hand and said, "What?"

Long ago, I made myself a promise that when the authorities came to arrest me, I would hold my head high. Look them in the eye and acknowledge my real name, unbowed by what I had done. But when the detectives got out of the car, I was thinking, Please, not now. Not on a perfect day like this. As if there were a good time for the law to come and take me away.

One of the cops was a tall, caramel-skinned guy with a goatee. He was wearing a cream-colored linen suit, which probably cost a week's salary. His partner was a bald white guy in baggy pants and a rumpled plaid sports coat.

"Evening, folks," the tall detective said. "We're looking for the owner, Adam Owens?"

"Yes, sir. I'm Adam." My heart was trying to punch a hole in my chest.

The cop offered his hand. "I'm Detective Martinez from the sheriff's office. This is my partner, Detective Holloway." He nodded politely at Gwen. "Mrs. Owens."

"No," she said, raising one eyebrow, "but I'm working on it."

Martinez frowned, annoyed at himself for his small mistake.

"Gwen Landry," she said, grinning.

"I'm sorry for the intrusion," Martinez said, "but we got a complaint down at the station. Guess one of your neighbors feels the music's too loud."

I didn't respond. I didn't think any of my neighbors lived close enough to be bothered by the band. Besides, the police wouldn't send two detectives to check on a complaint about loud music.

Martinez cocked his ear. "Is that an oboe?"

I nodded. "My son Elliot." The song coming from the backyard was slow and melancholy.

"Man, I love that sound." He grinned. "You don't have any cobras back there, do you?"

"Definitely a few vipers," Gwen said.

The detective laughed. His partner leered at her and showed his yellow teeth. We stood there, listening. The song ended, and the kids in the backyard let out a big roar.

Martinez shook his head. "I don't know how anybody could complain about jazz like that. I'd pay good money to hear your boy play." He shrugged. "Just tell the band to turn down the volume a notch or two when they crank up the guitars again."

There was an awkward silence. I realized the detectives had not come to arrest me. But it was like that feeling you get in the middle of a bad dream when you're fleeing a wild animal or about to fall off a cliff and you begin to realize that the dream isn't real. You know you're safe—all you need to do is open your eyes—but the dream is so vivid something holds you back. You want to know what happens next.

The Indolents started playing "Crazy Little Thing Called Love."

"I'll go tell the boys," Gwen said.

"Thanks," Martinez said. "I want you folks to have a good time. Fact is, my son Preston's here at the party. I was in the station when the call came in and figured I'd take it myself." The light bulb went on in my head. Preston was the goalie on the soccer team and a good friend of Ajit's. The resemblance between father and son was striking.

We watched Gwen walk toward the backyard in her white cut-offs, her legs taut and tan from running. Elliot came around the side of the house with his oboe, and Gwen said something to him and gave him a hug. He looked our way, and Martinez waved him over.

"Congratulations, young man," Martinez said. "That's a terrific sound you got going."

"Thank you." Elliot shook the detective's hand but kept his gaze on the ground.

"Who wrote that piece you were playing? Sounded like something by Wayne Shorter."

Elliot looked up for a second, then dropped his eyes again. I couldn't tell if he was pleased or offended by the question. I had never heard of Shorter.

"It's one of his own," I said proudly.

Martinez did a double take and looked at Elliot. "You're kidding me. You wrote that yourself?"

Elliot shrugged.

"He's written dozens of songs," I said proudly.

"That's fantastic. You keep it up. I got a nephew went to the Berklee College of Music in Boston. Great school. He's a percussionist, studio musician in New York now. Plays with some of the best jazz artists in the world."

Elliot gazed at his oboe as if he were hoping it might speak for him. I wished I could give my son the confidence to smile and look the detective in the eye, but he muttered his thanks and turned and went into the house.

The detective said to me, "He get his talent from you?"

"I wish. It's a complete mystery. One of those lucky miracles, I guess. I've got a tin ear. His mother did too." I couldn't remember the last time I'd had such a strong feeling of Lucy's presence, as if the police in their routine mission had brought her along for the ride. "She died a long time ago."

I felt a twinge of guilt and let it go.

∞

Over the next few years, Elliot continued to be a slacker in school. None of the needling from me or his teachers did any good. He did enough to get by, unconcerned about his grades. He had his heart set on going to Berklee. I guess it was Detective Martinez who had put the idea in his head. When it came time to fill out applications, I told him I didn't want to pay a small fortune for him to go to a trade school three thousand miles from home.

"What do you mean, Dad? Berklee is the *best*. You won't believe how many great musicians have gone there." He rattled off a bunch of names. The only one I recognized was Quincy Jones.

"Yeah, I know. I've read their literature. But most students who go there don't even bother to get a degree. They spend all their time playing music and graduate with what they call a *professional diploma*."

"Don't worry, I'll get a degree."

"Why not go to a liberal arts college with a good music department?"

"And do what? Minor in astrophysics?" He rarely got sarcastic like that. "I'm a musician, Dad. That's all I've ever wanted to be since I was in the fourth grade."

"You know Berklee's cutthroat, right? They've got kids coming in from all over the world. Every one of them scratching and clawing, trying to grab that little brass ring."

"And you don't think I can compete?"

"No, I just think you're—"

"Lazy and irresponsible."

"I never said that."

"Whatever."

"I love your music, El. I know how much it means to you. I just want you to consider other options."

"Don't worry. I'm going to apply to other colleges. I probably won't even get into Berklee anyway. But I want to *try*. Isn't that what you want me to do, aim for the top?"

I liked his spunk, but I kept coming up with reasons and incentives to steer him elsewhere. My arguments were legitimate. He'd get a much broader education at a liberal arts college. But it wasn't just the narrow focus at Berklee that concerned me. I didn't want Elliot to go back to Boston. I couldn't shake the feeling that if Lucy saw him, even if it was just a casual glance on the street, she'd recognize him in an instant.

Chapter 29
Lucy

Boston—November 1999

On the Sunday after Thanksgiving, Zoe and Eric Underwood invited Jill and Terry and my beau William and me to their house for leftovers. The gathering had become a tradition for the six of us over the past few years, and Zoe could make leftovers seem like a gourmet meal.

As we sat around the dinner table talking, Jill said, "Is that a new necklace, Luce?"

"Mmm-hmm." I touched the string of carnelian stones. "A present from William." I leaned into him, and he squeezed my thigh under the table.

"It's lovely," Jill said.

"You need to stop that, my friend," Terry said. "It makes the rest of us guys look bad."

"Understood," William said. "That's the last thing she ever gets from me."

"Let me ask you, William," Terry said, changing the subject. "What do you think about this whole Y2K business? Is it just a bunch of scare tactics, or is the whole world going to come crashing down around our heads?"

William was the CEO of a high-tech firm that made widgets for the government, the kind of stuff he wasn't supposed to discuss even if the bad guys spirited him off to some Third World dungeon and pulled out all his fingernails.

Before William could answer, Eric said, "It's going to be a nightmare, mark my words. Computers crashing all over the globe, power grids shutting down. People won't be able to get cash out of the ATMs. Missile systems hiccupping all over the globe." Eric taught marketing at Harvard Business School and often acted like he knew everything about everything.

"We're selling passes to the bunker in our basement," Zoe said. "Five hundred dollars a night per person. Bring your own booze and cyanide capsules."

We all laughed, no one harder than Eric. Zoe was always the quietest person at the table, but she had a knack for zinging her husband on his more outrageous statements.

William said, "This Y2K stuff is much ado about nothing. Our biggest problem is what to *call* the new decade. Here it is, less than a month away, and nobody can agree on a name."

Everyone had an idea—the *aughts*, the *zeros*, the *O-ties*—which led to some very good puns.

On the way home William said, "Well, Eric succeeded in making an ass of himself again."

"I know. He can be insufferable. But do you see how he looks at Zoe with that boyish devotion and laughs when she cuts him off at the knees? It helps me forgive his pomposity."

"Is that what you want from me? Boyish *devotion*?"

"At the very least. Diamonds would also be appreciated."

William and I had been going out for three years. The two of us were more like pals than lovers. We met through an adult literacy program we were associated with—I gave my time and William gave his money. There weren't any fireworks, good or bad, between us, just a solid, comfortable connection. We had both been married twice and didn't want to make another mistake. I didn't like to think of us as cynics, more as realists who had lived and learned.

I'd met my second husband, Drew Lofton, in 1991. In the eight years since the children had been kidnapped I'd gone back to graduate school for a degree in library science and taken a job in a small private day school, leaving my summers free for travel. Drew and I met in the Château de Chenonceau in the Loire Valley, then found ourselves at the same restaurant that evening. He was traveling with his two daughters, who were in their early twenties. My instincts told me to decline Drew's offer when he asked me to join them at their table—I could see those girls had no interest in sharing their father's attention—but I have never been good at following my instincts, at least not the cautionary ones.

Drew's wife had died the previous winter, and he and his daughters had come to France to spread her ashes in a place she loved. I didn't give him my address or phone number that evening at dinner, but he remembered my name and looked me up when he got home. A professor of comparative literature at Boston College, Drew was the most well-read person I had ever met, someone who could snatch a quote from Molière or Goethe out of the air as easily as a nursery rhyme, but he was a wounded man. His wife had spent the last few years of her life spiraling into madness before committing suicide. Drew needed to talk, and his openness pulled me in. We dated for a year, and he asked me to marry him. I accepted without hesitation, but we were at odds over where to live. He didn't want to leave his lovely old house in Manchester-by-the-Sea; I was adamant about staying in Jamaica Plain.

My house, I tried to explain to Drew, was both a prison and a sanctuary. I believed that as long as I lived there, my children might come home and find me, never mind that they wouldn't have remembered the address or a single thing about it. I didn't maintain it as a shrine. I had redecorated their rooms and, except for a few treasured items, had given away most of their clothes and furniture, the trampoline and swing set. But the house still held the sounds of their laughter, the rhythm of Sarah's quick footsteps on the stairs, the soughing of Nathan's breath in the night. I kept their pictures on the mantel in my bedroom, though I purged them from the rest of the house. I didn't want any questions from people who didn't know what had happened to me, no reminders of so much sadness for those who did.

Do you have children? In some ways that everyday question was the most difficult for me. Saying yes inevitably led to more questions— *How many? How old? Where are they now?*—ones which I couldn't answer without telling my story or telling a lie. My story had no moral, no end, only sorrow and pain for me. If I answered by saying I didn't have kids, it felt like I was denying their existence, admitting they were gone forever. I had never found a strategy to cut off that question before it was asked. I knew that people were simply making conversation, but it could seem like an unwittingly cruel reminder of what I was missing. Each time the question required me to do a quick mental calculation: Who was this person? A passing acquaintance? A new colleague at work? How would my truthful answer change the way that person saw me? How would I undo the lie if I chose to tell one?

In the first year or two after the kidnapping, when I'd be at work at Garbo's or walk into a room full of people, I'd notice some woman—it was almost always a woman—give me a furtive glance and whisper to the person beside her. I couldn't hear the words, but I knew what she was saying: *That's her, the woman whose husband kidnapped their children*. I didn't know if she was saying it in pity or blame, but at least there was some comfort in knowing that she and the person she was whispering to were already aware of my story. Sooner or later, when I had to tell a new friend or lover about the kidnapping, it was easier for me to make it brief and direct, sticking to the facts and trying to describe the whole thing as if it had happened to someone else. The reaction was invariably a mix of outrage and sympathy and curiosity. But I had learned over time that my sorrow and loss, even my anger at Matt, wasn't something anyone else could share. They were mine to endure *alone*, and they touched me most deeply when they came unbidden—when I was brushing my teeth or sitting at a traffic light or trying to pick out a ripe avocado in the supermarket.

Drew knew about sorrow and loss as well as I did. The more we talked and fell in love, the more we believed we could pull each other through. He agreed to come live with me in JP, and we were married in a small ceremony in the fall of 1992.

Drew's daughters put on their plastic smiles for the wedding, but both of them had disapproved of our romance from the start. Plain, prickly young women, they were unhappy in their jobs and neither had a man in her life—no one except their father. They felt he had gotten involved with me too quickly after their mother's death, which, in retrospect, was probably true. Drew and I convinced ourselves that the girls' resentment would diminish over time, but it only became more entrenched. One girl moved to France and rarely communicated, while her sister contracted a mysterious illness that left her debilitated and unable to work. Drew worried about both girls constantly. I said they were acting like spoiled brats, and he and I began to quarrel about them. Things came to a head when he got a vituperative letter from his daughter in France, a litany of perceived slights and wild accusations.

"Oh, Drew, I'm so sorry," I said when I read the letter.

"This is how it starts." His face twisted in anguish. "They get paranoid and lose touch with reality." He was afraid the girl was contemplating suicide. "I should go see her."

I looked into his sad brown eyes. It didn't matter if his daughter was a manipulative vixen or mentally ill like her mother; either way the drama would keep escalating until she had won her father back or descended into madness.

"Yes, you should go," I said.

I can't honestly say if letting Drew go was an act of generosity or cowardice, good judgment or bad. The older I get, the more I realize the answer to most questions is: *All of the above.*

The second week in December, I was in the teachers' lounge when Lewis came in. Lewis was the vice principal and our de facto computer expert.

"Lewis," I said, "what do you make of this whole Y2K problem?" I had recently finished computerizing the checkout system in the library.

"Why, Lucy?" He smiled. "Don't tell me you're worried about overdue library books?"

"Just curious. There's been so many articles about it in the newspaper lately."

"Forget about Y2K. It's much ado about nothing."

"That's exactly what another friend said. I wonder if Shakespeare anticipated this."

"Absolutely. The man was prescient. This whole thing is a *tempest*"—he dunked a teabag in his cup—"in a teapot."

"All's well that ends well?"

"Exactly. Which is just *as you like it*, my dear." He had a devilish glint in his eyes, waiting for my retort.

I paused, stumped. "You win, Lewis."

He chuckled and sat down across from me. "I saw Amy Vogel's mother today, and she was singing your praises."

"Amy's a doll," I said. She was in the third grade and one of my reading junkies, kids who read on the school bus, in the lunchroom, outside at recess. They'd finish one book and immediately start another, like a chain smoker lighting his next cigarette off the last. I wanted every child to be an avid reader, so I set up a challenge to give them some incentive. Each student started out the year as a Walker; after finishing five books and handing in a short report on each, he became a Jogger. The next level was Runner, then Sprinter, Jet Pilot, and Astronaut, with a small prize at the end of the year for every student who made it to Sprinter.

329

JAMES WHITFIELD THOMSON

When I was studying for my master's in library science, I pictured myself working in a university helping professors with their research and tracking down rare books, but the market was tight when I got my degree, and I took a job at an elementary school in Arlington. I spent the summer boning up on children's and young adult literature and found I really enjoyed it. Once school began, I fed off the energy of the kids. I loved their wide-eyed enthusiasm and candid reactions to books. It was such a pleasure to read to them, to pause before some dramatic moment in a story, anticipating their gasps of horror or squeals of delight. Parents began telling me how much their children enjoyed story hour, so I set up an evening workshop to help them improve their reading skills and discover new books for their kids. The workshop was so popular I turned it into a regular course at the Cambridge Center for Adult Education. I felt like I had finally found my calling.

I finished my tea and asked Lewis if he'd come by the library some afternoon to make sure I was backing up my computer system properly, just in case Y2K was real. He said he'd be glad to.

As I was straightening up the library at the end of the day, Sophie Reardon hurried in to pick out a few books. Sophie was a second-grader new to our school this fall, a delicate Asian girl with silky black hair that hung down to her waist. She was reading well above grade level and working her way through Judy Blume and Beverly Cleary. At the rate she was going, she'd be an Astronaut soon. I considered inventing a new category for readers like her. Moonbeams? Shooting Stars?

Sophie came up to the front desk with *Double Fudge*.

"Can you please find another good book for me, Ms. Thornhill?"

"Of course." We went to the shelves. "Have you read *Harriet the Spy* yet?"

She shook her head.

"Oh, you'll love that one, honey," a woman said behind us.

We turned around. Sophie said, "Mummy!" and ran and gave her a hug.

I recognized the woman instantly. She was wearing a stylish black coat and a fur hat, wisps of gray hair framing her face. She had Sophie's red jacket over her arm.

"Hello, Winnie," I said.

"Hello." She had a confused look on her face. "I'm sorry, I've forgotten your name."

"Lucy." People had only used first names at GrieveWell. "Lucy Thornhill." I never went back to the group after the night Winnie rebuked me.

"Yes, of course," she said, though I could tell she was faking it, trying to fix me in a time and place.

"Let me check these books out for you," I said to Sophie.

I wasn't surprised that Winnie didn't remember me. When I met her, she was still in the throes of grief and rage, eviscerating strangers like me and probably her loved ones as well. Perhaps I should have pretended I'd never seen her before. What good would it do her to be reminded of our brief acquaintance all those years ago at such a painful time in both our lives?

While I checked out the books, Winnie helped her daughter into her coat. Sophie pulled a white wool cap from her sleeve and put it on her head.

"Sophie has been telling me how much she loves coming to the library," Winnie said.

I nodded. "She's a terrific reader."

As Winnie tucked a strand of hair under Sophie's cap, I saw the light go on in her eyes. "How are you, Lucy?"

"I'm well." I smiled. "Really well."

"Me too." She returned the smile, her gaze firm and steady, the look of one survivor to another, free of longing or surrender or guilt. "Would you like to go have coffee sometime?"

"Yes, I would. I'd like that a lot."

∞

Monday evening five days before Christmas I was sitting on the couch, reading, when Sam came into the room and meowed at me. He hopped up into my lap, and I scratched his head and said, "I know, baby. I know." My dog Frodo had died two months before, and Sam missed him as much as I did. I kept promising myself I'd get a new puppy, but I wasn't ready. The book I was reading was *Open Secrets* by Alice Munro, each story so rich it felt like a novel. The kids' line rang in the hall, and I sighed and put my book down. I no longer felt a shiver of hope when I heard that phone or came home and saw the red light blinking on the answering machine, but I had no intention of having it disconnected. The phone went hand in hand with my superstition about staying in the house, another link to Sarah and Nathan. *Big nose, ice snows, jiggy wiggy piggy toes.* There were rarely more than two or three calls a month; usually it was a blank message or a recording from a telemarketer or political candidate, one machine talking to another. If I was home, I didn't pick it up when it rang, just stood in the hall next to the credenza, waiting as I screened the call, listening to the sound of my own voice on the answering machine.

Hello, you have reached 617-244-6673. This is Lucy Thornhill Drobyshev, mother of Sarah and Nathan Drobyshev. I have not seen my children since they were kidnapped by their father, Matthew Drobyshev, sixteen years ago, in June, nineteen eighty-three. But I have never given up hope. Nathan was two and Sarah almost five when they were taken. If you have any information about my children or their whereabouts, please leave a message here, or you can reach me at 617-464-2539. You may also contact my attorney, Arthur Hoyt, at 617-237-8821. Thank you... Sarah and Nathan, I love you and miss you beyond words. Every morning I wake up believing that today is the day you will come back to me. Every night I try to find you in my dreams.

Most callers would hang up as soon as they realized they'd dialed the wrong number, though occasionally someone would listen all the way to the end and leave a message. Over the years I'd had people say *Good luck* or *Hang in there*. One woman said *Miracles happen*; another told me she'd remember me in her prayers. A few years after the kidnapping, a man left a series of messages so filled with venom they brought me to tears.

Tonight the caller waited to the end of my message. After the beep there was a distinct pause, as if the person were trying to think of something to say. Then the line went dead. There was no caller ID on the phone. I'd thought about getting it, but that was Pandora's box; every time there was a blank message on the machine

I'd probably feel compelled to call the number back. I went into the living room and tried to read my book, but I couldn't concentrate. I kept thinking someone was on the other end of the line, reaching out to me. I stretched out on the couch and looked at the ceiling, one of those nights when I wished I still smoked.

Chapter 30
Adam

Encinitas, California—December 1999

Sara spent the first semester of her senior year in Paris, studying and doing research for her thesis on Cézanne. I smiled when she first told me she was going to major in art history. I rarely spoke about our lives before we left Boston, so she was surprised when I mentioned some of the paintings I'd seen and transported on the job as a courier. I told her about Vermeer's *Geographer* and *View of Delft* and how much they had moved me. It made me wish I'd kept my collection of postcards of my favorite pieces of art to show her. I had stopped going to art museums after I took off with the kids, as if I were no longer me, or didn't want to be reminded of the life I'd left behind.

Sara came home from France Saturday afternoon a week before Christmas. I was supposed to pick her up at the airport, but she left a message on my cell phone telling me Ajit would meet her instead. They were like two lovers in a country song, unable to quit each other or get it right. Aside from Ajit's parents' disapproval of the relationship, I wasn't sure what the problems were. Ajit seemed quite jealous. It made me uncomfortable thinking Sara might be unfaithful, like Lucy.

She had been up for twenty-fours straight when she straggled in Saturday night. I dragged her out of bed at noon on Sunday and took her out to brunch. In the afternoon we played a round of golf. I held my own through the front nine, then she pulled away. I teased her about how I used to let her win. That lasted until she was fifteen. I'd only beaten her a few times since. I tried to get Elliot to join us, but he wouldn't even go to the driving range. Except for his music, he didn't have a competitive bone in his body. He was finishing up his first semester at Berklee. I'd tried to talk him into coming home for Thanksgiving break, but he said he was too busy. He had a paper to write and was playing in a jazz quintet called The Spendthrifts. At my insistence he was taking a full load of academic subjects. He seemed interested in a contemporary American history course in which they were studying topics like Watergate and the war in Vietnam. It gave us something to talk about in our once-a-week phone calls. I missed the sound of his music wafting through the house. With him and Sara gone, I thought I'd get to work on some long-overdue projects, like repairing the back deck and adding a second bathroom, but I spent what free time I had reading or watching TV. I was between girlfriends and couldn't find the energy to look for another.

Sara and I had a beer in the clubhouse after our round of golf.

"When's El getting in?" she said.

"Tuesday afternoon. Around two-thirty. You want to pick him up?"

"Sure. I can't wait to see him. Has he told you about his band?"

"A little. We talk every Sunday evening. He's not exactly the world's best communicator."

"He's a college freshman, Dad. He's got a million other things to do." She wouldn't let anyone say anything remotely negative about him, even if it was true.

"I take it he's writing you two or three long emails a day."

"He keeps in touch," she said, ignoring my sarcasm, which probably meant she felt as out of the loop as I did. She sipped her beer. "I think he has a girlfriend."

"Really? That's terrific." Elliot had always been shy around girls. I'd catch him looking, but he could barely say hi, let alone strike up a conversation. In his sophomore year a girl who had been a classmate of Sara's started flirting with him. I tried to caution him but he was already under her spell. They went on a few dates, and I think she may even have taken his virginity, but she lost interest quickly. Elliot was devastated and retreated back into his music. He went to his senior prom with a girl who was a wonderful violinist, but he said they were just friends.

Sara went off with some of her pals Sunday evening. I called Elliot, but he was busy studying for his last exam and our conversation was brief. I went to bed early. I'd been busy at work and hadn't even done any Christmas shopping yet. Not that I was complaining. The dot-com boom was in full swing and business had never been better.

When we moved to California, I spent two years working as a carpenter and getting to know other guys in the trades. Then I got my contractor's license and went out on my own. My time with the courier company had also served me well. I made up my mind to work with people who saw me as a professional. I wanted clients, not customers. I told my prospects I wasn't interested in being the low bidder. I said my goal was to turn their visions into reality and keep their hassles to a minimum. Within a year I had two three-man crews working full time. I paid good wages and held my workers to strict standards—safety first, no foul language or loud radios on the job, keep conversations with the clients to a minimum. I had made my share of mistakes in the ten years I'd been in business, but my company had a reputation for excellent work. Most of my jobs came through referrals from former clients.

On Tuesday I got home from work at five-thirty and heard the sounds of Elliot's oboe coming from his room. It sounded like something new. A sad, sweet melody, not the usual jangle of notes he'd been playing all summer before he left for college. Sara was in her room with the door closed. I tapped on Elliot's door, and the music stopped.

I poked my head in. "Welcome home, bud."

"Hey, Dad."

He had a wispy mustache and a little tuft of hair under his lower lip. I resisted making a crack about it. We gave each other a hug, and I asked him how his last exam had gone.

"Fine," he said.

"Whadya say we go to Limoncello's for dinner?"

"Sounds great."

Sara came out of her room and joined us.

I said, "I liked that piece you were playing. Is that one of your own?"

"Yeah, the last thing I turned in for my composition course. The professor said it needs work."

"Sounds beautiful to me. What's it called?"

"'Lost and Found.'"

"El?" Sara said, a threat in her voice.

He gave her a dirty look. "Whatever."

I glanced at her, then at Elliot. She was bossy and he was as stubborn as crabgrass. They didn't fight often, but when they did, things could get ugly fast. Cross her and she'd go for blood. "What's going on here, guys?"

"Nothing." Sara's eyes flashed at her brother. "Nothing at all."

Elliot said, "Everything's fine, Dad."

I shrugged. "I gotta go clean up. We'll leave for Limoncello's in an hour." I said to Sara, "You want to ask Ajit if he wants to come too?"

"Ugghhh. You must be kidding."

"Well, *okay* then." It was no use trying to guess what she was upset about. I'd probably find out soon enough. I headed down the hall, singing, "'Tis the season to be jolly. Fa la la la la."

Sara dominated the conversation at dinner. She talked about Paris and how much she loved it. She said she could see herself living there someday. I asked Elliot about The Spendthrifts. Besides him, they had keyboards, saxophone, guitar, and percussion. He said the group had been offered a chance to play a free gig at a small jazz club in Somerville.

I said, "Where'd you guys get the name?"

"Our drummer came up with it. He said when you give a performance, you have to give it your all. You know, spend everything you got."

"Who writes your music?" Sara said. "Is it mostly yours?"

"No, we all do. So far it's been great with everybody contributing. But it's easy to see why bands are always breaking up. People start bickering about whose stuff is better and what gets played."

When I asked about Berklee, he said the musicians there were so good it was intimidating, but I could see in his eyes that he was holding his own. He told us how much he liked Boston. I noticed Sara give him one harsh look during dinner, but they seemed to have put aside whatever they had been arguing about.

When we finished eating, I said, "You guys interested in a movie? Or we could go get a Christmas tree."

Sara said, "I've heard *The End of the Affair* is excellent."

"Ahh, Julianne Moore," I said. "I could watch her sleep."

"You may have to," Elliot said. "That movie has boring written all over it. I say we go see *Deuce Bigalow, Male Gigolo*."

Sara and I laughed.

"Laugh now," he said, pretending he was miffed, "but that movie's destined to be a classic."

"Like *Evita*," Sara said.

Elliot clutched an imaginary knife in his chest. In his hierarchy, Madonna and Andrew Lloyd Webber ranked alongside Hitler and Pol Pot for the evil they'd unleashed on the world.

While we finished dessert, we laughed and tried to name the worst movies we'd ever seen. We ended up going to *The End of the Affair* and all agreed it was wonderful.

When I came home from work the next day, Sara was in the kitchen taking a pan of cornbread from the oven. The table was set, a bowl of bean salad in the middle. Sophomore year of high school Sara announced she was a vegetarian and would be taking over our meals. I had never been much of a cook and relied a lot on pizza and

Chinese and Mexican takeout. Much to Elliot's and my relief, Sara's vegetarian phase didn't last long, but she became a wonderful cook. Shellfish stew, chicken tetrazzini, goulash that would have made Sandor proud, great salads with homemade dressings. A few of my girlfriends made snide remarks about me turning my daughter into a surrogate wife, but it sounded like jealousy to me. As far as I was concerned, it was a perfect arrangement. Sara liked being in charge; Elliot and I loved the meals she made for us. When she left for college, he and I fell right back into our old habits.

I went to the sink and washed my hands. I could hear the sound of Elliot's oboe coming from his room.

"I have to admit I was wrong about Berklee," I said to Sara. "It seems like it's really been good for him."

"Seems like it," she said, but the tension in her voice suggested something different.

I dried my hands and put my arm around her shoulder. "You cut yourself?"

She looked at the Band-Aid on her finger and shrugged. "Occupational hazard."

Elliot came into the room. "Hey, Dad."

"Hey, El. You guys have a good day?"

"Yeah, it was okay." I knew the way he said it that things still weren't right between them.

"Sit," Sara said, pointing with a spatula.

She took the lid off the frying pan on the stove and served us each a wedge of the frittata stuffed with cheddar cheese, onions, mushrooms, and broccoli—the kind of thing you'd pay twelve bucks apiece for in a restaurant. Over dinner she told us more about Paris and her research on Cézanne. She seemed a little manic. Elliot was quiet and distracted, which wasn't unusual. Sometimes he'd be looking right at you, but you could tell he wasn't there. If he were a cartoon character, there'd be musical notes flashing across his eyes. He cleared the dinner dishes from the table while I made a pot of coffee. Sara brought out an apple cobbler she had baked, and we all sat down at the table again.

"Dad?" Elliot said as I was pouring sugar into my coffee. "There's something I—"

"Elliot, don't," Sara said.

"I'm sorry. I have to."

"No you don't. You don't *have* to do anything. You promised you'd wait."

"I said I'd think about it."

"Well then, *think*, you selfish little shit. This isn't only about you."

"Hey, enough," I said. "Come on, guys. What's going on here?"

She glared at her brother and jabbed a finger across the table. "I'm warning you, El. If this whole thing blows up, I'll never forgive you."

He paused for a second, then turned to me. "I was in the library on Thanksgiving weekend, working on a paper for my contemporary history course. Our professor likes us to do original research, so I was going through some newspapers on microfilm, and I came across a photograph from the *Herald* that won a Pulitzer Prize. It was a picture of a young woman and a little girl and some flower pots falling from a collapsed fire escape. In the photo you can't see the ground or the top of the building, just the woman falling head first like she's doing a clumsy swan dive and the little girl with her arms and legs spread out wide. It said in the caption that the little girl lived but the woman died." He poked at his cobbler with his fork but didn't take a bite. "That picture got me thinking about our mother and how she died in a fire too, and I started going through the microfilm to see if I could find the story in the newspaper. You never wanted to talk about it, Dad, or tell us how it happened. I wasn't…I mean, I don't know. I just wanted to read about it and maybe find a picture of her in the paper. All I knew was the year she died. It took a long time to scan each roll of film. I'd almost given up when I came across this."

He took a piece of white paper from his back pocket, unfolded the paper, and handed it to me. It was a photocopy of a newspaper article with a photo of him and Sara as little kids. The caption read, *Ex-cop disappears with children.* I glanced at the story without reading it. My heart was a jackhammer. I couldn't have spoken if I'd tried.

Elliot said, "I probably wouldn't have noticed the article if wasn't for Sundae." In the photo, Sara was holding the llama in her arms. Elliot looked at me. "She still lives in Boston. In the same house in Jamaica Plain, I think. Her number is listed in the phone book."

Sara said, "I can't believe you've known about this for a month." She turned to me. "He only told me about it yesterday."

"What was I supposed to do, Sar?" Elliot said. "You were in Paris. It's not exactly something you can talk about long distance."

"So, you wait till it's three days before Christmas?"

I was trying to get my bearings and think of something to say.

I said to Elliot, "Have you contacted her?"

"Not exactly. I called the phone number Monday evening and got an answering machine. I wasn't going to say anything if she picked up. Not without talking to you and Sara first. I'm not sure why I called or what I was expecting. Maybe just to hear her voice. On the machine she says she hasn't seen her children since you kidnapped us in 1983. She asks people to leave a message or call her other number if they have any information about us." He swallowed hard. "Then she speaks directly to Sara and me, except she calls me Nathan. It's really sad. She says she misses us every day."

I laid the photocopy of the article on the table and smoothed the creases with my thumb. In the picture the kids looked so cute. I had only a few photos of them before Elliot was about six. Another caution, I suppose—a way to keep the past unseen.

"Tell us what happened, Dad," he said. "Why did you take us? Did she hurt us or something?"

I blew out a long breath, still struggling for something to say.

Sara said, "You're the best father ever, Daddy. You don't have a mean bone in your body." She pulled the sleeves of her sweatshirt over her hands, wriggling with anxiety and love. "I know you did what you had to."

I picked up the newspaper article and looked at it for about ten seconds and put it back down again. "Listen, you guys deserve answers. It's just I…I'm feeling a little overwhelmed at the moment. I need to clear my head." I stood up. "I want to go outside and get some fresh air. Just for five or ten minutes, that's all. Then I'll come back and we can talk. I'll tell you everything." I kissed Sara on top of her head. "Please, honey, don't be angry at El."

The air was clear, and the stars shone bright in the sky. I walked down to the grove of lemon trees. Perhaps it was just a defense mechanism, but I had always believed that one day I'd be caught. Some nights I'd lie awake and imagine myself in a courtroom, explaining myself to a judge and jury. I would tell them what I had done might be wrong in the eyes of the law, but not as a father trying to protect his kids. My children were in danger. Sometimes justice works too slowly. I *had* to act. Yet for all my fine reasoning, I never considered what I would say to Sara and Elliot. What did it matter what verdict a jury might reach when the worst penalty could come from my children? Did I assume I would never have to explain myself to them? Elliot wanted to know what had been taken from him, a reckoning between the life he'd had and the one that might have been. In time, Sara would want answers too. The irony was that in my attempt to comfort my children for their loss, I had turned Lucy into the perfect mother. Now I had to tell them the ugly truths, the same ones I'd so often told myself.

"Well, here goes," I said, my voice cracking a little. We were all sitting at the kitchen table. "You guys have been my first priority since the day you were born. You are my world. Everything I do comes back to you. The trouble is, I told you a huge lie and committed a crime. I told you your mother was dead, and I stole you away. I could lie some more and say it was the hardest decision I've ever made in my life, but the truth is, it wasn't that hard at all. I did what I had to do to keep you safe. Over the years I've tried to pretend that Lucy was a good, kind, loving mother, but she was not a stable person. She was incredibly irresponsible and self-absorbed. When we were going through the divorce, my lawyer got her to admit to all kinds of bad stuff in a deposition. I tried to get full custody of you kids, but the court wouldn't allow it. The law bends over backward to protect a mother's rights. Do you guys remember anything about her?"

"Not really," Elliot said. "Just a few things you told us."

"I remember she was tall and pretty," Sara said. "She smoked. She liked to read to us. She used to call me sugar pop."

"Do you remember Griffin?"

Sara narrowed her eyes, trying to recall. "The name maybe. Was that her boyfriend?"

"Yes, he was a creep. They did a lot of drugs together. She was involved with him for a few years after college. They broke up and I came along, and Lucy and I fell in love. I did anyway. I think she *tried*. She got pregnant, and we got married. As far as I was concerned, I was the happiest man in the universe, but Griffin was like a dark shadow hanging over us. Sometimes I'd just look at her and know she was thinking of him. He came back, and they started having an affair. I caught the two of them in bed together. They were both high as kites. There was an altercation, and he gave me this." I pulled the hairs apart to show them the scar above my ear.

"Oh my god," Sara said. "It sounds like a nightmare."

I nodded. "With you guys stuck in the middle."

"Do you remember when you broke your wrist?"

"A little bit. I remember how itchy my cast was."

"Do you remember how you got it?"

"I fell off a trampoline."

"You were on it with Griffin. He was probably stoned out of his head. Lucy tried to dismiss it as a simple accident, but I kept thinking how you could have sailed into the jungle gym or landed differently and broken your neck."

Elliot gave me a questioning look. "And the courts wouldn't do anything?"

"I didn't even report it. I told my lawyer, but he just shrugged.

It's ridiculous how biased the system is toward mothers. A woman has to be an axe murderer before she loses custody of her children."

Sara said, "Is that when you decided to take us? When I broke my arm?"

"That wasn't the half of it. Every time I turned around, it was something new. Lucy would forget to pick you guys up at day care, send you outside in the middle of winter without your hats and gloves. You remember Nanda, your grandmother? She got arrested for drunk driving with you kids in the car? I couldn't believe Lucy let you ride with her when she knew the woman was a total lush. One day I found a burn hole in a cushion on your mother's couch, the kind that goes all the way down into the stuffing. It's a wonder the whole place didn't go up in flames. Lucy and Griffin would smoke dope and get so wasted they couldn't see straight. I'd go on business trips for three or four days and be sick with worry the whole time I was away. I was afraid I'd come home and…" I shook my head. There were tears in my eyes.

"Thank you, Daddy," Sara said, tears in her eyes too. She came to me and put her arms around my neck. "You did the right thing. I love you so much."

I couldn't read the look on Elliot's face. "I want to meet her," he said.

"Why?" Sara said. "What good would it do? She means nothing to us."

He looked at me. "I understand you were trying to protect us, Dad. You were afraid you'd come home and find something terrible had happened to us. But think about her. She really did lose her kids."

"You can't do this, Elliot," Sara said angrily. "If she goes to the police, they'll arrest Dad for kidnapping and put him in jail."

"I'll tell her not to," he said. "I'll say if she does, I won't see her again."

I said, "You can't control what she'll do, El. Why do you feel you have to see her?"

"She's my *mother*, Dad. Maybe she's changed. You should hear that message on the answering machine. She's spent half her life waiting for me and Sara to come home."

Sara said, "I'm not going to let you do this, El."

"How can you stop me?"

She glared at him. "Let me put it this way. If you go see that woman, you and I are *done*. I mean it. I won't have a brother anymore."

Elliot looked at me, his eyes sad and his mouth tight with resolve.

"I don't regret what I did, El. I felt like I didn't have any choice. Not if I wanted to keep you guys safe. But you're a grown-up now. I raised you and your sister to think for yourselves. If you want to go see Lucy, I won't try to stop you. You're my son and I love you, simple as that. Sara loves you too. She's angry now, but she'll get over it."

Sara looked at me like I was the enemy and went to her room and slammed the door. Elliot and I couldn't think of anything to say, and he went off to his room as well.

I sat at the table alone, wondering what my future held. I probably should have gone into more detail about Lucy's failings, but no doubt there would be more time for that. Elliot's description of that message on her answering machine was poignant, but I couldn't dredge up any pity for Lucy. There were so many unforgivable things she had done. For the first few years after I'd left, I used to find myself going down the list. Not a fun exercise, but I guess it was my way of reminding myself that I was right to have taken the kids. In time those bad memories began to fade. But the one that stuck with me as vividly as any was the photograph I'd seen on the mantel the night I'd gone into her house—her and Griffin and the kids smiling brightly in the snow.

My cell phone rang. It was a prospective client calling to clarify a few items. While I was trying to rush her off the phone, Sara stormed through the kitchen and went out the door. I heard her drive off. The woman on the phone said she was ready to give me the job. I told her I'd come by in the morning to get the paperwork signed and pick up a deposit.

Elliot came out of his room and sat across from me at the kitchen table. "I'm going to go to see her, Dad. I booked a flight online."

"When?"

"I'm going tonight on the red-eye. It was really expensive. I used the credit card. I'll pay you back from my savings."

"I don't care about the money, El. When are you coming back?"

"Saturday, around one-thirty in the afternoon. It was the only flight back I could get. We'll still have Christmas together."

"Did you call her? Does she know you're coming?"

He shook his head.

"I don't think this is the best plan. You don't know anything about her life. She may be going away for the holidays. She might not even be there." He shrugged one shoulder, a stubborn look on his face. Once he made up his mind about something, wild horses couldn't make him change. I stood up and said, "I'm going to make more coffee. You want some?"

"Okay."

He was silent while I got the coffee going and sat back down.

"I'm not trying to hurt you, Dad. I'm really not."

"I can see that, El. I've known you for a long time." I grinned at my feeble joke. "I think I understand you pretty well."

"When I was growing up, even when I was a little kid, I always felt like I was *different*. Not a weirdo or anything like that. But we were always moving around, and I felt like an outsider, even in our own family. You and Sara are so close. For me...I don't know. It's like I keep trying to understand how I fit in."

His words stung. I didn't want them to be true. I was afraid I was going to break down. "Did you think I loved Sara more than I love you?"

"I'm not talking about more or less, some number you can record on a chart. I know how much you love me, Dad. You tell me all the time. But with Sara it's like you don't even have to say anything. It's just there—the way you think, what you guys like to do, the things that make you laugh. I'm not jealous. I'm just...different."

"Do you think you can find that connection with your mother?"

"I don't know. Yeah, maybe."

A better father would have said, *I hope you can.* But I said, "I don't want to lose you, El."

He gave me a sweet smile. "You'll always be my dad."

I smiled too, but I could feel him slipping away.

Chapter 31
Lucy

Wednesday evening, three days before Christmas, William came to JP and I cooked him his favorite meal of wiener schnitzel and dumplings, a reminder of one of his mother's specialties from his childhood. He and I hadn't seen each other much over the past few weeks as he had been working sixteen-hour days, trying to get out a new release of one of his company's widgets. Over dinner he told me they'd gotten over their last big hurdle and were on track to meet their deadline.

"That's great," I said. "Maybe you'll have some time to relax a little?"

"You bet. Maybe we could go away someplace next week. Fly down to some island for three or four days and lie around in the sun."

"No, we don't have to go anywhere. I'd rather stay here and sit by the fire and just hang out with you."

"Done. Let's start this evening."

He went into the living room to build the fire while I cleaned up the dishes. When I was finished, I dried my hands and called Thorny.

"Hey, Lucy," he said. "How's my little girl?"

"I'm great. William's here. We just had dinner."

"You guys still planning on coming down for Christmas?"

"Of course, Daddy. We'll be there in the early afternoon."

Thorny lived at an upscale retirement community called Deer Hollow. His mind was as sharp as ever, but his physical ailments were mounting fast—macular degeneration, heart problems, a painful old spine injury from the Navy that sometimes made it difficult for him to walk. It wouldn't be long before he would have to transfer to the nursing home wing of the complex. He and Amanda had sold their house and moved into the community three years ago. They'd barely gotten the pictures hung in the new place when she was diagnosed with pancreatic cancer. She refused all treatments and was dead in seven weeks. Deer Hollow women started buzzing around Thorny like mayflies, but he wasn't interested. *Your mother was the only woman for me,* he told me without a trace of irony. *She had as much spunk as Amelia Earhart. Just as pretty too.* I figured his prostate surgery a few years before her death had slowed him down with the ladies as much as anything.

I said, "You want to go to a movie or something before we have dinner? There are a few good ones playing."

"Sure, why not? I haven't been anywhere in days."

I made a mental note to work on ways to get him out and about when I wasn't around, maybe hire a companion who could take him into the city once in a while. I kept worrying that he'd fold up his tent and start to die. My brother Mark and his wife and their two children were coming home for a visit the day before New Year's, so that gave Thorny something to look forward to. Mark's wife was a Swedish physician with Médecins Sans Frontières, and they had spent the past few years living in Zambia. I was always glad to see

Mark and tried not to be resentful that I'd been handling all this stuff with our parents on my own.

I said to Thorny, "What're you reading these days? You want me to bring you some books?" Meaning books on tape. With his eyesight even the large-size print was a chore.

"Oh sure, something by that *Get Shorty* fellow."

"Elmore Leonard."

"Yeah, that's the one. Funny as hell. Kind of like eating chocolate cake with nails in it."

We spent a few more minutes on the phone. When I hung up, I went into the living room and cuddled up next to William on the couch. He'd thrown some sticks of palo santo on the fire, and its sweet aroma filled the room. So far I had managed not to fall into my usual pre-Christmas depression, each day getting a little harder as the holiday drew near, thinking about the kids and where they were and what they were doing—not kids anymore, of course, but young adults, eighteen and twenty-one. I was still unwilling or unable to believe they were gone for good, which in some ways was the hardest part of all, the insidious side of hope. That was what I was trying to tell Winnie sixteen and a half years ago. What I told her again when we went out for coffee last week. People say, *Don't lose hope, miracles happen,* as if hoping might have some bearing on the outcome. But hope can be such a cruel companion. Hope never lets you grieve and be done with it. Hope is the abuser you keep hoping will change.

Thursday was the last day of school before Christmas vacation. The kids were too excited to have story time in the library, so I concentrated on helping them find books to read over the holidays. It was mostly wishful thinking on my part—they'd be too busy with their new toys and games to get much reading done—but there were always a few who would come back from vacation and surprise me, not only having finished their library books but telling me about the ones they'd gotten as presents. After school I went to Harvard Square to do some shopping, then stopped in at the Class Report Office where I used to work so I could meet up with my old friend Anita. She and I had reconnected a few years ago after I ran into her on the street. The two of us went out to dinner and a reading of *A Child's Christmas in Wales*. Afterward, we had a drink so she could tell me more about how she'd been dumped by her latest beau. I sipped a glass of wine while she downed two margaritas and got so buzzed I insisted on driving her home.

It was nearly midnight when I got back to JP. On my way to the kitchen, I noticed the blinking red light on the answering machine in the hall. Two messages. My mind immediately jumped back to the call I'd gotten Monday evening, the one where the person hesitated before hanging up. Hope, my old nemesis, tormenting me again.

I pressed the button and the machine said, "Thursday, one fifty-four p.m."

"Hello," a young man said. "Hello, this is your son"—he cleared his throat—"Nathan." I let out a soft cry. "I'm sorry. I know how nervous I sound, but please don't think this is a hoax. When we left Boston in 1983, my dad told us you died in a fire, but I found out recently that you are still alive. I talked to him, and he told me what happened. I love him. He's been a great dad and all, but I... He said it was okay for me to contact you. You are probably at work now, so I'll call you back around eight-thirty this evening. Thank you. Bye."

I was standing by the credenza with my fists tucked under my chin. The machine beeped again and said the next call had come in at eight twenty-nine.

"Hello, this is Nathan again." His voice was more assured now. "I hope you haven't gone away for the holidays. I'll try to reach you again tomorrow morning. I called you on your other line but didn't leave a message. Bye."

Sam came into the hall and rubbed against my leg; I picked him up and listened to both messages again. The fact that the boy said it wasn't a hoax seemed to increase the likelihood that it was. There wasn't anything in his message that couldn't have been gleaned from my outgoing message on the answering machine, but he sounded so nervous, especially on that first call. Then there was the way he said, *I love him. He's been a great dad and all...* Somehow that made the whole thing seem true to me. But what about Sarah? Why didn't he mention her? Had something horrible happened to her? I was reeling, unsure what to think. I needed to talk to someone. My first thought was Jill, who had been through it all with me, but she went to bed early and I didn't want to scare her by calling so late. William was a night owl. I went to the kitchen and got the portable phone and dialed, and he picked up on the second ring.

"William?"

"Hey, honey, what's up? Are you all right?"

"I'm not sure. I went out to dinner and the theater with Anita tonight, and when I came home, there were two messages on the answering machine in the hall. You know, the one on the kids' line?"

"Okay."

"I'm going to hold the phone next to the machine and play them for you. I need you to tell me what you think."

After he listened to the messages, William said, "Lucy, this is fantastic. Amazing."

"Really? You're not suspicious?" Hearing the boy for the third time, I was convinced it was Nathan—his voice was so gentle and conflicted and yearning—but I needed reassurance. "Maybe it's a prank."

"No one is *that* cruel, Luce. Or that good an actor. You must be jumping out of your skin. Do you want me come over?"

"Yes, William, please."

He lived in Winchester, a half-hour away even with no traffic. This morning I'd left the coffee pot to soak in the sink. I filled it with warm water and rinsed it out and started a fresh pot. I noticed a reddish stain on the counter and sponged it off, then my eye went to a greasy fingerprint on the toaster. Moments later, still in my school clothes, I kicked off my low heels and turned into the white tornado, huffing loose hairs from my eyes as I scrubbed and mopped and shined, thinking, Nathan, Nathan, Nathan. Sarah? Then William came in the door and I ran to him and he held me and kissed my temple.

He went over to the answering machine and said, "I want to hear the messages again."

My heart sank. I was afraid that he'd thought of something on the way over that convinced him the calls were bogus. But he smiled as he listened and pumped his fist, and I felt giddy again.

I said, "Come on out into the kitchen. I made coffee. I don't *want* to sleep. I'm afraid I'll wake up and find out it's all a dream." He sat at the table, and I poured him a cup. "Sorry for how I look. I went a little crazy cleaning the kitchen, waiting for you to get here. I wonder what time Nathan will call in the morning. I'm so glad I don't have school. Not that I'd go if I did, of course. I wouldn't leave the house for anything, but I get scared just thinking about the fact that he might have called when I was away traveling or something, like last summer when we were in England." I had a sponge in my hand, wiping the counters again, too worked up to sit. "We were gone two weeks. He could have given up and disappeared again."

"Lucy, Lucy, relax. It's gonna be all right. He'll call tomorrow."

"I wonder where he was calling from. I wish I had caller ID on that line. Is that something the telephone company can do remotely? Just add to your line from the central office? I should call them first thing in the morning."

"You need to sloooow down, honey. Nathan is reaching out to you. Just give it time."

"That's easy enough for you to say. You're not the one who's been waiting for half your life, waking up every fucking morning hoping *somebody* will call. You can just sit there and...*Arrrgh.*" I threw the sponge into the sink. "Oh, William, I'm sorry. Sorry. Thank you for being so positive. I know you're trying to help. But if this isn't real. If this is..."

He stood up and put his arms around me. "Let's go to bed, hon. I'll listen to you talk all night if you want. Or maybe you'll be able to get some sleep."

We went up to the bedroom. As William held me, I started

talking about Nathan when he was a little boy, how he was so quiet and contented playing with his trucks and trains, rarely calling attention to himself while Sarah was bouncing around, saying, *Look at me, Mommy*. Where was she, my little sugar pop? William let out a soft snore. I cuddled up against him, and he pulled me closer in his sleep. But my mind was still churning, and I got up and went downstairs and listened to the messages I already knew by heart.

∞

I woke up at twenty past six, surprised that I'd gotten as much sleep as I did. I went down to the kitchen, and William was mixing scrambled eggs. He'd already set the table, and I sat down and took a sip of orange juice. Maybe he was waiting for me to go first, or perhaps we both felt it would be bad luck, but neither of us said anything about Nathan and the messages. William had to go to work. As he was leaving, he said, *Call me*, and I said I would. I wanted to shower and wash my hair, but I was afraid of missing Nathan's call. I thought about phoning Jill or Carla or Thorny, but I kept thinking it would be a jinx. I put on a pair of tights and a loose-fitting shirt and did a few yoga exercises to try to calm myself down; then I went back downstairs and started cleaning again, triaging the kitchen drawers, getting the dead bugs out of the crystal globes in the chandelier in the dining room. Each time I looked at the clock, I got a little more discouraged. Then the phone in the hall rang.

"Hello," the boy said. He paused. "This is Nathan. Is this…?" He didn't know what to call me.

"This is Lucy Drobyshev. Is it really you, Nathan?"

"Yes."

"I'm sorry to be skeptical, but I've had…People can be cruel sometimes."

"I know. I was afraid you might think it was a hoax. I asked my dad how I could prove it was me, and he said to tell you your first date was at the Café Budapest. He was wearing his police uniform, and you put a rose in your hair."

"Oh my god, it really *is* you." For a moment I was too choked up to speak. Through my tears I said, "There's so much to talk about. Where do we start?"

He laughed nervously.

I said, "You're all grown up now. Nineteen next month."

"I, uh…I thought my birthday was February second?"

"Actually, it's January seventeenth." What other lies had his father told him? I said, "Do you go to college now?"

"Yes, I'm a freshman."

"What about your sister?" I held my breath.

"Sarah's a senior. She's a great student."

I felt a surge of relief, knowing she was okay. "I'm not surprised about that. You were both so smart. She started reading when she was three. Where do you…?" I was going to ask where he went to college but cut myself off. He'd been cautious so far, his answers short and spare on details; I'd have to be careful and not seem to be probing.

"Ma'am?"

"I'm sorry. I'm a little overwhelmed right now." A strong feeling suddenly came over me—a mother's feeling—and I realized he was nearby. "It's amazing to be talking to you like this. You sound like you're so *close*."

"Yes, I'm in Boston."

"And you've come to see me."

"Yes, but…I have to…I don't want you to call the police or anything. I don't want to get my dad in trouble."

"Oh no, no, don't worry. I won't do that."

"It's just, I mean…I couldn't stop you if you did, but…"

"It wouldn't be much of a reunion then, would it?"

"No, ma'am. I guess not. But Sarah said she…"

"You can trust me, Nathan. Would you like to come here to the house? Or we could meet someplace? Whatever makes you comfortable."

"I'll come to your house. I know the address. I could be there in about half an hour."

"That would be wonderful." I wanted to tell him to be careful, take your time, look both ways before crossing the street. "Would you like me to make some coffee? Or tea? I could walk up to the bakery and get some sweet rolls."

"Just coffee."

"Okay, see you soon."

I hung up the phone. Out in the kitchen my hands shook so badly I got coffee grounds all over the counter. I called William's cell phone, and he picked up immediately.

"It's him," I said. "It's really him. He's here in Boston. He's coming to the house in half an hour."

"Oh, Lucy, that's fantastic."

"I have to go get ready."

"Of course. Call me afterward."

I ran up to the bedroom, looking at one outfit then another, as conflicted as a teenager about to go on her first date. I settled on a white sweater and black slacks. "Nathan," I said aloud to the photograph on the mantel. This was about today, not all those lost yesterdays. But I would tell him about my journals, show him how I never stopped counting the days. I brushed my hair, took off the sweater and changed into a beige one, took off the slacks and put on jeans, pulled the sweater over my head and got a red Western shirt with mother-of-pearl buttons, ran a leather belt through the loops of my jeans and cinched it tight. I looked like a desperate divorcée in a honky-tonk bar. I went back to the white sweater and black slacks, brushed my hair again, and pulled it back with tortoiseshell hair combs. Lipstick? Something pale. No mascara, though my eyes looked puffy. I tried on a bunch of shoes and ended up in plain black flats, then went downstairs and peeked out the front window to see if I could see him coming up the street. I ran back up to the bedroom and got the photograph of him and Sarah to put it on the mantel in the living room.

When he knocked on the door, I opened it and smiled and said, "Come in."

He stepped into the foyer, a tall, thin boy with a backpack over one shoulder and a watch cap in his hand, a few nicks on his handsome face from shaving. My eyes were filled with tears and his with questions.

I said, "Did you have any trouble finding the house?"

He shook his head. "I took a cab."

He stuffed his cap in his pocket, and I hung his parka on the coat tree. Neither of us said more until we were in the kitchen and I asked him how he liked his coffee.

"Milk and sugar," he said.

361

"Just like your dad."

He nodded hesitantly, wary at the mention of his father, his eyes darting around the room as if he were looking for something he could remember. I put the milk and sugar on the table and watched him stir it in his coffee.

For the first few years after they were gone, I saw Sarah and Nathan everywhere—in playgrounds, in the lines of schoolchildren holding hands as they crossed the street, in shopping malls and movie theaters—embarrassing myself and scaring others as I'd stare and move closer, trying to get a better look. Intellectually, I knew that their faces would change as they matured. Still, I was convinced that when I saw them, really saw them, I would know them in an instant. Now, searching the boy's face, I could find only the slightest traces of the child I remembered: the green eyes and small mouth, Matt's coloring and dark wavy hair.

I said, "Let's take our coffee into the living room. We'll be more comfortable."

As I led him through the dining room, he paused and looked up at the ceiling. "I think I…"

"What?"

"I remember that fruit basket around the chandelier."

"That was one of first things I fell in love with when we saw the house. I repainted it myself."

"My roommate's family has one like it in their home. I had a feeling of déjà vu when I saw it there."

"Where does your roommate live?"

He hesitated, uncertain how much he wanted to reveal, then said, "Providence."

We went into the living room. He sat in an armchair, I on the sofa.

I said, "Have you...?" at the same time he said, "What do you...?" and we both laughed nervously and tried again. No one had invented a vocabulary for a moment like this. The two of us would have to make up new words and fumble with the old ones, as if we spoke different languages or came from different cultures, trying to discover what was acceptable and what was taboo.

I said, "It's hard to know where to start, isn't it?"

"Yes."

"And you're not sure you can trust me?"

He shrugged. "It's not...I mean...my sister's going to kill me when she finds out I came here. She and my dad are incredibly close."

I nodded. "She and Matt always were. Is that what he still calls himself?"

"No, it's Adam. My name was changed too. I'm Elliot."

"And Sarah?"

"She's still Sarah, only she spells it without the *h*."

He reached in his pocket and handed me a photocopy of the old newspaper clipping from the *Herald*. "This is how I found out about you. I came across it when I was doing research for a paper. Sarah still has the llama. That's how I recognized us."

I smiled and fought off my tears. "Thank you, Sundae. Your grandmother gave her that. Nanda. Do you remember her? She passed away a few years ago."

He shook his head. "I really don't remember anything. When I saw that article, I was in total shock. My dad told us the house burned down and you died. He didn't talk about you much. He said it made him too sad, which I think was true. He never got married again."

It was difficult not to show my anger. Over the years, there were moments when I honestly believed I could douse Matt with gasoline and never think twice about lighting the match.

I said, "You got this article from the library?"

"Yes, over Thanksgiving break. Then I found your number in the phone book. I didn't know what to do. Sarah was in France, studying. When I got home and showed her the newspaper article, she said we should forget about it. She wanted me to pretend I'd never seen it. She's afraid you'll tell the police and they'll send our father to prison. But I just couldn't...I wanted to meet you."

"Thank you."

He nodded but said nothing more.

"You said in your message your dad said it was okay for you to come here?"

"He could see it was something I needed to do. He said he raised me and Sarah to think for ourselves."

"Well, I'm glad he did. Your father and I, uh...there was a lot of bitterness between us. I don't know what he told you. I'm not sure I want to know. But, please, believe me, I'm not going to contact the police or try to punish him. The only thing that matters to me now is having a relationship with you and Sarah again." Relief showed in his eyes. "Would you like more coffee?"

"No, thank you..." He still didn't know what to call me.

"What's Sarah studying in college?"

"Art history. She's doing her thesis on Cézanne."

"Really? How wonderful. What about you? Do you know what you want to major in?"

"Music. I play oboe, also flute and cor anglais."

"Classical music?"

"Sometimes. But mostly jazz."

"I don't know much about jazz. Do you write your own music?"

"A lot of it. I'm in a band at school. The day I found that article in the newspaper I came home and stuff just started flowing. It was kind of crazy, learning you were still alive, and I used to have a different name and all. It felt like the whole world was turned upside down. I was trying to make sense out of what my dad had done. I guess music helps me deal with things. As upsetting as it was finding that article—I know this probably sounds strange—it also felt kind of cool. Sort of like an adventure. Like I was still me but somebody completely different."

"You must spend a lot of time alone with your music."

"Yeah, I do."

"I spend a lot of time alone too. How does it work? The music? Do you hear a melody in your head and just start playing it on your oboe?"

"Yeah, pretty much. I use a tape recorder. Sometimes it's almost like I can't keep up with myself. Things start pouring out of me, and I have no idea where the piece is going. I'm just trying to get it all down. It's kind of like being in a field of butterflies and you're trying to catch as many as you can, but some of the best ones keep getting away. After I've been playing for a while, I go back and listen to the tape and I'm surprised by half the stuff that's there. It's almost like somebody else came into my room and put a bunch of music on my tape recorder. Of course, a lot of it is pure crap." He laughed. "That's when the hard part starts, trying to figure out what to keep and what to get rid of. Anyway, it's pretty strange. A couple of hours before, none of that music existed. And now it does. I made it up, but I have no idea where it came from."

"That's how I feel about you at the moment. Like you fell out of the sky. Did you finish that piece? The one you started the day you found the article in the newspaper?"

"Sort of. I turned it in for my composition final. My teacher liked it, but he said I need to keep working on it."

"Did you bring your oboe with you? I'd love to hear it."

He went to the foyer and got his book bag and took out the instrument case. When the oboe was fitted together, he wet the reed with his lips and played a burst of warm-up notes.

"Well, here goes." The look on his face was eager and uncertain.

"What do you call it?"

"'Lost and Found.'"

He closed his eyes and began to play a slow, melancholy song. I sat on the edge of the sofa watching him, drinking him in. The oboe looked tiny in his long-fingered hands. I thought of all the things I had missed—first day of school, first lost tooth, first home run, first oboe recital, first crush. Matt took all that for himself. I wondered if I could ever forgive him. It was hard to imagine ever wanting to, but I would have to try. It might be the only way I could keep Nathan and find my way back to Sarah. I'd been broken for so long that I wondered what it would be like to feel whole again. A sudden trill of the oboe startled me. The tempo was quicker now, the melody sweet and airy; my son had found his way home. I had never felt so happy, or so afraid.

Chapter 32
Adam

The night Elliot left to go to Lucy's, I drove him to the airport to catch the red-eye to Boston. Both of us were quiet, but there wasn't any tension between us. He put on a jazz tape and fiddled with the snaps on the parka he'd draped across his knees. I assumed he was thinking about his mother, wondering what would happen when he knocked on her door. He'd said he thought she was still living in our old house in Jamaica Plain. I remembered what a cool place it was, with the marble hearths and the dentil crown molding. The way the light shone through the stained-glass windows by the front door. But Lucy ruined everything about it for me. To this day I could still see her coming down the hall in that kimono, looking like a hooker carrying a wineglass and beer bottle. It was hard to imagine her still rattling around in that big old house alone.

I wondered if she and Griffin had gotten married and had more children. That seemed unlikely. He wasn't the marrying kind, and she wasn't cut out to be a mother. But maybe the two of them had gotten caught up in the charade they'd been playing and decided to start a family of their own. The more I thought about that possibility, the more I hoped it wasn't so. I had a strong feeling that Elliot was going to develop a relationship with Lucy. Maybe, eventually, Sara would too. Discovering a younger half-brother or half-sister would only draw them closer to her. It made me wonder how our lives would have changed if I had gotten married again myself. Elliot might not have felt so different growing up. He probably wouldn't have gone looking for information about Lucy if he'd had another mother. Sadly, that hadn't been something I could give him. I'd met some fine women along the way, even came close to falling in love a few times. But marriages are built on honesty and trust, and I could never risk telling my secret to anyone.

Elliot and I got out of the truck at the airport and gave each other a hug. As I stood on the curb watching him walk into the terminal, he lifted his hand to wave goodbye without looking back. It was just past eleven when I got home. Sara was back from her date, warming a piece of apple cobbler in the kitchen.

"Where's El?" she said.

I hung my keys on the hook by the door. "Gone back to Boston. I just dropped him off at the airport."

"That's insane, Daddy! Why did you let him go?"

"What was I going to do? Lock him in his room? He's going to have to figure this out for himself. You will too, honey." That last line seemed to catch her off guard. She wanted me to tell her to hate her mother and never have anything to do with her. "I meant it when I said I taught you guys to think for yourselves."

"What if she tries to get you sent to prison?"

"I don't think she'll do that. It's not a pretty story. She's not going to want to air all the gory details for you and El to hear. But if she does…I'll just get up on the stand and tell my side to a jury." I set my jaw in defiance. "I'm proud of what I did, Sara. The only thing I'm guilty of is trying to protect you and your brother. Nobody's going to send me to jail for that."

She didn't look convinced. For all my bravado, I wasn't entirely convinced myself.

She said, "When is he coming back?"

"Saturday around noon. We'll have Christmas dinner and open presents together."

"Terrific," she said sarcastically. She tried to take the cobbler out of the toaster oven and muttered, "Shit," as she snatched her fingers away from the heat. "I can't believe he couldn't wait till after the holidays."

"Don't be too hard on him, Sara. This was something he needed to do. He's been carrying it around for over a month. I'm just glad he came home and talked it over with you and me before going to see her." I poured a cup of cold coffee and put it in the microwave. "Where'd you go tonight?"

"Out with Ajit. I didn't tell him what's going on."

"I suppose you'll have to, sooner or later." I hadn't begun to process how this whole thing would play out beyond the three of us. It wasn't something we could keep secret for long. "What's up with you and Ajit?"

"We're okay, I guess." The look on her face said something different. "He just found out he won a two-year fellowship to Oxford."

"Wow, that's fantastic."

"It is. But I'm tired of us always being apart." She'd been accepted into a prestigious apprenticeship program at the Getty Museum in L.A. starting in the fall.

"Ah, don't worry. You guys'll work it out." Or not. I wanted to be supportive, but I'd never seen two people in love who could make each other so unhappy.

She sat down at the kitchen table with the apple cobbler and a glass of milk. "What would you say if I went to England with him?"

"And gave up the job at the Getty?"

She shrugged. "I could take some grad courses. Try to get something at one of the museums over there."

"I'm not sure what to tell you, hon. It's your life. I could make a good case one way or the other." I retrieved my coffee from the microwave and sat down with her at the table.

"I think Ajit's going to ask me to marry him."

"Wow." I snapped to attention. "Really?"

She gave me an impish smile. "He's been hinting around." Her question about moving to England was just a way of leading up to a much bigger topic.

"What will you say if he does?" I hoped it would be something like, *Are you out of your freaking mind, Ajit?* They were too young. What would they live on? All they ever did was fight. I tried not to let my concern show on my face.

"I don't know, Daddy." Tears came to her eyes. "I don't want to lose him."

"Couldn't you guys just live together?" I didn't want to come right out and tell her I thought the whole idea was crazy. "Is this all because of his parents?"

She nodded. "They're starting to put the pressure on him." Ajit's parents were always kind to Sara, but he knew he was expected to marry a nice Bengali girl someday, just like his two older brothers. Now that he was about to graduate from college, his parents

370

probably wanted to start making introductions. They probably had a list of candidates lined up and waiting. But Ajit, for all his academic achievements, saw himself as a rebel. Perhaps he was truly in love with Sara, but I was afraid he might be using her to make a point with his parents. The more I thought about it, the more it pissed me off. But I wasn't ready to say that to her.

"I'm sorry, sweetheart," I said. "These things are never easy. The course of true love and all that crap."

She tried to smile. "How are you supposed to know when it is true love, Daddy?"

"Good question. People have been chewing that one over since the beginning of time."

"You used to say you fell in love the instant you met Lucy." It was interesting that she'd used her mother's first name instead of saying *Mom* the way she did when Lucy was still a ghost. For Sara, Lucy had become the enemy until proven otherwise.

"Yeah, I did. And to this day I still don't know if it was the best thing that ever happened to me or the worst."

$$\infty$$

I met with my new client the next morning and got the contract signed. It looked like it was going to be a great project. She didn't quibble about money and was already talking about other things she wanted to add. I spent the rest of the day working at another job site. All day I kept checking my cell phone to see if Elliot had called. When I got home, Sara and Ajit surprised me with the Christmas tree they'd put up and decorated. I showered and changed my clothes and took them out to dinner. Ajit talked enthusiastically about his fellowship. He had a great smile and his accent always got a little more pronounced when he turned on the charm. I didn't know if Sara had told him about Lucy yet or how she had explained Elliot's absence, but I was glad the subject didn't come up. She and Ajit were happy and playful with each other, touching hands and taking food from each other's plates. Neither of them made any hints about getting engaged. During the course of the dinner, it dawned on me that Sara might actually be the one who was pushing the idea of getting married. Maybe she was testing him, which wasn't a bad idea. Better to find out now if he would take a stand against his parents rather than being disappointed in a year or two, after she'd followed him to England.

After dinner Sara and Ajit went off to meet some friends. When I got home there was a message from Elliot on the machine. "Hey, guys, just checking in. No contact yet. I left a message on her machine. Guess I'll catch up with her tomorrow." He tried to sound matter-of-fact but was clearly disappointed. He was going to feel like a fool if she was away for the holidays and he had made the trip for nothing.

Christmas Eve was a day off for me and my work crews. Sara and I went to the driving range, then out shopping. I had always made a point about not going overboard on Christmas presents. She and Elliot and I often told each other exactly what we wanted, then made a joke out of being surprised by what we got. Later in the day we stayed busy wrapping presents then got some Mexican takeout for dinner. Neither of us had heard any more from Elliot, and we seemed to make a point of not talking about it. I watched a basketball game on TV, the Lakers and the Spurs. Elliot called about nine-fifteen, past midnight in Boston.

"Hey, El," I said. "I was hoping you'd call. Everything go all right?"

"Yeah, fine. It was pretty emotional. We talked for a long time."

"Tell me about Lucy. Did she remarry? Have any more children?"

"No. No children. She said she...She has a boyfriend. William. Real nice guy. He knows a lot about jazz. The three of us went out to dinner and talked."

"You back in your dorm now?"

"No, I'm still at her house. In my old room. She asked me to stay over."

"Cool. You can play with all your toy trucks." I meant it as a joke, but it came out sounding snide.

"She didn't keep it the same. Just saved some of our books and things."

"I'm sorry, El. I didn't mean..."

"I know, Dad. It's okay. It's late. Let's talk when I get home tomorrow."

"Sure. Okay. Good night. I love you."

"Night. Love you too. Oh wait, one more thing. I changed my ticket to a later flight. It gets in at quarter to eight." He was trying to sound casual, no big deal, just a minor change in the schedule, acting like he didn't know he was kicking me in the balls.

"How much did that cost?"

"Seventy-five dollars. I'll pay you back, Dad. I just want to, you know..."

"Sure, fine. Whatever. I'll pick you up." I didn't wait for him to say good night again. I ground my teeth and stared out the window.

He'd been with her less than twenty-four hours, and Lucy had already started to turn him against me. I imagined her sneaking out in the middle of the night, all the stores closed, desperately trying to find some Christmas presents for him. Or maybe she'd just rummage around in the basement and haul out a bunch of nostalgia. I wondered what kind of lies she'd told him about me.

I spent a restless night. In the morning, I was up around seven and went out back and inspected the rotten deck. With my pry bar and a hammer, I started ripping up the floorboards. Sara came outside in a San Diego Chargers jersey, hugging herself with her hands tucked under her armpits. It was uncanny how her body language often reminded me of Lucy.

"Jeez, Dad. What're you doing? It's 7:30 Christmas morning!"

"Yes, it is. And this is a present to myself. You have a good time last night?"

She pouted as if she hadn't. Then she grinned and stuck out her left hand to show me her ring. The diamond was as big as a jelly bean.

I gave a low whistle. "Did Ajit win the lottery or something?"

"It's fake, Dad. He got it for fun. You know I don't care about crap like that."

"Oh, Sara, I'm so happy for you guys." I put down my tools and wrapped my arms around her. "I can't wait to walk you down the aisle."

"Thanks, Daddy. That means the world to me." She knew I had my doubts, but there was no sense in my saying anything. People never want you to tell them they're wrong about love.

"When is Ajit going to break the news to his parents?"

"This afternoon. We're going out to lunch with them. Ajit

figures we'll have less chance of a total meltdown if we tell them in a public place. I should be home by the time you and El get back from the airport."

"He changed his flight. He's not getting in till this evening."

"What the fuck!" She knew how I hated to hear her say that word, but she didn't even try to apologize.

"I don't want to talk about it, honey. We'll deal with it as it comes."

I wished her luck when she left for lunch with the Banerjees, and she said she'd need it. But when she and Ajit came by the house in the late afternoon, they were giddy. Ajit said he had talked to his father in the morning, and his father had acquiesced.

"I can't say he was surprised when I told him," Ajit said. "Maybe a little disappointed. But he's an economist. He knows things in the real world don't always work out the way you want them to. I guess he figured, why fight the inevitable."

"He was really sweet about it," Sara said. "He said we were a couple of contrarians."

"What about your mom?" I said to Ajit.

"She didn't say ten words. She likes being a martyr."

Sara took his hand. "She'll be fine as soon as we have kids." It stunned me to hear her say it. She was still a kid herself.

When Ajit went home, I asked Sara if she'd told him about the situation with Lucy. She said not yet, she'd made up a story about Elliot going back to Boston to play with some big-time jazz musicians.

I said, "I think you need to tell him, honey. Sooner rather than later."

"I know. I just want to hear what El says first."

∞

We picked up Elliot at the airport. Sara showed him her ring, and they laughed and chattered. I think we were all grateful for the distraction of the engagement. None of us wanted to talk about Lucy yet. We were all famished when we got home, and Sara made spaghetti for a late dinner. In the living room our Christmas gifts provided another distraction. The forced cordiality between us was growing, as if we were clinging to harmony when everything was about to come undone. There was a small pile of presents under the tree. Elliot said he'd had a chance to do some shopping in Boston but didn't have time to wrap anything. He got me an alligator leather belt and a geode, a silk scarf and silver necklace for Sara. Expensive things, bought with a touch of guilt, I guess. I finally asked him about the trip.

"I'm not sure I can put it into words," he said, taking a deep breath. "It was like watching a movie, only I was the one who was in it. I had to keep reminding myself that it was real. I left two messages on her answering machine and called myself Nathan, which was truly weird. When I talked to her on the phone the next morning, she invited me to come to her house. I didn't know what to call her. It's kind of hard to say 'Mom' to someone you just met. Anyway, she's real nice. She works as a librarian in an elementary school and loves her job. She also teaches a night class for adults on reading aloud to children. We didn't talk about what happened between you and her, Dad. She said it would just lead to a lot of ugliness back and forth and make everyone miserable." I gave Sara a quick glance as if to say, *I told you so*. Lucy would never want all the sordid details to be revealed. "I was pretty cautious with her at first. I said I was called Elliot now, but I didn't tell her our last name or where I went to school or anything. She could see I didn't trust her, so she came right out and said she wasn't going to turn you in to the police, Dad. She made me a promise."

"Well, that's a big relief," Sara said.

"Great," I said. "Did you get that in writing?" Another joke that fell flat.

He told us the two of them went out shopping for groceries and she cooked Hungarian goulash for dinner. I wondered if she was still in touch with Sandor. Nearly everything Elliot said felt like it carried a hidden message from Lucy to me. She had given him a stash of photographs from our life together, which Sara was curious to see. The only photo I had of them as little children was the one I'd had in my wallet when we left Boston. Lucy also included a recent photograph of herself, kneeling on the grass next to an ugly brown dog.

Sara said, "God, she's so beautiful."

"No argument there," I said. Her hair was streaked with gray, her face a bit drawn and angular, but her smile was radiant.

Elliot said, "The dog's name was Frodo. He died a few months ago. She wants me to go to the animal shelter with her and help pick out a new pup."

I tried not to react. Lucy was already making plans for when he came back. I could see her insinuating herself into his life. Inviting him for dinner all the time, going to see The Spendthrifts play. How long would it be before he moved into her house? Sara started asking him questions about Lucy. As I shifted in my chair, a muscle spasm gripped my lower back and I let out a groan.

"I'm sorry, El." I stood up, wincing. "I tore the deck off the house today, and my back is seizing up on me."

Sara said, "Do you want me to get you a heat pack?"

"No, no, I'll be fine. I just need to go lie down."

I gimped off to my bedroom and fell asleep in my clothes.

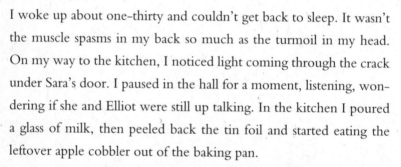

I woke up about one-thirty and couldn't get back to sleep. It wasn't the muscle spasms in my back so much as the turmoil in my head. On my way to the kitchen, I noticed light coming through the crack under Sara's door. I paused in the hall for a moment, listening, wondering if she and Elliot were still up talking. In the kitchen I poured a glass of milk, then peeled back the tin foil and started eating the leftover apple cobbler out of the baking pan.

"Hey, Dad," Sara said, coming into the kitchen.

"Hey, honey. Can't sleep?"

She shook her head.

"Is it Lucy or Ajit?"

"Her. I called Ajit and told him everything. I was afraid he'd think we were a bunch of lunatics, but he was great about it." She ate a few crumbs from the pan with her fingers. "Lucy gave El a present to bring home for me. Can I show you?"

"Sure."

Sara went to her room and came back with a tattered copy of *Eloise*.

"It was almost like I knew what it was before I opened it," she said. "I remembered how much we liked reading it together. This letter was tucked inside." She took out a small piece of pale blue stationery and read aloud. "Dear Sarah. Merry Christmas. It's three o'clock in the morning, and I have spent the last two hours trying to write this letter. Elliot told me why you didn't want him to come see me. I can understand why you feel the way you do. I know how much you love your father and want to protect him. Please believe me when I say that I will not contact the authorities or try to settle any score with him. Nothing can be gained for any of us by deconstructing the past. All I want is to see you again. But that isn't something I can control. You are a grown-up now, and I don't want to intrude on your life unless you want me to be a part of it. My hope is that you will find it in your heart to reach out to me and let me earn your trust. With all my love, Mom." Sara turned over the page and kept reading. "Yikes! Every time I try to write this letter, it gets worse. I'm not sure why it's so hard to sound like me. I've actually written to you and your brother in a journal hundreds of times since you've been gone. Maybe one of those entries will work better. All I really want to say is that I have never stopped loving you or missing you, and tonight I miss you more than ever."

It took me a second to reply. I wasn't sure what Sara expected. "Powerful stuff," I said.

"Yeah." She took a folded sheet of paper from the back of the book and handed it to me. I sat down at the kitchen table to read, my life unraveling in photocopies from Boston. I recognized Lucy's cramped handwriting.

7-21-95 (12 years, 1 month & 7 days gone) Sarah, I'm sorry I missed your birthday yesterday. It wasn't that I forgot. I was thinking about you all day, but I was sightseeing and museum-hopping and I kept putting it off, waiting for the right time to sit down and try to say something meaningful, which is the kind of thing that never works out the way you plan—not for me, anyway. I'm in France, traveling with my new beau, William Hufnagel. Have you ever been to France? I was your age the first time I came. I visited a girl who had been an exchange student in our high school. She lived in Saint-Malo on the chilly coast of Brittany. William and I are on the other side of the country, exploring the Riviera. This morning we drove up into the hills above Nice to see the Matisse Chapel in Vence. I'd read about the chapel in guidebooks but had never seen it before. It was the last big art project he did before he died and his only piece of architecture. The place is breathtaking. I'm not a religious person, but when you sit inside the chapel, bathed in the blue and green and yellow light, you know God must have inspired Matisse to do it, one last surge of creativity before the angels whisked him up to Heaven. (If Matisse didn't make it, I don't want to go.) At the moment I'm in the garden outside the chapel while William goes off to get some bread and wine and cheese for our lunch. It's strange, I almost never go into a church back in Boston, but when I'm in France, I can't get enough of them. Not so much the big cathedrals, though you'd have to be a cold fish not to be awed by Chartres or Notre Dame. I prefer the churches in the villages—some sturdy little Romanesque église with faded frescoes above the altar and the names of the dead soldiers from the Great War on a plaque on the wall, five or six brothers from the same family, sorrow beyond human understanding. I would love to bring you here to Matisse's chapel someday. We could sit quietly in the sanctuary and breathe in the light and think about that old man in his wheelchair with a paint brush on a long stick and an imagination as big as the sun. It's enough to make you believe in miracles, sugar pop, which is how I feel right now. I know I'm going to see you again.

I looked at Sara. We both had tears in our eyes.

"You know what's really crazy?" she said. "I went to that chapel with some friends about a month ago."

I blew out a long breath. "You have to make up your own mind, honey."

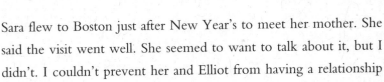

Sara flew to Boston just after New Year's to meet her mother. She said the visit went well. She seemed to want to talk about it, but I didn't. I couldn't prevent her and Elliot from having a relationship with Lucy, but as far as I was concerned it was "Don't ask, don't tell." I never wanted to hear Lucy's name again. But I knew that wasn't going to be possible.

In the middle of January, shortly after the kids were back at school, Ajit's father called me and asked if we could have lunch together. The few times I'd met him he seemed like a nice guy. He was tall and handsome like Ajit, but a little stiff. Even at soccer games he always wore a coat and tie. When he spoke, it sounded like he'd learned English from a textbook. I was concerned when he called to set up the lunch. I thought he might have concerns about Ajit and Sara's engagement and wanted to see if I felt the same. But it was nothing of the sort. We met at a restaurant near the university where he was a professor.

"My wife and I are so happy for Sara and Ajit," he said, smiling. "I apologize for not getting in touch with you sooner to send my good wishes."

"Likewise. I'd like to take the two of you out to dinner together sometime."

"Yes, thank you, that would be wonderful." We chatted for a while. Then he said, "You know, we are very proud of Ajit for winning a fellowship to Oxford University. He will be coming home for spring vacation in March, and we were thinking about giving a party in his honor. Ajit suggested that it would be appropriate to use the occasion to celebrate his betrothal to your beautiful Sara as well. Kill two birds with one stone as they say. Ha ha." I could tell he'd been rehearsing the lines.

"Sure, that would be great." I had a feeling this was more Sara's doing than Ajit's. "Were you thinking of a dinner party?"

"Oh yes. Traditional Bengali food. It will keep my wife busy planning the menu. Some music perhaps, so the young people can dance."

"That sounds terrific. Shall we split the cost?"

"Thank you. That is most generous of you." He seemed relieved.

I called Sara's cell phone on my way back to work and left a message. "Hey, kiddo, I just had lunch with Mr. Banerjee. I guess you already know about the party they're planning for you and Ajit. Just tell me the date and time and I'll be there with bells on my toes." I was smiling to myself as I hung up.

Sara waited nearly two weeks to tell me she was inviting Lucy to the party, something I should have guessed all along. She said she hoped I didn't mind, though she knew how much I did. I suppose I could have issued an ultimatum. *Her or me. I never want to be in the same room with that woman again.* But I didn't want to back Sara into a corner.

As the day of the party approached, Sara acted as an intermediary. She said Lucy was coming to California two days early and wanted to get together with me "to clear the air."

"That isn't necessary," I said. "We're both adults. Neither one of us wants to make a scene."

"Please, Dad. I think she's right. You guys need to talk. Do this for me, okay?"

I was dreading it, but I felt like I had no choice. Sara arranged for us to meet at the bar in the hotel in Del Mar where Lucy was staying. I was seated in an out-of-the-way table in back when she came in. She was wearing a pair of gray slacks and a lavender blouse. She looked around and spotted me. No smile. I thought about the first time I saw her crossing the street in Copley Square. She still carried herself with that slow, catlike grace. Men still turned their heads. I stood up to greet her.

"Hello, Lucy." I pulled out a chair.

"Hello, Matt."

"Adam."

She shrugged, her eyes fixed on mine. We were like two boxers at a weigh-in, sizing each other up, neither of us wanting to show any fear.

"This seems like a nice hotel," I said. "Is your room okay?"

"Yes, fine. Wonderful view."

"Have you ever been here before? To the San Diego area, I mean."

"No, it's lovely. Seems like a great place to raise children."

It was a solid body blow. I tried not to let it show. "Yes, terrific weather. Sara can play golf year-round. Did she tell you how good she was?"

"She did."

The waitress came over and asked for our drink orders. I said I'd have a soda water with a lime. Lucy asked for white wine.

"Well," I said, "you look as lovely as ever."

"Thank you. You look good yourself. Maybe we should think about getting back together." Another hard shot to the ribs.

"Sara said you wanted to clear the air. How nasty do you want this to be?"

"I don't know." She paused. "One part of me wants you to die. I don't mean that figuratively. I've had fantasies about murdering you myself. Another part tells me to try for forgiveness. I'm having trouble getting traction on that one."

"Fair enough. You want to go first or should I? How far back do you want to go? How about the night you went off with Griffin and came back and told me you were pregnant with Sara?"

"Wow, that *is* far back."

"You slept with him that night, didn't you?"

"I did."

"And started our marriage with a lie."

"Which you never really believed. The lies you wanted to hear were the easiest ones to tell."

I didn't respond. The waitress brought our drinks.

She said, "I was a terrible wife, Matt. I'm sorry. You deserved better. But I wasn't a terrible mother."

I curled one corner of my mouth. "Right."

"No, I'll never accept your judgment of me on that."

"Would you like me to start enumerating your failings?" I tapped my finger hard on the table. "Isn't that why you told the kids you don't want to *deconstruct the past*? Because you don't want them to know what a fuck-up you were?"

Her eyes never left mine. "Oh, you don't have to do any

enumerating for me. I've gone over my failings more times than you ever will. I've bored therapists, written about them in my journal, had the most egregious ones etched in stone so I could beat my head against them. You can't tell me anything bad about me I don't already know." She took a sip of wine. "I'm sure you believe that what you did was right, Matt. That no jury would convict you after hearing what a horrible mother I was. You think *I'm* the criminal, not you. Okay, fine. Guilty. I won't try to defend myself. So, tell me, what should my penalty be?"

She waited. I said nothing.

"I mean it. I want an answer. What's my punishment?"

"I couldn't risk leaving the kids with you, Lucy. The stakes were too high."

"Answer the question."

"Sara's broken arm, Amanda driving them around drunk. Dropping cigarette ashes on—"

"Guilty, guilty, guilty. The accused has freely admitted to her crimes and thrown herself on the mercy of the court. All you have to do is render a sentence."

"I did what I thought was best for the children."

"Why can't you say it? Why can't you tell me what my punishment should be?" She looked at me with disgust. "You didn't drag me into a court of law, Matt. You played *God*. And the judgment you handed down was that I should never see Sarah and Nathan again. Never hear their voices, never know where they lived or what became of them." Tears were rolling down her cheeks. "I spent sixteen and a half years waiting, wondering if my sentence would ever end. I would have spent less time in prison if I had committed manslaughter."

"You were out of control. I couldn't sit around for a year or two, waiting for the justice system to figure out that you were an unfit mother. Like you just said, you were guilty. What do you want from me? Do you want me to tell you I'm sorry?"

"What I want from you is this. I want you to go home tonight and look in the mirror and say, *Lucy got what she deserved.* Have you ever done that, Matt? Talked to yourself in the mirror? I've tried, and let me tell you, it's *really* hard. Hard to tell yourself the truth. Even harder to believe your own lies."

"I have no regrets, Lucy. Sometimes you have to make a decision, and once it's made it can't be changed."

"Try it, Matt. *Lucy got what she deserved.* Five little words. Look in the mirror and see if you can make yourself believe them."

Someone laughed loudly at the bar, and we turned our heads to the sound. When I looked at Lucy again, something in her eyes seemed to soften. She swirled the wine in her glass and put it down without drinking.

"Thank you," she said. She stood up. "I feel much better now. I don't have to hate you anymore."

I watched her go. I felt hollowed out, not angry or sad or guilty or hopeful. Just empty. Wondering how she could still do that to me.

The party was at a small club in Encinitas. Lucy and I weren't seated at the same table and didn't talk to each other. The food was great, a sitar player providing background music. When it came time to make toasts, no one spoke too long or said anything embarrassing.

They'd hired a DJ to provide the dance music. Sara and Ajit got things started, jitterbugging to "Oh Boy" by Buddy Holly. I'd never been much of a dancer, and I went out to the terrace to get some air. Three Indian gentlemen were out there smoking cigars. They offered me one but I declined. I listened to them talk about cricket but didn't know enough to join the discussion.

When I went back inside, there were about twenty people on the dance floor. Marvin Gaye's "Heard It Through the Grapevine" was playing. Sara was dancing with Elliot. It was uncanny how she moved her body like her mother, quiet shoulders and snaky hips. Like me, Elliot was an awkward dancer, but he was having a great time. Lucy was talking with a man who made her laugh. She was wearing a sexy green dress. I thought about the night we met. I could still see her standing outside the Café Budapest with one hand on her hip and a rose in her hair. Did she ever have a clue how much I loved her? The song ended and the DJ put on "What a Feeling" from *Flashdance*. Sara let out a squeal and grabbed Lucy's hand and the two of them spun each other around. Elliot and Ajit joined in, all of them dancing in a pack. As she twirled around, Lucy scanned the bystanders and caught my eye. Her smile was luminous. Unconquerable.

I walked out to the parking lot and got in my pickup. I headed north on the 5, my hands tight on the wheel. I couldn't get that image of Lucy out of my head. The way she looked at me with that smug smile. I'm sure everyone else could see it.

A deputy sheriff's car raced by with its blue lights flashing, and I eased off the gas.

I tried to ratchet up my anger, but the more I thought about it, the more I started to wonder if she really was being smug. I never could read her very well. Maybe it was her way of asking me if I wanted to come join the dance. Wouldn't that be something? All of us bopping around like one big happy family?

Just past Oceanside, traffic slowed to a crawl. Up ahead the deputy's car was stopped in the middle lane behind an old Dodge station wagon with its hood up and smoke pouring off the engine. Cars were jockeying for position to get past the tie-up. I let another driver merge in front of me, and the guy behind me honked impatiently. I looked at him in the rearview mirror for a second, then looked away.

Traffic picked up speed after I got past the broken-down station wagon. As I settled back in my seat, I looked in the rearview mirror again, but all I saw were my own eyes.

"Lucy..." I said aloud, but I couldn't make myself finish.

It was a beautiful evening, the moon hanging over Mt. Palomar. I thought about turning around as I approached the next exit. But I kept going.

Reading Group Guide

1. From the first date on, it is clear that Matt is more taken with Lucy than she is with him. Is it the norm in most romantic relationships that one person falls more deeply in love than the other? After the confrontation in the bedroom with Lucy and Griffin, Matt says to Lucy, "I never had a chance, did I?" Do you think Lucy ever really tried to make the marriage work? Does Matt bear responsibility for their breakup?

2. Matt says that taking the children was his "fate" and he had no other choice. Is this simply a rationalization, or was the kidnapping justified? In the end, would you say Matt has been a good father or a bad one?

3. Lucy feels as if she can't quite figure out how to be a good mother, yet she is unable to broach the subject even with her best friend, Jill. Do you think this is a common feeling among women? How do Lucy's relationships with other women define who she is and what we think about her?

4. Lying is a key element of this novel. Who do you think lies more, Matt or Lucy? What is the worst lie each of them tells? For most people, there have been times when they would

rather have heard a lie than the truth. In what situations has this been true for you? When have you lied because you felt that is what the other person wanted to hear?

5. When Lucy goes to the GrieveWell meeting, she finds that one woman feels that Lucy's is "a second-class sorrow." Is it possible to compare one person's grief to another's? Do you think that most people measure and compare their losses to those of others?

6. Once the children learn the truth about their past, Sara remains fiercely loyal to her father while Elliot is pulled in the opposite direction. Why do you think this is so? Have you ever encountered a startling revelation in your own life or in that of someone you know that caused you to rethink your entire world?

7. Lucy quotes her mother as saying, "Any fool can be happy. The hard part is feeling like you matter." What do you think about this statement?

8. Lucy's journal-keeping has a profound influence on her life. Do you keep a journal yourself? How has it affected your own life?

9. Is there any validity in Matt's contention that the court system is biased toward a mother? When adjudicating domestic disputes, does the legal system today give fair consideration to the rights of both parents?

10. Did Lucy give up too quickly in trying to find her children? The children's disappearance takes place before the age of the Internet. How would Lucy's search be different today?

11. The last thing Lucy says to Matt is, "I feel better now. I don't

have to hate you anymore." But she doesn't offer him forgiveness. Are there some acts that are simply unforgivable?

12. Matt cannot make himself say the words "Lucy got what she
deserved." Did she?

13. When talking about the difference between movies and films,
Matt says, "Movies were entertainment, stories that made you
laugh or cry and kept you on the edge of your seat. Films had
meaning and subtitles, slow, tortuous stories with bleak endings or no ending at all." He likes movies; Lucy likes films.
Which is true for you? If *Lies You Wanted to Hear* were made
into a motion picture, would it be a movie or a film?

A Conversation with the Author

1. **Jim, at 67, you are one of the oldest first-time authors we've published at Sourcebooks. Tell me a little about your journey. Did you always want to be a writer?**

   Yes, I guess I did. I wrote some poems in high school, mostly your typical teenage stuff about love and angst, then one long, obscure poem in college that I kept revising and revising. My roommate used to joke with me about publishing it in a chapbook called *The Collected Poem of James Whitfield Thomson*. After college, I spent three years as the navigator of a Navy supply ship off the coast of Vietnam, then I went to grad school and wrote my dissertation on the work of Raymond Chandler, but I never tried to do any creative writing myself. I landed a job as an assistant professor in the English Department at the University of Miami but quickly realized I wasn't cut out for academia. I joined a start-up company as a salesman and loved it. It was such a relief to be able to measure my performance in terms of dollars and cents. Our company grew fast and I was very driven, but I still had dreams of becoming a writer.

2.   **What inspired you to make that dream a reality?**

In 1985, I was turning forty and a close friend died, so that provided the motivation. I wrote a short story called "The Spice of Life" about a man who's trying to decide how to dispose of a dead friend's ashes. The story wasn't autobiographical, but I was obviously thinking about my friend. I sent the story out to a few magazines but got discouraged after a few rejections and stuck it in a drawer. Three years later, Christopher Tilghman invited me to be a guest at a workshop led by the great short story writer Andre Dubus. At the end of the evening, Andre asked me if I wanted to come back the following week and read to the group. I was thrilled. This was my big chance to find out if "The Spice of Life" was any good. I don't remember a single comment anyone made about the story, but the consensus was clear: *Not bad for your first effort, pal; now go write another one.* It was like the proverbial light bulb went on in my head. Writers write. Time for me to get to work.

3.   **Did it take you long to discover your own style?**

Yes and no. I could always construct good sentences, but I think my academic background hurt me a lot. I wanted to write *serious* literature, so I kept trying all these stylistic flourishes to prove how clever and lyrical I could be. It took a long time to realize that the goal is to keep the reader engaged in the story—anything that distracts the reader and makes him think about the author is just a writer's way of showing off. Let me give you an example from another art form. No matter what role Jack Nicholson is playing, there always seems to be a moment when he cocks an eyebrow and gives the camera that devilish grin of his, and everyone in the audience suddenly thinks, *There's* Jack. Jack Nicholson the *actor*, not the character he's portraying on the screen, which completely breaks the spell. I can't say I never give my readers that same sort of grin, but I try to do it as little as possible. I want them thinking about the story, not about me.

4.   **If you could describe your style in a single word, what would it be?**

Clear.

5.   **Are you a fast writer or a slow writer?**

Painfully slow. It took me four years to write *Lies*. There are plenty of days when I'll spend several hours working on a single paragraph. In an interview, Ernest Hemingway told George Plimpton he wrote forty-seven endings to *A Farewell to Arms*. Plimpton was dumbfounded and asked him why. Hemingway said he was "trying to get the words right." That pretty much sums up the struggle for most writers. I have no idea how prolific authors like John Irving and Joyce Carol Oates do it. If my full-time job were to *type* the stuff that Stephen King writes, I'd be a year or two behind.

6.   **Who are some of the writers you admire?**

For my money, the greatest living writer is Alice Munro. She can write a thirty-page story that feels richer than most novels. She starts a story with two people who disappear ten pages later, and somehow that seems perfectly logical. She's so good it's hard to learn anything from her. I like Dan Chaon, Philip Roth, Raymond Carver, Daniel Woodrell,

Margot Livesey. *The Vanishing Act of Esme Lennox* by Maggie O'Farrell and *The History of Love* by Nicole Krauss are wonderful novels. Two recent novels I loved are *The Devil All the Time* by Donald Ray Pollock and *Billy Lynn's Long Half-Time Walk* by Ben Fountain. The books I like best all tell a good story. I think that's what most readers want. It's why airport bestsellers are mostly thrillers and mysteries. I'm not saying plot should be a writer's first criteria, but I tend to lose patience with novels that plod along and never seem to go anywhere. I hate to admit, but I tried to reread *Madame Bovary* last summer and gave up after fifty pages. There's only so much nuance my mind can endure.

7. **All the authors you've mentioned are fiction writers. Are there other genres you like to read?**

Yes, I read a fair amount of nonfiction—history, memoir, biography. There's a book by British journalist Anthony Loyd called *My War Gone By, I Miss It So*, about the war in Bosnia. Terrific title and a heartbreaking account of what it's like to be a correspondent on the front line in a world gone mad. I also admired *We Wish to Inform You That Tomorrow We Will Be Killed with Our Families* by Philip Gourevitch about the genocide in Rwanda. There's a memoir called *Gone Boy* by Gregory Gibson about the murder of his son at Simon's Rock College. The book came and went in a nanosecond, but it's a searingly honest account of a parent's grief and his attempt to find out the truth about his son's death.

8. **What is one thing you know now that you wish you knew when you started your writing career?**

    I wish I had known how long it would take for me to get my first book published. If I had, maybe I would have set a goal that was more realistic, like becoming pope or the host of *Jeopardy!* Last summer, when I got word from my agent, Laura Gross, that Sourcebooks had accepted *Lies*, I could hardly believe it. When I told my wife Elizabeth, she said, "It's like you've been pregnant for twenty years." It's great to finally be published, but in retrospect, I spent too much time letting the desire to be published distract me from the simple joy of writing.

9. **Did you get discouraged by all those rejections?**

    Yes, very much at times. The whole process feels very personal. People are telling you your work isn't good enough to make the cut. There were several periods of four or five months when I hardly wrote a word, but I kept going back to it. I went to a reading by an author whose novel was rejected something like forty times before it ended up selling a gazillion copies. At the reading someone in the audience asked him how he could explain this, and he said, "The cream always rises to the top." His book is wonderful, but I disagree with his response. I think there are hundreds if not thousands of fine novels languishing in drawers because the people who wrote them simply gave up.

10. **That's one good piece of advice for aspiring writers: *Never give up*. Anything else?**

    The only thing *any* writer can do is write the next line.

You don't have to escape to a cabin in the woods for three weeks to get something done. If you're lucky enough to have that opportunity, sure, go for it. You may get an entire short story written or the first chapter of a novel. But when you come back to your everyday life, you have to find a way to keep it going. The trick is to let the story take hold of you. You can write the next line when you're out jogging or standing at the deli counter in the supermarket. Actually, once you get going, the hard part is trying to find a way to leave the story behind and join the real world from time to time. People get annoyed when you're having dinner with them and you've got that faraway look in your eyes. They want you to pass the salad dressing while you're sitting there wondering if your heroine should tell her husband about the money she found hidden in the basement.

11. **Is that what you love about writing, getting caught up in a story?**

Absolutely. I love it when the characters start talking to me. My wife thinks that is slightly crazy, the idea that there are imaginary people floating around out there telling me all sorts of stuff. But that's what happens. Of course, half the time the characters are mumbling, so I can't really hear them. Other times the things they say or do are so trite and predictable that I have to slap them around and demand something else. But that's all part of the process. A wise person, I wish I could remember who, once said, "Writer's write to find out what they didn't know they know." That's a great description of what is exciting about being a writer—allowing your mind to take you places you never thought you'd go. Some of those places can be pretty scary or very hard to get to, but the best writers find a way to dig down and take us on that journey with them.

12. **How do you know when a story is finished?**

Andre Dubus used to say that a story is never really finished, it's just abandoned. That's not quite true for me, but what does happen is that sometimes I think a story is finished, then I let it sit for a while, and when I go back to it, I find there are changes I want to make.

13. **Let's talk about *Lies You Wanted to Hear*. What inspired you to write this story?**

Around 1998, there was a front-page article in the *Boston Globe* about a man who was arrested for kidnapping his children eighteen years before. He'd been turned in by a lawyer who found out his secret and was hoping to collect a reward. The kidnapper had two daughters who were accomplished young women in their early twenties, and they stood behind him completely. They refused to even meet with their mother—who had become an academic research scientist—unless she agreed not to press any charges against him. According to the newspaper coverage, the man had difficulty telling the truth and lived off the money that came from a succession of rich wives, but he appeared to be a great father to his daughters. I let the story marinate for about a year before trying to turn it into a novel. When I began writing, I started with the premise that both the kidnapper and the mother who loses her children were essentially good people. The story didn't have much appeal to me if either of them were a monster. Beyond that, I always knew that in my novel I wanted it to be one of the children who discovered the secret of their kidnapping. I can't say why I felt this so strongly, but it obviously adds another dimension to the story that is missing from the original. I wrote about sixty pages before I lost interest. Ten years later the story started speaking to me again. Even though I'd kept a file folder with all the old newspaper articles from the true-life case, I decided not to reread them until I had finished writing the novel. I didn't want the facts of the true story to interfere with my imagination.

14. **How did you come up with the idea of the alternating chapters for Matt and Lucy?**

My goal was to let both characters have their say and see how readers responded to them. In the first draft, I wrote in the third person, limited perspective. In the second draft, I decided to try first person with the hope that it would force me to look at my characters more deeply. That turned out to be exactly what happened, especially when they began to explain to the reader why they did what they did.

15. **Is there one character in the novel you feel most closely connected to?**

No, I can't say that there is. Lucy turned out to be a lot more complicated than I had anticipated, so it was interesting to see where she would take me, but I don't feel any closer to her than I do to Matt. Maybe it's like having kids; you love each one and couldn't possibly say which is your favorite.

16. **What's the next book you're working on?**

It's a novel called *The Jukebox King*, set in 1962 in Pittsburgh, where I grew up. My rock 'n' roll novel. The protagonist is an inveterate entrepreneur who has a complicated relationship with his wife and two sons. I wrote a draft of it about fifteen years ago. Now I'm having fun revisiting it. There's a good story there, but I feel like I'm a much better writer now.

Acknowledgments

I would like to thank the people who helped make this book possible. My first mentor, the late Andre Dubus, never stopped encouraging me to make my work deeper and richer. Leslie Epstein, writer extraordinaire and poker pal, has been a constant source of advice and laughter.

Don Arbuckle read every draft of *Lies You Wanted to Hear* and occasionally talked me down off the ledge. His belief in my work, along with that of my friends Jack Herlihy, Pete Hogg, John Pennington, and Dan Roble has been unflagging.

Susan Barrett, Nat Butler, Donna Cameron, Joan Crockett, D.A. Hayden, Chris Konys, Jan Levin, Margot Livesey, Amelia McCarthy, Danielle McCarthy, Helen Peluso, Flippy Polikoff, Connie Thomson, Jessica Treadway, and Peter Weinbaum all read drafts of the novel. Their feedback sometimes made me sulk or argue, but their willingness to be honest with me ultimately made this a much better book.

Lt. Brian Grassey of the Natick Police Department assisted me in establishing various points of fact regarding Massachusetts law and procedure. Dale Smith, Linda Champion, and Dell Redington of the Morse Institute Library answered numerous questions, as did Maria Young, the librarian at Memorial Elementary School.

Libby Plum cheerfully printed many versions of the manuscript.

Adriana Flores made sure I got the Spanish right.

Debby Smullyan proved to be an incomparable line editor, rooting out typos that were hidden like termites on every other page.

Simon Lipskar believed in me when so many publishing insiders did not.

Walt Bode challenged me to take the novel to another level and offered insight and guidance every step of the way.

My agent Laura Gross looked me in the eye the first time we met and said quite simply, "This novel will be published." Her unflagging effort on my behalf has been amazing, and I thank my lucky stars to have found her. Kudos as well to her very efficient assistant, Amaryah Orenstein.

Shana Drehs is just what I wished for in an editor. She has been enthusiastic and responsive, never demanding more from me than she asked of herself. Her suggestions about the text, which ranged from major cuts to small word changes, were wonderfully discerning.

The entire staff at Sourcebooks has been terrific: Katie Anderson, Heather Hall, Heather Moore, Valerie Pierce, Nicole Villeneuve, and the entire production and design team.

My artistic children, Meg, Brett, and Kelly Thomson, have all championed my work over the years and helped me keep the faith. Ditto for my stepsons, Brian and Kevin McCarthy, along with Jodi Sperbeck Thomson and Tim Edwards.

My wife Elizabeth never lost patience with my quixotic undertaking. (Well, almost never.) I cannot thank her enough for her many hours of careful reading and editing, and for her constant love and understanding.

About the Author

James Whitfield Thomson grew up on the North Side of Pittsburgh and attended Harvard College on scholarship. After graduation he served three years in the Navy as navigator of a supply ship off the coast of Vietnam. Jim earned a Ph.D. in American Studies at the University of Pennsylvania, writing his dissertation on the detective novelist Raymond Chandler.  Following a brief stint teaching literature in academia, he joined a start-up venture as a salesman. The company's rapid success allowed him to retire early and devote himself to writing. He has published stories in a number of literary magazines including *Agni* and *The Ledge* and has been a Massachusetts Council for the Arts grant recipient. Jim and his wife, Elizabeth, live in a Victorian farmhouse outside of Boston and have five globe-trotting children. *Lies You Wanted to Hear* is his first published novel. You can find him on Facebook or at www.jameswhitfieldthomson.com.